"You wish to keep your husband?"

Tamsen stared at Prince Igor, numbly, her fist clenched on the table. "Keep Dan? Of course I do! What are you talking about?"

Igor took her hand, uncurling the fingers one by one, and brought it to his lips. "Then, dear lady, listen to what I have to say if you value your safety. My sister is like a tigress when she cannot have what she demands. Your husband wishes something from her—a chance to reach the ear of the Tsar; she wishes something from him, a few moments of dalliance. It can do no harm—"

Tamsen was on her feet. "My God! Are you trying to tell me—?"

"I am trying to tell you nothing, except that you are in Anya's way. I do not wish to see you hurt..."

Tamsen smouldered at this suggestion. Did he imagine that she would agree to her husband's satisfying that woman's lust to buy her own safety? Princess Anya should be worried about her own security because Tamsen Tallant could defend herself!

Books by Aola Vandergriff

Wyndspelle
Wyndspelle's Child
The Bell Tower of Wyndspelle
The House of The Dancing Dead
Sisters of Sorrow
Daughters of the Southwind
Daughters of the Wild Country

Published by
WARNER BOOKS

DAUGHTERS
OF THE
WILD COUNTRY

by Aola Vandergriff

WARNER BOOKS

A Warner Communications Company

WARNER BOOKS EDITION

Copyright © 1978 by Aola Vandergriff
All rights reserved

ISBN 0-446-82583-2

Cover art by Jim Dietz

Warner Books, Inc., 75 Rockefeller Plaza, New York, N.Y. 10019

Printed in the United States of America

Not associated with Warner Press, Inc., of Anderson, Indiana

First Printing: June, 1978

10 9 8 7 6 5 4 3 2 1

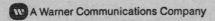 A Warner Communications Company

For Jackie, not my oldest but the one
I've had the longest, with love.

CONTENTS

PROLOGUE

Late in the evening of a June day in 1856, guests at the great house on the hill, Baranov Castle, gazed out over a twilight world. The sun had set, but with the peculiarity of an Alaskan summer day, it would be light enough until midnight to see the forested islands that studded the bay, breaking the swell of the Pacific; it would be light enough to view the perfection of the extinct volcano, Mt. Edgecumbe, or St. Lazaria as it was called by the Russians who claimed this kingdom.

To the north, Harbor Peak stood like a silvery outline. There, too, were The Sisters peaks with their crowns of ice and snow. Beyond the bay to the southeast, mist-wreathed mountains appeared as soft smudges against the sky.

The small stockaded settlement of Novo-archangelsk seemed blurred into a kind of beauty. In the gardens that surrounded the tea houses on the knoll, the Sitka roses paused in their folding for the night. The foundry shipyards had ceased their clangor, and there was none of the customary brawling and loud laughter of the *promishleniki*, who were the Russian hunters.

Only the bell of St. Michael's, the domed Russian Orthodox cathedral, broke the silence as it chimed to welcome a ship in the harbor. To the innocent

7

onlooker the scene was the picture of complete serenity. But it was a false serenity, for here, in this Eden, was a veritable cauldron of ambitions, jealousies, and hatreds. All these feelings mixed liberally with the rum that was both the downfall and mainstay of the settlement since the time of Baranov's great dream: the dream of extending the Russian Empire to include the wealth of Alaska.

The fur supply was now depleted, and all trade had declined sharply. Complaints had reached the ears of Tsar Alexander Nikolaevich, and governor-general followed governor-general in corrupt administrations. The present ruler of the area, Stephan Vassili Voedvodski, was a man who lived with the fear of being replaced, the fear of foreign interests taking over, and the fear of the Indians who lived outside the stockade—and there he had some reason to be scared. Only the year before, the proud and warlike Tlingits had risen against the settlement once again, though this attack was less severe than the massacre of 1802.

Voedvodski distrusted the English because of the Hudson's Bay Company's encroachment on what he considered Russian lands. But the English threat paled before this newer one from the United States. A move, spearheaded by Baron Edouard de Stoeckl, that urged the sale of Russian America to the United States, was underway.

Voedvodski had no intention of giving up his realm. Allied with him was Ivan Furuhelm, a Finnish engineer with designs on the governorship for himself. The Finn agreed with Voedvodski on the need to impress the tsar with plans for Russian expansion and development of the country's natural resources. Knowing Furuhelm's ambitions, Voedvodski kept a close eye on him. An experienced administrator could use such a man, if he kept him under control.

The true danger came, not from within his regime, but from without. Therefore, the emissary from the United States, Daniel Tallant, together with his lovely wife, Tamsen, headed the governor's list of people to watch.

BOOK I

BARANOV CASTLE

CHAPTER 1

Tamsen Tallant was angry. The picture she made as she stood, her dark eyes smoldering, in the crimson-draped chamber, was not lost on the aging man. Guiltily, he bowed his head before her wrath and stammered answers to her questions.

"What were you doing at my husband's desk? What were you looking for?"

"Only a bit of paper—on which to outline today's lesson."

She glared at him in disbelief. There was a sheaf of blank paper on the desktop in plain sight, and he had been opening drawers when she walked in. Gregor Illyitch Liedenov had been assigned to her by the governor as her Russian language tutor. He was an elderly man, pensioned off with a few rubles for his service with the Russian-American Company, and he'd seemed happy to earn more through his teaching. But she could trust Gregor Illyitch no longer. Evidently, someone was paying him more than she.

"Consider your services at an end," Tamsen said stiffly, as she held the door open. "And now, goodbye."

Closing the door behind him, she wished once more that Dan had installed a bolt before he left on his trip. Gregor had found nothing, she knew that. Dan, whose position was that of advisor on transportation and communication to the governor-general, had already turned over his maps of land and coastal routes to Voedvodski. Tamsen knew that Dan kept smaller, more detailed charts for himself concealed in an oilskin packet he kept inside his shirt at all times.

The mineral samples brought back from his journeys were another matter. So far, the false bottom in Tamsen's old cashbox had sufficed to keep them hidden.

She went to a small chest where her underthings were kept. Nothing had been disturbed. Lifting the cashbox from its nesting place among perfumed lace and ruffles, she opened it and began identifying its contents as her husband had taught her.

Gold, silver, lead, copper, iron, zinc—Dan's proof that this new land was rich beyond belief. One day, these samples, along with the miniature maps pinpointing the locations where they were found, just might tip the scales toward the purchase of Alaska.

Dan entrusted Tamsen with their keeping. And she was happy to do it, proud of her husband's work. But was it worth it? She wondered, night after night in her lonely bed, if any job were worth such loneliness. Dan had been gone for more than three months. She couldn't be certain if he were dead or alive. The country was big and filled with such dangers as treacherous straits and avalanches in the spring, to bears and wolves all season round. He had no right to leave her behind!

Fiddlesticks! Her eyes filled with tears. She dashed them away. There was an American ship in the harbor. Maybe there would be someone from home on it. Governor-General Voedvodski had proclaimed a *praznik*, a holiday, to honor the newcomers. It would not do to be red-eyed for the evening's revels.

Later, when she went down to the great hall, she must look her best, even though the wives of the noblemen looked down their noses at her and the Aleut women pretended to ignore her.

I don't give a damn, Tamsen thought angrily. If they couldn't keep their men's eyes from roving, it was their fault, not hers. She hadn't tried to attract any masculine attention, that was for sure. But it would serve the women right if she did! Dan, too, for that matter! He'd left her here to be snubbed and spied upon—

She was moody, that was all—spring fever—and needed a distraction. She would write once more to her sisters, telling them of the beauty of Sitka, which was known as the little Paris of the Pacific. She would be able to send her letters to San Francisco with the returning American ship.

How wonderful it would be if she could entice one or both of them here for a visit. Em's last letter had been filled with questions.

Tamsen conjured up a picture of her older sister; lovely Emmeline, domestic and gentle, soft gold-brown hair framing a sweet face. Em's letters would have been written at night, Tamsen supposed, since Em was not one to neglect her household duties. Little Martha would be abed, and Em's husband, Senator Donald Alden, would be nearby, smoke from his pipe wreathing his silver hair as he read his paper—

A knot of homesickness gathered in Tamsen's throat as she imagined the scene. She could almost hear Em saying, "I'm writing to Tamsen, Donald. Is there anything you want me to ask about?"

That would account for Em's unusual desire to

know all about the Russian-American Company, since her only real interest lay in keeping house and seeing to the comfort of her husband and child.

Tamsen picked up her pen and began to write. She explained how, years ago, the Siberian fur traders had pushed eastward—ahead of the tsar's tax collectors and Cossacks. Eventually, a number of small fur trading companies were formed. Then Gregory Shelikof, a Siberian merchant, conceived the plan of combining the fur trade in one great monopoly and secured a charter from Emperor Paul in 1799, under the name of the Russian-American Company. Alexander Andreevich Baranov became the first administrator.

Baranov had chosen Novoarchangelsk on the island of Sitka for his capital. Though he had been repulsed by the Indians in 1802, he returned to conquer them and build a small empire in the name of Russia.

"Don't let the American part of the Russian-American Company mislead you," Tamsen wrote. *"This place is Russian to the core! It's only because it's on the American continent."*

She sat thinking for a while, the tip of her pen to her lips. It would do no harm to tell Em and Donald. After all, Donald was in politics, himself, and her words would go no further.

"It may truly be American one day," she wrote. *"This is a secret, of course. Dan is here on the pretext of mapping the area and helping the Russians. But he's making a series of small charts showing the location of gold and precious minerals. He hopes this will tip the scales in favor of purchasing Russian Alaska for the United States. Our stuffy senators"* (her lips quirked as she thought of Donald Alden) *"must be convinced there are profits to be made."*

16

A dull letter, she thought wryly, finishing it with a few more personal notes. But Em would like it. Writing Arabella would be more difficult. Her beautiful red-haired younger sister had asked no questions. Her last note, sprawling across a page in violet ink, had done nothing but extol the virtues of Juan Narváez, the handsome young Spaniard who had given up his career with the *cortes* in Spain and become an expatriate in order to marry Arab.

At her last writing, Tamsen had described the splendor of the Russian splinter court. She'd written of the bigness of the country, telling of the grandeur of the castle, an immense wooden structure crowned by a cupola which served as a lighthouse from its position on the hill, or kekoor. Had she described the sumptuous dining hall? The priests in their splendid robes, the glittering uniforms of the Russian naval officers? And there were the paintings, the beautifully bound books in the library, the priceless collection of museum pieces.

She remembered telling of the Russian hospitality, avoiding any mention of the unfriendly attitudes of the women. And she had discussed the tall samovars, and the Russian insistence on a guest partaking of *penatchit copla*, or fifteen drops. Their fifteen drops consisted of at least half a tumbler of very strong spirits, Tamsen learned to her dismay. She'd not said anything about the Bacchanalian endings of the constant feasts, and also concealed the fact that these people seemed half-barbaric to her mind.

After all, she did want to coax them to come here, if only for a little while. She was so lonely! But how to capture Arab's interest?

She thought of Arabella, who even as a little girl was impetuous and venturesome. Arab always loved

17

the stories Tamsen invented especially for her, making them dramatic and frightening. She could still see the child—green eyes wide, shivering deliciously at the scary parts—of course, the castle ghost!

"The castle is haunted," Tamsen wrote. *"It truly is."* And she told the tale of a beautiful Russian princess, in love with a midshipman but forced to marry an old roué. Her true love appeared as the rites ended, and the princess thrust a dagger into her heart. Her lover used the dagger then to end his own life.

"Some say the princess was Mary, daughter of Governor-General Wrangell. Facts seem to bear this out. Others say she was niece to Etolin, another administrator. Her spirit is variously referred to as the Woman in White, the Woman in Black, and the Woman in Blue. Since the Russian wedding gown is blue, and since she appears wearing her wedding crown, the last is most likely.

"Her room is right across the hall from mine. And, Arab, it's gorgeous! Sometimes, I think I can feel her presence. Wouldn't it be exciting to see her?"

Now, what to say? Arab wouldn't have much interest in the crumbling empire of the Russian-American Company. And Tamsen certainly didn't want to describe the wily Governor-General Voedvodski, or tell of the constant surveillance she was subjected to!

Nor could she write in glowing details about her life with Dan, as she did earlier. She had gone with Dan on one journey far to the north, and it had been as she had dreamed: the two of them together beneath fur robes, the warmth of his body close as the dog team sped through the long night. She

18

shuddered at the ecstatic memory.

But this time he felt that he had to leave her behind as he went into rough, uncharted terrain. And this time, she hadn't taken it with good grace. The night before he left, she'd flirted madly with the Russian, Yuri, as a way of getting even. And Dan was angry.

She'd been penitent, later. But Dan had said, "I've forgotten the past, Tamsen. I trust you, because I love you. And if you love me, don't ever give me reason to doubt."

He'd held her close, and they'd renewed their love in a moment of tenderness. But the incident had haunted her, and would until his safe return.

She buried her face in her hands and didn't hear the silent entry of a barefoot Tlingit girl.

"Ret'a rihin," the girl murmured.

Tamsen raised her head and blinked. "The water is warm," she guessed. The girl nodded, pleased.

The girl, Helena, was Indian in appearance, though she was the child of a Tlingit woman and a Russian *promishleniki.* Helena had been educated in the school founded by Father John Veniaminov, now Metropolite of Russia. Then she had left Veniaminov's orphanage, to attend Madame Etolin's school for girls. Thus she had escaped the disfigurement of the labret, a wooden, spoon-shaped plate the Tlingit woman inserted horizontally in the lower lip.

Adept in languages, Helena was soon able to communicate with Tamsen, her new mistress. In turn, Tamsen was eager to learn the Tlingit tongue.

Watching the girl as she moved to fill a basin, Tamsen thought how lovely she was. Her dark hair was parted in the center and drawn back like wings

19

framing her eyes, calm pools in a serene face. Odd that a servant should be her only friend in this place.

Or was Helena a friend? Given the opportunity, would she, too, rifle the room seeking information for the Russians? She had been educated by them and been given a Christian name to replace her true name, which was Sket-u; was she also their tool?

I'm too suspicious, Tamsen thought. It comes from all this time of being alone. She had always had responsibility for someone—Em, Arab, Dusty, Nell, the girls—her present life of aimless luxury was difficult to endure. Especially with the spying and prying the Russians seemed to indulge in.

"This dress nice." Helena drew a white brocade from the armoire.

It was Tamsen's wedding dress. She had worn it the night she'd eloped with Dan. The ceremony had been performed on the wharf beneath the stars just before they sailed to Alaska.

Tamsen hadn't worn the gown in Alaska, though her other gowns had appeared time and time again. The dress brought her good luck before. It might once more.

"It will do," she said and began to dress.

Her long hair was still down as she surveyed herself in the mirror. She would leave her hair loose, the way it had been on her wedding night. At Helena's suggestion, she donned a lacelike jeweled tiara.

"You look like princess," the girl said reverently.

Tamsen shuddered, thinking of the ill-fated princess who haunted the room across the hall. But it was only a story. She had her love. She must just wait for him.

Then the thought of being at her best, of going

20

below to face the admiration of many men, began to rouse an old excitement in her; a feeling out of her past—gone but not forgotten.

CHAPTER 2

The sailors poured off the American ship, dressed in their best uniforms, which they had hoarded through the journey for this occasion. Shore leave in the little Paris of the Pacific was an experience to be savored. The Russian hospitality was famous. There would be drink, women, and merriment.

The ship's only passenger followed the crew, but he moved slowly. Edwin Devon, who had traveled from England to San Francisco, from San Francisco to Sitka Bay, was well aware of his limitations. All his actions now were dictated by the seed of death already germinating in his breast.

"Move slowly," his physician had said. "Moderate exercise. And you have perhaps a year—"

With the sentence of death upon him, Devon had made a decision. No one must know of his illness. He would seek adventure in the remaining days allotted him. And when the time to die came, he hoped to disappear into the wilderness.

Breaking all connections with anyone who might mourn him, he was led by his romantic, poet's nature to America's western borders. But he had found that San Francisco did not offer the seclusion for which he searched, so he had boarded a ship carrying goods for Alaska.

Debarking onto the hulk that was used as a

landing stage, Devon went on to enter the dusky tunnel of the warehouse, which was built of huge, hewn logs. He paused a moment, touching the marks of tools in the scarred wood, feeling a kinship with the hands that had made them.

Then, turning, he looked back at the vessel. My last voyage, he thought. Here was a place in which one might die with dignity. Devon slowly followed the others, who were out of sight now, only their ribald shouts trailing behind them. Then with determination he essayed the steps that led upward to Baranov Castle.

Inside the castle, he was grabbed by a burly, jovial Russian in full dress uniform who pressed a drink into his hand. Dazed by his efforts in climbing the stair, Devon was confused by the splendor before him: a long room, paneled in cedar, silken draperies, and costly mirrors that reflected myriad lights set in silver candelabra. On one wall were enormous gold-framed pictures of the tsar and tsarina. Swinging lamps of pungent, exotic incense burned before ikons and holy images. Floors with a glasslike sheen mirrored the shining boots of uniformed, courtly officers and the brilliant dress of ladies with midnight hair. They were Russian ladies, Aleuts, and an occasional Tlingit beauty.

Once he grew accustomed to the glitter, he watched as a knot of attentive gentlemen parted for a moment. Suddenly, for Edwin Devon there was only one woman in the room. A small girl-woman, in virginal white, with a golden-olive face and dark hair hanging to her waist...a flower, on a pale and slender stem.

"My word," he whispered. "My word!"

The officer, his self-appointed host, looked at Devon sharply when he muttered the English words and disappeared to find the governor-general and report a possible Hudson's Bay man in their midst.

Devon didn't see him go. He was too intent on waiting for the girl to reappear. She didn't belong in the middle of a noisy banquet room, but in the shrine-like corner where incense burned. For surely she was an angel.

Tamsen did not sense his rapt attention. She only felt the envious eyes of the other women upon her as two of her admirers, Yuri and Petrov, escorted her to the table. The two men vied for the privilege of seating her, and she gave permission to Yuri in a queenly manner.

"But you," she promised Petrov, "will be my first partner for the dance."

The banquet was a long, lavish affair made up of many courses in which fish and wild game predominated. Drink flowed freely, and with it the Russians shed their courtliness. Conversation grew louder. Impromptu speeches were made, toasts given, waving glasses slopped contents over a table laden with bird and bones; the linen was soiled and its edges were used to wipe grease from many a bearded mouth. An officer began to paw the giggling woman at his side, evoking lewd remarks from those nearest him. Discussions turned into arguments. One drink-flushed gentleman stood, overturning his chair.

As if at a signal, the music began. The governor-general stood and offered his arm to his lady. He led her into the dance, and the good humor of the assembly returned.

Edwin Devon, retreating to a position near a samovar, accepted a glass of the thick brew, tempered with hot water from the spigot below. He refused the brandy he was also offered. Alcohol sometimes loosened one's tongue and induced self-pity. He had not come here for that.

He watched Tamsen. He had noticed that she drank little, though many of the other women were as drunk as the men. How had she come here, he wondered. She seemed out of place among these barbarians. The Russian officers who had escorted her to dinner were both inebriated, he thought with distaste. They seemed spoiling for a fight.

Tamsen stepped back quietly as the two men, Petrov and Yuri, glowered at each other, their heads lowered like angry bulls. They had forgotten the pact made before dinner, and each claimed the privilege of leading Tamsen into the dance. Weaving back and forth, they growled Russian obscenities. The alarmed Devon forced his way through a crowd of onlookers as Yuri struck the first blow and the fight began in earnest.

Tamsen, backing from the fray, felt a hand at her elbow. She looked up to see a tall, grave man with intensely blue eyes in a pale, aesthetic face. Without a word, the man led her to the door as other drunken men leaped joyously into the battle behind them. Outside, her rescuer looked at her helplessly for a moment, then drew a handkerchief and wiped his forehead.

"Jove!" he said huskily.

Tamsen's eyes sparkled with delight. The single word was one from her past, bringing her old friend, Dusty—William Winston Wotherspoon—to mind. Though there was no resemblance between this gentleman and the lovable, alcoholic little reprobate, she suddenly felt at home with the stranger.

"You're English!"

It was Devon's turn to react with pleasure. "My word! I thought you were Russian!"

25

"No. I'm from the United States. Tamsen Tallant. My husband, Dan, is an advisor to Governor-General Voedvodski."

"Edwin Devon," he introduced himself. Then, with a note of disapproval, "I did not see your husband. Why didn't he come to your rescue?"

"He isn't here at present," Tamsen said in a small voice. "He's on a mapping expedition for the Russian government."

"It must be quite important to have left you at the mercy of these—" He did not finish his statement, for the lady's eyes looked suspiciously wet.

"I'm sorry," he apologized. "I didn't mean to fault your husband. Do you—do you wish to return to the hall?"

A full-throated, animal-like roar emanated from the room they'd left; the onlookers, crazed with blood lust and drink, were cheering the contestants on. Tamsen shuddered.

"I don't think so."

"Then would you care to walk?"

At her assenting nod, he extended his arm. Together, they walked down the stairs, Tamsen a bit bewildered at her feeling of ease with a strange man, Devon wondering what kind of husband this woman had. Imagine, leaving her like this for any reason at all! He decided he did not like Dan Tallant.

Tamsen paused. "I didn't think—I'm taking you away from the festivities." She had noticed his slow pace and read reluctance into it.

"I am grateful. I take no pleasure in that sort of thing."

She laughed. "Then it's lucky you didn't visit in the famous Baranov's time." She went on to describe how barrels of rum were poured into an enormous cooking kettle and how everyone in a circle tried to

26

see who could drink the most. Those who didn't drink were plunged into the kettle, or pushed off a rock into the sea.

"It would appear they're still at it," he said wryly.

Tamsen's hand tightened on his arm. She could not see the person following them in the shadows, but she sensed a presence as she had so many times before. She had a feeling that all her actions were observed, all conversations reported. She must take care that the English gentleman said nothing that would bring discredit upon himself—yet, to reveal that they were under surveillance would cast a pall upon the evening.

"Let's walk to the tea houses," she said hastily. "The gardens there are lovely."

They strolled toward the knoll where the tea houses stood empty at this hour; Tamsen talked nervously about the golden age of Baranov. Reaching the gardens with their splendid view, they both were silent. The brief night had begun to fade, revealing a slate-colored sea studded with shadowy islands and the silhouettes of sailing vessels being drawn to shore.

Devon drew a shuddering breath. *"Through a glass, darkly,"* he said in a somber voice.

Tamsen, startled, looked up at the grave face above her. "What did you say?"

"I was just wondering," he said, "if dying is like this. Beauty fading, dimming, the last picture frozen on the retina forever?"

Sensing Tamsen's confusion, he apologized. He waved his hand, as if to erase his comment. "I did not mean to interject a morbid note into this enchanted atmosphere. I—writing is my avocation. Poetry, small essays. I suppose a poet often dwells on death."

"You should find many things to write of, here."

"True." Devon tried to return to lighter conversation. "I should consider something in a more humorous vein." He gestured toward the castle on the hill. "The Russian aristocracy at play. But who would believe it? I have never seen such behavior—"

His words were cut short as Tamsen stumbled, pitching forward into his arms. "My ankle," Tamsen said on a sob, "I've twisted it. A stone—"

With an exclamation of concern, he half led, half carried her to a small bench. His every nerve was conscious of the warm body pressed against his own, of the night wind, soft with a scent of lingering blossoms. Seating her, he knelt to examine the injured limb with trembling fingers. And Tamsen bent above him, her lips close to his cheek.

"For the love of God, be careful what you say," she implored. "There is a man behind a shrub, listening. All you say will be reported. These people do not take kindly to criticism."

He tensed with shock. Spied upon? Surely the lady was joking—or endowed with an overwrought imagination.

Unless her husband had set a watch upon her. Perhaps he was concerned for her safety, and rightfully so. For Edwin Devon felt such a surge of passion that his heart was thundering out of control.

Tamsen, too, was shaken. She hadn't been so close to a man since Dan's departure. Drawing a deep breath, she said, "My ankle is all right, I think. It has stopped paining me. Let's just rest here awhile."

"My pleasure."

"And do go on with what you were telling me. You are going to write of the wonderful Russian hospitality, aren't you? And incorporate the exciting

28

history of the Russian-American Company. That's why you've been encouraging my chatter."

Heart still palpitating, Devon could only take the easiest course, which was to agree. Mystified, he listened as Tamsen pointed out the wonders of Novoarchangelsk in glowing words. She indicated the shop and the storehouse, pointing out the tannery for furs, the barracks, the office buildings, and the school, bakery, and joinery. And where could one find a more beautiful cathedral than St. Michael's with its treasures?

Perhaps he might write of the industry: shipbuilding, the foundry for casting bells, a sawmill. Did he know ice from a nearby lake was shipped all the way to San Francisco? And all of this thriving business was controlled by the Russians in their impregnable fortress behind an eighteen-foot log wall, with one hundred fifty cannon to protect it.

She talked feverishly. Devon agreed in monosyllables as he searched the shadows for a lurking figure. Spotting him at last, he grew angry. Not so much at being spied upon, but for the intrusion into this perfect night.

He dared not remain in the vicinity of this girl who stirred such emotions in him. Tomorrow, he would leave and go into the interior to meet whatever came, like a man. Tamsen Tallant was a stranger, a married woman. He had been drawn to her through the knowledge of his own mortality.

"Perhaps we should return you to the castle," he said abruptly, "if your ankle will permit. It is approaching dawn. I am rather weary, as you must be—"

"I have been talking too much. It is a fault of mine."

"Not at all. I have enjoyed it."

29

The walk back to the castle was rather stiff, the conversation formal. Tamsen limped, aware of the shadow at their heels. Edwin Devon wondered, uneasily, if his first assumption, that Tamsen's husband was having her watched, had been in error. But why would the Russians trouble themselves to spy on a small, defenseless woman? Perhaps she needed a protector....

"I will not come in," Devon said at the door, "but will return to the ship."

"You're not leaving when it sails?" Tamsen's eyes were troubled. For a few moments, her loneliness had been forgotten.

Devon's mouth was dry. "No," he admitted. "I plan to go up the inland waters, to find solitude in which to—to write."

"But not right away!" There was a pleading note in her voice. "There is so much to see here."

Devon succumbed. "Perhaps a day or two." A pause. "Maybe you would be kind enough to show me, by day, the things you pointed out in the darkness."

She gladly agreed, and he took his leave, hating himself for his weak will. But there was something afoot here. Something that frightened the girl. And that, he told himself, had influenced his decision to stay, not the lady herself. After all, he had the good part of a year. What did a few days matter?

Turning at a parapet, he looked back to watch the small figure limned against the light. And he thought of Anne, at home in Sussex, who had broken their engagement when she learned of his illness.

This girl would stand by a man. She looked like an angel. But why would an angel be beset by Russian spies? He would try to find the answer to that another day, he decided as he made his way back to the ship.

As she entered the castle, Tamsen came face to face with Niklas Kovalski, the governor-general's chamberlain. The man's bearded features were grim above the glitter of his uniform. The governor-general wished to see her. Would Madam Tallant please accompany him?

Tamsen felt her knees crumple. Dan! Something had happened to Dan, and word had been brought in her absence! How could she have left the castle, even for a moment! With an effort, she stiffened her body and followed the chamberlain. Edwin Devon was forgotten. Only one name thundered in her ears.

Dan! Dan! Dan!

When Tamsen reached the chamber where the governor-general waited, she saw that he was not alone. Standing beside the governor was Ivan Furuhelm, the engineer who was in agreement with Dan regarding the exploitation of the country's resources, but opposed to the sale of Russian America to the States.

Neither gentleman spoke for a moment, then Stephan Voedvodski, the administrator of Novoarchangelsk, cleared his throat.

"I regret to inform you, Madam Tallant, that there has been a death."

CHAPTER 3

The governor-general's mouth was moving, and a part of Tamsen's mind watched, fascinated. The words so slow in coming hung in the air, but suddenly they began to make sense. She sighed with relief.

Yuri Chelov stabbed Petrov last night. Petrov was dead, not Dan. Petrov, whose face she couldn't remember. . . .

It was some time before she realized that she was being held responsible for the murder, accused of provoking the quarrel. Voedvodski's eyes glinted with a kind of glee as he voiced his subtle accusations. She looked at him in bewilderment.

"I don't understand. You're blaming me? I had nothing to do with it. They'd been drinking—"

He raised a placating hand. "It is most understandable, madam. This is a small settlement, more than a thousand men and less than sixty true Russian women. It is no place for a courtesan."

A courtesan! Tamsen was rigid. "You forget yourself, sir! You are speaking to the wife of an emissary from the United States. I demand an apology."

"An apology, *Madam Franklin?*"

Tamsen froze at his words. He couldn't know! He couldn't possibly know! "You—you are in error,"

32

she stammered. "My name is Tallant—"

Voedvodski shot a triumphant look at the puzzled Furuhelm, who had been called from his bed to attend this meeting. The governor needed a witness for his coup, and he intended to show his friend and rival how a true diplomat handled a situation.

"Do not judge us all by the antics of a few amorous officers and ignorant *promishleniki*, madam. We are not fools. I have here a record of your past." He indicated a sheaf of papers on his desk. "And I have here a further record, one you might not wish to reach the eyes of your husband." He extended a folder toward her.

The lines of writing danced before Tamsen's horrified eyes. The dossier consisted of a record of her activities in these last three months, since Dan had been gone. It was true Yuri had come to her room at night, but she had forced him to leave! It was true that she had gone into the back of a warehouse with a clerk and remained for an hour. But they had been searching for a bolt of silk in a certain color. Incident after incident, signed by witnesses. And they had all taken place, but they were twisted, misrepresented, making her look like ... like ...

"These are lies," Tamsen choked. "All lies! What are you trying to do to me?"

Governor-General Voedvodski assumed an injured expression. "Nothing at all, my dear lady. I am trying to help you. I am prepared to overlook the Petrov incident. And I am certain you would not indulge in shoddy affairs such as these." He plucked the papers from her icy hands and thrust them into a drawer.

"But will your husband be equally understanding?

33

I believe there was a minor quarrel regarding your—adventures—before he left."

Tamsen's face flamed. "Listening at keyholes is also part of your duties?"

"You are overwrought. I will overlook your accusation. Novoarchangelsk is a small place. Rumor spreads rapidly. It is not surprising that word reached my ears. I think we should return to the problem—that of keeping this knowledge from Mr. Tallant. Dissension between married couples is so sad, don't you think?"

Tamsen's shoulders sagged. "What do you hope to gain by this?" she asked, wearily. "What are you trying to do to me? I'm certain you have your reasons for this . . . this blackmail!"

Voedvodski looked shocked. "My dear woman! I'm only trying to help you. I cannot hide the fact of Petrov's death. It is public knowledge. I pray you may be able to convince your husband of your innocence in the affair. As for this other scurrilous information, it is yours to destory."

But he made no move to return the list. Tamsen stared at him. Such an ordinary man! His face wreathed in a smug smile, cheeks pink at his own cleverness. She shifted her gaze to Ivan Furuhelm. He only looked confused and embarrassed. It was evident Voedvodski hadn't briefed him beforehand. She turned once more to the governor-general.

"I suppose you've put a price on the papers. What do you expect for them?"

"A price? Not at all. Let us say a *trade*." He leaned forward, pausing a bit to savor the moment before he continued. "I want the charts your husband has made."

His words shocked Tamsen. She realized that he'd

somehow got wind of Dan's secret papers, but still she tried to dissemble.

"He has given you the maps you requested."

"But not all. Not those showing the locations of our country's natural resources. The ones he plans to use to influence your stuffy senators toward the purchase of Russian America—"

Stuffy senators! Her letter to Em! She should have known Voedvodski would open her mail.

Trapped, she turned to Furuhelm. At Voedvodski's words, he had leaned forward with an expression of avid interest. It was clear his mind had grasped the import of what the governor-general was doing. The charts, once obtained, would be equally effective in influencing the tsar.

Tamsen assumed an attitude of angry amusement. "I haven't the slightest idea what you're talking about," she said. "Furthermore, my husband will see through this farce in a minute! He won't believe a word of those accusations!"

Voedvodski's self-congratulatory smile disappeared. He leaned across his desk; his eyes were hard, his voice smooth as silk. "If he doesn't, in the light of your past, madam, then he is a fool. And in Russian America, fools often meet with fatal accidents. It would be a pity, would it not?"

Tamsen shrank before his expression. He was no longer an ordinary little man, pompous and sly. Recalling that he was the man who had turned cannon on the Tlingit Indians when they rebelled last year, she realized that he was not making an idle remark, but a threat.

Then, as quickly as it had gone, his geniality returned. "But we need not think of such things. He has a wise wife, who will look after his health, yes?

35

We must return to the business at hand. I do not press you for a hasty decision. You may have the full day to consider my proposition. Now, if you will excuse us?" He waved a languid hand toward the door.

She was dismissed. Tamsen stormed past the chamberlain, white-faced and trembling.

As the door closed behind Tamsen, Voedvodski turned to Furuhelm. "Well, friend Ivan, that was handled well, eh?"

"I would not have done it in that manner," the engineer said stiffly. "I would have dealt with Tallant himself. I have no stomach for persecuting ladies—"

"A lady? Mrs. Tallant? Take a look at this report on her background before she came here."

Furuhelm took the dossier from the governor-general's hand. It had been prepared by a detective agency in San Francisco; it was written in English. Though the Finnish engineer spoke the language well, he was not adept at reading it. When he finally managed to puzzle out its content, he was round-eyed.

"I cannot believe this! A dance hall entertainer! Operator of a brothel, under the name of Madam Franklin—Holy Mother of God!"

Voedvodski nodded. "I've had the dossier for some time, wondering how to put the information to use. As you know, I was not in favor of Tallant's coming here. I sensed he was something more than he pretended to be. Still, I could not refuse to accept the services his country so generously offered, for fear of antagonizing them. But to be on the safe side, I did some checking, and the lady's past came to light. I had thought of using it to effect Tallant's recall; then I realized they would only send someone to replace him."

He leaned back with an expansive sigh. "So, I waited—and watched. A good administrator knows how to gather information, and when to use it to his advantage."

His tone implied that Furuhelm might not have done as well. The engineer reddened. "It still doesn't seem right," he persisted. "If you believe Tallant guilty of spying on his country's behalf, you could arrest him, force him to give you the charts."

Voedvodski shrugged, pettishly. "He is a stubborn fellow, and extraordinary measures would have to be employed. He represents the government of the United States, and I wish no quarrel with them. Diplomacy, my dear friend, is always preferable to violence. The lady will cooperate. And this way, no one will be hurt."

Furuhelm acceded with reluctance and left to return to bed. Voedvodski leaned back in his chair, his hands clasped comfortably over his stomach, and reflected on his triumph. The Tallant woman had been uncomfortable when her past was mentioned, but that alone did not carry much weight. Of course, when the record of her recent activities was added to the first, she'd been most definitely shaken. He had an idea, however, that the veiled threat to Tallant had been his masterstroke. Despite her sordid past, the woman seemed to love the man. Voedvodski was not without a degree of sentimental feeling. Still, one must do what must be done. . . .

And he'd managed to show Furuhelm his own superiority in the diplomatic field. He knew of the man's plans to unseat him and take the governorship for himself. It was necessary that Furuhelm recognize he was facing an able adversary. For when the charts were delivered to the tsar, there would be no more talk of selling Russian America. And

Voedvodski might be assigned permanently to the position he now held.

Tamsen had rushed blindly to her room, dazed with the tumult raging in her brain. She sank into a chair, her hot face in her hands. If she did not produce Dan's charts, that—that pack of lies would be given to her husband. Would he believe them? Whether he did or not had no bearing on the decision she faced. Voedvodski's last words had terrified her. *Fools often meet with accidents....*

She was the fool, for she had set down her husband's plans on paper for his enemy to read! After the way she'd been watched, spied upon, she'd been too stupid to consider her letters might be intercepted. Because of her thoughtlessness, she'd placed Dan's life in danger.

"You have the full day to consider my proposition," the governor-general had said. As if she had a choice! She would do anything to keep Dan safe! There had to be some way out of her dilemma.

She would let the governor-general think she intended to do as he wished until Dan came home. Then she would tell Dan the whole story the minute he arrived.

Ah, God, no! Dan had a terrible temper! He'd try to take on the whole Russian settlement and get himself killed. That might just be what Voedvodski wanted him to do!

Oh, *damn* those charts! How her head hurt!

"You have *tach-tsin?*"

Tamsen looked up. Helena stood beside her, eyes filled with sympathy. At Tamsen's blank expression, the girl placed her hand over her heart. "A hurt here?"

Tamsen smiled. "I suppose I do."

Helena had been waiting to help Tamsen get ready for bed. But she left quietly when her mistress explained that she had *achschan-renik*, an aching head, and wished only to be alone.

Tamsen went to the window. The rising sun had tinted the sky a faint pink, echoed in the snow and ice-capped mountains. Another sunny day had dawned, one of the few in this land of forever-rain. But this morning, nothing could lift Tamsen's spirits.

She thought drearily of the past she'd left behind her. As Madam Franklin, she'd operated Madam Franklin's Parlor for Gentlemen, a high-class brothel in San Francisco. She'd used the name of Poppy Franklin once before that, as a song-and-dance girl in a Texas cantina. Her dossier must have provided the governor-general with some interesting reading!

But nowhere would those pages have mentioned that she'd been the sole support of her sisters, Arabella and Emmeline! That she'd been a shy, terrified girl trying to earn a living, forced into circumstances beyond her control.

They wouldn't state that she and the girls had been orphaned when their father died along the trail, or that they'd reached the outskirts of Magoffinville cold, hungry, Emmeline ill, Arab just a child. And that someone had to find work—

The only job was in a riverfront cantina. Her father's friend Dusty had taken her there, and Dusty's sweetheart, Nell, had hired her to sing and dance. Tamsen had found herself in an abbreviated costume before an audience of leering men. She'd had no voice at first. But when she began to sing, at the first taste of success, she'd experienced a sense of power...

No matter how it looked on paper, she had not been bad. Nor had most of the people she consorted with. William Winston Wotherspoon, better known as Dusty, was more of a gentleman than Governor-General Voedvodski would ever be. And Nell, the manager of the cantina, who was running Madam Franklin's Parlor now, was a lady inside—where it counted.

Tamsen's past had risen to haunt her again. If Voedvodski hadn't learned of her background, he might not have troubled to use it as he did, spying upon her every move, reading her letters, forging his collected information into a weapon.

Again, she went over the alternatives. If she told her husband of Voedvodski's blackmailing attempt, he would react in anger. If she did not tell him, and didn't produce the charts for Voedvodski, then the governor-general would face Dan with proof of her misbehavior during his absence.

"Don't ever give me reason to doubt," Dan had said.

Surely, the document would give him reason enough. But whether Dan believed those fabrications or not made little difference. Once he'd seen those papers, Voedvodski's hold over Tamsen was gone. The governor would have to resort to other means to obtain the charts. And Dan would be in danger.

She shivered at the thought. She could not steal the maps. Dan would never forgive her. There had to be another way. But now she was tired, too tired to think. She fumbled at the buttons of the gown she'd worn for good luck.

Through the open window came a keening sound. It came from the village beyond the fortress wall. Helena had explained that mourning wails began the

40

moment a Tlingit died and continued through the four days before cremation, the corpse sitting dressed in full regalia against the wall of the tribal house. There had been three deaths this night: Petrov, an unknown Indian, and her belief in her own security.

Petrov would be buried on land or at sea. The Indian would be placed upon a funeral pyre, his spirit rising with the smoke. But Tamsen must go on somehow.

She looked down at the dress that had been her wedding gown, hating it, and yanked savagely at it until the buttons flew off. And then the tears began.

CHAPTER 4

At a respectable hour the next afternoon, Edwin Devon presented himself at the door of the castle, which was just beginning to stir. A sleepy sentry announced his presence to Tamsen's maid, Helena, who conveyed the word to her mistress.

Tamsen, who had just risen from a nap, had difficulty in recalling the afternoon's engagement. Even the man's face eluded her memory. Too much had occurred in the intervening hours. Perhaps it would be best to say she was indisposed. But then she would only be alone with her thoughts.

Suddenly, it seemed imperative to escape from the familiarity of the suite. She chose a brightly colored gown to wear and tried to pinch some color into her cheeks. But she knew her efforts had failed when she saw the gentleman's stricken gaze.

"You're exhausted," he said, contritely. The dark circles beneath her eyes had surely not been there the previous night. In the light of day, she looked weary, fragile. "I've been selfish. Perhaps you would rather rest."

"Indeed not!" Her voice was gay but brittle with nerves. "I've been looking forward to our tour."

Not quite daring to believe her enthusiasm, but wishing he could, Devon proffered his arm.

She led him on a tour of Novoarchangelsk,

coming to life again in the holiday atmosphere. The huge gates to the stockade had been opened temporarily to allow trade at the Indian market. Enthralled by the Indians' beautiful workmanship, Devon purchased a delicately woven basket for his guide, a bowl carved in the shape of a comical frog, a wooden ring trimmed with beads such as the Tlingit girls wore to hold their braids at the nape of the neck.

"Enough," Tamsen said, finally, "or I shall be spoiled!"

"My pleasure," Edwin said. How he wished he had the right to give this girl everything in the world.

For a while, they walked along the shoreline where they studied the Tlingit bidarkas, large boats carved from a single cedar log, commenting on the beauty of their painted designs. Tamsen explained the system of potlatch, whereby a Tlingit gave a feast and invited wealthy friends to whom he gave all his property.

"There's a catch," she explained. "Each friend is then obligated to give a feast and return the favor, with even larger gifts."

Devon listened with interest, then started as the keening began again. "Good God, what's that?"

"Someone died," Tamsen said nervously. "Come, I think it's about time they close the gates." She walked away, hurrying so that he was hard put to keep up with her. Once inside the fortress, he paused from force of habit to rest a moment, but he suddenly realized that he was not winded at all! For a space, he dared to hope.

They left the area of industry and barracks, and Tamsen led him inland, past the orphanage established by Veniaminov many years before. They walked on to the lake where ice was cut for shipment to San Francisco, and on to the Indian trail which

Tamsen and Dan had walked together upon arrival.

"We are alone?" Devon asked suddenly. "I've been watching. It would appear we are not being followed today."

He was right, Tamsen realized. For the first time in days, she had not seen or sensed a shadow. There was no point in further espionage; Voedvodski had all the information he needed. "Perhaps they've decided we're harmless," she said.

"Then we are alone."

The ardor in his statement disturbed Tamsen. After all, the Indian trail was known as a lover's lane. She had never walked here with anyone but Dan. To cover her thoughts, she became a guide once more.

"The hill up there," she gestured, "was once covered with totems with carvings indicating the families of the dead. Their ashes were placed in a sort of repository in back. The early missionaries thought they were idols and burned them."

"Pity," Devon said.

His mind was elsewhere. Normally, he would have stopped to consider the permanence of death, those dead and gone leaving no imprint. Now, all he could think of was his own sense of well-being and the girl beside him who caused that feeling.

"The Indians had a good life," Tamsen said wistfully. "Fish from the sea. And look at the berry bushes. They all grow wild here. Currants, huckleberries, blackberries, raspberries. And there are snowberries, strawberries, and crowberries. They dry them for the winter. The animals in the forest provide meat and furs. It would be wonderful to lead such an uncomplicated life, wouldn't it?"

"And yours is complicated?" He took her by the arms and turned her to face him. "Mrs. Tallant, what are you afraid of?"

44

For a moment her eyes filled with tears, and she seemed to melt toward him. Then the brittleness was back. "Afraid? I'm afraid of nothing. Not even ghosts. Do you know there are graves of two lovers near this trail? They committed suicide rather than be parted and therefore couldn't lie in the churchyard. The girl's ghost haunts the room across from mine—"

As she told him the story of the ill-fated lovers, she moved ahead of him until they reached a flat rock. He sat down. She hesitated, then took her place beside him. As they talked, he drew in the soil at his feet with a sharp stick. A map of Novoarchangelsk took shape, with the placing of major buildings as he remembered them.

Tamsen leaned to see his work, studying it with a critical eye. "Almost right," she said. "But St. Michael's is a little farther to the left. There—"

He took a small notebook from his pocket. "I'd better copy it here," he said. "It wouldn't do to have such an impressive structure in the wrong place. My word! I might have written this up for posterity, and my readers would never have caught the error!"

He looked to Tamsen for an answering smile, but her face was still, her eyes filled with a dawning wonder. A map with something out of place! And if she hadn't corrected him, he'd not have known. And the cathedral was a tangible thing, not something as vague as a site where minerals might be found.

She'd found the answer to her problem. And Edwin Devon had provided it for her. Impulsively, she leaned to kiss his pale cheek. "Don't ever leave this place," she said passionately. "I need you! I can't tell you any more than that. But you'll never know how much you've helped, just being here."

Then and there, Edwin Devon came to a decision. The remainder of his life was going to be inextricably entwined with that of this enchanting, unpredictable creature. What was left of it belonged to her. He reached out to her in an agony of need, and Tamsen, shocked at her own impetuous action, stood hastily.

"It's growing late," she whispered. "I think we'd better go."

The summer light still persisted, refusing the night its due, as they slowly returned to the castle. The *praznik* was still in force. Today there had been no clanging anvils, no shrill sawmill noises. Only the servants at the castle scurried about their duties, removing the ruin of the previous night's feast, preparing for yet another since the California ship would sail with the tide.

"Tonight, then?" Devon took Tamsen's hand in his own, reluctant to leave her.

"Tonight," Tamsen echoed. But as she went to her apartments, she was still undecided. She hadn't mentioned Petrov's death to Devon. All afternoon, she'd tried to erase it from her mind. There would be people pointing fingers and gossiping tonight, but to stay away would be to admit her involvement.

She must keep up appearances. For Voedvodski would be there, waiting for his answer. She would tell him that he had gained the upper hand with his fraudulent papers, and that she would provide the charts he asked for.

Devon had given her the clue that would solve her predicament. She would copy Dan's charts in great detail. And hand them over to Voedvodski—with minor alterations. By the time the Russians checked the validity of the material she gave them, the true charts would be in American hands.

That night Edwin Devon waited glumly in the banquet hall. The assembly seemed to be even more dazzling than the night before. The American contingent was already far from sober, preferring brandy and rum to the Russian version of tea. Even Devon was not immune. A drunken Russian, overwhelmed with a sense of hospitality, had splashed some liquor into Devon's glass, shouting *"Penatchit copla!"*

Devon sipped at it as he searched the room for the figure of the only woman in his world. Without her, the evening was a loss, though he had sought out the governor-general, to impress him with details of the story he wished to write. In return, he had received an invitation to occupy an apartment in the barracks and found himself being regarded as a very important person, despite his nationality.

Why hadn't Tamsen informed him of last night's fatal stabbing? He'd only learned of it tonight. Was this what kept her away? Embarrassment at being the reason for the tragic quarrel?

At last, he was led to the shimmering table by Voedvodski himself and seated at his right hand. When the governor-general stood to make his second speech to the Americans, first in Russian, then in English so that all present would understand, Devon was amused. He heard his own name mentioned in the flow of foreign words, then discovered himself being introduced as a famous writer from England, who had come to depict the wonders of the Russian regime.

Devon rose, bowed gravely in acknowledgment, then seated himself once more. The governor-general ended his speech to a round of applause. At its ending, there was a silence. Then a whispering began, eyes turning toward the door behind Devon.

He turned. Tamsen Tallant stood in the doorway, a regal figure in a flowing scarlet gown. For a moment, she was still, knowing full well she was the focal point of the assembly, her lips curved slightly in a self-confident, mysterious smile. After all, this was no different from an entrance into the cantina, coming down the stairs at her establishment in San Francisco. The majority here were men. And were not all men interested in the same thing?

As she posed, her eyes searched the table. No place had been reserved for her among the aristocracy. There was only an empty chair at the table of the cadets.

She moved forward gracefully and stood behind the empty chair until the two astounded young men at either side revived enough to scramble to their feet. Awkwardly, both wrestled with the chair before one gave in, red-faced, to step away.

"Thank you," Tamsen said graciously, with the air of an empress bestowing her favor. She did not look toward the governor-general, nor at Devon, but devoted her attention to the bemused young men at her side.

"Bravo," Devon thought, sinking back. He had half-risen to his feet, recognizing the tone of the whispered Russian comments, if not their content. It was evident the ladies present had no love for Tamsen, but the young woman had carried the situation off, and beautifully!

As the meal progressed, Devon's eyes were more on Tamsen than upon his plate. A troupe of Russian soldiers, arms folded, performed their incredible dance—squatting and kicking outward. An aria, sung by the wife of a nobleman, followed. Then the governor-general stood.

"We have just learned that we have had an artist in our midst in the person of Madam Tallant, wife of our esteemed American representative. She has, it

48

seems, quite a reputation"—he paused here—"as a singer and dancer. Perhaps she will entertain us with one of her creative efforts."

A round of applause rose from the American seamen as Tamsen turned, first white, then scarlet, at Voedvodski's words. When the Americans would not be hushed, she stood, her humiliation replaced by fury.

She had half a mind to sing a naughty song from the cantina! Let these stuck-up snobbish Russian women see how their husbands reacted to a few provocative movements!

No! She was not Poppy Franklin, here; she was the wife of a man who represented the government of his country. She must be discreet. Hands clenched at her sides, she bowed acknowledgment of the governor-general's request. Then, her face an oval of purity, she lifted her eyes and sang.

"Black is the color of my true love's hair..."

The song had been the favorite song of her father, Scott McLeod, who died along the trail to Santa Fe. As she sang it, remembering him helped to obscure the sea of foreign faces and their hostile stares.

Few of the Russians spoke English. But Tamsen's oddly husky voice, the shine of tears that moistened her eyes, touched every masculine heart. When she finished, even the ladies stirred uneasily, hypnotized by the emotion the frail figure beneath the shimmering candles had evoked.

"My word," Devon said softly, under his breath.

But the governor-general wasn't finished. His eyes narrowed a bit as he thanked Tamsen for her rendition. "But I understand you also *dance*," he said. "May we see a sample of your dancing?"

Again, thunderous applause from the American contingent. But Tamsen seemed to be upset, her face chalk-white once more. Devon sensed she had reached her nerve's end.

He stood, his tall figure dwarfing the figure of Voedvodski beside him, his hair shining golden in the candlelight.

"Forgive me, sir," he said to the governor-general, "but I feel I should speak in the lady's behalf. Last evening, she became quite distraught, due to an— unpleasant altercation going on around her. I took it upon myself to remove her from the scene, on pretext of seeing some of the buildings housing the great commerce of your wonderful colony. Unfortunately, she stepped on a loose stone and sprained her ankle. I think it best to advise her against accepting what must be so flattering an invitation—"

Voedvodski looked disgruntled, but only for a moment. Then he bowed, waved for the dancing to begin, and led his lady to the dance floor.

Devon went straight to Tamsen and rescued her from the young cadets who seemed about to stage a repeat performance of the previous night.

"Thank you," she whispered.

"Delighted to have been of service." He was still a bit bewildered. Why had the governor-general's suggestion that she dance aroused such a reaction in her? For a moment, he'd thought she would faint. But apparently there were going to be no explanations. "Shall we leave the dancing? Would you like to walk once more?"

Tamsen had regained control. She wrinkled her nose impishly, her eyes sparkling as she said, "You forget, sir! My *ankle!*"

He touched his forehead in mock distress. "Ah, yes! How forgetful I am! So clumsy of me!"

Tamsen caught sight of the governor-general

50

standing nearby, his fierce gaze fixed on her. Smiling at Devon, she said lightly, "Perhaps a cup of tea might mend it. Then later we can slip away."

Feeling absurdly like a love-sick boy, elated at the notion that she wished to be alone with him, Edwin Devon pushed his way across the crowded room to a samovar. And Tamsen, with a few quick steps, was at Voedvodski's side.

"You will have your maps," she hissed angrily. "I do not know how I will get them, or when I can get my hands on them. But in the meantime, you will treat me with the respect due a lady! Otherwise—"

Voedvodski bowed low. "Of course," he said in a mocking tone. "Of course, my dear."

He walked away, chuckling to himself. His insinuations tonight had been understood. Madam Tallant would not allow her status to be diminished. Tonight he would sleep well.

Tamsen was in place when Devon started back across the room, a glass held in either hand. Her eyes met his, and she thought about how kind he was, so considerate, with the soul of a poet. The woman he loved would be a lucky one indeed.

She saw him turn at a change of sound in the front of the room. They looked toward the door as others did. In the doorway stood a tall, bronze-skinned, trail-worn man in checked flannel shirt and soiled denim trousers, searching the room until he found Tamsen's stunned face. His own lit with an expression of delight, and he smiled—a lazy, teasing smile.

"Dan!" Tamsen cried. "Oh, Dan! Dan!"

Then she was running, flying like a bird toward him, her arms outstretched. As she reached him, she paused, conscious of the eyes that watched them.

"Dan!" she said in a broken voice. One hand went

51

up to touch his lean, bearded cheek. "You're home."

"Home," he said huskily, his eyes dark with emotion. "Oh, God, sweetheart, I've missed you!" They stood for a long moment, then his dark face crinkled in amusement. "So help me, Tamsen, if we don't go find some privacy, I'm going to kiss my wife in front of everybody!"

"Then we'd better go—"

Edwin Devon found himself staring at an empty doorway. He stood looking at the blank space for a long time, two glasses balanced carefully in his hands. Finally, he managed to shake himself into awareness. Walking to a table, he carefully set both glasses down.

He had a lot to do tonight. All his belongings must be removed from the ship. Tamsen had begged him to remain, had said she needed him, though she couldn't tell him more than that. Seeing Tallant, trailworn and unkempt, holding Tamsen's gaze for that long moment, like a snake hypnotizing a small and trembling bird, had solidified his intent.

He could not leave Novoarchangelsk and the gentle, cultured girl who was tied, through some mischance, to a barbarian.

CHAPTER 5

All Tamsen's worries were relegated to the fringes of her mind. She watched Dan close the door of their apartment against the noise of the banquet hall, her knees still trembling from the shock of his sudden appearance. He was here, and he was safe. For the moment, that was all that mattered. Weak with love for him, she waited for him to take her in his arms. Instead, he pushed her away.

"I just want to look at you for a moment," he said, his voice rough with emotion. "I want to be sure you're really there." He studied her, seeing the pale oval of her face in the light of the single candle, observing the quickened pulse in her throat as she pushed back her dark hair; he saw the happiness in her eyes.

"Tamsen!"

With one long stride, he reached her. She was in his embrace, his mouth on hers, hot and searching, the heat of his body burning through her clothing as she pressed against him, whispering his name like a poem. His lips left her mouth and moved to her throbbing throat. "Ah, God, Tamsen! Sweetheart!"

Then he held her away from him again. "I said I missed you, Tamsen, but I lied! You went with me, did you know that? When it was cold, you curled up against me and kept me warm. Then I'd wake up and reach for you, and you'd be gone. Don't ever leave me!"

"I won't, Dan! I couldn't! I love you!"

He buried his face in her hair. "I shouldn't hold you like this. I've slept in the open, in Indian houses. I smell of smoke and fish. I promised myself a bath first—"

She laughed, softly. He smelled of cedar, of woodsmoke and the clean outdoors. "It doesn't matter," she said. "Oh, Dan, I've waited so long."

"I was afraid you wouldn't be waiting," he said soberly. "I was scared. Scared as hell. The way I blew up before I left, accusing you of flirting with that Russian, what's-his-name, I wouldn't have blamed you if—"

Her small cold hand covered his mouth to stop the flow of words, and Tamsen stiffened in his arms. Startled, he released his hold and she pulled away. Going to a corner of the room, she pulled the cord that summoned Helena.

"You will want your bath," she said.

Somehow a curtain had dropped between them, and Dan tried to recall what he had said. She did not appear to be angry, just remote.

"Tamsen—"

"You haven't told me where you've been. Did you make any new discoveries?"

"Yes," he said, frowning, "but—"

A tap at the door signaled Helena's arrival. The girl said that she was pleased to see he had returned safely. She would have bath water brought immediately. When she left, Dan moved toward Tamsen. She was on her knees beside a chest, rummaging for clean clothing for him. He put a tentative hand to her hair. "You are glad I'm home?"

A tremor shuddered through her at his touch. "You know I am."

"Then tell me about it?"

He lifted her to her feet. As she looked at him, seeing the stark need that darkened his eyes, her own slid away evasively. "I've missed you," she faltered. "I love you."

"Tamsen, is something wrong?"

"Of course not."

His arms went around her once more, pulling her close. She could feel the thudding of his heart beneath the flannel shirt. Her own responded, her body melting as she clung to him. For a moment she felt like blurting out the happenings of these last days—Petrov's death, the way she'd been spied upon, blackmailed, the governor-general's ultimatum—

The door opened, and Dan released her with a sigh. Helena entered, followed by a train of kitchen boys carrying pails. A wooden tub was set up behind a screen and filled with steaming water. When the others were gone, Tamsen walked to the window and stared blindly into the night.

Dan looked at her bent shoulders in bewilderment. It was clear she had something on her mind. Intuition told him to wait for her to come to him. He pulled off his plaid shirt, exposing the oilskin packet that held his secret charts. Placing the packet on a chair, he folded his shirt over it. When he slept, it would be beneath his pillow, close at hand.

Tamsen, turning, saw his action and felt ill. There were the maps she must get her hands on, and copy. Though she intended to mark them falsely, it was still not being honest with Dan.

He stood before her, clad only in his denim trousers, broad-shouldered, lean, hard-muscled and brown from the out-of-doors. So many nights she'd dreamed of resting her cheek against his familiar shoulder—

"Something is the matter, sweetheart, tell me. What is it?" His voice was perplexed.

"I guess I'm still in a state of shock," she said, forcing a smile. "Now, take your bath. I'll ready myself for bed."

Tallant went behind the screen, frowning. This wasn't the homecoming he'd dreamed of. Tamsen seemed stand-offish, even—shy. He'd been gone for a long while. Was that the problem? Was he going to have to woo her all over again? Hell, he'd never understand women. Soaping himself vigorously, he thought for a moment, then grinned.

"Tamsen, come here."

Leaving the window where she'd been staring at nothing, Tamsen crossed the room and went behind the screen. Her heart stopped at the sight of his gleaming, bronzed body, the dark hair falling over his forehead dripping above a devil-may-care grin.

"Still dressed? We'll fix that." Reaching out with a soapy hand, he gripped her own and pulled her, fully clothed, into the water with him.

"Dan, you fool!" Laughing and sputtering, she struggled as he tore at the buttons of her sopping gown. "Dan!" They slipped and slithered, water splashing to the ceiling. As a grand finale, the screen came crashing down. They lay beneath it, laughing until they couldn't breathe.

"You hurt?" Dan finally gasped.

Tamsen realized she was. "I'll have a black eye in the morning," she said in mock accusation, "and everyone will know who did it."

Sobering, Dan moved the screen and lifted her gently, touching her face with gentle fingers. Then his hands moved down, removing the layers of sodden clothing until it lay in a heap about her feet. He stepped backward, saying her name on a harsh and ragged breath. She answered with a small moaning sound, her hands outstretched. Then she was in his arms and he carried her toward the massive Russian bed with its canopy.

Covering her against a chill, he lay beside her, his lips tender on her bruised cheek. His hand traced the line of her mouth, her throat. "Getting to know you," he whispered as he had on a far-away moonlit hill above San Francisco. His mouth found the curve of her shoulder. Her trembling had ceased. She was burning with an inward fire that matched his own.

"Are you warm now?"

"Yes, Dan. Dan—please! Oh, please—"

He drew the covers back and smiled down at her. The woman who had bewildered him was gone. This was the Tamsen he knew; willful and wanton, her slim body golden in the candle's light; eyes dark with passion, her mouth a flaming flower—

He snuffed the bedside candle and turned to her with love.

Tamsen woke in the morning with a sense of security and well-being, the governor-general's threats forgotten. Drowsily, she reached a hand toward Dan's pillow, remembering. It was empty. He had already risen.

Tamsen sat up, dark hair falling over bare shoulders, to see Helena at work cleaning up the water spills from the night before.

"You are awake," the girl said cheerfully. *"Agan tache."*

"The sun burns hot," Tamsen guessed.

And she also correctly interpreted Helena's next statement. Pointing at Tamsen, the girl giggled and said, *"I-ssran."*

"You love."

After slipping into a pale blue silk robe, Tamsen sat before the mirror and brushed her hair, dreaming of Dan's returning. He'd left word with Helena that he was taking his new maps to the governor-general and shouldn't be long. She would not dress, today. This day was theirs.

Then she received two messages, one on the heels of the other. The first was from her husband. He would be closeted with Voedvodski most of the day. She was not to wait for him, but to take advantage of the rare Sitka sun.

Closeted with Voedvodski. The fears that had been quieted during the night in Dan's arms were with her again, intensified. Dan would surely learn of Petrov's death. What would the governor-general say of her part in it? He might even make a few sly insinuations, to keep her dancing like a puppet....

She should have told Dan about the Yuri-Petrov affair last night. And now it was too late. Tamsen was pacing the floor when the second message came. It was from Edwin Devon. Stiffly formal, he requested an introduction to her husband. He would be honored if Mr. and Mrs. Tallant would be his guests at tea, morning or afternoon, at their convenience. His messenger would wait for their answer.

Tamsen felt a surge of relief. The company of Devon would help her take her mind off her problems. If she stayed in her apartment, she would go out of her mind with worry. It was better to wait and see what had been said to Dan. No point in anticipating.

"Tell Mr. Devon, Mrs. Tallant is happy to accept," she said. "And the morning will be nice. We'll meet at the foot of the knoll at ten."

It was nearly that time now. Hastily, she dressed in an apricot gown, grabbed a sunshade to match, and hurried to meet the young Englishman.

Devon had had a bad night. He had blamed it on the unfamiliar quarters, but the truth was that he kept conjuring up pictures of the happy reunion of husband and wife. If Dan Tallant were worthy of Tamsen, well and good. But if he were the savage he appeared to be, the lady would need a friend.

Devon's happiness when he saw her coming, and alone, knew no bounds. He hastened to meet her with his long stride, forgetting the doctor's cautioning words.

Tamsen did not see his thoughtful expression as she explained her husband's absence. Only a boor would desert his wife, for any reason, on his first day home was Devon's private conclusion. And the faint mauve line along her cheekbone was not a shadow cast by the sunshade!

"Shall we go in? Or would you prefer tea in the garden?"

Tamsen opted for the garden. The day was so lovely. Devon assisted her to a bench in the shade, then hurried in to order tea. How wonderful it would be, Tamsen sighed to herself, if only Dan were with her. She folded her sunshade and watched a small ruby-throated hummingbird, surely a visitor from California, as it sipped from bloom to bloom.

Devon, returning with a tray of tea and small Russian pastries, was first enthralled at the picture she made, then appalled. The mauve line was clearly a bruise.

Seeing his expression, Tamsen remembered. Guiltily, she touched her face. "I—I bumped against something in the dark," she lied. For after all, there was no way to explain what had really happened.

Devon, his face set in stern lines, managed to make small talk, but all in all, it was an awkward tea, their old rapport missing. At Tamsen's suggestion, they walked once more along the Indian trail, where she gathered her arms full of flowers. She smiled to herself, thinking how she would bring Dan here on the morrow, and Devon, watching her, thought, "Poor, brave little girl!"

It was quite late when they retraced their steps, time for tea again. Tamsen gave in to Devon's insistent invitation, though she was beginning to long to return to the castle. Surely, Dan's conference would be done by now.

With her instinctive knowledge of men, she decided it just might be a good idea to let Dan wait for a while, to let him wonder where she might be. And it was pleasant here in the sun among the birds and flowers.... The bells of St. Michael's began to ring, and people were running toward the wharf, waving. A ship was coming in.

Devon drew a small collapsible spyglass from his pocket, opening it to its full length. "A Russian ship," he said. "An enormous one. With well-dressed people at the rail. Evidently we're about to receive a visitation of notables—"

"Another feast," Tamsen moaned. "And we shall have to attend! I don't think I can bear it!"

But at least it gave her a chance to get away, gracefully. "I must get back to the castle, see to my wardrobe—"

Devon escorted her as far as the open spot at the foot of the kekoor. I dare not let her go, he thought, without some knowledge of the way I feel. She must know there is someone she can come to, in time of need. He bowed over her hand, kissing it, then, looking into her eyes, quoted the last two lines of a poem he'd written for her the previous night.

"To drown within my loved one's eyes

60

Would be to wake in Paradise—"

Good Lord, Tamsen thought, amazed. He means it! And I had no idea! For the first time, she saw the blue lines bracketing his mouth, the fine sheen of perspiration on his upper lip. He didn't look well. What a strange, kind man he was.

"I must go," she stammered. And, whirling, she ran toward the steps, almost bumping into Dan. He gripped her wrists, his eyes hard and angry. But when he spoke, it was in a half-teasing way.

"Just what was that about? And who is your friend?"

"An English gentleman," she gasped. "A writer. He—he sent an invitation asking both of us to tea, and since you were occupied—"

"You handled the social graces, right? And very well, too, considering the tender parting I just witnessed."

"Dan!"

"I'm not angry," he said, tensely, "just disappointed. After what happened here the other night—"

"Who told you?"

"Who hasn't, for God's sake! Do you think you can keep something like that a secret? A man's dead!"

"Dan, I swear it had nothing to do with me. Yuri and Petrov had both been drinking, and they—"

"They chose to fight over my wife, who was, as usual, indulging in a little harmless flirtation. Dammit, Tam, you're just about as harmless as an earthquake! When are you going to learn?"

Tamsen whirled, catching the gaze of a sentry who listened curiously, not understanding the words that were exchanged, but clearly enjoying the quarrel. She turned back to Dan.

"If you have anything more to say to me, I suggest you do it in the privacy of our apartment." Haughtily, she attempted to brush by him. He caught at her, spinning her to face him.

"I'm sorry, sweetheart. I know you mean no harm. You just don't know what you do to a man." He touched her cheek with a forefinger in an attempt to reestablish their relationship, but Tamsen looked stonily ahead.

"Look, Tamsen, you've got to understand how this hit me, coming home to find you were involved in an ugly mess, then seeing you with that—"

"Are you coming?" she asked, icily.

He spread his hands. "I can't right now. I'm going down to meet the ship that just came in. There are some people aboard I must see—people who can help me. The Baron de Stoeckl has just returned from an interview with the tsar, trying to push the sale of Alaska to the States. I need to find out if he made any headway—"

"Then go," she said. "I'm certain his information won't wait. It's more important than settling our own problems."

"Tamsen!"

He was talking to thin air. She'd left him and was hurrying up the steps. He made a move to follow, then said, "Oh, hell!" He shook his head and made his way to the shore, where the newcomers were being welcomed with pomp and ceremony.

Tamsen's anger had begun to cool by the time she reached the apartment. Naturally, Dan had been upset, hearing the gossip from others. And maybe she was to blame, after a fashion. Courting the admiration of men had been a trick of the trade when she operated her establishment in San Francisco. The fascinating Madam Franklin, who sang, danced, maintained a stable of girls—but would not go upstairs for any man. Had the old habits stayed with her? Had she, subconsciously, become a woman who promised with no intention of following through?

Had both Yuri and Petrov been given reason to believe they should do battle for her favors? And Devon! Poor Devon! Well, she could fix that! Tonight, at the banquet, she would see that he met Dan, let him discover she was married to a most wonderful man. She would show him where her true affections lay and perhaps gently propel him in the direction of another girl.

It was very late when Dan returned. Tamsen had already readied herself for the feast, in her most unbecoming dress. Plum-colored, with touches of black lace, it was an unattractive color for her, and the lines were too matronly for her small figure. But it would surely serve to discourage admirers. She would behave most sedately tonight.

She was brushing her hair when Dan entered. He approached cautiously, lifting the silken mass to kiss the back of her neck. "Forgive me?" he asked.

She reached up to pull his face down to hers. "Of course," she whispered. "And Dan, I think you were right. I will take care!"

He patted her, absently. "That's my girl. Now, I must dress—"

"Dan!" She caught his hand, feeling a need to return to last night's blissful state. "Dan, let's not go tonight. Let's stay here, the two of us alone. I need— I need you."

"And I need you, sweetheart." He smiled, crookedly. "But duty calls. As I said, there are some important people here, people who can help me. But you don't have to go."

"Try leaving me behind!" She smiled mistily, "Just you try!"

Both of them dressed and ready to leave the apartment, Tamsen paused at the door. "Do I look all right?"

Dan looked at her gown, frowning a little. "I suppose there isn't time to change—"

"Change! What's the matter with what I'm wearing?"

"Nothing," he said feebly, "nothing at all. Except perhaps something a bit richer-looking would have been in order. There are people here we must impress."

Wordlessly, Tamsen walked ahead of him, heels tapping, toward the banquet room. What did the man want? First, she must be a demure little wife, not attracting male attention. Yet at the same time, she should outshine the other women in the room.

She made a rude sound. And the dignified manservant at the door blinked. He could have sworn that when he stared at her, startled, the wife of the emissary from the States stuck out her tongue at him.

Tamsen saw Edwin Devon near a samovar as they entered the great hall. She decided to get the introductions over as soon as possible. Turning, she said, "Dan—"

But Dan Tallant's eyes were fixed upon someone across the room. She followed his gaze. In a far corner, amid the colorful costumes of Russian noblemen, a central figure stood out with clarity. The figure of a Russian girl, blond among the dark women, dressed as a princess would dress, glimmering with jewels. Surely the most beautiful woman in the world.

"Dan," Tamsen said once more, but he didn't seem to hear her.

"Excuse me," he said absently, setting Tamsen aside with one hand.

As Dan wove his way through the crowded room, Tamsen watched helplessly. The Russian girl's face lit with a charming smile of welcome, and she greeted TaHant with outstretched hands.

Tamsen stood still, her heart clenched in an icy grip of fear. Then, head high, a stiff smile on her lips, she made her way to where Edwin Devon waited with a look of sympathy and understanding in his eyes.

CHAPTER 6

Tamsen again made her excuses for Dan as she greeted Devon. "I wanted him to meet you, but he had business with the people who came in on the ship. Perhaps later."

"Here, allow me to get you some tea." Filling a glass, which the Russians preferred to a cup, he presented it to Tamsen, who sipped the tea absently, her eyes on the gaily plumaged nobles across the room.

"Who is she, do you know?" Tamsen asked.

"As it happens, I do know." Devon leaned against the wall behind him. "I've been speaking to her brother, who has a creditable command of English, as does the lady, I understand. They are the Prince and Princess Mischerski, distantly related to the tsar himself, and favorites at court. The brother is Prince Igor." Devon gestured with his glass. Following his gesture, Tamsen gasped at sight of a young man fully as beautiful as his sister.

"And the princess is Anya, known variously, according to her loving brother, as *duschechka*—or the darling—and *melki bes*, which, translated, means the little demon."

"She sounds like a fascinating woman," Tamsen said caustically.

"I wager she's not. I say, Tamsen—forgive me,

Mrs. Tallant—perhaps you might like to join the group. May I have the honor of presenting you to Prince Mischerski?"

She turned a dazzling smile on him. "Do call me Tamsen," she cooed. "And I shall call you Edwin. And—yes, I think I would like that."

She crossed the room on Edwin's arm and was soon introduced to Prince Igor, who studied her intently, his bold eyes sparkling with mischief. Then she felt Dan's hand at her elbow. He moved her to face the princess, introducing her as his wife.

Princess Anya Mischerski's gaze was bold, too, assessing Tamsen in one look. But where her brother's eyes glittered with mischief, hers were slits of ice, as brilliant as the diamonds she wore in her hair. No taller than Tamsen, her bearing was arrogant, overwhelming. Tamsen felt dowdy and small in contrast as she acknowledged the introduction.

Turning, she gripped Edwin Devon's arm, unaware that he felt the chill of her small hand through his coat. Stiffly, she uttered the proper words, addressing Devon to the princess and then to Dan, who had been prepared to meet this man on a friendly basis. But at the look of dislike in the gentleman's eyes, an instant antagonism sprang into his own. Who the hell did he think he was, anyway? Typical Britisher! Stuffed shirt!

Then Tallant remembered he had some news to break to his wife. "Tamsen, sweetheart, I have the honor of escorting Princess Mischerski to dinner. I told her you would not mind."

"Not at all." Tamsen's voice was frigid, and the princess smiled a slow triumphant smile. Then her brother, Prince Igor, broke in.

"Since your husband is spoken for, Madam

Tallant, would you settle for second best? I would be honored—"

"Thank you," Tamsen said, inclining her head graciously, "but I've accepted an earlier invitation. Mr. Devon will take me in to dinner."

Dan's face went white, then red. Dammit, Tamsen couldn't have known he'd be forced into this spot. Yet she'd already made arrangements with that Englishman!

"I'm sure," he said curtly, "Mr. Devon won't mind—"

"But Mr. Devon would mind," Edwin said, meeting Tallant's glare head-on.

"For which I do not blame him," Prince Igor broke in. "I can only hope to have the pleasure of dinner at another time."

"I shall look forward to it." With a slight curtsy that included the group, Tamsen turned to take Devon's arm and they swept away. He could sense that she was trembling.

Out of their hearing, Tamsen whispered, "I'm so sorry, Edwin. I don't know what made me say that! Forgive me. If you have other plans—"

He stopped short. "Madam Tallant, will you allow me the honor of escorting you to table?"

A wry smile touched her lips. "Mr. Devon, I accept with pleasure."

"Then, now that the formalities are over, shall we go?" With great ceremony, he extended his arm.

Tamsen sat beside him, unable to swallow a morsel of the typically heavy meal. She only glanced toward Dan once, noting that he was seated between the princess and Baron de Stoeckl. Dan, however, glanced often toward the couple at the end of the table, glowering at the man who had appropriated his wife. He himself was in a spot. The Baron de

Stoeckl had advised him to seek the princess's favor, since she had Tsar Alexander's ear. The princess's charm was far too intense.... He had a feeling he would have some explaining to do this night.

After the banquet ended, Dan looked for Tamsen in vain. The Princess Anya regarded him as her personal property for the evening, and he couldn't gracefully get away. As he danced with the princess, looking over her golden head for Tamsen, he heard her small, amused laugh.

"If you are seeking your wife, sir, I am certain she is in good company. She left with the English gentleman at the banquet's end."

Tamsen had left the banquet hall as soon as possible. Pleading a headache, she returned to her apartment. Edward Devon went to his lonely rooms at the barracks where he would spend the remainder of the night composing another poem to his love.

Pulling off the plum-colored gown, Tamsen wadded it up and pitched it into a corner. She would never wear the thing again.

Dan's actions this night had been unforgivable! He had devoted his attention to that cold-eyed Russian witch! And the assessing look the girl had given her was that of one who studied her—competition—and found it unworthy of concern!

And Dan! Dan had made a fool of himself over the hussy! After daring to criticize Tamsen for her own actions! Being jealous of poor Edwin Devon, who had comported himself like a gentleman! Well, what was good for the gander was good for the goose! She would show him!

Pulling on a bedgown Dan hated, because he swore he couldn't find her among all those yards of cloth, Tamsen finally went to bed—the bed in which

69

she'd been so close to heaven the night before. She lay awake, still fuming as the skies took on their early summer light. She was still awake when she heard noise and laughter in the hall, though she feigned sleep.

Dan Tallant entered with a sense of vast relief to find his wife in his own bed, where she should be. He'd always loved her mule-headed unpredictable nature. But angered, there was no telling what she'd do. And she had every right to be angry, he thought, uneasily. He'd be glad when this damn fool business was over and done with.

But for now, should he wake her? Have it out now, or wait until morning? What the hell! Might as well get it over with.

"Tamsen?"

Her cold and stony silence told him she was awake.

"Tamsen, sweetheart—"

She sat up. "Don't you sweetheart me," she hissed. "And don't touch me! Go chase that predatory Russian blond, if you've got any romantic ideas! I'm not interested in anything you have to do or say!"

"Tamsen, Tamsen," he sighed. Sitting down on the edge of the bed, he put his arms around her fierce unyielding body. "You've got to listen to me, honey. You're my wife! I love you!"

Tamsen felt her resolve melt at his touch and fought against it as he went on speaking. "Please hear me out! I'm only trying to do my job—"

"And she's doing one on you! Princess! She's a dreadful, flirtatious little—"

His hand went over her mouth. "Hush! She's in the room across the hall! She'll hear you!"

Across the hall? The haunted room? Perhaps she

70

thought it was worth it—being close to Dan. "Convenient," Tamsen said bitterly.

He released her and stood up to pace the length of the room and back again. Finally, he spoke, his voice firm. "First, I want to apologize. You can accept that apology or not, as you will. Then I want to explain my actions, and why I let myself get in a corner.

"You know why I'm here. Supposedly, I'm an advisor to the Russians. Actually, I'm checking to find if this land's worth buying. And it is. These goddamn Russians are sitting on a gold mine and don't know it!

"All right, so the land's worth it. Now what's the next step? I've got to convince the President and the Senate of the United States. This is an election year, and God knows what changes will take place. Even at the best, it'll be a problem."

He frowned at Tamsen, who sat unmoving, head bent. "When the President and Senate are convinced, then there's the tsar, Alexander II, himself. And he's like a weathervane, the weak-willed sonofabitch! De Stoeckl's talked till he's blue in the face. Then it's yes, until some of Furuhelm's following talk him out of it. But he'll listen to this young woman—"

"And why would he do that?" Tamsen's voice was sweet. Too sweet. "A man of de Stoeckl's experience is ignored, but he'll listen to *her?* For the same reason you do, I suppose?"

Dan fought the urge to grab his wife and shake some sense into her. Slowly, painstakingly, as if he were speaking to a child, he told the story he had heard from Baron de Stoeckl.

The prince and princess were distant relatives of Tsar Alexander. Their parents were killed when revolutionists made an attempt on the life of

71

Nicholas, the present tsar's father, and the orphaned children were reared at court. Alexander looked upon the Princess Anya as a beloved younger sister. Prince Igor he tolerated, affectionately, regarding him as a rather effete young man. So it was Anya he sent to study the situation and advise him as to the practicality of selling the colony and its possessions...

Dan neglected to mention something else the baron had told him. The lovely princess had been in a spot of trouble—with a married nobleman. Tsar Alexander had seized upon the Alaskan situation as a solution to the problem, sending her here.

"The best part of it," Dan said finally, "is that the baron has talked to the princess. She can be bought—"

"I'm sure she can. And just what is her price?"

Dan threw up his hands. "I've had one hell of an evening! I know land and rivers, horses, minerals and where to find them, guns, hunting, trapping—but I'm sure as hell no goddamn diplomat! If I was, I'd know how to handle my wife. Here I plan on coming home, spending a week in bed, just loving you—and you're a half-mile down a table talking to a love-sick Britisher, while I'm stuck at the other end with a man-hungry female—"

Tamsen made a small sound, suspiciously like a giggle. He looked at her warily, and at last she raised her head. Her eyes were streaming with tears, but she was laughing and crying at the same time.

"Oh, Dan, hold me! Hold me! Never let me go!"

Dan sat down on the edge of the bed and gathered her in his arms, tipping her tear-wet mouth to his. "This is what I should have done in the first place," he said unsteadily. "I don't know why it is—when we try to talk things out, the sparks seem to fly. But touching, like this, we know each other. Our

72

misunderstandings fly out the window. Have you noticed that?"

She had. Perhaps everyone was the same. Two people tried to be individuals, standing apart, when they were meant to be one. Only in Dan's arms did she feel whole and content.

"I wish to hell I'd caught on to this trick earlier," Dan said fervently. "Every time we crossed swords, I should have grabbed you and held you till we both calmed down."

She laughed, remembering their stormy courtship, and he understood the reasons for her laughter. "I guess I'd have been holding you most of the time," he said, sheepishly.

"I think I'd have liked it," she said. "Oh, Dan, we lost so much time with each other! It was so foolish!"

"We'll have to make up for that lost time now." His mouth touched hers tenderly, then became more demanding as his passion mounted. "Tamsen," he finally groaned, "I can't find you! Will you get rid of that damned *shroud?*"

She rose, removing the gown she'd put on to repel his advances. It fell around her feet, and she kicked it beneath the bed. Tomorrow, she would give it to Helena.

Later, warm in the curve of Dan's arm, Tamsen thought of the girl across the hall in the haunted room and gave a silent prayer.

"If it's true, and there is a ghostly spirit, and she's listening to me, please, oh, please, haunt the hell out of her, will you?"

She chuckled a little at her own fancies, and Dan stirred. "Mmm?" he mumbled, sleepily.

"Nothing at all," she whispered. "It's nothing." She curled closer to him, feeling sleepy and warm and much loved.

The next morning Tamsen woke, the sun on her

73

face, to the sound of movement in the room. Stretching lazily, she said Dan's name. When he didn't answer, she sat up, the covers falling away, to see Helena. The girl, dustcloth in hand, wore an odd expression.

"The husband is not here, Mrs. Tallant. He walks through Novoarchangelsk, with the Princess Anya." The young woman was stammering with agitation. "But there are messages for you—"

Tamsen seized them eagerly, hoping one would be a note from Dan. The first was a long and passionate poem from Devon with a postscript inviting her to tea. The other, accompanying a package, read, *"Perhaps this will repay, in part, for sharing your husband with my untrustworthy sister. May I have the pleasure of your company in seeing the sights of this small settlement?"* It was signed merely *Igor.*

The package contained a Russian cross of heavy, hammered silver, set with precious stones.

"Convey my gratitude to both," Tamsen said, "with my regrets that I am indisposed." She drew the chain of the cross listlessly through her fingers. "And please return this gift."

Helena vanished to do her bidding, and Tamsen rose to walk the floor. How little she really knew about men, she thought. Her days of managing the parlor in San Francisco had not led her to place much trust in them. Reputedly happy husbands had passed through those doors, had vainly sought her own attentions—and gone upstairs with Katie, Carmen, or whoever was at hand.

Yet she must trust Dan. It was the princess she didn't trust.

CHAPTER 7

In San Francisco, the chill gray fog blanketing the city reflected the mood of Nell Campbell, now owner and proprietor of Tamsen's former place of business, Madam Franklin's Parlor for Gentlemen.

Nell lumbered to her feet and closed the crimson velvet draperies against the depressing day, then returned to her desk. Her chair groaned as she lowered her massive bulk, clad in her favorite robe, pink silk with ostrich feathers dyed to match. She'd donned it with the notion it might lift her spirits. But she was lower than a snake's belly, that was for sure.

Spread on her desk were papers covered with figures. And any way she juggled those numbers, they added up to one thing. Ruin.

Gawdammit, she wished that Tamsen girl was here! Puny little mite, but she had a head on her shoulders. Never give up on nuthin'. She'd figger out some way to keep this joint afloat.

Her worries were justified. For in this last year, San Francisco had gone from boom to bust. In February of 1855, the St. Louis home office of Page, Bacon and Company had gone bankrupt. When the news reached San Francisco, the immediate run on the local branch caused it to default. Runs on other banks forced them to close their doors. Business after business had gone under. And from the looks of Nell's figures, Madam Franklin's Parlor, herself as owner and proprietor, just might be next.

In the meantime, her head ached. She needed to talk to someone, to get her thinking straight. And Dusty was better than nobody. Rising again, she made her way to the door of a small anteroom. The little Englishman who had been her friend and lover for so many years was sprawled on a cot, a bottle close at hand. His wispy mustache twitched with each bubbling snore. Nell looked at him for a moment with loving eyes, then shook her head and closed the door quietly.

It was a dumb-headed idea, anyway. Not much the little sonofabitch could do to help, so why get his bowels in an uproar over something that couldn't be mended? Somebody around here oughta be happy. Dusty'd been feeling low enough anyway. He'd been moping around ever since Tamsen got married and took off for the north. You'd think she was his own kid.

Maybe if the two of them had got hitched a long time ago, and had half a dozen of their own—

Helluva time to think of that now! Anyway, kids were nothing but trouble. And husbands brought nothing but grief. She should know, in her business.

Grunting at her wave of sentimentality, she seated herself once more, sweeping the papers from her desk. Breaking out a new deck of cards, she began to deal with a most professional hand. If worst came to worser, she told herself, maybe she'd find some well-heeled sucker and get a game going. If there was anybody with money left in this town.

"Pretty damn slick," she muttered, as she viewed the hands she'd dealt herself and an imaginary partner. Two aces showing for her opponent, nothing down. Two treys for herself. She smiled, turning over the down card, exposing another trey. And someone tapped at the door.

"Gawdammit," she bawled, "don't bust the door down! Whatcha want?"

Maggie, clad in a faded wrapper and still wearing last night's paint and powder, pushed the door open. She had an odd, rather frightened expression on her face. "Some—some people here to see you," she said.

"I'm busy," Nell barked. Then, "Oh, hell! Send 'em on in! Probably some more of them gawdamned bill collectors."

Maggie stepped back, ushered the visitors in, and closed the door behind them. For a moment, Nell was unable to speak. Her face blanched at the sight of two ladies, dressed in subdued finery, hatted and gloved, their own faces wearing strained smiles.

"I'll be damned," Nell finally grunted. "Arab and Em! Never thought I'd see you two in this place. Tamsen'd be fit t'be tied!" Then her eyes darkened with alarm. "You ain't brought bad news? The girl's awright, ain't she? Tamsen—?"

Emmeline Alden spoke quickly, afraid that the woman might have a stroke. "Tamsen's fine. We haven't heard from her in several months, but she was fine—and very happy."

Nell tried to pull herself together. "I think a lot of that girl. She's got guts! Now, I ain't foolin' myself that this's a soshul visit. Whatcha got on yer minds?"

"We wondered what you had heard from Tamsen," Em evaded. "We miss her, you know."

"Hell, yes," Nell said gloomily. "Me, too. But ain't no cause t'worry. No matter what that girl fell in, she'd come up smellin' like a rose. Got a letter here somewheres. Dusty read the damn thing to me." She flushed. "Guess I gotta get some specs. I see fer figgerin' awright, but readin's somethin' else—"

"But she sounded happy in your letter?"

"Sure as hell did. Livin' in a castle, all them Rooshians fallin' at her feet. More'n a thousand men an' about sixty 'er so wimmen. All kinda in her line of work, so to speak." Nell's voice trailed off as she realized what she'd said. "Don't git me wrong, I know she's married an' all, but Tamsen ain't one t'crawl in a hole an' pull it in after her—"

"I know, I feel that way at times." Arabella Narváez spoke for the first time. "I danced with Lola Montez, you know. And now, even though I'm happily married, I still miss—some things."

Nell eyed her sharply. Was it possible all wasn't rosy in the Narváez household? Juan Narváez was certainly a man to write home about, but Arab had never struck Nell as the homebody type.

Now Em, that was different. Em was more the mincey housewife, the kind beyond Nell's understanding. Rather make a pie than a man, any day. Last time Nell saw Senator Donald Alden, she'd bet he'd gained fifty pounds. An' Em was prob'ly proud of ever one a' them. If it wasn't fer th' guts she showed having her baby along the trail, Nell wouldn't believe she was Tamsen's sister.

"How's little Martha?" Nell asked abruptly.

"Just fine," Em answered. "She's growing like a weed."

"Thass good."

A long pause followed. Nell finally struck the desk with a hamlike fist. "Awright, dammit! Let's git to the point. You girls don't belong here. You know it. I know it. If you come, you come fer a reason. Let's git it out in the open, an' to hell with the soshul chitchat."

Emmeline and Arabella exchanged glances. Then Em leaned forward, the color high in her cheeks.

"You know about the bank failures?"

"Hell, yes," Nell said fervently.

"What you may not know is that my husband, Donald, feels he is in some way responsible. He was on the board of directors of several banks. As a former senator, and as an attorney, he advised clients who invested money on his recommendations. Therefore, he feels at fault."

"I gitcha."

Em's voice was nervous as she continued, "There have been attempts to blacken his character. You remember his stepbrother, Adam?"

"Sure as hell do."

"Adam had friends who contributed to the present situation. For example, 'Honest Harry Meiggs,' who defaulted and went to South America, owing something like a hundred thousand dollars to the people of the city. And he was friendly with other men who bilked them."

"An' they're blamin' the senator? Sonsofbitches!"

"No," Em shook her head sadly. "The senator's blaming himself. He—he's sold the seaside property that was to be our new home. He's also disposed of the house that was his stepmother's, where we've been living. We're staying in the rooms back of his offices now, and he's talking of selling that. To make restitution."

"You mean he's paying off them gawdam bastards?"

Em flinched. "Every one."

Nell looked at Arab. "What's yer beef?"

"Juan is tarred with the same brush, since he took a job as Donald's assistant. Like Donald, he puts honor above all else. I know he's been in communication with his uncle, General Narváez in Spain, who disinherited him when he married me.

79

He keeps saying I'd be better off without him to drag me down." Her face twisted with pain as she said, "I'm afraid he'll leave me."

"Donald's been failing this last year," Em put in. "He's older than I, but not that much older. I can't bear to watch what this is doing to him."

There was another long pause, and finally Nell said, "Well, hell! It's a damn shame things turned out like that, but whatcha want from me? You didn't come here to cry on my shoulder. Go on, speak your piece. Never did like dealin' with a cold deck!"

Em bent her head, twisting her hands in her lap. "We haven't discussed this with Donald or Juan, Nell. But Arab and I, we've thought of opening a small dining place. I would do the cooking, and Arab could wait tables. But it would take money, and we have no collateral."

Nell fixed her with a beady eye. "Hankerin' to go into bizness? Or are you that hard up?"

"That hard up," Em confessed. "Our husbands can't find work. We thought we'd try—"

"An' you come to get some money from me." Their guilty expressions showed Nell she'd guessed correctly. Well, she might as well set 'em straight.

"You could borry it, if I had any. But I ain't. Things is bad all over. Tamsen turned this here place over to me, lock, stock, and barrel; I was makin' money hand over fist. So I sez to myself, 'Hell, Nell, yer in big bizness now. Put the gawdam stuff in th' bank, so's it'll be safe.' Then th' bank went broke. Shows it don't pay to be honest, don't it?"

"I'm sorry," Em whispered.

Throughout the conversation, Arabella had been working at the fingers of her mended gloves. Now she looked up, her eyes filled with determination. "Are you going to ask her, Em, or shall I?"

Em remained silent, and Arab turned to Nell. "If you can't lend us money, can you—can you give us a job?"

"What was you thinkin' on doin'?"

Arab could sing and dance, she told her. And Em was an excellent cook. Perhaps she could help Mrs. Faraday, who cooked for the Parlor now?

Nell rubbed her chin. She'd had to let Birdie Faraday go. She'd closed the dining room. And she'd cut back on the girls until only Carmen and Maggie were left. Things had plumb gone to hell in a bushel basket.

"Good thing, too," she said. "If things was good, I might give you a job. An' what'd that do to them men of yers? Senator Alden's wife the chief cook in a whorehouse? An' yer man, Arab, that high-toned furriner, think he'd go fer his wife kickin' up her heels in a place like this? Hell, no!"

Em and Arab were both in tears. "I'm sorry," Arab finally said. "You're right, Nell. We—we didn't know where to turn. Thanks, anyway."

Nell screwed her eyes up in thought. "There's always Tamsen," she reminded them. "Dan's well-heeled, got him a good job. She might give you a loan. Hell, yer men ain't doin' too good here. Why not head fer Alaska?"

Em wiped her eyes. "We don't want to tell Tamsen our troubles. She's really happy. Perhaps for the first time in her life. She's always taken the responsibility for us. It's our fault she got into this kind of business." She reddened, realizing what she'd said, then lifted her chin. "What I'm trying to say is that it wouldn't be fair to unload our troubles on her. We'll manage some way."

"Sure you will," Nell said heartily. "Sure you will."

She studied the two girls, Emmeline Alden, with

81

her gentle, sweet blue eyes grave in a fair face, crowned by gold-brown hair. And Arabella, with slanting green eyes and hair like flame. They were not her kind of people and never would be. But they were Tamsen's sisters, and they unleashed a wave of nostalgia for the girl.

Nell reached into the bosom of her robe and brought out a handkerchief knotted around a few gold coins. "Ain't got much," she said hesitantly, "but yer sure as hell welcome to what there is—"

Em was on her feet. "I'm afraid we painted the picture blacker than it really is," she said brightly. "It will be all right. And thank you." They went through the polite motions of farewell. They reached the door, and Arab turned. Quick as a flash, she reached the desk and placed a kiss on Nell's cheek.

Nell sat rubbing her cheek for a moment, then said, "Well, I'll be damned!"

She couldn't help Arab and Em, but she had a new idea. Why not think about Alaska herself? More than a thousand Rooshians, only about sixty women. If all else failed, one of her customers had mentioned the way the Esky-moes set the old and useless flat on their ass on a cake of ice, leaving them to the hand of fate. Better than the seat she occupied now, about to be yanked out from under her by bill collectors. Hell, why not?

Going to the door of the small anteroom, she yelled, "Dusty? Dusty, git th' lead out! I'm headin' north. You goin' with me?"

William Winston Wotherspoon sat up. "Wherever you are, Nell," he said gallantly, "there is Eden."

"That's what I figgered, you little sonofabitch," Nell beamed fondly. "That's what I figgered. So sober up, gitcher long-handles an' snowshoes together, an' let's git goin'."

Tamsen was going to be in for one hell of a surprise! But even this was going to take some doing. Nell returned to her desk, grinning at what Dusty would think when he really woke up. The little bastard would be surprised what he'd agreed to. She began to plan.

She'd stall off the bills for a while by closing off all but one room downstairs and two above; she would strip the others and sell the luxurious contents piece by piece. She had no hope of selling the place as a whole. She'd already tried that. But she could shut the house down, under pretext of renovating, and turn the rest of the furnishings to cash. With a few months' income, no matter how meager, and the money from the furnishings, they'd walk out and leave the stripped buildings for the wolves to fight over.

This should give her enough money for her fare and Dusty's—and Carmen's and Maggie's, of course. They had to have something to start with, and she didn't know what those Esky-mo women were like at the trade. Heard they only rubbed noses.

Shaking her head, she snuck a quick look in the mirror on the wall. The men up north liked their women with a bit of blubber on them. She wondered if she might be able to turn a trick or two, then virtuously dismissed the thought. Dusty wouldn't like it, not at all.

So there it was. Maybe it wasn't honest to skip out on the bills, but the banks hadn't been honest with her either, closing their doors and keeping her hard-earned cash. Thank God she wasn't afflicted with Donald Alden's conscience. Seemed to her he ought to give more thought to the woman he loved, and her child—

Must of cost those girls a lot to get up the nerve to

come here like that, today. She frowned a little, wishing she could help Em and Arabella in some way, then dismissed the thought. They were young. They had husbands to care for them. It would all work out some way.

"It'll work out," Arab told Em as they walked from the parlor to the rooms behind Donald's offices which they now called home. "And Nell was right. We couldn't have worked there. It would have destroyed Donald and Juan."

"In the meantime, what Donald is doing is destroying us," Em said. "Arab, do you realize there's no money coming in? And Martha needs new clothes? She's growing so—"

"And we're a drain on your finances and your patience," Arab said drearily, "just crowding you out of the small space you have to live in—"

Em stopped. "Don't ever say that! We're in this together, Arab! Our reputation has spilled over to Juan! If it hadn't been for that—that *damned* Adam!"

"Em!" Arab began to giggle helplessly at her prim sister's choice of words, and Em finally joined her.

"We'd better hurry home," Em said at last, "or the men will be wondering where we've been. I don't think we'd better tell them, do you? And, maybe, just maybe, one of them will have found a job today."

That hope was unfounded. The sparse evening meal was shadowed with gloom. Juan had applied for two clerical positions. The first prospective employer had scowled at Juan's dark features, his combination of Spanish-born and British-educated accents. "Ain't hirin' no damn furriner," he'd growled. The second knew of his connection with Senator Alden.

84

"Some say he's a crook," the man had said, spreading his hands. "Now, I don't say I believe it. Never heard a whisper against him until this last couple of years. But like the old saying goes, where there's smoke, there's bound to be fire. And I can't afford any loose talk in my business."

"The positions were already filled," Juan told the group assembled around the table. "What about you, Donald, did you have any luck?"

"Ran into another fellow who lost his shirt because of my sage advice." Donald smiled painfully. "I told him I'd see what I could do to help him." He turned to Em. "We are going to have to sell this place, my dear. Keep out just enough to start over again—"

"Are we going home?" Little Martha's eyes had lighted. "Mommie? Daddy? Are we going home to our house on the hill?"

Donald looked stricken, and Em picked Martha up from her chair, carrying her, protesting, off to bed. How did one explain to a child that home was no longer there? That it had been sold to satisfy her adoptive father's debts of honor?

Arabella and Juan repaired to their own room, silently readying themselves for bed. They lay apart, each lost in a separate world, until Juan said, "Arab! Little Arab! What have I done to you? You cannot live in my country. I cannot live in yours—"

Arabella turned to him fiercely, putting her lips against his to stop his words. Then, cradling his head in her arms, she tried to comfort him.

"Don't think like that, sweetheart! There have been good times here and there were good times in Spain. Remember the fountain, the flowers?" She was lost in a memory: their bodies white and gold in the Spanish moonlight, the way they'd laughed and played like children until, at last, drugged with love and the scent of blossoms, they'd lain upon the grass...

"I can only remember how you were stolen away from me, how your life was endangered," he said soberly.

"Forget Spain, then! Think of our wedding day, in Em's garden!"

"And remember that, since, I have failed you."

"Oh, Juan!" Now it was she who was weeping, in need of comfort. They couldn't seem to communicate any more. His blasted pride stood between them. Somehow, somewhere, she must find an answer.

Somewhere! If she were not welcomed by his family in Spain, if he could not find work here in San Francisco, maybe they should find a totally new beginning!

"Juan," she whispered, "what would you think of going to Alaska? Tamsen says—"

At the same moment, in the other bedroom, Em was having identical thoughts. Donald, ordinarily not overly demonstrative, had turned to her in passionate need of reassurance.

"No," she said, "not with Martha in the same room. She might waken—"

With a muttered curse, totally unlike Donald Alden, he sat up. "Dammit," he said, "the child's asleep. How long do you intend to go on like this?"

"This was your idea," she told him stiffly. "You sold the house, putting your honor above your home. And you weren't at fault, Donald! You didn't owe those people anything—"

He turned away from her, and she was instantly contrite. "I'm sorry, Donald. I know you did what you had to do. Please!"

86

He lay unmoving, and in a small frightened voice she said, "It's all right. Just let me check on Martha, first, to see if she's really sleeping."

"Never mind, Em," he said sadly. "I don't feel like a man right now. More like a failure."

"But you're not!" Her breath caught on a sob. "You're my Donald, my love, the most wonderful man I know! And everything's going to be all right. Sell this place, Donald! I don't mind."

"Then you do understand?" There was a note of pleading in his voice.

"Of course I do. And, Donald, you mentioned starting all over again. At first, I was afraid of it, but then I had the most wonderful idea . . . ."

"Yes?" he prompted.

"Let's go to Alaska!" She was half-laughing, half-crying. "It's a brand-new country, and Tamsen's there! She'll help us. I know she will! Tamsen can do anything—"

Donald Alden rose. Em said his name and he didn't answer. She could hear the sounds of his dressing in the dark. Then the door closed behind him. At first she was alarmed. Such actions were not like Donald. Was he angry about something? Probably he'd only gone out alone to think over what she'd said. And he'd come to the same conclusion she had, that it was the only thing to do. She, Em, might not approve of all that Tamsen had done, but she'd managed to bring them all through times of adversity. And she would do it again.

Secure in the knowledge that Donald would see it her way, feeling safe already, in knowing that Tamsen would look after them, Em fell into a restful sleep for the first time in months.

Donald Alden, striding through the night, was beset with a kind of fury. He'd tried to be lover, husband, friend, and protector to his wife. But in a time of need, her thoughts had turned to her younger sister.

He didn't feel the dampness of the San Francisco fog, so deep now that it soaked through his clothing like rain. He paused for a moment beneath a street lantern and caught a glimpse of himself in a storefront window. A blurred image of an aging man, white hair standing on end like a lion's mane, slightly pudgy with the added fifty pounds he'd put on this year. A senior statesman, former senator, he thought wryly, but without the dignity; he felt like an old fool.

Perhaps if he hadn't been so besotted with Em, so occupied in trying to create the magic he'd known with his first girl-wife, dead these long years, he might have seen disaster coming. Instead, his mind had been on building a house by the sea, an honorable retirement, with Em and little Martha at his side.

San Francisco had gone under, financially, and his good name with it. He'd spent every cent he had, trying to buy it back. Was Em right when she accused him of putting his honor above his home? He supposed she was. And just how honorable was he?

For a long time, he'd guessed at something Em herself didn't know. Though she loved him, it was not the passionate love of a woman for a man, but something else. A deep affection, born of respect. Em was in love with being a wife, a mother, having a man and a child to care for, a kitchen to cook in, a house to clean, respectability.

She had been emotionally wounded when he met her, with a small child, born of rape. He'd offered her marriage, a home, a father for her child. And now he'd taken that security away. Em was another casualty of his recent mistakes. Another debt of honor that he must try to rectify.

He looked at the figure reflected in the window. A dull, aging man. Perhaps a little absurd. "But honorable to the end, old boy," he said aloud. "Honorable to the end." Turning, he plodded back toward the office building, a lonely figure, the fog misting his face like tears. He had made his decision, and now he knew how to pave the way for Em.... He hoped her trust in Tamsen was justified.

In the weeks that followed, Tamsen's letter arrived, bearing out Em's contention that Russian Alaska was, indeed, a promised land. Em and Arab planned together, alive with excitement over the impending move. The office building was put up for sale. They chafed with impatience when nobody came to buy.

In the house on Stockton Street, Nell cursed the weather, the meager clientele, and the tight money situation. To avoid the eyes of creditors waiting to pounce, the furnishings of the establishment had to be sneaked out, piece by piece, under cover of darkness. And it didn't move as fast as she'd have liked. Some of it went to the Bella Union—Madame Simone Jules knew a bargain when she saw one—some to the houses on Portsmouth Square, and some to Sydneytown.

The last item to leave the parlor was the shining grand piano that had been Tamsen's pride. Nell added her bulk to the rear of it as Dusty and the girls fought to push the piano through the back door into a dray that had been backed to the steps.

With it gone, Nell returned to the echoing empty

room, and ran her fingers along the mahogany bar that must remain, her beady black eyes glistening with unshed tears.

"Glad to git rid a' th' gawdam place," she insisted to herself. "Allus was too plush fer an' ol' horse like me. Never should'a left th' cantina."

But it would sure be good to see that Tamsen girl. Nell managed an affectionate grin. Never seen such a one for getting herself in trouble and out again. Be good to find what the hell she was up to, now!

CHAPTER 8

Tamsen stood at her window in Baranov Castle, idly tracing the passage of raindrops on the pane. For the last few weeks, it had rained incessantly, but that was to be expected. Sitka had had its vaunted ten days of sun. Two hundred inches of rain would fall before another brief summer.

The landscape below was wet, trees and foliage intensely green, the parade ground a sea of mud. Unpainted buildings had soaked up the moisture and stood black and charred-looking against a gray sea.

Only the Russians were undaunted. They scurried about their duties, heads bent against the downpour, as though they enjoyed it. Tamsen wanted no part of it. In the days on the wagon train, she had been wet, cold, sometimes hungry. At least this room held all the creature comforts.

Turning from the window, she thought of how homelike this room had been during the last year's rains. The firelight flickered on the dull red walls, pointing up the gold-framed paintings, the heavy silver lamps with their red glass bowls, the fine oriental carpet and velvet draperies. It was a room to be warm in.

She walked to the heavy, high-backed velvet chair before the fire, touching it. Here Dan would sit, resting his dark head on the back, and she would nestle there at his feet, his hand on her hair, shutting out the Russians and the rain.

Now they both intruded, the rain keeping Tamsen a prisoner in this room, while she listened to the laughter across the hall. Every day, the Princess Anya held court in her suite, lying languidly on an enormous, canopied bed with silken hangings of a pale and delicate blue. Above the bed, the high ceiling was decorated with an array of Cupids and sun-gods disporting themselves among misty clouds. The walls were hung with hundred-year-old tapestries, and the finely carved furniture was upholstered in satin and damask.

A room fit for a princess. Complete with admiring audience—and Dan Tallant, Tamsen's husband. Tamsen wondered whether the reputed ghost of the lady who died for love was numbered among the laughing crowd. And if she was what she thought of her room's present occupant—and Anya's husband-stealing tactics.

I must trust Dan, Tamsen thought wearily. It was just that Anya's designs were so obvious. But then, she seemed to use her wiles on any man. Dan's young aide, Ivan, was so smitten over the woman he didn't have good sense! Fawning over her like a fool!

Tamsen hugged her folded arms against the empty feeling she always seemed to have these days. Maybe Dan was right, she thought ruefully. She was jealous at the attentions the princess received; she didn't like being beaten at her own game. Well, perhaps so. The princess outshone her as Tamsen Tallant, American lady, married and properly behaved. But she'd bet that Poppy Franklin would have given her a run for her money!

Her musings were interrupted by a tap at the

door. She opened it to find Prince Igor standing there, rather comically balancing a tray of small Russian cakes.

"I have here another gesture in exchange for your husband," he said, his blue eyes dancing with malicious merriment. "When Anya heard that you were indisposed, she insisted that I bring you refreshment, to show her concern. And a very pretty and convincing show she made of it, too."

Indisposed, indeed! So Dan was making excuses for her! He'd urged her to attend , but after several such occasions, forced to watch Anya's blatant flirtations, she'd declined. He might think it politic, but she still had the right to accept or reject invitations if she chose.

Igor's quick eyes caught her flash of anger, and he laughed. "Aha! As I thought, you're quite well. You have no stomach for my untrustworthy sister's little games. *Duschechka* to the men, perhaps, but *melki bes* to all women. Alas, I know her tricks too well."

Despite herself, Tamsen had to smile. The slight, handsome blond boy, she'd come to realize, was a bit of a troublemaker. Life was a huge joke to him, and he delighted in pitting friend against friend, husband against wife, his eyes sparkling with mischief when a few well-placed words struck fire. "You're quite wrong," she lied. "I have a dislike for crowded rooms and noise."

He nodded sagely. "You have need to take the air. And no husband to escort you. May I offer myself? We shall go to the tea house on the hill and drown our sorrows, forget my evil sister's machinations."

He swooped past Tamsen, set the teacakes down, and looked at her expectantly. "Your cloak?"

Tamsen sighed. She had no desire to go out in the rain. If she did, she should put the time to good use.

She'd heard Edwin Devon was ill and had been petitioning Dan to call on him. It would not do to go to his barracks apartment unattended. Perhaps Prince Igor would escort her there.

She broached the subject, but he refused, making a compliment of it. Here he had an opportunity to have a lovely lady all to himself—since her husband was otherwise occupied—and he didn't intend to waste a minute making sick calls on a rival. Let the servant, Helena, ask after the gentleman—he gestured grandly toward the tray—with a gift of cakes.

She despatched the girl on the errand, and Prince Igor assisted Tamsen into her cloak, a utilitarian wrap of oilskin lined with warm flannel.

"Too bad," he said, adjusting the hood. While the woman is beautiful, the cloak is plain. You should be swathed in furs."

Tamsen flushed. She'd forgotten for a moment that Igor was a nobleman and that her everyday garb might be an embarrassment to him. "I have a beaver. Let me change—"

He shook his head. "Beaver will not do. It must be a white fur, to complement your dark hair, a royal fur to match your loveliness. Perhaps ermine. This husband of yours, can he not give you ermine?"

Igor continued in a flirtatious vein as they walked down the steps and onward to the knoll where the tea house stood. Though she seemed to have his full attention, Tamsen sensed his bright eyes missed nothing, storing up bits of information for later use like a squirrel—a golden squirrel.

In the tea house, with glasses of spiced brew fresh from the samovar, his attitude seemed to change. He looked at her steadily for a long moment, so steadily that she felt a tinge of red touch her cheeks.

"I must talk to you," he said quietly. "And I must be serious and truthful." There was a flash of his former gaiety as he said, "And for me, that is most difficult to do, you understand." Before she could answer, the question came.

"You wish to keep your husband?"

Tamsen stared at him, numbly, her fist clenched on the table. "Keep Dan? Of course I do! What are you talking about?"

Reaching out, he took her hand and, uncurling the fingers one by one, brought the hand to his lips. "Then, dear lady, listen to what I have to say if you value your safety. My sister is like a tigress when she cannot have what she wants. Your husband wishes something from her; she wishes something from him. The ear of the tsar, in return for a few moments of pleasurable dalliance. It can do no harm—"

Tamsen was on her feet. "My God! Are you trying to suggest—?"

He still had hold of her hand, and he drew her down to face him once more. "I am suggesting nothing! I know that Anya feels you are in her way. I do not wish to see you hurt."

"I'd like to wring the she-devil's scrawny neck!" Tamsen said fiercely. Then, remembering she was talking to the girl's brother, she forced herself to be calm. "Why are you telling me this? Was it her idea? To face me with this—this obscene proposal?"

"No," he said candidly, "it was my own. I know the way Anya's mind works. Your husband is a most attractive man. And my sister is filled with superstition. She has destroyed what she believes to be an unlucky number of marriages and is determined to add one more to that number. It might be wise to look the other way."

Anya, superstitious! That cool blond girl with eyes like chips of ice? Not so flawless, after all, if that

95

were true. "You're joking," she said. But his face showed that he was not.

Tamsen began to laugh, a ripple of amusement that quivered at the edge of hysteria. For she had just had a wonderful thought. "Tell me," she finally chuckled, wiping tears of mirth from her eyes and leaning toward the startled Igor, "does she know about the room she's occupying?"

He shook his head warily.

"That room is *haunted*."

"Haunted?" Igor looked at her in disbelief, then his expression changed. Once again, he was the merry golden squirrel, collecting tidbits, brimming with malice. "Tell me," he pleaded, "tell me all! How I will enjoy repeating the story to my beloved sister!" He rubbed his hands in anticipation. "This should be delicious!"

And so, Tamsen related the story of the ghost of Baranov Castle. The afternoon passed pleasantly, now that they had become friends. As they climbed the steps to the castle, Tamsen was almost sorry it had ended. But as he left her at her door, his face assumed sober lines once more.

"Do be careful," he told her. "And think about what I said."

Entering, Tamsen found Helena, who helped her remove her wet cloak. Shaking the droplets from her hair, Tamsen asked after Edwin Devon.

"*Tschaltakat chtlingit Kog-kana*," the girl said dolefully. "All human beings must die."

"Die?" Tamsen's heart thudded in shock. "My God! He's not dead!"

"Not dead. But the mark of it is upon him. The *ich'ta* should be called—"

Tamsen stared at her. "The shaman? Medicine man? Helena, this is an English gentleman you're talking about! Not a barbarian! And I shall go to see for myself. Tomorrow."

The next morning, Tamsen set forth in the rain. She had thought of Devon all night, seeing his grave face before her eyes, recalling his kindnesses. Dan wouldn't like her going alone, but he'd planned his schedule this morning before she had a chance to suggest that he accompany her. For a moment, as she walked, a trace of the old Tamsen surfaced. To hell with convention, she thought.

Climbing the stairs to Devon's second-story rooms, she paused for a moment. What if he were as ill as Helena said? Oh, God, what if he were dead? Steeling herself, she rapped at the door.

To her vast relief, Devon opened it himself. At first sight, his face seemed gray, lined beyond his years. Then his face lit up with a boyish smile, and his coloring returned as he grasped Tamsen's hands.

"My dear lady! How kind of you to come. But as you can see, I'm now quite well. Though I did appreciate the cakes you sent by that pretty girl of yours."

"But she said you were ill, very ill," Tamsen said in confusion. "In fact, I was afraid—"

"Afraid I'd be abed," Devon said. "And I assure you that I have been, these last several weeks. Else I would have been unable to keep from seeking out your charming company. Am I—am I compromising your good name by inviting you in?"

"Not at all," Tamsen said recklessly. "I see no harm in a respectable matron calling upon a sick friend." Matron! What a terrible thing to call one's self, she thought with amusement. Apparently Devon was amused, too, because he almost smiled.

They spent a pleasant hour in conversation and Tamsen said her farewells, Devon assuring her that

97

he'd be out and about soon, that she was not to worry. Watching her from his door, he thought of Helena and her uncanny prescience. Perhaps her Tlingit blood had endowed her with an extra sense. A chill touched the nape of his neck, and he felt suddenly afraid his time was running out.

No, this attack was over. He would have many good days yet. Best of all, Tamsen had come to see him, of her own will, and unaccompanied. Tallant must be a cad to let her come alone.

Dan Tallant was, in fact, waiting for Tamsen upon her return. "Where have you been?" he wanted to know. "You said something about wanting to go out this morning, and I cut my work short—"

Tamsen removed her cloak, shaking the rain from it. "I've been to see Edwin Devon. His health is improved."

"Alone, Tamsen? Was that wise?"

She looked at him steadily. "I'm my own person, Dan. You were gone for months, and I did not require your permission for any activity. I've seen so little of you since your return that I feel the same rules still apply."

"I'm sorry, Tamsen, and you're right." She'd never seen him look so worried. "These last weeks have been hell. But Anya sails for Russia soon. A month or so, I think. Then I'll make it up to you. I promise. And in the meantime..."

"In the meantime?" she prompted him when he paused, with a futile gesture.

"In the meantime, I've had a damn good idea. It's been a year since you saw Arab and Em. I know you've been missing them." His false exuberance faltered as she stared at him with watchful eyes. "While I'm winding this up, since you have to be alone so much, why don't you think about going home for a visit? Just for a while."

Tamsen closed her eyes, recalling the things Prince Igor had said of his sister and Dan. "Your husband wishes something from her, she wishes something from him. The ear of the tsar, in return for a few moments of pleasurable dalliance. It can do no harm—"

Tamsen's lip curled. "Not on your life," she said bitterly. "Whatever happens, I intend to be around to watch. Just remember that!"

"But Tamsen—"

"Get out!" she raged. "I'm in no mood to talk to you now! Go back to your work—which I'm sure you enjoy!"

Face stained an angry red, Dan turned and left, slamming the door behind him. He did not go to Princess Anya, as Tamsen expected, but straight to Baron Edouard de Stoeckl.

"I'm giving up," Dan said simply. "Quitting for the first time in my life. There's nothing more important than my wife and my marriage!"

"Not even your work for your country?"

"Not even my work for my country. Not when I have to put up with hints from that little bitch Anya—hints that some harm might come to Tamsen if I don't climb in her bed. I can't take any more of it!"

"Then why not send your wife somewhere? Home for a visit, say?"

"I just suggested that," Dan said morosely. "And she's mad as hell!"

"Maybe that's the answer," de Stoeckl speculated. "If the princess thinks you're estranged, your wife's safety should be assured."

"I can't do that to Tamsen! Let her suspect—"

De Stoeckl shrugged, wearily. "I don't see where

you have much choice. Either you talk your wife into going home, or she stays here. If she stays here, and Anya believes her to be an obstacle, it is very possible that she'll instigate some act of violence against her!"

"I can see that Tamsen doesn't trust me any more. I've tried to explain the situation, but Anya keeps me dancing at her beck and call. Dammit, Baron, can't you see my dilemma? If Tamsen ever left me—"

"Where would she go? Sitka is a small island. And for that matter, where would you go, if you chose to give up on this project? There are no boats from the States in the harbor. Anya doesn't want to deal with me. You know that!"

"I don't know anything," Dan said in desperation.

"Then let things stand as they are for now. It will resolve itself. You've raised the price you offered to Anya for her help?"

"To the hilt," Dan said. "What I was empowered to offer, and all the personal funds I have with me. Until I receive my salary from Washington—"

"I will give you a draft to make up the difference," the baron said. "Do not forget, I am with you in this. It is something we both believe in."

Their conversation ceased as the governor-general entered. "Glad to have found you together," he said heartily. I'm planning a small dinner party tonight. Only fifty people or so, and I wished to extend a special invitation to you, Baron de Stoeckl, and to you, Tallant, along with your good wife. We've seen little of her of late."

"She'll be there," Dan said grimly. "If I have to drag her."

He flushed at the governor-general's startled look, which stated plainly that Daniel Tallant was no gentleman. Well, he wasn't. He'd never pretended to be. And he was sick and tired of intrigue and pussyfooting around. All he wanted was to get this assignment over and get the hell out of here.

But first things first. Right now, he was going directly to his rooms to get everything straightened out with his wife.

CHAPTER 9

Dan's explanations achieved exactly nothing. After all, it had all been said before. The facts, Tamsen pointed out with cold politeness, were as plain as the nose on his face. The princess was a man-chasing vixen, and Dan was certainly not resisting her!

"I have no interest in the woman!" he shouted. "You know that!"

"Do I? Then why are you sending me home? I must say you seem to enjoy your work. I remember how you used to go upstairs with Katie Ryan at the cantina and the parlor. Just a little side benefit of government espionage. All right! So you're doing your duty! Trying to get that—that hussy—to present your case to the tsar! But there are limits!"

"And I intend to stay within those limits!"

"Do you? But you want me to go home."

"Damn it to hell," Dan yelled. "There's no use trying to reason with you!" He swept a candlestick from the table and it hit the floor with a crash. For a moment he glared at her. Then he said, "To hell with it! I've got to get some rest. I'm worn out!"

"Naturally," Tamsen said sweetly. "You put in such late hours."

Ignoring her, Dan collapsed across the bed.

Tamsen, busying herself ostentatiously about the

room, made a pretense of being too occupied to notice him. She glanced at him furtively from time to time, unable to believe her eyes. He was asleep! Just like a man! Faced with an unsolvable problem, just go to sleep! She hated him for his ability to shut out the things that were destroying them. She felt like flying at him, pummeling him awake!

At the same time she wanted to lie down beside him, to cradle his dark head in her arms and try to coax him into loving her. She put the candlestick back in place with a thump, walked to the armoire, and pulled out her cloak. As she fastened it on, she looked at Dan once more, hoping he'd wake up and stop her. Then she walked from the castle and out into the rain, moving blindly, with no idea of where she was going.

She found herself in the Indian market. For a time, she stood before one of the small stalls, watching a woman weave a basket. The woman's face was serene beneath the raven wings that framed her temples. A small brown boy played at her feet. Tamsen looked at the child with yearning.

She'd wanted a baby, but it had been Dan's idea to wait. They were in a foreign country with strange customs, he said. Better for a child to be born in civilization.

But Martha, Em's child, had been born along the trail from Magoffinville to California during an Indian attack. And mother and baby had both survived. Tamsen could still remember the feel of the small new creature in her arms, and the memory left her aching inside. Now she wondered if there would ever be a little one that was truly hers. Hers and Dan's—

The Indian woman looked up, her dark eyes questioning. Tamsen realized she'd been staring

103

fixedly. With a forced smile, Tamsen pointed to the basket.

"Ssik-gu, kletch-uschku," she said. "Pretty, beautiful." And then she fled.

At the water's edge, she walked among the brightly painted bidarkas moored there. From this point, she could see the row of solid wooden houses, some of them with their kwan symbols painted above the door. She wondered in which the Indian woman lived—and the little boy.

A flurry of activity at the gates of the settlement indicated it was time for their closing. Listlessly, Tamsen returned to the castle, wishing she were a Tlingit woman weaving baskets... that life were simple.

When she reached their apartment, where Dan still slept, she prepared herself for the evening's dinner, careful to choose a gown that he had always liked. She needed help with the buttons that closed the tightly fitting bodice, but she'd be damned if she'd wake him! Finally, she managed to get dressed.

Dan woke and changed, not speaking. In icy silence, they went to dinner. Together, but miles apart.

Tamsen had come to a determination. She would not give up without a fight! Heretofore, she'd been sitting back quietly, letting the princess steal the show! She was still capable of exciting the admiration of men! A look into the mirror had told her so. And the flush of anger on her cheekbones reflected the apricot color of her gown.

Leaving Dan to fend for himself, she swept into the room, immersing herself in the shimmer and glitter of the evening. Here tonight were only the elite, the common seamen and *promishleniki* omitted; this evening was for the nobles and their honored guests.

A quick glance sufficed to tell Tamsen her appearance surpassed even that of Anya, and her own tiara might well be a crown.

A familiar face appeared at her right hand. "Niklas," she cried, "ah, how handsome you are in your uniform tonight. And you, Dmitri! It seems days since I saw you last. And there's Ivan! Dear Ivan, I would so like some tea—"

She linked an arm through that of Dan's young aide, who had been staring forlornly toward the Princess Anya. He was startled at first, then assumed a rather foolish grin. He had not noted how lovely the wife of his employer was! As beautiful even as the princess he worshipped. He led her to the samovar. They were followed by a small retinue and by the eyes of many of the gentlemen present.

"Penatchit copla?"

Fifteen drops. "Of course," Tamsen said, extending her glass for the generous amount of spirits. Let Dan frown, she thought rebelliously. After all, why not?

Bored with the attentions of the group surrounding her, Tamsen saw Igor approaching with a feeling of relief. Grudgingly, the other noblemen gave way before his royal presence, and soon Tamsen and he were standing alone.

"Your sister doesn't seem her sparkling self tonight," she told him. It was true. Anya sat quietly, her face set in lines of discontent that did not become her.

"The princess is sulking," Igor confided. "For one thing, you outshine her this night. And there is yet another worry. You recall I told you she is most beset with superstition?"

"Yes."

"Tonight is her birthday." He smiled with a hint of malice. "She has also attained that same unlucky number of married men she seduced over the years. And now, she has learned that she must sleep in a haunted room—too late to make changes at this hour."

Tamsen burst into laughter, and Dan, across the room, watched morosely. He had never seen Tamsen look more beautiful.

Moving back into the clusters of Russian nobles, Tamsen was toasted and besieged with invitations from gentlemen who wished to escort her to dinner. Refusing them all, not wanting to be seated at the head of the table near Dan and Anya, she chose young Ivan, much to his amazement. Ivan, least important of the whole assembly, would surely be placed at the foot.

It was a wise choice. Throughout the evening, all eyes were directed toward Tamsen, rather than toward the sulking princess. Anya did not respond graciously to the banquet, the speeches, the entertainment arranged to celebrate her birthday. A pall seemed to settle over the assembly, dampening its normal orgiastic trend as the evening wore on.

When the floor was cleared for dancing, Tamsen remained apart, content to be surrounded by an ever-growing group of admirers. Then the governor-general approached. "Forgive me," he smiled, "but I must take this lovely lady away for a moment."

He led her graciously into another room, then his gallantry fell from him like a cloak. "It has been brought to my attention that your husband has been treating with the Princess Anya as a means of gaining the attention of the tsar. Is this true?"

Tamsen's face crimsoned. "I do not know. I haven't seen him much of late." She wished she could have bitten the words back at Voedvodski's knowing expression.

"Ah, you find the princess a problem, too?"

"I don't suppose I think of her, one way or another."

"You may be pleased to know she is leaving soon. There is a ship due in next month, with supplies from Russia. On its return, it will take the long way around to Russian shores in order to avoid the terrible Siberian winter. She plans to board that ship in preference to staying in our small settlement until spring."

Tamsen tried to hide her pleasure at his words, then he continued.

"When the ship departs, I plan to send a small vessel to land a messenger at Okhotsk, on the Siberian coast. Even with 5,000 miles of difficult terrain to cross, he will reach St. Petersburg well before the princess."

"Why are you telling me this?"

"Because my messenger will carry the maps you will obtain for me," he said testily. "It is important that I have them as soon as possible. With those in hand, I don't think the tsar will place much credence in what Anya or Tallant will tell him. It is imperative that you find them before your husband goes."

"Before he—goes?"

Voedvodski's brows lifted. "Is it possible you do not know? My informant believes Mr. Tallant will accompany the princess on her voyage home."

Tamsen's mouth was dry. At last, she said hoarsely, "No, I didn't know. Though I might have guessed. You will have your maps."

Seeing how white her face was, her huge eyes blank with shock, the governor-general felt a momentary qualm. "I'm sorry if I've been the bearer of bad news. And I do not wish to press you about the charts, but, as you can see—" He spread his hands.

107

"You will have them."

Tamsen returned to the banquet hall. Both Dan and Anya were gone.

Dan Tallant was having his own troubles. The princess had approached him with an imperious demand that he follow her. Dan paused for an instant.

"I'm prepared to accede to your terms," Anya said, "with one stipulation, which I wish to discuss. If you do not hurry, I shall change my mind."

Still hesitant, yet hopeful that the situation would be resolved, he complied, following her up flights of steps to the tower. He hadn't been here before, and he looked about with appreciation. The sides of the structure were windowed. A large stand with three sets of arms, each supporting four shallow square cups of seal oil burning there; a reflector three feet in diameter projected the light about six miles at sea.

Anya stamped her foot. "You can inspect lighthouses some other time," she pouted. "Pay attention to me."

He turned to her, and she repeated her former words. She would accede, but with a stipulation. She was soon to return to St. Petersburg—and had decided the monies offered for her intercession with the tsar were quite sufficient. His wave of relief receded as he heard the stipulation. He was to accompany her.

"I cannot and will not," he said firmly. "It is impossible."

"I will give you an hour to think about it." She yawned prettily. "You will find me in my room when you make your decision. I will be waiting." Brushing past him, she flew down the stairs.

Tamsen, too unnerved by the governor-general's words to bear another moment of social chatter, brushed off the admiring men who immediately clustered about her. Leaving the banquet hall, on pretext of a headache, she hurried toward her room. She must reach it before she gave way to angry tears.

She slowed her steps as she saw the figure of Anya ahead of her; her fists clenched tightly at her sides as she watched the princess enter her own suite. Odd that she would leave the festivities so early, but then she had been sulking all evening. God, how she wished she might give her something to really be angry about!

Voedvodski had to be in error. Dan would never dream of going to Russia with that conniving woman! If he did—it was the end.

Her fury grew as she entered her room, preparing to remove the apricot gown. Again, the buttons proved recalcitrant. Fumbling at them, in a rage, she finally reached for a letter-opener, an ornate imitation of a dagger with a razor-sharp edge, and hacked the buttons away. She pulled on her pale blue robe and went to the mirror, reaching to lift the tiara from her hair. She stopped, her heart thumping. For a stranger looked back at her—a blurred figure in blue, the breast of her gown stained with blood, who wore a crown on her head.

Tamsen let her breath out with a sigh. For a moment, she thought she had seen a ghost. Her hand went to her breast. Pulling the robe open, she discovered a paper-thin cut. In her anger, she'd wielded the paper knife too savagely. For a small cut, it had bled quite profusely. The robe was ruined.

Moving back to the mirror, she studied the apparition that had frightened her. With the candle behind her, her features were not recognizable. Just a white face with enormous shadowed eyes, beneath a tiara-crown. Her fright had been understandable.

She wished it had happened to the Princess Anya.

Her eyes widened, and she thought—why not?

Across the hall, Anya had hastily stripped off her regal gown. Unpinning her hair, she shook it about her shoulders and surveyed herself in the mirror. Was she getting plump with these incessant feasts? God, she hoped not! But her hair did seem to be darkening, thanks to the dampness of this devilish place. She reached for a filmy nightdress, then thought better of it and climbed beneath the silken sheets as she was.

It had not been a good day, she thought, her mouth sullen. The first thing this morning, seeking to prove her luck hadn't changed, she had laid out the cards. An ace and a queen of spades! And Igor, the beast, had laughed. Then the governor-general had talked with her, hinting that she might be happier elsewhere. She imagined that she could see Igor's fine hand there, too.

And then, tonight! That Tallant woman daring to try to outdo her! And Tallant himself, countering her offer with, "I cannot and will not."

Well, she smiled to herself, he could and he would! She knew that this transaction meant much to him. He was not a gentleman, but he was an ambitious man. He would come, and soon, if he wanted her to help him get to the tsar. Meanwhile, she was alone in this room purported to be haunted, and it gave her an eerie feeling. With only a single candle burning by the bed, the place was filled with moving shadows.

She listened for footsteps. There were none. But when she heard the door open softly, she stretched like a cat, showing just enough of the rosy shoulders beneath the sheet, but not too much. Then, as though just awakened, she turned drowsy eyes toward the door, preparing to say Dan's name in a husky whisper. Instead, she emitted a startled cry.

For there in the doorway stood a specter, the ghost of the lady in blue. The bosom of her silken apparel was stained with blood, and she held an uplifted dagger in her hand, its jeweled surface reflecting the candlelight as did her crown. Anya shut her eyes, taking a long indrawn breath to precede a scream. And the shadowy figure stepped backward, gliding away.

Downstairs, at the samovar, Dan dropped his glass as the first shriek echoed through the castle. As though it had opened a floodgate, there followed scream after scream. The entire party stood transfixed for a moment, then converged toward the door. A little late, for the source of the screaming had come to them.

Baranov Castle, though it had been the setting of many an orgiastic banquet, had never quite seen anything like the scene that followed. A naked princess ran into the banquet hall.

The hubbub rose incredibly. Finally, a group of ladies surrounded the babbling girl, hiding her with their skirts, and the men turned away at last. The evening ended very quickly after that, but not before some present had drawn their own conclusions about the event.

Dan Tallant hurried to his suite to find his wife. But Tamsen appeared to be sleeping the sleep of the innocent, her dark lashes curled against her cheeks. Dan stared at her for a long time, suspicion in his eyes. If he knew Tamsen, she'd had a hand in tonight's affairs. But how?

In the morning a messenger delivered a gift for Tamsen. A princely gift, dispatched by a princely hand. It was from Igor. And it consisted of a cloak of ermine—luxurious white furs.

CHAPTER 10

Moments later, another messenger arrived. The word he carried was not so welcome. Written in a flowery script, by the governor-general's own hand, it offered his sincere apologies for the inconvenience that he must now put them to.

It appeared the Princess Anya had had a severe shock the previous evening. She insisted she had seen the castle ghost, and she refused to occupy her apartment any longer. Certain that the Americans would be compassionate regarding her plight, the governor-general had promised the princess the quarters they now occupied and had made arrangements to have their things moved to a small house he hoped they would find suitable for their needs.

The unpainted house was small and square and reeked of the wet of rain-soaked lumber. Its windows were unscreened and the interior unfinished. As if to make up for the lack of comfort, the governor-general had been lavish with wall hangings, oriental carpets, heavy furnishings, and paintings in ornate frames. Tamsen thought of a store in San Francisco, operated by an elderly Chinese gentleman, where beautiful things rubbed shoulders with junk. She could not suppress a bitter laugh. Her actions had brought them to this. But it was worth it.

Dan, hearing her laugh, looked at her hopefully. They'd been quiet all day. Too quiet. When he asked a question, she answered. When he put his arms around her, she submitted. But that was all.

"It isn't so bad, is it?" he asked.

"No, it isn't so bad."

"And it'll be good to have our own home. We'll be away from all that damn partying."

"Yes," she said listlessly. "There's that."

"Tamsen," he said, "now, look, I don't want you to blow up at me, but dammit, I've got to say it once more. If you want to go home, you can."

She looked at him with expressionless eyes. "No, Dan. I don't want to go home."

He couldn't figure it out. A Tamsen who didn't laugh or cry, who didn't react to his attentions, who didn't even get angry. She wasn't herself. Maybe she was ill. Perhaps a doctor...

"No, Dan," she said when he broached the subject. "I'm fine. No reason to see a doctor at all."

What ailed her no doctor could cure. Only Dan could do that. The night before she hadn't slept, wondering what to do. Should she tell him she'd learned of his impending trip to Russia? Have it out then and there, and tell him it would be the end of their marriage?

She'd decided to wait. She hoped he wouldn't withhold the information until the last minute before he sailed and try to pretend it was a sudden decision! She could bear anything but a lie from him.

In the meantime, she would have to endure his embraces, knowing that part of him was secret, locked away from her. And she would copy the charts for the governor-general, improvising, to keep Dan's integrity intact.

But how could she live after he had gone? She

113

could not go home and face Arab and Em with the fact that she'd made yet another mistake. Perhaps, she thought hopefully, the princess was not so appealing now. The shrieks last night had been most unprovocative. And the ranting that followed, shrilling through the castle, was definitely not appealing. And that embarrassing entry into the banquet hall! Igor had recounted it to Tamsen this morning, with great glee. She'd bet the lady wasn't receiving company today!

Tamsen was correct in that assumption. After her things were moved into Tamsen and Dan's former apartment, the princess refused to see anyone. She paced the rooms, her mood veering from anger to humiliation. She would remain in seclusion until the ship came. At home, in Russia, no one would know.

Anya's lips tightened. Igor would tell. He would make a story of it at every court function, embellishing it with details of his own. She would see to it that he remained behind. Her anger turned from Igor to Dan. If he had come to her room, as she expected, none of this would have happened. The ghost might have appeared, but she would not have been alone—to run from the room—

Muttering a Russian imprecation, she threw a vase at the wall. It was days until the ship was due. She would go mad!

And in the meantime, there was some unfinished business. She'd been a fool to insist on this apartment, thinking the occupants would be moved to some cubbyhole in the castle. Now, somewhere out there in the shrouding rain, Tallant and his ninny of a wife were in their own home—probably locked in an embrace of passion. She would have to plot carefully to see that her plans for them went smoothly.

The princess was only half right. In their bed, that night, Dan turned to Tamsen in an agony of need, but she was wooden in his arms. His urgency unmatched, he fell away unsatisfied. She was tired, he tried to convince himself, after the move today, but he lay awake, troubled, for a long time.

Tamsen was on edge as she listened for the deep, even breathing of his sleep. When it came, she rolled closer to him and his arm reached automatically to gather her close. For a moment, she lay still, then carefully she slid her free hand beneath his pillow. Her fingers closed on the oilskin packet he kept there, and she withdrew it, slowly . . . slowly.

She moved away from him, as if she were moving in her sleep. Hearing his mumbled "Mmm?", she waited to be sure he dreamed on undisturbed; then she slipped from bed and went into another room. Here there was a desk, writing materials, and a half-finished letter to Em. If she were caught, she would sweep all but the letter out of sight and pretend she was writing because she couldn't sleep.

With trembling hands, she lit a candle, then slipped a chart from the packet. Unable to get her nerves under control, she took the better part of an hour to copy it, and when she finished, she closed her eyes and touched the pen to the map. X marks the spot, she thought with satisfaction. Tonight, she would only do the one. And now, she must return the packet in the same manner in which she had taken it.

There were few opportunities to copy the charts in the next week, for Dan was not sleeping well. He was desperately worried about the success of his mission. Anya's silence since the night of her fright was ominous. Baron de Stoeckl had tried to see her, but with no results. She was seeing no one.

A change in her attitude, after days of seclusion,

115

came about because of Dan's young aide, Ivan. Mooning over the absence of the princess, he'd purchased a Tlingit amulet, a good luck charm, and sent it to her by messenger.

Inside the door to her apartment there were many gifts from many men. But this one, with its worshipping note attached, appealed to her superstitious nature, and it led her to view the other gifts with a different eye. Perhaps, she thought, preening herself, the incident hadn't been the disaster she'd thought. Maybe it only added to her appeal.

"Tell the sender I have not been well," she said to the boy who delivered the gift, "but I would be honored if he would call, so that I may thank him in person."

An excited and flattered Ivan presented himself at her door within the hour. A husky voice called for him to enter and he complied, but stopped short at the sight of slender arms stretching drowsily above a golden-haired figure in the canopied bed. The sheet slipped down, revealing a glimpse—not too much—of rosy, unclad shoulders.

"Ivan," the voice thrilled. "It's you!"

When Ivan stumbled away at last, dazed at the thought that this glorious creature was actually his, Anya rose and dressed. Fitting diamond earrings to her ears she was pleased to see that they matched the sparkle in her eyes.

She smiled. She had learned what she wanted to know. Ivan was a bore, but the time spent was well worth it. She'd mentioned the incident in the banquet hall, blushing prettily, and he'd answered. "But you can't imagine how lovely you were! That's all any man would remember." Thus reassured, Anya sent a messenger for Dan.

Tallant received her summons with mixed

emotions. He'd tried to convince himself that Tamsen's unresponsiveness and her occasional guilty secretiveness were because of another man. But it had all begun with Anya, and his attempts to use her for his own purposes required that he behave in a manner alien to his nature. Today, he would be himself. If she brought up that nonsense about stipulations again, he'd tell her to to go to hell and walk out.

He went as he was—flannel shirt, faded denims— throwing on only a fisherman's slicker as concession to the weather. His boots marred the carpets of the hall as he headed toward the princess's apartment, steeling himself for the coming interview.

He knew instinctively that the fate of a national project depended on the outcome. If Anya did not work with him, she'd work actively against him.

He drew a deep breath and tapped at her door. He was shown into the familiar suite, but the girl who received him was almost a stranger. Wearing a demure dark dress, the flashing of diamonds at her ears reflecting eyes bright with tears, Anya was subdued and ladylike.

"Dan," she said softly, extending her hands. She drew them back quickly. "Dan, come in—"

He entered, grinning at his fears. He'd built her up into some kind of monster in his mind. And, hell, she was only a scared girl. Maybe they could come to terms on this deal, after all.

"I wish to apologize for putting you out of your rooms," she said. "And please convey my apology to your wife. I know I should have done so earlier, but I have been ill. The shock—"

"It must have been a pretty eerie experience," Dan agreed, a smile playing at his lips as he recalled the scene in the banquet hall. "Glad to oblige,

117

ma'am. We're comfortable where we are, thanks."

Anya eyed him suspiciously. Was he laughing at her? Lowering her head, she plucked at a fold of her gown. "The ship comes soon. I shall miss this place, with its mountains and tall trees. The court at St. Petersburg is stultifying. I am lonely there."

Here it comes, he thought, his mouth tightening. "We will miss you here," he said. "All of us."

His dark eyes met ice-blue ones head-on. Except that now the ice was melting. A single tear marred the perfection of Anya's cheek. Her small pink mouth quivered into a smile.

"And I have another apology to make. I was wrong to insist you accompany me. I had no right to disrupt your life. I felt I needed someone at my side when I faced Alexander, someone who knew more of this country than I. But the Baron de Stoeckl has promised to attend me—"

"Then you're going to speak for us?" Dan was dumbfounded. "You're going to accept our deal?"

The princess looked at him, uncomprehending. Her command of English was extensive, but the phrase was unfamiliar. Her face finally cleared. "The deal, yes. The deal. I have intended to help you always." She flashed one of her old flirtatious smiles as she added, "I withheld that information as a way of getting attention. It is the way I have been reared at court. We are not honest and forthright as you Americans are. We love intrigue."

"You're going to help us!" Dan couldn't stop the grin that spread over his dark features. After all his worry, things had worked out fine for him and Tamsen. He couldn't wait to get back to the house, to tell her it was all over and done, that they'd soon be going home. There'd be a trip to Washington, first, to deliver his maps. Tamsen in Washington!

118

"I'm certain you have much work to do," Anya said, "so I will not keep you. But I wished you to know." With warmth and graciousness, she saw him to the door and closed it behind him. She leaned against it, her lip curled, her eyes hard once more.

Miss this place, indeed! The tall mountains and trees! What of the rain, the mud, the biting gnats and flies? The whole coast smelled of fish, of dirty Russians, dirty Indians! No, she would not miss it. Not at all. She would not miss Dan, either, for she had plans.

Only this morning, searching for a ring that had rolled into the dark recesses of the armoire, she had found an unusual object. A robe of pale blue silk, wadded into a small bundle and thrust into a corner. She shook it out, frowning as a dagger-like letter-opener clattered to the floor. The bosom of the robe was stained with blood.

At that moment Anya began to make plans for Tamsen Tallant, too....

Dan left the castle and walked through the rain, whistling. All was well with his world. With Anya's promise to help, the sale of Alaska was going to be easy. After a trip to Washington, he would get into some other kind of work. Maybe a ranch, down near the City of the Angels. A hacienda. And Tamsen could have those kids she'd been wishing for.

De Stoeckl was coming toward him, his cloak dripping wet. But he, too, wore a broad smile.

"You've heard the good news," Dan said.

"By special messenger. A note in the lady's own hand. I'm to accompany her to Russia. She will press for the sale. It is all we could wish for." Then, uneasily, "I wonder what happened to change her mind?"

"I don't know," Dan admitted, "but I'm all for it." He gripped the baron's hand.

"One thing," De Stoeckl said, surreptitiously massaging his fingers, "I overheard a conversation that troubled me. Voedvodski and Furuhelm were discussing some charts, showing where gold and mineral deposits might be found. I thought I heard your name mentioned, though they ceased talking as I approached. If you have made such discoveries, it would leave the situation open to a new interpretation—"

Dan's body tensed. The governor-general and Furuhelm couldn't know of the charts he carried on his person. If someone had seen them, perhaps his Indian guide, there was no way of judging their content. He hadn't discussed his findings with anyone, even with de Stoeckl, his ally. If it were known Alaska held such riches, his mission would founder. The Russians would never let go.

"You must have misunderstood," he said, lips tight. "You've seen the maps I drew up for the governor-general. They're on the walls of his office. I charted rivers, mountains, Indian trails. They're hardly treasure maps."

The baron's brow cleared. They talked for a few moments about other things, then Dan walked toward home, his euphoria dimmed. "Impossible," he said to himself. "Dammit, it's impossible!" Only someone with access to his person, a knowledge of his intimate habits, could know they existed.

His mind went to Helena, the Tlingit-Russian maid who served Tamsen. More Indian than Russian, she moved silently. It was his habit to place the packet on a chair, his clothing over it. Could she have gotten a look at them then?

No, not long enough to study them, he was sure of that.

From beneath his pillow, then? Good God, he'd slept with one eye open, his gun at his hand, for years. Many times, in Indian country, his alertness had saved his scalp. Helena couldn't have approached his bed without his knowledge. And that was the only place she could have found them. Now, the charts were in their packet against his heart. Like Anya, he was seeing spooks.

Still, Voedvodski and Furuhelm were too close to the truth for comfort. A guess, that's all it was. A guess. At least the baron's words had created enough of a diversion to cool him off. He'd been on the verge of heading home to Tamsen with his good news. The fact that he'd gone rushing off when Anya sent for him would be damned hard to explain, if he knew Tamsen. He'd keep his good news to himself until Anya sailed. Then he would say, "Sweetheart, it's all over. We're going home to start that family."

He didn't know the news of his visit to the princess had preceded him. Tallant arrived to find Igor taking tea with Tamsen. Dan didn't like the young man, and he didn't appreciate the prince's attention to Tamsen, but he greeted him warmly. Throwing off his dripping slicker, Dan accepted a cup of steaming tea and launched into an account of his walk in the rain, his meeting with de Stoeckl, omitting the details of their conversation—and his visit with Anya.

Igor left and the evening wore on. Tamsen was silent and uncommunicative. Helena served their evening meal quietly. The girl's hands were deft, Dan noticed. He found himself trying to reconstruct what might have happened. Perhaps Helena saw the packet on the chair as he bathed behind the screen. Her Indian eyes might have detected its imprint beneath his pillow when she made up the bed in the morning. It would be possible that she might slip it out at night, study the contents, replace it, and go to Voedvodski with what she'd learned.

In that case, he might wake up one morning with his work here made useless. The only flaw in that theory was that Helena couldn't have managed it without waking him. True, he wasn't a boy any more. Maybe he was getting soft. But to sleep while someone reached beneath his head? Impossible! Better to suppose it could be done, though; from now on, he would remain alert.

Tamsen, who was looking out the window at snow-capped mountains obscured by blowing rain, decided that the wind-whipped waters of the bay were as depressing as her thoughts. For Igor had given her another bit of news.

He would be remaining in Novoarchangelsk. Not from choice, he said laughing, for he dearly loved St. Peterburg with its gossip and intrigue. Had he told her his sister, Anya, handled the purse strings of the family? She had actually *paid* him to remain behind. It was some man, of course. A shipboard romance she wished to keep to herself. Surely not the sedate de Stoeckl! He shrugged his shoulders and made a face.

Tamsen knew who that man would be. And now that Igor had gone, she could stand it no longer. She turned from the window to face her husband. "Dan, you've got something to tell me, so why not come out with it?"

He looked up at his wife with an abstracted smile. By all rights, he should tell her his news now—that Anya had come through and they'd soon be going home. But this thing about the charts still worried him. Best to wait, in case there were complications. "I do have something to tell you, sweetheart, but not now. I want it to be a surprise."

Her fists clenched for an instant as she prepared to flare back at him. Then her shoulders slumped in defeat. A day at a time, she thought wearily. I've got to take things a day at a time. Tonight she must try to get hold of the maps again.

That night, they lay far apart. Dan had learned to take his cue from his unresponsive wife. Besides, his mind wasn't on lovemaking tonight, but directed toward Helena. If he slept at all, it must be lightly. If she were trying any funny business, he'd catch her in the act. Finally, believing Tamsen to be asleep, he forced himself to breathe deeply and evenly, his ears alert to any sound. None came.

At last, Tamsen moved in her sleep, rolling toward him. He grinned to himself. Maybe the true Tamsen took over when she was not awake. He would lie still and let her make the first approach. One small hand touched his shoulder. He felt her soft breath on his cheek, his passion beginning to surge through him. God, it had been a long time . . . .

He stiffened suddenly, feeling her other hand slide beneath the pillow. Not Helena, he thought, horror-stricken, but Tamsen! Oh, my God, Tamsen! My own wife!

Secure in the knowledge that she had managed this last time, Tamsen rolled away. She lay still for a moment, to make sure. Then quietly she rose and tiptoed into the other room.

CHAPTER 11

Reaching the desk, Tamsen seated herself. She carefully laid out the unfinished letter to Em that was to be her cover if Dan woke and came to look for her. Extracting a map from the oilskin packet, she slid the packet in the drawer, and left it ajar just enough to open easily, if she should have to sweep the work she was doing out of sight. One more map and she was done. Her one satisfaction was that if the Russians found what they searched for, it would be purely accidental, and Voedvodski would be a most unhappy man.

She dipped her pen and began to trace the chart when a hand gripped her wrist and twisted it hard. The ink overturned as she struggled; her pen went flying across the room. She was picked up by one arm with brutal pressure and the chair kicked out from under her; Dan turned her to face him. His face was black with anger.

"Just what the hell do you think you're doing?"

Though the evidence was on the desk behind her, she could think of nothing but her manufactured excuse.

"I couldn't sleep. I was writing to Em." And, as his grip on her arm increased, "Dan, you're hurting me!"

"I ought to break your damned neck! Goddamn it, maybe I will!"

"I can explain. It isn't what you think."

Dan looked at the face upraised to his: white, dark eyes terrified but steadfast, her lips pressed together with pain. His anger faded, and he released her arm. No matter what she'd done, this was Tamsen, the woman he loved. But she had betrayed him. Oh, God, he felt sick!

He backed away, dropping his arms to his sides, and stared at the girl who swayed before him, one hand clutching her bruised arm. She looked so small, so—so goddamn *pure*. And he'd caught her in the act of what amounted to treason. How could he believe anything she said?

"Start talking." His voice was hard.

How could she explain to him so that he would understand? In the state he was in, he'd go straight to the castle and beat the governor-general into a pulp. Then he would be hanged, or sent to Siberia. She swallowed hard and tried to smile.

"It isn't what it appears to be, Dan. You still have your maps. I only made some copies—harmless copies. Let's go back to bed now. I'll tell you the whole story in the morning." She moved toward him, not realizing that her outstretched hands gave an appearance of invitation.

She had betrayed him, and now she intended to seduce him into forgetting the whole thing. A bitter taste rose in Dan's mouth. She was still the Tamsen of the old days; song-and-dance girl, madam of the brothel, where everything had its price...even he. She'd let him think she'd returned his love, and all the time she'd been working against him—

"You'd sell everything from flesh to government secrets, wouldn't you?" he said jerkily. "What's Voedvodski paying you? Enough to start another whorehouse?"

"Dan, you don't know what you're saying!"

"I only know what I see. And I don't like it. You haven't changed, have you? Still the same old Tamsen, out to get what she can. You can set up all the paying customers you want from now on, because, my dear, I'm through!"

Snatching up the maps, he replaced them in the oilskin bag, and thrust it inside his shirt. Then he rummaged in another drawer and extracted his pistol. He walked toward the door, where he turned to look at her, his image looming dark and dangerous against the stormy night.

He's going to shoot me, Tamsen thought. She wished he would. She couldn't know that, when the door slammed behind him, Dan Tallant stumbled through the rain-swept night, his eyes wet with tears. The anger that had sustained him had dissolved into hopeless misery. God help him, he still loved her, despite her betrayal. His wife was a traitor—and he was a fool.

By morning, Tamsen's feeling of guilt was replaced by anger. She'd gone through pure hell for Dan's sake, still falsifying the maps despite her fears that he was going to Russia with Anya. She should have faced him with *that* last night when he chose to draw such ugly conclusions.

She'd told him the charts were harmless, but he didn't listen. If he hadn't behaved like an angry bull, they could have discussed the whole situation rationally, and he would have understood. But maybe he didn't want to understand. It could be his way of getting off the hook regarding his trip to Russia. He'd used his own guilt feelings to accuse her of unmentionable behavior, throwing her past in her face.

Well, let him believe she was a traitor, a bad woman! Let him! She went to the window. Last night's blowing rain had resolved into a freezing drizzle. The small sailboats in the harbor were ghost ships, ice-frosted masts silver against a gray sea. She hated the cold.

But she was going out anyway. First, she would go to the company store and purchase materials for a new gown. When Dan went away, she would see him off in style. Then she must find a way to endure the remainder of the day; Igor had asked her to tea, so that would ensure a busy morning. Since Devon's health had improved, she could take tea with him in the afternoon. Tomorrow, Ivan and Dmitri.

One thing for sure, she wasn't going to sit around and wait. If Dan Tallant ever wanted to come back, it would be on his knees. But for now, she must prepare to venture out on her own onto the great skating pond Novoarchangelsk had become. Dressing warmly, she bound her boots with strips of rawhide, so that she could achieve traction. She'd learned the trick the previous year—the hard way, though she had incurred no serious injury. Dan had picked her up—she would not think about last year, she told herself. Nor about Dan.

Fingering the bolts of material in the store, she was fascinated by one of black satin...how it shimmered and caught the light. Yet it was not suitable for a gown. The Russian noblewomen wore velvets and heavy brocades. Moving on, she discovered a measure of tulle, also in black. She slid one hand beneath a single fold, seeing how glowingly it shone through like translucent pearl. It would have been perfect for Madam Franklin's parlor, she thought with a small smile. She was still thinking like a flesh-merchant.

Passing the tulle by, she turned for a last look. To hell with fashion, she thought recklessly. She would set the castle on its ear! And in a gown so decorous, no one could take exception to it. She asked that the materials be delivered to her house and set about her plans for the remainder of the day: morning with Igor, afternoon with Devon.

If only she didn't have to face the long and lonely night.

Tallant, on the pretext of having work to do, had arranged for a cot in the small office he shared with de Stoeckl. The baron was agreeable to the situation, though it was evident he didn't believe Dan's excuse for sleeping there. His Russian mind put two and two together. A beautiful princess and a jealous wife could provide only one answer. Ah, well, the departure of Anya would soon resolve it.

The truth was that the work had long been done. A complete package in favor of the sale of the Russian-American Company's holdings to the States had already been drawn up, corrected, and approved. Dan read it over three times. Then he turned to his charts, the maps which had been of such value, to be used to influence a new President, the Senate—

He tried to whip up his anger once more, but he could feel only a terrible heartsick weariness when he thought of what Tamsen had done. Why would she betray him as she did? For she had done it. He'd caught her in the act. But *why?* Jealousy, perhaps? She'd never quite believed his lack of interest in the princess. Oh, Lord! Would that have led her to do such an awful thing? He knew some of the things he'd said last night were unfounded. And he'd left her in a bad state. No telling what she'd do—he shoved the oilskin packet inside his shirt and went out to look for his wife.

She was not at home. Entering, he gathered up a few clothes and waited. The clothing would be his excuse when she returned. Giving up, finally, he returned to his office-room, meeting de Stoeckl, who remarked, offhandedly, "I saw your wife at the tea house this morning, with Prince Igor."

Anger drove Tallant back to his house again. Here he'd been worrying himself sick and his wife was evidently off having a fine time. She still had not returned. He went back to his room and sat brooding. There was a view of the knoll where the tea houses stood, and his heart lurched as he saw Tamsen approaching, accompanied by Edwin Devon.

Trust Tamsen not to waste any time! They entered a tea house, and Tallant sat by his window, unable to see them—but unable to tear his gaze away.

Devon seated Tamsen and ordered tea. Much more of this, Tamsen thought, and I'll turn into a samovar! But she couldn't remain in her house. Not today. When the tea came, Devon began to give a résumé of the bit he was writing for the governor-general's eye. It was imaginative and overdrawn, each sentence with a double meaning. Voedvodski would see his words as complimentary; an Englishman or American would see them as derogatory.

Tamsen laughed until she cried. "Oh, Edwin," she said, clasping his hand, "you're good for me!"

"I hope so." The blue English eyes were troubled. With a pang, Tamsen saw the toll his illness had taken, the grave young face lined prematurely. "I hope so," he repeated. "Tamsen, there's something

129

wrong. I knew the minute I saw you. If it is none of my affair, tell me so, and forgive me. But if I can be of service—"

"It's nothing," she whispered. "A personal problem."

As the afternoon wore on and turned into early evening, Tamsen did not express a desire to go home, and Devon's concern grew. It was almost dark when she reluctantly said, "I suppose I must go—"

"I will walk you home," he said gallantly. "I'm sure your husband's worried by your absence."

"I doubt it." There was a world of bitterness in her tone.

Ice was sheathing their vision as they walked through the freezing mist, her hand on his arm. Reaching her house, she did not offer to release him, but began to shiver a little. "Don't go," she pleaded. "Come in—get warm before you go—you've been ill—"

Knowing Tallant would not welcome his intrusion but feeling disturbed at Tamsen's nervousness, Devon complied. Inside the door, she turned to face him, her features crumpling like a child's.

"Dan's not here. He'll be sorry to have missed you. No! That's not true. He's left me! Dan's left me!"

Taking the sobbing figure in his arms, Devon tried to soothe her. All she could say was that there had been a misunderstanding and Dan refused to hear her out.

The savage, Devon thought. The damnable, bloody brute! If he, Devon, were a well man, he'd punch his blinking nose for him! If duels were still the fashion, he'd call him out! The girl was too good for the fellow, by God! She was better off without him. But he had the good sense to remain silent while he held her close and let her have her cry.

Dan, drawn to follow, in spite of himself, had a good view of the whole proceeding through the window. Fuming, he stamped away into the darkness of the frozen night.

CHAPTER 12

The next several days were rather uneventful. Tamsen busied herself morning and night by designing and stitching her new gown. In the afternoons, she held soirees, successfully gathering the elite of Novoarchangelsk into her small unfinished house.

"It is not the house, but the lady we come to see," Igor said gallantly, and his words were echoed by her other guests. By this time, word of the Tallants' estrangement was going the rounds. And Igor thought it was all to the good, since Tamsen was now free to hold her own small court.

"You don't really mind that he's gone, do you?" he asked anxiously.

Tamsen looked at him with steady eyes. "Igor, have you never loved anyone?"

"I suppose not," he said comically, "but I've tried. Many times. Many women. Oh, how I've tried." He rolled his eyes, and Tamsen had to laugh. It seemed there was a lot of laughter these days, but all of it was on the surface. Deep inside, she could feel her heart still bleeding.

Since the evening with Devon, she had taken refuge in numbers. The Englishman's sympathetic embrace had soon tightened into one of passion. It had been difficult to ease away. There would be no more close attachments—never again. They hurt too much.

She didn't shed another tear until the two ships came in; one was a large supply ship carrying materials from Russia; the other, a small trawler bound for Okhotsk. The larger of the two would pick up passengers—the Princess Anya and Dan among them—and sail around the globe to reach its destination. It would be in port for several days, but the smaller ship would leave on the morrow.

Tamsen wasn't surprised at a summons from the governor-general. He knew there was one remaining chart. She had explained that she was removing them one at a time, replacing them with folded paper, leaving the rest so the packet looked untouched. The last one was to have been removed just prior to Dan's leaving, when in the flurry of preparations he would not notice.

Now she stood before Voedvodski defiantly. She could do no more. Dan had caught her with the packet, she said, and discovered his papers were missing. Their marriage was over. But the last chart was unimportant, anyway, showing only traces of lead and zinc as it did.

Tamsen's eyes were darkly circled, and her mouth trembled as she spoke. The governor-general looked troubled. "I'm not a cruel man," he began. "I only did what seemed expedient. I'm sorry that—"

"If you will excuse me," Tamsen said stiffly. *"Sorry!"* she raged as she left the castle. "He's *sorry!* I hope he rots in hell!"

Looking after Tamsen, Voedvodski rubbed his chin. Though he'd just accomplished the greatest coup of his career, his conscience pained him. A firm believer in holy matrimony, he had disapproved of the arrangements between the local officers and the

Aleut and Tlingit women. A pity to break up a marriage; he was not proud of what he'd done.

There might be a way to mend the situation. At least, he would get them together so that they might work things out. Now he could lean back and congratulate himself. His luck had improved of late. The Tlingits had been kept down this year. And he had the maps showing gold and mineral locations to send to the tsar. Thank the good Lord, too, he would soon be rid of the Princess Anya.

He could well afford a sentimental gesture. In the meantime, there was much to do. A banquet tonight would suffice to welcome both ships and provide a farewell to speed the trawler on its way. And there was his message for the tsar to brief. Affairs of state sat heavily on his shoulders. Therefore, when he took pen in hand to write two ornate invitations, he was overwhelmed by a sense of his own generosity. Each requested the presence of Daniel Tallant and his lady at the governor-general's dinner. One was sent to Tamsen, the other to Dan.

The invitation was more of a summons, Tamsen thought. And a rather malicious gesture, since Voedvodski knew she and Dan were estranged. Perhaps this was a way to ensure that she did not attend at all. But she wouldn't give the governor-general that satisfaction! She would go, and she would wear her new gown. She would arrive late, in order to make an entrance. And she would go alone.

The next evening, dressed for the feast, she surveyed herself in the mirror. The costume she had created was absolutely wicked—and equally becoming. She had made an underdress of the black satin. Cut daringly low, it molded to her body and gleamed with highlights; it was slit up one side to the knee like a dancer's costume. But the overdress conformed to all of decency's standards: high-necked, with long bell sleeves, straight in front but full and sweeping behind and made of tulle. It was both covering and revealing. Much of a golden Tamsen showed through.

She would set the place on its ear, she thought with satisfaction, as she put her little black dancing slippers in a matching reticule and pulled on the sinew-bound boots she must wear to traverse the icy terrain. She would change when she reached the castle and leave her boots in the foyer.

Last of all, she donned Igor's gift of white ermine, wearing the fur cloak for the first time. It fell about her, soft and luxurious. And she was ready to go—

She stepped out into the darkness and gave a small cry as someone seized her arm.

"Dan!"

He bowed mockingly. "The governor-general's invitation was quite clear. I'm to escort my wife."

"And if she doesn't wish your company?"

"That's her problem. You're coming with me, and that's it. Let's get going. I don't like this any better than you do, and I've been standing out here in this goddamn cold for an hour, freezing my—

"Always the gentleman," Tamsen said sweetly. "Such pretty speeches."

For an answer, he gave a tug at her arm, forcing her to move despite her intentions. They walked in silence to the castle and climbed the steps together. In the foyer, Dan knelt and pulled off her boots, sliding her small black slippers on her feet. He seemed to be taking an uncomfortably long time at it. Looking down at his dark head, Tamsen fought back tears. Then he lifted the ermine cloak from her shoulders, turning to hand it to an attendant. Turning back, his eyes widened.

135

"My God! You're not going in there in that!"

Stunned, Dan reached out one hand toward the attendant, as if to retrieve the fur cloak. Tamsen skipped away from him and hurried to the banquet hall, pausing in the doorway.

All eyes turned toward her. Igor's eyes danced with delight. Devon's face reddened. But they both came toward her. In an instant, she was surrounded by a crowd of men.

"I haven't seen so much of a young lady since my sister graced the hall," Igor whispered.

Edwin Devon didn't know what to say. The girl looked breathtakingly beautiful; her creamy shoulders glowed through the black, sheer material. But, blast it, the dress wasn't decent! Though for the life of him, he couldn't decide what was indecent about it. She was more covered than any woman in the room. Still, it wasn't something he'd want his wife to wear.

And she'd come in with Tallant! He'd thought that was over. And the bumbling clod had left his wife standing here in that—that provocative gown— and headed for a bottle-laden table.

Devon moved forward, took Tamsen's hands in his, and said gravely, "You look lovely, my dear."

I'm an embarrassment to him, Tamsen thought, intuitively. But still he is kind. The evening was a whirl of success for Tamsen. She was shunned by the women, especially Anya, who had chosen to dress to suit her new character—that of a young girl, demure and virginal. Decked in white ruffles, she felt like a fool, which was a sensation she did not like, since she was far from being one.

Worse, Dan Tallant had escorted his own wife to table. Tamsen was furious at being captured and led away from her coterie in such a high-handed way,

136

but managed to cover it by speaking only with Igor at her left. Dish after exotic dish was served. Great heavy platters of silver, ornately scrolled, reflected back the glitter of candles. A peacock, brought by ship, occupied the center of the table; it had been roasted whole and its feathers replaced.

Around the table, the noblemen outshone the peacock's vibrant colors. What a successful party, the governor-general thought with satisfaction, except for the icy silence between the Tallants. He had more or less forced them into close proximity tonight. Even though Dan Tallant was a threat to the colony, and even though his wife's dress was outlandish to the point of disgrace, Voedvodski hoped things would mend between them.

Imagine, Stephan Vassili Voedvodski playing Cupid! He laughed comfortably and sipped at his drink. Then he met Tallant's eyes and choked a little. It was plain the man knew who had his maps, but he would not dare to cause trouble. Voedvodski had set Dmitri and Niklas to watch him, "Let him know you are watching," he had said, "and that you are armed."

There would be no problem. And soon Tallant would be gone, either sailing for Russia with Anya, as was rumored, or returning to the States with his wife. Voedvodski would enjoy the festive evening.

Tallant, a man of action, was not enjoying anything. His every instinct urged him to haul the posturing governor-general out of the room and beat his face in. Diplomacy, hell! With effort, he controlled himself and turned to watch Tamsen. Her attention was on the nobleman at her other side. She had him bewitched. The man's dinner partner, a Russian woman, was livid at being neglected. Tamsen was up to her old tricks. She needed a good

137

shaking! Again, Dan controlled himself.

The feast ended and the speeches began. Waltz music signaled for dancing. Tallant gripped his wife's arm and led her to the floor. For an instant she swayed against him, and he felt his pulse pounding. Then he recovered his senses. The move had probably been calculated, as was everything Tamsen did.

"I suppose you know you're making a spectacle of yourself tonight," he said harshly. "That dress! The way you've been behaving—"

"It's no concern of yours. You told me to do as I wished."

"By God, you're still my wife!"

"Am I?" Her eyes filled with angry tears. "You were the one who went off into the wilderness, leaving me to face the spying, blackmail—"

She stopped short at the expression on his stone-hard face. "Blackmail? What the hell are you talking about?"

She pulled away from him. "Tamsen!" He followed her, losing her in the crowd of dancers. Dammit, he had to find out what this was all about! He could see only the top of her head through the shoulders of a surrounding group of royally clad officers. If he forced his way through to drag her out, she would surely refuse to come, and there would be a scene.

He must talk to her. No matter what she had done, he loved her, and he had judged her without giving her a chance. Blackmail, she'd said. His eyes went to the governor-general. If the man had persecuted Tamsen in his absence, he would kill him! For now, it was important that he do what he should have done that first night. Get Tamsen off alone, take her in his arms, and hold her until they reached a basis of understanding. He shut his eyes, imagining the small figure standing before him. Clutching her bruised arm, saying, "I can explain."

And what had he done? He'd flown off the goddamn handle, in typical Tallant fashion. If he couldn't get her out of that crowd, maybe someone else could. He looked around the room, rejecting Devon—damn Britisher—and Igor, mischief-making young fool. He finally spotted his young aide, Ivan, who stood with Anya, and made his way to him. "Tell my wife she's wanted in the governor-general's office. Don't answer any questions. Just get her there as quickly as you can."

Turning on his heel, he walked away. To his dismay, the princess followed, tucking her hand in the crook of his arm. "Dan, we must talk. The money you promised me—"

"You will have it in the morning. Now, please excuse me. I have something to discuss with my wife."

"But I don't want it in the morning," she pouted. "That's what I wished to ask. Gold is heavy. I cannot carry it. And I would trust no one else. Will you bring it to the ship just before it sails?"

"I'll bring it. Now, please, for God's sake—"

Anya had caught sight of Tamsen approaching in Ivan's company. "Until the ship sails, then,"she said loudly. Then, "Oh, Dan!" She threw herself into Dan Tallant's startled arms. Tamsen stood stunned. Ivan made a harsh sobbing sound and fled. Before Dan could disentangle himself, Tamsen, too, was gone.

"Now, what the hell was that for?" Dan growled at Anya.

"A thank you," Anya said demurely. "And to seal our bargain." With a smile, she left the room. Too

139

bad, she thought, that Ivan had also viewed the scene. But he had served his purpose; now he was expendable.

Tamsen reached the foyer, a part of her mind telling her what to do. Smile at the attendant. Ask for your wrap. Exchange slippers for boots. Then her emotions took over. Run! Run out into the darkness. Run home—anywhere—but get away from this place. The door closed behind her; the cold mist hit her hot face...and she ran.

She didn't realize she had slipped until she was falling, tumbling down the icy steps that led to the bottom of the hill. Then her cloak caught on a projection and she pitched to one side and struck her head against a stone wall; there was darkness everywhere.

For an instant, she regained consciousness. For some strange reason, she was in Dan's arms, and someone was talking about her boots—

"Should have had ice guards," the Russian sentry said. "No wonder she fell. Her cloak catching like that was all that saved her—"

"But she did," Dan said. "I saw them! Oh, God, help me get her inside! Tamsen! Sweetheart—"

Ivan stood quiet as the sentry held the door so that Tallant could carry his wife into the castle. He was beginning to understand the scene he had witnessed immediately following the feast. He'd gone in search of his adored princess and found her in the foyer, a pair of small boots in her hand. Seeing him, she'd seemed flustered.

"Do you like these?" she asked. "I'm thinking of having a pair made like them. Do you think they'd suit me?" She thrust out a tiny foot, exposing a liberal amount of slim ankle, and the bemused Ivan had forgotten all else.

140

Now he knew that his idol had feet of clay. Her protestations of love for him had all been lies. She wanted Tallant enough to kill for him. He, Ivan had been used.

CHAPTER 13

Tamsen's condition was serious. She was removed from the castle to the small Russian hospital, and she lay in a deep coma. The Russian physician pronounced her injury a fracture of the skull.

A series of distinguished visitors besieged the hospital, including the governor-general, but the doctor was adamant. No one was allowed to see her. Even Dan was only allowed two five-minute intervals during the day, no more. The remainder of the time, he paced outside her door, stricken with guilt at his treatment of her, beset with memories. Memories of a small dark girl bending over a fire on the trail to Santa Fe touched him. He'd loved her even then, though they struck sparks whenever they met, bringing out the worst in each other.

He recalled her in Magoffinville: the singer, dancer, and cantina girl, who struggled to support her sisters in any way she could. In Magoffinville, she could have been his. And what had he done? Ridden off like a fool to do his goddamn duty, leaving her behind. Another assignment, like this one, had come between them.

He'd left her behind when he went into the wild country, fearing for her safety. And she had not been safe here. The word *blackmail* still lodged in his mind. When she recovered—oh, God, if she recovered—he would find out what had happened in his absence, and he and the Russian governor would have a confrontation.

He wished she would wake, if only for a moment, so that he could tell her how he felt. He loved her. No matter what she'd done, he couldn't live without her. But she lay in there, her white face below a swath of bandages, lost in darkness. Alone. What the hell happened to the thongs that bound her boots, anyway? He knew they'd been there—

Three days of it. Three days of pacing, waiting, thinking, and Tamsen didn't recover enough for him to tell her all his deep feelings for her. Then a messenger arrived with a note from Anya. The ship would sail on the morrow. She wished him to deliver the promised payment.

Dan groaned. Hell, de Stoeckl was going. Let him take it! No, most of the gold was government funds. It had to be accepted and signed for, and it would take two people to carry the small, heavy chests. He would take one, and Ivan could carry the other, though he need not know its contents. It shouldn't take more than an hour, if he hurried, and he wouldn't leave if Tamsen showed any signs of waking.

The next morning, her condition was unchanged. Dan and Ivan collected the chests and went on board ship where the usual farewell ceremonies were in progress, liquor flowing freely, the emotional Russians alternating speeches with tears.

Anya was caught up in the hubbub. "Take the chests to my stateroom," she whispered, "and I'll be down to sign for them immediately. And you,

Ivan"—she smiled at the young Russian—"you can return to join in the festivities."

Dan, however, had other ideas. He didn't wish a repeat performance of Anya's earlier embrace. "You will remain with me," he instructed his aide. "I must only wait for a signature on some papers."

The two men waited, ill at ease. Anya's mark was already on her stateroom. The silken sheets on the bed were turned back, a filmy gown thrown over the foot, and there was a scent of perfume in the air. They waited five minutes, ten; the vessel would soon sail. "I'll go get the lady," Dan said, finally. "Ivan, you wait here—"

There was a harsh grating sound at the door. Dan and Ivan looked at each other with a wild surmise. Then Dan moved toward it. The knob turned, but the door didn't move. It had been barred from the outside in some way. Dan cursed himself for entering without checking.

"It is locked!" Ivan stated, his eyes wide. "But why?"

Dan moved backward, then threw his shoulder against the metal door with all his weight. It didn't give. He tried time and time again, his breath sobbing between his gritted teeth. He was still trying when the ship began to move.

An hour later, Anya stood in the doorway, pretending surprise at the sight of two grim-faced men. "I'd completely forgotten you," she said. "Did someone lock the door? How dreadful! And we're already under way."

Dan went toward her, murder in his eyes. "You damn, lying little slut," he snarled, "I'm going to kill you with my bare hands."

Two burly Russian seamen appeared in the door,

144

one at either side of her. "You heard what he said." The girl pointed to Dan. "He threatened me! Put him in irons!"

Dan felled the first one who reached him with a mighty blow, then whirled to face the other. But the fallen man lifted himself to twine his arms about Dan's legs. As Dan struggled to free himself, the other seaman brought a club down upon his head. Once, and again, then the struggle was over.

Anya watched the seamen carry Tallant away, her eyes wide. "Such a violent man," she murmured. Then she turned to Ivan with a wistful smile. "I'm so sorry this happened," she whispered. "Such an awful mistake. But perhaps I can make it up to you. It will be a long voyage. And I'll be lonely."

But Ivan was no longer the callow youth who had melted at her touch. His eyes were hard as he said, "A pity. But I am sure you would not enjoy my company."

He walked from the stateroom, leaving her standing open-mouthed. He must find de Stoeckl, tell him of Dan's plight, and try to arrange for his release.

Dan came to in the hold of the ship, his head bursting, and with a raging thirst. Desperately, he tested the chains that bound him; they were heavy iron cuffs on his wrists and ankles, and he was chained to the wall like an animal. He cut his wrists, trying to break the chains, but they didn't come off, and he was certain there was no way to escape. His mind went to Tamsen. If she woke, she would not know where he was, nor why he had gone. She would think he had deserted her. And she would never know that he loved her, forgave her, that he hated himself for his cruelty toward her—oh, God—and if she died, she would die alone.

Dan had never been a religious man, but he began to pray. Not for himself, but for the girl he loved. The small girl who was so many things to him: lover, sweetheart, friend—and enemy. For the first time in his life, Dan Tallant knew what it felt like to cry.

CHAPTER 14

For several days, Tamsen escaped into a land of dreams, her life passing before her in segments: Arab as a toddler, playing about the steps of their old home, auburn curls shining in the sun. Em, sweet-faced, aproned, working in the kitchen. And Papa—but Papa was dead. He had died along the trail to Santa Fe. . . . Magoffinville and the cantina. Dusty, Nell, *Dan*. . . San Francisco and the Parlor . . . *Dan*—

"She's coming along splendidly," the Russian physician beamed at the governor-general's query. "A bit confused and disoriented at this time. But a day or two should bring full recovery."

"Good," Voedvodski grunted. He'd been concerned by the girl's plight. Especially since Tallant had apparently absconded with Princess Anya. How she would take his defection, he didn't know. He had been most woefully mistaken in judging Tallant's character. That a man would go off with a beautiful woman, he could understand. But not when it meant leaving his wife at death's door.

Dan Tallant! Tamsen sat up with a cry. "Dan! Where is he! Where is he!"

Firm hands pressed her back to the pillow. A voice in a foreign tongue, which she strangely understood, was entreating her to lie still . . . to be quiet . . . she'd been ill.

She complied. And after a while, she ceased to ask for her husband. For her memory had fully returned, and she knew that she had last seen him in another woman's arms.

When she could receive visitors, it was Igor who told her that Dan had boarded the ship and not been seen again. It was evident that her husband had sailed with Anya.

Finally, she was able to return to the small house. Edwin Devon had tactfully removed all traces of Dan's occupancy. He helped a shaky Tamsen from the hospital to her home, building up a fire as soon as they got inside. He placed a fur robe across her knees.

"I don't know what I'd do without you," she said honestly.

"Don't ever try to do without me," he said with passion. He was feeling better now than he had in a long while and was beginning to dare to dream. "Tamsen, I have little to offer, but—"

"But I'm a married woman," she said. "Even though my husband is gone. And we must remember that."

Edwin Devon wished mournfully for a miracle. Perhaps the fellow would fall overboard!

Igor's proposal was perhaps the most touching. Arriving with delicacies calculated to stimulate an invalid's appetite, he seemed strangely quiet and shy. He hadn't much in the way of worldly goods, he said haltingly. His sister handled the purse strings. But whatever he had was at her disposal, along with his protection. Then if her husband ever—if she ever—if she wished—. He bogged down. Igor serious was a far different creature from his more naturally whimsical self.

She thanked him, telling him she would call upon

him if need be, and he took his departure, leaving Tamsen to mull over a new problem. There was no money in the house. Evidently Dan had left her unprovided for. With a pang, she realized she couldn't even afford Helena, who had been hovering over her since her return.

Helena did not share her realization. Tamsen had been kind to her, treating her like a person, not a being who was half animal, half Russian. Her people, the Tlingits, were wealthy, not in the way the Russians were, but in fish, berries, and furs—things that counted. She felt it her duty to care for the little American woman until a ship arrived to take her to her own country. Tamsen shed weak tears over the girl's generosity. She would find a way to repay her.

The governor-general's visit failed to arouse such an emotion. He felt the situation was somewhat his fault, he said expansively. Therefore, she was welcome to be his guest at the castle as long as was necessary. Or, if she preferred, she was welcome to the use of this house.

Tamsen chose the latter. "I will see that you are well paid when my husband returns."

From his expression, she could tell that he knew, as she did, there was little likelihood of that eventuality.

The time for condolences had passed. Beyond the window, the sea was shrouded by a screen of softly falling snow. But spring would come and with it a ship. She had no money for passage, but she would sell her jewels one by one. And she would do as Dan suggested, return home.

But not to Em and Arabella with their safe and settled lives. She would go, instead, to Nell. Nell, who knew the undependable natures of men and accepted them for what they were—profiting by the knowledge. She wouldn't accept the Parlor back from Nell, to whom she had deeded it without qualifications. But she could work there; sing and dance for her room and board, and depend on no one.

She laughed ruefully. For an independent woman, she was in one hell of a mess—dependent upon a Russian for her lodging and a half-caste Indian girl for food. But here, too, she tried to pay her own way. She went to the armoire and withdrew the ermine cloak. Helena had cleaned it, lovingly, and mended the tear where it had caught in time to save Tamsen's life; she had sponged away the mud and the bloodstains. Tamsen draped her in its folds.

Seeing Helena's bewilderment, she said, "It is for you. A gift." Not a muscle moved in the girl's serene face, but the dark, liquid eyes brimmed with tears.

"*Ach-tlak*," she said softly. "My sister." Then, "*Achtu wassigue*—I love. My heart cares." She touched Tamsen's cheek with a gentle finger.

The passing days seemed to deepen the friendship between Tamsen and the Tlingit-Russian girl. And at last, Helena came to her. "I have spoken with the elders of my people," she said seriously. "I have told them you are the sister of my heart. My mother accepts you. The daughter of *ach kak*, my uncle, is to marry. I have been told I may invite you, since you are of my family."

"Helena—I am honored."

"The Russian governor will not like this. It must be secret. And you must remain outside the gates until they open once more." The girl's voice was troubled.

"Then we must arrange to make it appear I am at home," Tamsen said. She thought a moment, then laughed. "I shall invite Edwin Devon to dinner in the presence of others. He will spend the evening here, lighting the lamps. Then he will go, after putting them out, leaving only a small candle in the bedroom."

"You will not laugh at my people? Our customs are not like yours."

"I'm certain their customs are better than many of ours," Tamsen comforted her.

Edwin Devon was not so sure. He reminded Tamsen that these same Indians were the ones who had stormed the walls of the settlement less than two years before and were only brought to bay by the use of cannon fire. Since that time, the gates of the stockade were closed at night. The Russians had good reason.

As for Tamsen, this might be a plot. She could be kidnapped and held for ransom, used to bring the governor-general to terms. But Tamsen would not be dissuaded, and he finally gave in with reluctance. He would cover for her, while she attended an Indian wedding.

On the day of the ceremony, Tamsen walked through the gates of Novoarchangelsk with Helena, carrying a market basket on her arm. Her dark hair was braided, worn in a coronet. Once in the Indian marketplace, she exchanged her cloak for a blanket Helena had provided. With the removal of a single pin, the braid fell down her back. When she entered the house of Helena's family, it would have taken a close observer to say she didn't belong with the throng of guests attending the wedding.

Outside, the snow was still falling. But in the windowless building with its single square door, it was hot. Too hot. The room was enormous, and in its center, the floor had been dug down about a foot deep. An earthen bank ran the distance of the house

151

and was curtained off with blankets and boards. Here, Helena whispered, were storage spaces and sleeping chambers. A second tier above them was also divided into such rooms, to accommodate her large family.

Nervously glancing at Tamsen from time to time, Helena led her to the innermost room. The area was floored, except for a space in the middle, where a fire blazed. The firelight flickered on monstrous masks, and the elders' faces were painted red and black, in true ceremonial custom. Smoke billowed to the firehole above, with much of it remaining entrapped in the room. This could have been a scene from hell. The scent of furs, smoke, fish, and crowded Indian bodies made Tamsen choke.

A hush fell. The wedding was about to begin. Helena hurried Tamsen to a corner where she might view the proceedings. The bridegroom, a young man in ceremonial clothes, came through the door. Not looking to right or left, he strode through the room and seated himself proudly on a white fur rug. Tamsen, blinking from the smoke, recognized it as the ermine cloak she had given Helena. Igor would never believe the use his gift had been put to!

The moment the groom was seated, songs and dances began. The purpose, Helena whispered, was to lure the bride from her hiding place. Then skins were spread on the floor to the spot where the bridegroom was sitting, and the little bride, in finest ceremonial clothing, walked across them to seat herself beside the groom; she bowed her head shyly.

Soon again the singing and dancing began. And through it all, the young couple sat like carved, brightly colored statues—the young man with his arms folded, his eyes staring sternly ahead, the girl with downcast eyes.

152

During the festivities, Tamsen was ignored. It was as if she were not there. Occasionally, dark eyes turned to look, not at her, but through her. She could not suppress a little shiver. Then an old woman, bent a little and with a waddling walk, shuffled toward her. Standing before Tamsen, she studied her with fierce eyes for a long time. Then she nodded, and from around her neck she took a pendant, a slender thong with a black stone carved into a raven's image, and placed it over Tamsen's head, settling the stone into place between her breasts.

"*Ach-ssi*," she said, simply. "My daughter." And then she was gone.

"Now," Helena said, squeezing Tamsen's hand, "you are of the Raven clan. My people."

The singing, dancing, and feasting went on until morning came and went. Only the wedding pair did not partake of the food or the pleasure. They must fast for two days before they can be together, Helena told Tamsen. And the marriage would not be binding for yet four weeks.

"The gates will be open now," she continued. "If you wish, we will go."

"I would like to thank your mother—"

"She knows."

Leaving the house belonging to Helena's kwan, Tamsen felt that she was returning to a different world. Her hands went to her hair, and she pinned the errant braid into a crown once more. The cloak came out of the market basket, and the blanket went in.

Passing the Indian market, the two girls entered the gates. There, Edwin Devon waited, the color high on his cheekbones from the cold, his eyes lighting at sight of them.

153

"Lord," he said, "I thought you'd never come."

He escorted them to Tamsen's small house, accepting her half-hearted invitation to tea. She didn't want an intrusion on her memories of the Tlingit village so soon. Devon plied her with questions, and she evaded many of them. It had been an intensely private experience which she did not intend to share.

After Devon's departure, Helena mentioned that Tamsen was the first white woman to spend the night in an Indian house as a guest.

"Perhaps I'll come to your wedding one day."

"That will not be possible. I shall not marry," Helena said solemnly. Tamsen stared at the girl.

"What marriage could there be for me? My mother is a Tlingit, my father an unknown *promishleniki*. I was taken from my mother after six winters, and put first in Father Veniaminov's orphanage, then in the girls' school of Madame Etolin. I read; I write; I speak the language of the Russian. No Tlingit man would want me."

"You are half-Russian."

"To the Russians, I am half-Tlingit. The best I could expect would be an arrangement with some man who is lonely for a wife in Russia. I do not want a Russian."

That night, readying herself for bed, Tamsen pondered Helena's words. The girl was made for love. Was it possible she could live out her life without a man? Tamsen had noted her yearning eyes during the wedding ceremony. She supposed she'd have felt the same way at a wedding in the style performed at home. Hopeless, with Dan gone.

With an odd sensation, she realized this was the first time in more than twenty-four hours that he had entered her mind. Perhaps she now could reconcile herself to the years ahead, to being alone.

Fingering the raven amulet, she thought again of the ceremony she'd witnessed. Grotesque in a way to a stranger's eyes. Yet there had been a dignity, a nobility in the ritual at the same time. Two days of fasting, of sharing deprivation together. Four weeks of testing before the marriage was declared valid. And the system must work. According to Helena, adultery was the rarest crime in the Tlingit code, considered even worse than murder.

CHAPTER 15

Spring approached and brought warm rains that melted the snow and ice which plagued Novoarchangelsk. The days grew longer, and occasionally a brief morning respite from the downpour showed the snow-covered mountains tinged with pink from the sunrise. Their petticoats of green inched higher as spates of snow-water ran down upon the settlement or into the sea.

Like last year, Tamsen thought. When it had been a time of waiting for Dan to return from his expedition. Except now there was nothing to wait for, except a ship returning to the States. There had been several, but none that would accept a lone female passenger.

In preparation for her journey, she'd sold her jewels and much of her clothing. Her afternoon soirees had been abandoned because of her new poverty; only Igor and Devon were encouraged to visit. And there had been a new type of visitor: the ladies of the settlement who had snubbed Tamsen before.

When the word went out that the American was selling her possessions, Russian women flocked to her door to buy her things and to stay for tea. Their attitudes were a mingling of avarice, curiosity, and pity, for they all knew the story—that her husband left her at death's door and ran away with the princess. Tamsen was angered by their pity at first; then she shrugged it off. Let them think what they would. They were buying; she was selling.

She also found something else to sell. Her dressmaking talents. For the visitors were wild to buy her gowns, certain that, if they wore them, they would be magically transformed. But when one broad-beamed lady was near tears, coveting a particular dress that would never have fitted at any time in her life, it was Tamsen's turn to have pity. She offered to make a gown for the woman on the same style. From this, a fairly lucrative business grew. There were days when Tamsen was desperately homesick, and there were days when she wondered if it might not be best to stay here and try to support herself by sewing. Her pride had kept her from writing home of Dan's defection.

It was at this time that an American ship was sighted in the harbor. Tamsen, stitching away at a gown for a Russian nobleman's wife, heard the news with a mingling of excitement and dread. Now she might be forced to make up her mind . . . to go, or to stay.

She pricked her finger, making a minute bloodstain on the material, and uttered a small sound of annoyance. Luckily it was beneath the hem where it would not show. And she had promised the gown for this afternoon.

She would finish it. She would not go running to the shore as the other residents did when the ships docked. There would be a welcoming affair at the castle tonight, and for the first time since her illness, she would attend. She could make arrangements with the ship's captain then—if she decided to go.... Painfully aware that she was stalling, she stitched away.

The garment was nearly completed when she was startled by a rude banging at the door. Leaping to her feet, she spilled the gown to the floor. Again the impatient pounding sounded.

Wondering, Tamsen went to answer the knocking. She swung the door open with a frown, then staggered a little in shock. For the doorway was completely filled by a wet and enormously fat woman in purple velvet, wearing a huge hat with bedraggled feathers. Below the feathered disaster, small beady black eyes glinted in a face wreathed with a foolish-happy grin.

"Colder'n a welldigger's ass out here," Nell's voice said. "Well, hell, honey! Ain'tcha gonna ast us in?"

"Nell! Oh, dear God, Nell!" Tamsen burst into tears and threw herself sobbing into the big woman's arms.

Alarmed at the violence of the girl's emotions, Nell held her to her bosom and patted her awkwardly on the back with a heavy hand. "Awww," she kept saying, "gawdammit, Tamsen." Then, finally, desperately, "Aww—hell! It's rainin' on my behind, an' yer soppin' up my front. Wettest gawdam place I ever seen. Helluva welcome! Rainin' pitchforks an' you keep me a-standin' here like a gawdam frog—"

Tamsen drew back. "Nell, I'm sorry! I'm just so glad—so glad to see you." Her voice broke. "Nell, Dan's gone."

The broad face arranged itself in funereal lines. "He dead?"

"No. Nell—he went away with another woman. He—he left me."

"Then th' sonofabitch oughta be dead," Nell said,

158

entering the room and pulling off her dripping, feathered hat.

And for the first time, Tamsen saw the others who had been standing behind her, waiting patiently in the rain. Dusty, Carmen, Maggie. And her tears began to flow again. She didn't need to go home, for home had come to her.

CHAPTER 16

Throwing her arms about Dusty, Tamsen repeated the scene she'd made with Nell. Dusty had stood beside her in all the crises she'd faced since her father died. He'd led her to the job at the cantina—and to Nell. Now he was here again, when she needed him most. She sobbed her heart out against his shoulder.

Red-faced, grinning a little foolishly with pleasure, he patted her awkwardly. "My word," he said. "Jove! Oh, I say, Tamsen, chin up, old girl!"

Nell, seeing his expression of fatherly affection, again felt an odd pang of bereavement. "Dammit, Tam," she boomed, "I'm drippin' on yer rug!"

Tamsen pulled herself together and greeted the others: pretty Mexican Carmen with her shining gold front tooth and slew-footed Maggie, both of the girls who went upstairs at the cantina—and later, at Madam Franklin's parlor—for money.

Tamsen set Helena to building up the fires while she herself brought towels for the drenched visitors. Now that her shock at seeing them had evaporated, her brow was wrinkled in perplexity. What were they all doing here?

A friendly visit from Nell, from Dusty? It was unexpected, but most welcome. But her relationships with Carmen and Maggie were only

160

due to the sharing of their business experiences. How odd that they'd come along on the journey. Had the Citizen's Committee closed the parlor down? Well, Nell would tell her in her own good time.

In the meantime, it was good to see them all. Nell held forth in the big chair, Dusty staring soulfully at her, misty-eyed with whiskey and adoration as she recounted their adventure of disembarking from the ship.

"We come through that tunnel buildin', an' there's all them people, grinnin', shakin' han's. I took me a look aroun' 'n' all I see is a mess of mud an' wood houses. I figger this is th' wrong place.

"Whurs this here castle? I says. An all I git is a lotta furrin jabber. Finally, I says, 'Bare-in-off,' an' this Rooshian points up an' says '*Keekoor.*' Tamsen, whut th' hell's a *keekoor?*"

Nell didn't wait for an answer before she continued, explaining how she'd seen this big wooden house, biggest one she ever saw, and figured this must be it. She described how they'd tromped through the mud and labored up the steps—oh, them goddamn steps—only to receive a cold reception by a man in a monkey suit.

"I tolt him," she said with satisfaction. "I says, 'Find me somebody what don't talk pig Latin. I ain't a-leavin' here till I sees his royal Hiney!' Say, Tamsen, that there castle would make one helluva cathouse. Figgered you wuz back in bizness the minute I walked in!"

Tamsen's tears had been replaced by the desire to giggle. She could imagine the sentry's face, confronted by the indomitable Nell. And the governor-general! What he must have thought!

The governor-general hadn't been too ready to

161

cooperate, either, Nell admitted. He'd asked questions about who they were, what they were doing here, and why they wished to see Tamsen—how long did they intend to stay anyway, he had asked.

"None of his goddamn bizness," Nell growled, her cheeks shaking with indignation. "But I didden tell him off. I got manners. I just says I come with a message fer you from yer sis, who just happens to be hitched to a senator in the good ol' U. S. of A.!"

"Em! You have a message from Em?"

"Hell, no. But it sounded good. Got us here, didden it?" She looked to Tamsen for approval, but Tamsen's mind had flown to Em and Arab, in San Francisco.

"Have you seen them lately?" she asked eagerly. "Or read anything about them in the papers? Has Donald retired? Juan taken over his business? The baby, Martha, has she grown much? Are they all well? Oh, Nell, I'm dying for news! They haven't written in so long!"

Nell's eyes shifted uncomfortably, as she recalled the day, months back, when Em and Arab came to her seeking help. That was not something to tell Tamsen, who had enough worries of her own. If they'd wanted her to know, they'd have told her, wouldn't they? It was their business—and probably all straightened out, by now.

"Hell," she said irritably, "how would I know? Oney one kinda soshulizin' atween high-mucky-mucks an' places like the parlor is. An' them men of theirs ain't been in. A-course," she added, slyly, "there's other houses—"

"Nell! You know better than that! Donald and Juan—"

"Is men. Ain't no man woman-proof at times.

162

That's whut keeps us in bizness."

Tamsen, thinking of Dan, swallowed. "Speaking of business," she said, taking her cue from Nell's last word, "how are things going for you at the parlor?"

Nell looked at the faces of the others and got no help. Tamsen had to know sooner or later. "Ain't no bizness," she said, harshly. "Ain't no parlor. It's all gone. Shot t'hell."

She went on to explain the financial situation in San Francisco. How "Honest" Harry Meiggs had skipped out, leaving a gap to the tune of eight hundred thousand dollars. Then a big-cheese bank in St. Louis folded and caused a run on its local branch. There were runs on other banks. One after another, they all "went busted—"

Nell banked the profits from the business in Tamsen's name. And when the dust settled, all she had left was a bit for operating expenses, in the safe, "an' some coins I keep stuffed down my front in a hankercheef," she added, dolefully.

The big bust had affected the clientele. The men just didn't come in any more. She'd had to let the newer girls go, one by one. She closed the kitchen—

"What happened to the cook, Birdie Faraday?"

"Married ol' Ben. Now he can get his pie to home. That worked out awright. But I shut the place down, fin'ly, an' snuck outta town, owin' ever'body. Figgured we'd start over again, in a new place."

The meaning of her words penetrated Tamsen's mind. "Not—not *here!*"

Nell looked defensive. "Well, you said it wuz th' gawdam promised land! Didden figger on findin' a mudhole."

Tamsen put her head in her hands. How to explain the settlement of Novoarchangelsk to Nell? A group of lusty, laughing, cheerful barbarians, the

163

Russians were. Yet they felt their religion deeply; the three churches in its walls attested to that. And the noble wives who came from Russia were held in deepest respect. A man might flirt outrageously— might even attempt a pinch or a kiss—but he wouldn't dream of being less than faithful.

Those whose wives and families had remained in Russia had taken Aleut or Kolosh wives as a matter of convenience. They, too, did not stray. With a compliant, submissive bedmate, why should they pay for the same services?

Here it was so different from San Francisco, that roaring, brawling town where miners came in with a poke to spend and looked for a woman to spend it on, where shopkeepers and businessmen satisfied a need for adventure by patronizing a brothel, where politicians and tycoons sought a discreet place so their names would be confidential—

Yet she had thought the Russians barbarians. Her head whirled as she wondered who was truly civilized.

"It won't work, Nell," Tamsen said, flatly. "Not here."

"I don't see why," Nell said in an injured voice. "Men's men, even if they's Rooshians."

"It won't work!"

"We could give it a try. Yer place here—ain't much fer size, but it's fixed up nice. We could name it sump'n fancy, hang out our shingle—"

"And we'd be drummed out of town, immediately. The priests...the governor-general...! We could be listed as undesirables, put in prison, sent to Siberia!"

"Gawdam," Nell said with feeling. "Whut we gonna do? Ain't even got passage home. Shot our wad a-gettin' here."

Tamsen closed her eyes. "You might as well

164

know," she said, "that I'm flat broke. I was ill when Dan left. He—he took every cent we had, leaving no money for my support."

"The sonofabitch!"

"I sold my jewels and some clothes," Tamsen went on, doggedly, "so there's some cash, but not enough to take us home. There—there seems to be a need for sewing here. We might consider setting ourselves up as a sewing establishment."

Nell's groan was echoed by Carmen and Maggie. "When we tried it afore," the fat woman said glumly, " I stuck my gawdam fingers so full of holes it looked like I'd tangled with a porkypine. But if they ain't no other way—"

"There's no other way. And, Nell, it would be better for business if the—if we kept the past to ourselves. Agreed?"

"Sure thing. Right, Dusty? Girls?"

She wasted her breath on Dusty. He was asleep. Carmen and Maggie nodded their understanding. But for now, they wished to explore the settlement. On the way to the castle, they'd seen some small eating places—or bars—

"Tea houses," Tamsen said.

Both girls looked doubtful, but they had been imprisoned on a small ship for a long time, with no interesting men. Perhaps even a tea house had possibilities. Tamsen watched them go, dubiously. She hoped they'd comport themselves properly. Everything hinged now on not attracting too much attention.

"They'll be awright," Nell said, settling back. "Now we're by our lonesomes"—she looked at Dusty and amended, "well, almost. You wanna gimme th' dope on Tallant? Never figgered you two'd split."

Tamsen told her the whole story, confiding the

things she'd never told anyone. First, the governor-general's blackmail—

"Gawdam Rooshian," Nell interjected.

Tamsen went on to tell of the Princess Anya, how she'd been after Dan, and Dan didn't seem to mind too much. She described the way she'd first heard of Dan's plan to go to Russia with the girl, and the trick she'd played on the superstitious princess. Nell laughed until she split a seam.

Tamsen told of copying the charts, of the way Dan caught her, and of the unforgivable things he'd said. She went on to tell of finding Anya in Dan's arms and how she'd run from the castle and fallen, sustaining an almost fatal injury. Then, in a low voice, she painfully related waking from her comatose state, to find Dan had really gone—

"Don't sound like Dan Tallant to me." Nell squinted, thinking. "Dan Tallant I know wouldn't have run out on you when you was down."

"But he did, Nell. That's all that matters. He did."

Nell sat for a long time, with a speculative expression. Then she said, "Them two men you mentioned, that Igger, and Ed something' er other. S'pose you could figger a way to make a few bucks offen them?"

Igor? Edwin Devon? "My God, Nell!"

"I guess not," Nell said sadly. "Well, we'll give this here dressmakin' a whirl."

CHAPTER 17

In the days that followed, Nell began to worry. Coming here had been one helluva mistake, for she couldn't fail to miss the poverty of Tamsen's establishment. The house belonged to the governor-general, and even the furnishings were on loan from the castle. She eyed the shining samovar and made a face. If things could be sold, that'd be the first gawdam thing to go.

Even the food they ate seemed to be donated by that Indian girl. She'd overheard Tamsen telling her she'd repay her. Tamsen, who never took nothin' off nobody. And there wasn't enough work coming in to take care of the whole crew.

"We're hangin' around her neck like some gawdam albertcross," she thought gloomily.

The bright spots in the day were the visits of Igor and Devon. Nell liked that Igger. His small, perfect physique was like Dusty's must have been; he was the son she'd never had. And there was a streak of naughtiness in his nature that appealed to her. Igger's a real humdinger, she told Tamsen.

And the feeling was mutual. There was much in the tough old woman that the effete young prince admired. They got on swimmingly. She also developed an intense affection for Edwin Devon. Born an Englishman, like Dusty, he charmed Nell with his

167

manners and accent. Anything made in England, she told him, was hunky-dory with her.

Startled at first, and then amused, Devon found himself liking the outrageous woman. He had a feeling that she was honest, according to her lights, despite her foul language. He found it difficult to believe she was the seamstress she pretended to be, recalling the dull little creature who did sewing for his mother.

He and Dusty got on well, too. It was good to talk with the old fellow, despite the fact that he was hardly ever sober. Good to remember the rolling green meadows of England, so neat and tidy, a miniature country compared to this place where everything was larger than life.

As he and Dusty conversed, Nell would study him, seeing him as a prospect for Tamsen. He was a handsome man, well set up. Yet there was something kinda sad about him, a shadow that she couldn't place. Something that gave her a kinda funny feeling...

Devon appeared to have money, and he was heels over appetite in love with Tamsen. She could tell. Frowning, her eyes went to Helena. For she'd guessed something Tamsen didn't know. The Indian gal was sweet on Edwin Devon, sure as hell. If Tamsen wanted him, she'd better mind her P's and Q's.

Jabbing a needle through a piece of heavy brocade, Nell returned to her major worry. Somehow, they had to find a way to get the hell out of here. Alone, Tamsen might survive. She would tell Dusty and the girls to keep their peepers open for any kind of opportunity.

In the meantime, Nell thought glumly, she'd et so damn much fish and washed it down with so much

Russian tea, it was startin' to swim upstream.

Maggie and Carmen took Nell's admonition to watch for opportunity very seriously. They, too, wanted to leave the small island and return to a larger civilization. Their visits to the tea houses had been unsettling. After a few curious glances, they'd been left to sit in a corner, unnoticed. And the language barrier presented a problem.

But with the coming of spring, the lone traders and trappers, the *promishleniki*, came drifting in. Here, the language between man and woman was universal. Maggie and Carmen were presented with furs which they dutifully traded at the company store on Nell's orders. Hell, Nell thought, what Tamsen don't know won't hurt her. An' we gotta do somethin' to pay our way

A messenger came, just as Tamsen and Nell had completed a gown for a Russian nobleman's wife. The woman tried it on and preened, surveying herself in a mirror with satisfaction.

"You look lovely," Tamsen said in Russian.

Nell assumed a look of profound admiration. "Jus' like th' north end of a south-bound mule," she said with enthusiasm.

The Russian woman beamed, thanking them in a spate of her own language. To the fee, she added a generous number of rubles to show her gratitude. Then, still smiling happily, she was gone.

"Nell! What am I going to do with you?" Tamsen groaned.

"Well, it worked, didden it?" The fat woman smiled complacently.

Tamsen opened the note from the messenger. The governor-general would like to speak with Mrs. Tallant at her convenience, within the hour. It was not an invitation, but an order.

She was apprehensive as she climbed the steps to the castle for the first time since her fall. There had been no communication from Voedvodski since the arrival of Nell and the girls. Invitations to festive occasions at the castle had been conspicuously absent. The governor-general knew who her guests were. He had it all down on paper, the results of his investigation. She'd been wondering if the Russian ruler would take action—or ignore the presence of her friends. It would appear that he'd reached a decision.

A sentry went ahead to announce her arrival. Summoning up her courage, Tamsen entered with a smile. A smile that faded into her pale white face at the scene that confronted her. Voedvodski was seated at his desk, his expression grim. To the right stood Carmen and Maggie, an armed Russian guard at either side.

Oh, dear God!

"Your friends, madam." The governor-general gestured toward the frightened girls. Maggie stood flat-footed, head lowered, her face blank with fear, while Carmen's eyes darted from side to side as if seeking an avenue of escape. Tamsen pulled herself together.

"What is the meaning of this?" she asked, icily.

"Your friends have been plying their trade. I've been keeping a close eye on you people, expecting such an eventuality. I do not intend to suffer an intrusion of your American morals. We are a civilized people here; we have churches, schools, a hospital, a museum. We do not need a brothel. There are certain standards of decency."

"Decency! My God!" Tamsen exploded. "Civilized! A bunch of rum-soaked despots, half of them with wives in Russia, living with Aleut or Indian women!"

"A matter of expediency," the governor-general said, flushing. "And such affairs are conducted with decorum."

Tamsen drew a deep breath. She was going at this all wrong. It wouldn't do to anger him further. "What are you going to do with them?" She gestured toward the frightened girls.

"That is a point I have been pondering. Our small prison here is hardly adequate, merely a place for drunken *promishleniki* to wait out the night. I might have them transported to a penal colony in Siberia. Or—"

Tamsen placed both hands flat on his desk, leaned toward him, her face set with fury. "My brother-in-law," she said in a tight voice, "has influence in Washington. You dare harm these girls! You just *dare!* And there will be repercussions all the way to St. Petersburg! A report on your treatment of United States citizens, your part in the Indian affair in 'fifty-five, the incompetence of the Novo-archangelsk administration, the feasting and drinking while the settlement deteriorates—"

Voedvodski was on his feet, his face suffused. "Madam!" he said. "Madam!"

They glared at each other for a long moment, then he sat down, struggling for composure. "Very well. Then I shall issue an ultimatum. Your husband has gone. You have no authority here. I must insist that you and your party depart the premises of Russian America within the month. Do I make myself clear?"

"Perfectly. And we will be happy to comply with your ultimatum! Come, girls."

Voedvodski barked a command at his guards. They lowered the butts of their guns to the floor. Taking each girl by an arm, Tamsen led them, shaking, from the castle. As they walked in silence toward Tamsen's house, an eerie keening sound from the Tlingit village announced a death.

A council of war with Nell, Dusty, and the girls led to nothing. They counted their assets. They'd be lucky if they could raise the fare to Vancouver. Though, as Dusty pointed out, they'd be among people of their own kind in that area. Tamsen doubted it. The British could be as stiffnecked as anyone. There would be no wealthy noblewomen to sew for.

"Mebbe we could git us a game goin'," Nell offered. "Hell, I could deal cards." And Dusty suggested he might be able to clerk in a Hudson's Bay store.

"We'll keep thinking," Tamsen said wearily.

The council was interrupted by a frightening apparition. Helena, her long silken hair cut short, her face painted black. Nell jumped. "My God, what's that there!"

But Helena went straight to Tamsen, taking her hands in her own. Very simply, she said, "Our mother is dead."

Tamsen had attended a wedding; now she attended a funeral ceremony. The whole affair lasted four days—days in which Helena sat with her fellow Tlingits, singing the mourning songs, which were accompanied by rhythmical body movements.

Tamsen participated in the gift-giving ritual where cloth, blankets, and other property were distributed among the guests by grieving relatives. A relative by adoption, Tamsen took a few yards of the cloth she'd purchased for sewing: velvets and silks were highly prized. Yet they would only be dead weight on their journey—wherever it was they might go.

She entered the Tlingit house, feeling as if she were returning to a familiar home. It was packed with men squatting around the fire and women sitting along the walls. Ten or twelve people sat in a cleared space just inside the door; among them were several women, including Helena and the recent bride, her cousin. They held long poles with which they beat time to the mourning songs, occasionally rising to accompany the chanting with beautiful, willowy swaying.

The body of the dead woman sat against the back wall of the house, dressed in full ceremonial garb, watching the festivities with fixed eyes. Remembering the old woman's fierce gaze and the feel of the steady hands that placed the raven amulet about her throat, Tamsen swallowed tears as she quietly took her place along the wall.

The distribution of gifts began, the cloth passed from hand to hand, without a break between the unwinding of one piece and the start of another. Another symbol, Tamsen thought, that linked these people together. And then the cloth was cut and shared—to a monotonous chanting—as the names of the guests were called. The Indian husband of the dead woman was required to give away all his possessions. Material objects were doled out all through the long night as berries, sugar, and tobacco were served to the guests. And through it all, the dead woman watched, unblinking.

On the fourth day, the body would be placed on a funeral pyre behind the house made of tree trunks piled in criss-cross fashion. The old woman's face would be painted then, and she would be covered with a beautifully designed Chilkat blanket. The mourners watched, some singing and pounding on boards with their long staves, as the fire was kindled. It blazed up brightly, signaling that all were free to leave.

Tamsen stumbled away, her face tear-streaked, knowing that she was something of a spectacle to the stoic Tlingits. The mourning was over now. All was done. After the fire burned down, Helena and her cousin would pick some charred bones from the ashes to be wrapped in cloth and placed in a wooden box to be carried to the grave house.

The cremation, too, had been a symbol to Tamsen. A symbol of her old life, now dead and gone. Leaving here, she would be leaving behind all traces of a life she'd shared with Dan. She returned to her house to find a condition approaching bedlam. "Wash th' Indian stink offen you, an' start packin'," Nell roared. "We're a-sittin' purty! Th' little bastard's gone an' done it again!"

Dusty smiled with smug modesty as Nell revealed her good news. He'd got to drinking with a sailor off a British ship in the harbor. And he'd learned of a big gold strike in the English-held territory, on the Fraser River. Nuggets big as hen's eggs! Thousands of Californians pouring into the area! "Gold," Nell shouted happily. "And all them men an' no wimmen! Hell, Tamsen, it's a natural! A couple a' tents, mebbe a log house later, with upstairs rooms! Singin', dancin'—expand!"

Tamsen was carried along on Nell's wave of enthusiasm. To take nothing and build something from it once more . . . ! Then her face darkened. "I can't do it, Nell," she said flatly. "When I worked in the cantina, it was for money to take care of Em and Arab. Then the parlor—" She blushed. "I suppose I fooled myself into thinking it was for Em and Martha. But I can't go into that kind of business again."

Nell was incredulous. "Why th' hell not? It's just bizness! Them miners'll be buyin', we'll be sellin'.

174

Can't sell somethin' nobuddy wants! Besides," she said practically, "don't see how you got no other choice. Gittin' run outten here, ain't we? An' I can't see where behavin' yerself got you nowhere, nohow."

She was right, Tamsen thought, listlessly. She thought of Dan's words on that last night. *You'd sell anything, wouldn't you.* And *You can set up all the paying customers you want from now on, because, my dear, I'm through!*

Her past had followed her here, intruding into her marriage. She might as well make use of her experience in the only thing she knew how to do well.

One morning a little less than a week later, Tamsen walked along the Indian trail behind the more heavily settled area of Novoarchangelsk. She walked alone by preference, though Igor and Devon both offered their services as escort.

She and Dan had strolled together here, hand in hand, bemused with love, when they arrived almost two years ago. She wished to recreate that scene. As a way of saying goodbye to this place that had been the scene of the happiest and unhappiest hours of her life. As if to suit her mood, the rains ceased temporarily. The snow-clad mountains gathered the ragged mists to themselves, like veils, and the bay was heartbreakingly blue. Vines clustered among the Sitka spruce were in early leaf, beginning to tremble with new life that would eventually burgeon into fruit.

Tonight Tamsen and her friends would board a small and shabby boat that would take them to Asquamalt. From there they must walk to Fort Victoria. Then to New Westminster by steamer, and from there, by sternwheeler, to a settlement on a rocky ledge of the lower Fraser where it was reputed to boil out of the canyon. This was the end of navigable water; from here, the journey to the gold fields would be on foot.

Edwin Devon would be traveling with them. The roaring atmosphere of a gold camp should be grist for a writer's mill, he told her. But she wasn't blind to the fact that it was an excuse, developed through his need to be near her.

He would change his mind, she thought, ruefully, once he learned the real reason for the trip to the gold fields. The thought of having to face his disillusionment made her feel ill. But he'd refused to be dissuaded, and he was a grown man.

Igor had been more sensible. Even Novoarchangelsk was too roughhewn, too elemental for his tastes. He painted a humorous picture of himself in his elegant clothing among the rough mining men. No, he would say goodbye and think of Russia.

Helena was most difficult. She, too, wished to go. They were going to open a business. She'd heard them discussing it. She was certain she could do anything Carmen and Maggie could do. And she was alone now that her mother was gone—

Tamsen was heartbroken at leaving the girl, but her heart would ache worse at seeing Helena, proud Helena, assimilated into a bawdy-house atmosphere. She refused her.

Now, kicking at a stone in the path, she knew she must put thoughts of Dan, of Helena, behind her. She had not come here to mull over the things that made her head hurt so, but to commune one last time with this place which surely must be the most beautiful spot in the world.

There was the rock where the Indians sat. And somewhere, hidden in the tangle of undergrowth, beneath bunchberry or devil's club, licorice fern or soapberry, lay the graves of the star-crossed lovers, together even in death.

A chuffing sound roused her, and she stepped off the trail as she'd been told to do. A brown Sitka bear ambled past, winter-thin, a bit comical in his loose-fitting fur. But only for a moment. Reaching the spot where she had been standing, he reared to his hind legs, sniffing the air. Now he was menacing...a killer. She could smell the rank scent of him, and she stood very still. Again, he dropped to all fours, a clumsy, humorous creature once more as he wandered on down the path and turned off to lose himself in the verdant growth beneath the trees. Tamsen returned to the settlement, to the hustle and flurry of getting their few possessions aboard ship.

In the morning, they sailed without ceremony. The Russian custom of coming aboard with governor-general, priest, and prayers, was conspicuously missing. Only Igor arrived, carrying something in a folded bit of paper. "I wanted to give you something," he told Tamsen, serious for once. "Something different. Don't open it until you've sailed."

She kissed the boyish cheek. Though Igor was associated with her time of trouble, she was fond of him, and it was difficult to say goodbye. Then he was gone, and the ship began to move. Blinking back tears, Tamsen turned to see Nell hugging a large, blanket-wrapped object to her bosom. Catching Tamsen's eyes on her, Nell looked defensive.

"Awright, dammit, so I took sumpin' I shouldn't of. But I figgered the gov'nor owed us sumpin'—and I got kinda attached t' th gawdam thing!"

Unrolling the blanket, she revealed its contents. The shining Russian samovar.

Tamsen stood at the railing as the small vessel navigated the island passages and saw Novoarchangelsk with its clustered wooden structures, the great Baranov Castle on its high hill looking out over it all, and thought of her and Dan's dream. It was a dream of a city, under the American flag, teeming with commerce.

She wondered if Dan's work was any closer to fruition. Then she wondered, wistfully, if he ever thought of her at all. The scene blurred and tilted before her eyes, and she turned to enter her cabin. Then she remembered the folded paper Igor had given her, now clenched within her hand.

Smoothing it, she opened it up, to reveal a bruised and crumpled Sitka rose. It brought back memories of Dan, now aboard a ship sailing around the world on a perilous journey. A pain caught at her heart as she wondered if he were alive—or dead.

CHAPTER 18

Dan Tallant leaned against the rail of the small travel-weary ship. He was having thoughts that were much the same as Tamsen's. They were somewhere off the coast of France and would soon negotiate the channel that led into the North Sea, thence into the Baltic.

And upon reaching St. Petersburg, he would be tried for intent to murder. He would not think of that now. He would think, instead, of Tamsen, of walking with her along the Indian trail. It would be nearing summer now, and the Sitka rose would be in bloom. The fragile wildflower reminded him so much of his wife.

Tamsen! Had she survived her injury? If he only knew, he could face the ordeal ahead of him with courage. He struck the rail with his fist, thinking of Anya, who had brought things to this pass, cursing her, consigning her soul to hell.

Tallant had three visitors in that first week as he lay in chains. First, Baron de Stoeckl came with the ship's captain, who was a small man with a ferocious red beard and evasive eyes.

"This is an outrage," the baron said. "This man is an official of the United States government. You will lose your command over this, I promise you!"

Captain Shelov fingered his beard; his eyes darted

like frightened mice as he pondered the baron's threat. It was true that the man held an important position, but the princess—she was a member of the tsar's own family. One must not make hasty decisions in a matter as crucial as this. He would wait until he heard what the princess had to say. Maybe, he thought, looking at Tallant's muscular shoulders with admiration, the lady might change her mind.

"Perhaps," he said cautiously, "this is nothing but a lover's quarrel?"

Dan laughed harshly. "Anything but that. I would suggest you set me ashore—or leave me in irons."

Captain Shelov retreated before the prisoner's murderous expression. "Calm yourself," he said placatingly. "I will speak with the princess. I pride myself that I am a just man."

It was several days before the captain had an opportunity to speak with Anya. As they headed south and westward, passing below Kodiak through the Aleutian chain, the small craft began to plunge in storm-tossed waves, with rain icing on the sails. Anya remained secluded in her cabin, and Captain Shelov, fighting the elements, almost forgot the touchy situation in which he was involved.

By the third day, the winds had ceased, and the ship glittered on a calm sea. Anya, wearing small boots bound with thongs against the ice-encrusted deck, appeared and turned her charms on the tired sailors. They forgot their exhaustion and went to work with a will, each conscious that she had eyes for him and him alone.

Tiring of her conquests, she saw Ivan at the rail. She approached him, linking her arm with his. "I've missed you," she said in a soft whisper.

He stared down at her, eyes expressionless. "Should you be on deck? It's rather slippery."

"I've taken care." She laughed, lifting a thong-bound boot. "Remember, I am accustomed to such weather."

"I do not like the climate. If you will excuse me." He bowed, sardonically, and walked away.

"Ivan." Her voice stopped him. "It is warm in my stateroom. Very warm. Perhaps tonight?"

He didn't turn, but the back of his neck stiffened. Anya laughed softly to herself. He would come. And now the good captain was approaching. An odd little man, but a most interesting beard. She put on her devastating smile.

The captain took note of it, but he also noticed something else. The lady's eyes were strange, like splinters of ice—as cold as the frozen spray that turned the deck into a mirror. He felt an odd twinge of fear, but stubbornly said what he had to say, avoiding her gaze.

The man in irons was someone of importance. Baron de Stoeckl had spoken to him on the gentleman's behalf. Was it possible Her Highness might forgive the American's unfortunate remarks? Perhaps he'd spoken in anger, due to the pressures of finding himself accidentally entrapped in her cabin. Now that he'd had time to think it over—

"You may be right," Anya said. "But I am afraid of him." She looked at Shelov, pleadingly. "May I confide in you? Oh, I'm certain that I may! You have such a—kind face." She paused for a moment, turning to the rail, gripping it with both hands, head bowed.

"The truth is that his wife was very—jealous of me. They were estranged, and she—had a tragic accident. I suppose he feels guilty. And he has threatened me before."

"Perhaps if you spoke with him?"

181

"I will try." She turned to face him, wearing a look of fear. "But you will be there? You will come with me?"

Red beard bristling, shoulders squared, Captain Shelov said, "Of course I will."

Dan, still shackled in the hold, hunched his shoulders wearily, trying to find a comfortable position. During the storm, he'd had to remain on guard. Every erratic dip of the ship threw him against its metal bracing; his body was bruised, and the irons chafed at his wrists and ankles.

A hatch opened, revealing a square of daylight. And the square framed the delicate figure of the Princess Anya, herself. She came carefully down the iron ladder, followed by Captain Shelov and one of the seamen who had brought Dan here. Tallant recognized him as the one he had downed before he was knocked unconscious by the other. His fist itched to strike out again, but he kept silent as the party approached. Probably, he thought grimly, she's talked them into throwing me over the side.

"Dan!" Anya's voice was plaintive, filled with sympathy. "Oh, Dan! I feel awful, seeing you like this!"

"I'll bet you do." The words dragged from him, dark with hatred. Then he closed his lips tightly. She was up to something, since she'd brought witnesses. He must hold his temper at all costs.

"But I mean it," she wailed. She came closer, reaching a small hand to touch his rough, unshaven face. "Oh, Dan! I know your wife hated me. But it wasn't your fault she was jealous—or mine, and she's dead now. Can't we be friends?"

She's dead now! The words roared in Dan's ears; his head rocked back as if he'd been struck. Tamsen dead! Ah, God, not Tamsen! But how had the prin-

182

cess received the news? How did Anya know?

He looked at the woman, his eyes bleak with agony, and he saw something that startled him—a look of triumph. She was lying!

"You she-devil," he rasped harshly. "You lying little bitch! I'll kill you—" His hand swung out, barely enough to raise a welt on her cheek before it was caught short by the chain that held the iron cuff. Maddened beyond endurance, he swung again and again, the irons tearing at his wrists as Anya moved nimbly out of his reach.

She turned sad eyes to the captain. "You see?"

"The man's a maniac," Shelov huffed. "My dear lady, are you hurt?"

The ice-blue eyes melted with tears. "No, not too badly. But I'm certain Alexander would wish him punished. Perhaps a touch of the whip would bring him to his senses."

The tsar's name had its desired effect. "Ten lashes," the captain said nervously to his aide. Then, "Come, Your Highness."

"I shall stay to see the whipping properly administered," Anya said, "as a representative of the Crown. But please, do go. It will be easier to—to retain my courage, without an audience."

Shelov's face was a study in doubt as his eyes darted from Anya to Tallant and back again. But he reluctantly took his leave. Satisfied that he had gone, Anya turned to the burly seaman. "Whip him," she said.

When the sailor hesitated, she snatched the whip from his hand, bringing the lash across Dan's face. Then the startled Russian was galvanized into action. He took the whip from her fingers.

"This is man's work, Your Highness."

Methodically, he laid nine stripes across Tallant's

183

back and shoulders. Dan's traitorous body flinched beneath the blows, but his eyes, terrible in his face, never left Anya's, and he did not make a sound.

Finishing, the seaman looked at Anya with barely disguised loathing. "It's done, Your Highness. Now, if you will return to the deck—"

Anya realized she was smiling. Quickly, she turned the corners of her mouth down. "I'm sorry, Dan," she said. "I—I only hope you'll think things over, and that you'll feel differently when next we meet."

The awful eyes in the bloody face never left hers. And the words that came in a dark, heavy intonation emerged from Dan's lips, but without any conscious thought of his own.

"Your luck's going to run out," he said. "It's going to run out. And soon—"

Anya paled. Turning, she scurried for the ladder. Reaching the deck, she took a deep breath of the clean, cold air in an attempt to pull herself together. And then she saw Ivan. He was watching her, staring. She forced a smile, then hurried to her cabin, where she erased Dan's terrible prediction from her mind with thoughts of Ivan.

He was still interested in her. She could tell. At least, this night, she would not sleep alone.

She was correct in believing she'd aroused Ivan's interest, but wrong in assuming the reasons behind that scrutiny of his. For he'd seen the blood that stained the bosom of her gown. Listening to the talk among the Russian sailors, he'd learned that the lady had insisted the prisoner be whipped, that she had struck the first blow herself, and that she'd enjoyed the man's punishment.

When dusk fell, Ivan let himself down into the hold carrying a ship's lantern and a bottle of rum he'd filched from the vessel's stores. Dan had been semiconscious, tossing in a dream born of delirium, but he was instantly alert as Ivan approached.

He relaxed when he saw the face of his boyish aide, strangely altered in the flickering light of the lantern. Ivan looked old, the shadows beneath his eyes thrown into sharp relief, giving him a skeletal appearance.

If he looks like that, Dan thought wryly, I must look like hell. He struggled to sit up and managed a smile, despite his swollen features. "I'd offer you a chair," he said, "but you see how it is." He waved a hand, only to be brought up short by the chain.

"Damn her," Ivan choked. "Damn her!" For a moment, he was frozen with rage. Then he squatted before Tallant. "This will hurt," he said.

He laved Dan's wounds with the stinging rum, pouring it onto the marks of the lash, the places where his wrists and ankles bled. Dan's breath hissed between his clenched teeth. And then he gratefully finished the remaining liquid in the bottle. "Thanks," he said. "That helped. At least I don't have to worry about infection—"

"Dan, I have something to tell you. Something I should have told you before. But I could not believe the princess is—what she is."

Slowly, painfully, Ivan told the story of what had happened the night Tamsen was injured. How he and Tamsen had seen Dan and Anya in an ardent embrace.

"Good God," Dan said. "Then that's why she fell! She was running away, thinking that I—that I—"

"And there's more." Ivan described how he'd found Anya in the foyer, a small boot in her hand, earlier that evening. He didn't believe her guilty of removing the thongs from it, not then, because he hadn't wanted to believe it.

"Now you know her for what she is! A monster!

185

Ah, God! Ivan, if you can find a way to let me loose—I'll kill her with my bare hands!"

"That kind of death is too good for her," Ivan said. His eyes in the leaping lantern light were pools of blackness, sunken into a hollow-cheeked face. "I had to tell you. To ease my own conscience."

"Thank you," Dan said, closing his own eyes against the tears that threatened. "Now—I am very tired. If you don't mind—"

"Of course." Ivan turned to go. At the foot of the ladder, he turned back. "I will do what I can for you," he said in a muffled voice. "And now—goodbye."

Ivan reached the deck, noting with satisfaction that the ship was once more slanting heavily in the swells of the sea. The wind had risen again, though the sky was cloudless and clear. He hoped the condition would continue until the morning.

Moving from one object to another to keep his footing on the icy deck, he made his way toward Princess Anya's cabin. She was waiting for him. And that night, he made love to her with a mastery he'd never known before. When she slept at last, satiated, he rose quietly.

In one corner of the room, across a chair, she'd thrown her clothing. And beside the chair was a pair of little boots, wrapped with thongs. He set himself to removing them. Then he returned to his own quarters.

Anya woke drowsily and reached out an exploring hand. Nothing. She sat up, her drowsiness replaced by a rising anger. Last night had been a most exciting experience. And she'd expected more of the same this morning. Yet he had gone and left her to wake alone. How dared he!

Rising, she dressed hurriedly, took a hasty look at

her appearance in the mirror. Satisfied, she threw open her stateroom door. Ivan stood opposite it against the rail, watching a pale late sun rise, touching a slaty sea that rolled to the horizon.

"Ivan," she called reproachfully.

He turned and smiled, beckoning. And she started toward him, hesitating at the slippery feel of the deck beneath her feet. The thongs weren't holding! She looked down, her face a mask of surprise.

Then the ship yawed and tilted. She found herself flat on her back and sliding across the deck, beneath the railing, toward the wintry sea. Clawing desperately, she managed to get one hand on the frozen rail, to hang there, sobbing with fear. Ivan's figure leaned over her. "Help me," she whimpered.

His face impassive, he pried her fingers loose, one by one. She slid downward, the dark waters closing over her head, choking off her final scream. A seaman had witnessed her fall, and he shouted for help as he ran toward the rail. Ivan calmly took off his coat, handed it to the horrified man, and dived after the girl. Reaching her, he wrapped his arms tightly about the struggling figure... they sank together.

Down in the hold, Dan could sense that the ship had stopped, wallowing in the choppy seas. He heard the scrape of a lifeboat being lowered over the side and wondered at it.

Much later, a grim-faced Shelov approached him and he learned what had happened. According to a sailor, Ivan had seen the girl strike the water, but had stood idly watching the girl's struggles until the seaman approached. Then he leaped in, ostensibly to save her. But another seaman witnessed Ivan's descent into the hold the previous night. And here was an empty rum bottle to prove it. The assumption was that Tallant and Ivan conspired to murder the

187

girl, and that Ivan, trapped, chose suicide. Ivan escaped justice, but Dan Tallant would stand trial for murder in St. Petersburg.

With the influential princess gone, de Stoeckl brought pressure to bear on the unhappy captain. Shelov was in a quandary. He had seen Tallant's attack on the girl. It seemed unwarranted, unprovoked. Yet he had heard the story going around—the lady's use of the whip, her obvious enjoyment of Dan's punishment. And the scar was there on the man's face for all to see. He, Shelov, must account to the tsar.

The decision was to allow the prisoner freedom of the deck while at sea. In port, he was returned to his chains in the hold. In this fashion, they rounded the world.

In Shanghai, the vessel's burden of seal oil and Sitka furs was exchanged for one of tea and exotic spices. The men who went ashore returned with a retching sickness that would plague them for the remainder of their journey. As the crippled ship fought onward, Dan volunteered for many of their duties. It was he who saw the cone of fire as they passed through the straits of Sumatra, he who leaped to the captain's aid, holding the wheel hard when the great wave came, nearly capsizing them, leaving them floating in a sea of ash.

Off the Gold Coast, they were attacked by a piratical crew, bent on plunder. Dan conducted himself well in the ensuing hand-to-hand battle, though two more of the ship's crew were killed. Since that time, he'd been free, giving his word of honor that he'd remain aboard ship. And he'd worked night and day to supplement the efforts of the decimated crew. He welcomed the physical labor. It gave him less time to think, as he did now, of Tamsen.

Still lost in a dream of his wife, Tallant turned blind eyes at the approach of de Stoeckl and Captain Shelov. Seeing the man's haunted, brooding face, de Stoeckl faltered. It was as if they were intruding. But the captain had something to say.

After preliminary greetings, de Stoeckl stood back while the captain began. "We will be nearing our homeland in the month ahead," he said soberly. Dan scarcely heard him. He was noting the way the small stubby pipe was lost in the fiery tangle of beard, the smoke emerging from it giving the impression that the beard was afire. His lips twitched. Tamsen would have been amused at the sight.

"And when we arrive in Petersburg," Shelov continued, "I have an unpleasant duty before me. I must inform the tsar of the Princess Anya's death. You understand?"

Dan nodded, his features grim.

"It was a sad affair, I shall tell him. An affair of the heart. One of the tragedies of love."

Tallant stiffened, angrily, and the captain went on. "Two lovers, Anya and Ivan—they had spent the night in each other's arms, did you know? And they wished to see the sunrise together. Young Ivan dressed and went to the rail, in gentlemanly fashion, leaving the lady to compose her own garments. In the heat of passion, she neglected to take safety precautions with her footgear."

Shelov coughed. "The thongs with which she habitually bound them were discovered beneath her bed. And of course, she fell. The gallant Ivan leaped after her in a futile attempt to save the girl he loved, but met, instead, his own death."

189

Tallant's head whirled. He recalled Ivan's last words. *"I will do what I can for you. And now— goodbye."* Ivan had been planning Anya's death, even then. And by the same means that had caused Tamsen's fall. Divine retribution.

"And that is what I will say to the tsar," Shelov ended. "You understand?"

Dan understood. He was free. Free to return home to the woman he loved—if she was still living.

The captain walked away, and de Stoeckl moved closer. "The gentleman has had quite a struggle with his conscience," he said. "But he has developed an admiration for you of late, and common sense won out. And perhaps some good has come from this, after all. You will have your own audience with the tsar."

"I must go home," Dan said in a dazed voice. "On the first ship—"

"Which will take months," the baron reminded him. "And you will have lost a golden opportunity." His eyes evaded Dan's. "To no avail, should your lady have—not survived her fall. Perhaps the tsar has received a communiqué from the governor-general in regard to her condition. And I will dispatch a messenger through Siberia, upon arrival, to assure her of your safety."

"I can't take any chances. I have to return."

De Stoeckl's face hardened. "The captain's will is easily swayed, as you have seen. A word or two from me will convince him that his earlier suspicions were correct. I sympathize with your plight, but I must consider not what is expedient for you, but for my country. Think about it carefully before you make hasty decisions." He walked away.

Tallant, remaining at the rail, agonized over de

190

Stoeckl's words. The baron was almost fanatic in his belief that Russia should sell Alaska to the United States. He feared another repetition of the Crimean War and knew the small settlement could not be held in isolation; he would use any means at hand . . . even blackmail. De Stoeckl had made no idle threat. Dan rubbed at his wrists, which bore the scars of his incarceration. He must concede to the baron's wishes if he were ever to see his wife again.

Looking out to sea, where the dying sun glimmered palely on endless waters, he thought of Tamsen, left sick and penniless, her belief in him shattered. Would she turn to Igor or to the Englishman for aid? The thought was intolerable.

No, he told himself. Somehow, she would manage to make her way to San Francisco, home, to Em and Arab. There she would be safe, cared for.

Rounding the vessel, he looked to the north and the east, already shrouded in darkness. Somewhere out there lay St. Petersburg and the court of the tsar. He would get his business done and take the short route, across the Siberian wastelands to Okhotsk. Then to Novoarchangelsk, and if Tamsen were not there, he would know where to find her.

He visualized their meeting. He would climb the steps to the Alden home and knock at the door. Tamsen would answer—he would take her in his arms—

He stirred uncomfortably. Something about his dream picture did not ring true. What if the princess hadn't lied? Perhaps a messenger had reached the ship before it sailed, with the news of Tamsen's death. Perhaps he'd lost her, after all.

The ship's bell signaled the time, and Dan Tallant walked, stumbling a little, to his post.

CHAPTER 19

Dan Tallant's wife was neither waiting in Novoarchangelsk, nor living in San Francisco. And she was not lost, though she definitely had a feeling of being misplaced. The journey had taken longer than expected. First, the small steamship on which they'd taken passage broke down, wallowing in the waves enough to turn the most experienced sailor green. Nell and the girls were not experienced sailors. The trip from Westminster, up the Fraser by sternwheeler, hadn't done much to ease the situation. There was no cabin space, and the deck was crowded to the rails with gold-seekers.

Closing her eyes against the sight of surging, clay-colored water, the towering walls of the Fraser valley, the ant-like scurrying of miners already at work—hanging from those walls by ropes, working the bars—Nell rebelled.

"Can't go on," she insisted. "I'm sick ez a gawdam mule!"

She was still proclaiming it among lusty groans as she sat flat on the ground near where the ship had docked. All efforts of Dusty and the girls to get her to her feet had failed. She could go no farther, though it was a helluva place to die.

At least her complaints gave Tamsen an idea. From this point on, the journey must be made on foot. She knew nothing of the terrain, except that it was supposed to be rough going. Perhaps if they could get Nell to her feet—and on a mule—they could continue at their own pace, gently.

One thing was certain. They couldn't stay here. She'd learned the Yale settlement, a grouping of shacks and saloons, was considered the most wicked town in the world. It was filled with outlaws and murderers. The corrupt gold commissioner had secured a fifty-year lease on most of the surrounding territory, and charged enormous ground rents.

Too, this was merely the jumping-off spot. The rich finds were ahead. There, in their own new place, her girls would be the only girls. The small place she would set up for entertainment would be in the midst of the activity. And she, like the gold commissioner, would be able to set her own rates.

Tamsen held a whispered conference with the others, all except Nell, who was intent on her own immediate, dramatic death. This was a town of daylight robberies and night assaults. Murders were said to be the order of the day. Yet they must somehow find lodgings here for the night to give the big woman time to recuperate and to locate some means of transportation for her on the morrow. She would check with some of the residents of Yale.

"I shall go with you." Edwin Devon had not stood the journey well. His face was pale, but his eyes were steady, his jaw set with determination. Tamsen smiled up at him. She would be grateful for his presence. But there was the problem of Nell and the girls. She had seen Dusty eyeing the saloons thirstily.

"Dusty, you will stay here with Nell, won't you? You won't leave the girls without a man's protection?"

He glared at her, his white hair standing on end,

the wispy mustache hiding his two missing front teeth trembling in indignation. "Leave these frail ladies alone? At the mercy of lewd characters such as those?"

He inclined his head toward a knot of amused men watching Nell's death agonies. "Jove, Tamsen, what do you take me for!"

Satisfied, Tamsen set out with Devon, walking along the main street of the settlement. They were shouldered aside by hurrying men, rough miners who carried six-shooters, rifles, bowie knives. From the saloons came shouts and sounds of breaking glass.

The exuberance of the place touched Tamsen with a thrill. It brought back memories of the cantina, of the streets of San Francisco in the earlier days. Except that the atmosphere in Yale was intensified. She had never seen its equal; thousands of men were so fevered by gold that they scarcely noticed a woman in their midst.

But wait awhile, she thought with satisfaction. Now they were new arrivals from more populated areas; their minds were on seeking their fortunes. But in the mining camps, their thoughts would turn to female company, games of chance . . . she would supply them both.

Poor Edwin, she thought, glancing up at him. He had no idea what the small packs of her group contained: two provocative gowns apiece for the girls, a hundred decks of cards, a hammer, saw, and small axe, some dried berries and fish, supplied by Helena, and a woolen blanket for each of them, to use as a half-shelter until some type of structure could be built. She was confident that eager miners would supply the rest.

The old feeling of a challenge to be met and

overcome swelled inside her. Edwin Devon, seeing her glowing face, was mystified. Dusty Wotherspoon's extravagant talk about looking into mining properties with an eye to investment no longer impressed him with its truth. And though he liked Nell—one could not resist an affection for the big woman—she and the girls were definitely not Tamsen's sort. Nor did Tamsen belong in this kind of place.

He looked with distaste at the rip-roaring town around them and at the harshness of the landscape. The island of Sitka had been soft and lovely, a blurred mixture of misty greens and blues and grays, reminiscent in a way of his beloved England's climate. But here, with the raging torrent of a river roaring between sheer rock walls, life could be merely a struggle for survival.

Certainly it was no place for a small slim girl, as fragile as a flower. "Tamsen," he said, "I can't understand why you intend to go further with this thing. It is uncivilized enough here. But up the river—"

She looked at him as if she'd forgotten he was there, then laughed gently. "But the opportunities are up the river, Edwin. We certainly can't stay here."

"Then why remain in this country at all? My word, Tamsen, it's no place for a decent woman! I suggest we return to Novoarchangelsk, or even to the States. Tamsen, I will accompany you wherever you wish to go, you know that!"

"And I'm going up the river. But you needn't go with us. You're welcome to go back to Sitka if you like."

With a pang, he realized that she'd sounded eager. That she might prefer that he leave the party. But he had no intention of leaving her in this savage wilderness. He shook his head doggedly. "I will go where you go."

Devon beside her, Tamsen fought her way through a crowd to enter a small general store. It was filled with men purchasing mining supplies, all of them impatient to be waited on. Tamsen caught the arm of a clerk and shouted above the din; she asked where one might find a room for a short time, or where a pack mule might be available.

The man shook his head. "Ain't none," he shouted above the clamor. He returned to the business of collecting money for goods.

Undaunted, Tamsen tried two saloons. In both, there were faro banks, games of three-card monte; the gamblers were so intent on their cards they didn't notice the strangers. The crowds around the bar made it unapproachable. To Devon's consternation, Tamsen insisted on stopping miners on the street. A look of irritation, followed by one of appreciation, always elicited the same answer. "Dunno, lady, I'm a stranger here myself."

"I shall make the inquiries henceforth," Devon exploded, finally. As they approached the stables, Devon insisted Tamsen remain just inside, near the door, while he moved toward a group of tobacco-chewing men. Tamsen, smelling the acrid atmosphere of the stable, ran her eyes over the few mounts in the place. All looked gaunt, whip-scarred, and overworked. Well, she'd gotten most of the way to Santa Fe with less.

Devon returned, his expression grim. "No horses or mules for sale," he said tersely. "No rooms in town." He didn't mention that one of the men had said upriver was no place to take a woman, or that another had come up with a far better place to take one, looking toward Tamsen with lascivious eyes.

196

Devon's fists were still clenched. Should have struck the blighter!

Tamsen, still undaunted, headed toward a small shop where deer carcasses hung before the building, black with flies and small stinging gnats. As they neared the shop, a small dog ran from the structure with a piece of raw meat in his mouth. He was followed by the cursing butcher, a meat cleaver in each hand. The man let fly with the one. The blunt end of it struck the dog's skull, grazing it, but dazing the animal. The butcher, in his bloodstained apron, took aim again.

He was foiled by a small boy who flew into him with flying fists. "You leave my dog alone!" he shouted.

The furious man slammed the child with a ham-like hand and knocked him backward. Scrambling to his feet, the boy bored in again.

"My word," Devon said as he saw the murderous intent in the butcher's face. He began to run. But Tamsen was quicker.

"Leave that child alone," she ordered.

"Like hell I will! The little bastard needs a good lesson!" He raised his hand again—this time, to find himself facing the muzzle of a small gun the lady had drawn from her skirts. It pointed at him steadily, held in a firm hand.

"Touch him again, and I'll kill you," she said.

She meant it. A look of fear entered the man's eyes, to be replaced by a sly, apologetic smile. "Wasn't gonna hurt him. You"—he jabbed a finger at the child—"git the hell outta here, an' keep that goddamn dog away, y'hear?" Then, to Tamsen, "Sorry, ma'am. I just try to keep a clean shop—"

Tamsen looked at the flyblown carcasses. "I see," she said, frigidly. The gun in her hand lowered, but only a little. "Now I need some information. I'm looking for a room, and some kind of pack animal."

"Ain't no sech in town." His face was red now, seeing the incident had not gone unobserved. A group of watchers would have it around before nightfall, that'd he'd been faced down by one little girl with a gun. He'd no longer be thought of as the meanest sonofabitch in Yale, a reputation he traded on.

When Tamsen showed no sign of moving, an idea struck him. His eyes glittering with spiteful delight, he said, "No sech in Yale, but you might try Hill's Bar, couple miles down the river. Try McGowan's place."

He grinned as the man and woman walked away. Down there, they might just find a leetle mite more than they bargained for. He figured he'd evened the score.

"We've got to get Nell on her feet," Tamsen worried as she and Devon returned to the riverbank where the others waited. Edwin Devon walked in silence, still unable to absorb what he had just seen. He would have tackled the butcher with his fists— and probably have lost the battle, he thought ruefully. But a lady of Tamsen's quality, with a gun! It was beyond belief. She was, however, an American. His shock was replaced by a mounting admiration.

It was dusk when the little party approached the collection of shacks and tents that was known as Hill's Bar. It took half an hour to convince Nell she could get to her feet and another fifteen minutes to hoist her into position. The trail they followed was a mule track, and their progress was slow as they looked down on the turbulent waters from dizzy heights. Their packs were rubbing their shoulders raw, and the girls complained. Devon was short of breath and pallid from exertion. Dusty kept dropping back to take a pull from his bottle. Nell dug in her heels every few minutes, refusing to take another step. Only Tamsen's indomitable courage kept them going.

Hill's Bar, if anything, had a more evil appearance than Yale. Two men, stripped to the waist, were fighting in a central area amidst a cheering crowd. Bets were being placed on who would emerge the winner. Tamsen caught a glimpse of silver; they were fighting with knives.

At least they created a diversion. The newcomers managed to slip past unseen, and head toward the only large structure in Hill's Bar, a two-story log building. If there were rooms to be had, here was where they would be.

A tap at the door brought a slack-jawed, heavily breathing boy. His eyes popped as he saw a group of women. He didn't know about a room and a mount. But he'd find out soon, he answered to Tamsen's questioning. Ushering them into a large common room, he left them, hastening to the space where the fight was still in progress, tugging at the arm of one of the onlookers.

"Mr. McGowan—"

The man shook him off, but he returned like a persistent fly.

"Mr. McGowan. I've got to talk to you. It's important. We got company. Wimmen!"

Gaining the gentleman's full attention, he went on to describe the people waiting at the house. Three pretty girls. One fat old lady. Two men, one old, the other kinda weakly. Looked like they could be took, easy.

McGowan thought quickly. "Put the women in the front room, upstairs. The men at the back." He motioned to a man standing across the ring in which the combatants fought, now slippery with blood. Let the boy settle the tenderfeet in for the night. He and John Bagley would take care of the rest.

The boy, Shanks, returned to the big house. He showed the women to their room first, his eyes sliding slyly over each of them as he assessed their qualities. The one doing all the talking was purty as a picture. The other two would do, especially the Mex. But hell, any of them was better than old wore-out Indian Annie, the only female in town.

He wagged his head, thinking of Ned McGowan's luck. He'd been talking of importing some women to the bar. And here they were, ready to hand. As soon as they got rid of the men. He left the girls in the large room, assuring Tamsen he'd see to finding a mule in the morning.

"Don't like it," Nell said, plopping herself on a ticking stuffed with fir boughs. "Somethin' here smells fishy. That Shanks feller's a sneaky little sonofabitch. Liable to wake up with our throats cut."

"Nell, for heaven's sake!" Tamsen was exhausted, the woman's words pushing her beyond endurance. "It's not my fault we had to double back! Not my fault we had to find a place for you to rest, a mule to carry you—"

"Blame me," Nell said in an injured voice. "Helluva way t'treat a dyin' woman!"

"A dying woman," Tamsen said grimly, "wouldn't insist on lugging a—a damned samovar over a trail like we took today."

Nell refused to dignify Tamsen's statement with an answer. Flopping over, she pretended to go to sleep.

Tamsen lay awake for a long time. Nell had been

200

right. There was a bad feeling about this place, despite the boy's eagerness to aid them. She didn't like the way he'd looked at her and the girls, for one thing. And the loud voices, profane and argumentative, drifting through the window on the night wind reminded her of something she'd heard: Nearly every major outlaw in the west had drunk the waters of the lower Fraser.

She was being overly imaginative. Nell had put these doubtful thoughts in her mind. She must try to sleep. There was a long hard trail ahead, and she might not rest in a real bed under a roof for a long time.... A hand on her shoulder woke her; Nell's face was close to hers, her gruff whisper rasping in Tamsen's ears. "Gawdammit, girl, wake up! Lissen!"

Sounds of the hell-raising outside still punctuated the night air, but mingled with the racket was a sound of familiar voices raised in anger. The words were muffled, but the tone was clear. Dusty and Edwin Devon! Were they—quarreling?

"Heered some fellers come up th' stairs," Nell hissed. "Then it sounded like all hell busted loose back there. Somethin's wrong. An' lissen! Now it's too damn quiet—"

It was. The voices had stilled. But a step creaked loudly in the sudden silence. Again. And two more noisy squeaks.

"Two fellers come up, an' four went down," Nell said flatly. "Don't like it. Don't like it at all."

Tamsen rose, shaking out the skirts she had lain down in, checking for the small gun. "Stay here, Nell. Wake the girls. It may be nothing, but be ready to go if we have to."

Slipping from the door, she went silently down the steps. The recalcitrant one creaked only a little beneath her slight weight. The common room stood empty, shrouded in shadows. But a darker square beside the stairs revealed another opening. Timorously, she descended into blackness, a step at a time, holding to the wall. At the base of the steps, there was another abrupt turn. And Tamsen found herself in a cave-like place, hewn from solid stone. A labyrinth of tunnels branched from it. And in the distance someone was swinging a lantern, its faint glow dispelling some of the shadows that lapped at the edges of the cavern.

There was a roaring in Tamsen's ears. Apparently, this was an underground entrance to the river. She stopped to listen, and above the tumult came a sound.

"Jove!" a voice said. "You men will hang for this!"

Dusty! Gathering up her skirts, Tamsen began to run toward his voice.

The tunnel opened into a larger cave, illuminated by the lantern. Beyond the cave, in the half-light of a northern summer night, the tawny river churned against bleak walls. And silhouetted in the cavern's opening were two men, backs to the river, arms upraised.

Tamsen's breath caught. Dusty and Edwin Devon. And they were facing guns in the hands of two menacing figures who stood before them, their backs to Tamsen. The intent of the gunmen was clear. They were going to shoot her friends and let them tumble into the water. The river would carry their bodies away.

Devon's face was white, beaded with moisture, but his voice was strong. "You harm those ladies, you bloody bastards, and you'll rot in hell! Shoot us if you will, but let them go! I beg you!"

Dusty's white hair was standing on end, seeming to crackle with his fury. "Don't you blighters dare

202

lay a hand on my Nell," he threatened, "or I'll—"

One of the gunmen chuckled. "We've got a use for those women. And that's more than you'll have, where you're going. I'd say you're looking at things from a purely selfish attitude." He looked at his companion. "Well, Judge?" He raised his gun.

"Wait a minute," the more portly of the two said. "I rather like the cut of the tall one's trousers. And he won't be needing them."

"Oh, hell," the other growled. "Those pants? With that big belly of yours? Forget it! Let's get on with the job—"

"Drop your guns."

The small, deadly voice came from behind them. The portly man complied, raising his hands with a whimper. The other man whirled, blinking into the shadows beyond the lantern's light. A single shot and his weapon spiraled from his hand. He stood shaking his numbed fingers and gaping foolishly at the small black-haired girl who stepped forward.

"Edwin," she said crisply, "Dusty, pick up those guns. And you two—" She stopped. It was Tamsen's turn to stare in amazement.

Ned McGowan broke the silence. "I'll be damned," he said. "If it isn't Madam Franklin! Owner of the fanciest whorehouse in Frisco. Fancy seein' you here! Listen, if I'd known it was you—"

Edwin Devon stepped forward, cuffing the man across the face. "You dirty-mouthed blighter! This is Mrs. Tallant! You will please watch your language when addressing a lady!"

Dusty made a strangled sound, and McGowan shot Tamsen a keen glance. "Tallant? So you snagged the big-shot hero, huh? Well, Tallant, Franklin, or McLeod, it's all the same to me. You're still a fancy-woman. And I ought to know."

Devon drew back his fist, and Tamsen stepped between the two. Her shoulders sagged a little as she said, forlornly, "Perhaps I should perform some introductions. Edwin, this is Ned McGowan, former judge, member of the California legislature, newspaper editor—and perhaps the crookedest politician the vigilantes ever ran out of the state. Apparently he hasn't changed his ways. And this gentleman"—she turned to the portly one—"was also a leading politician in San Francisco. I would imagine he's also here to preserve the state of his health."

"You—know them?" Devon's voice was laced with incredulity. "You can't know these people!"

"You'd better believe it," Ned McGowan chortled. "Hell, I wrote up her sister's wedding when she married old Alden. Did it up nice, though I hated the senator's guts! I've even been in his home. Though I'll have to say I enjoyed my visits to Madam Franklin's Parlor *better*. Those girls you had, say-y-y!" He licked his lips.

"Now, I've got this idea. I've got a good thing going here. The gold commissioner, Hicks, is under my thumb. And I've been planning on importing some girls, sort of a money-making sideline. We can work together. I'll set you up, you run the place— and I'll see that you get a good cut—"

Devon swung, knocking McGowan to the rocky floor. He lay there, half-reclining, wiping the blood from his split mouth, glaring at the Englishman with malevolent, snake-like eyes.

"You won't get out of Hill's Bar," he threatened. "You've just signed your death warrant!"

Edwin Devon pulled a dirty kerchief from the man's pocket, stuffing it into his mouth. "There's rope over there, Dusty." He pointed to a coil in the

204

corner. "Get it. Then you hold the gun. I'll tie them up."

The eyes he turned on Tamsen were dark with disillusionment, but still held traces of love. "Get the girls," he said. "We will have to leave before dawn."

Tamsen returned to three nervous, waiting women. There was no time to fill in the details. It was sufficient to say that if they valued their lives, they must leave immediately.

Leaving them by the back door, she went to the railed corral, where she selected two mules. One she loaded with their packs. She and the two girls, with much effort, managed to get Nell astride the other. Her skirts rode up over her fat knees, and she kept tugging at them. "Tain't decent," she said, indignantly. Then, "Hand me my sammyvar."

Holding it cradled in her arms, she glared over it until the men appeared. Then, as silently as possible, they moved off into the night.

The return to Yale, with the mules to carry Nell and their possessions, went speedily. The thought of the danger that lay behind them hurried them on their way. The early summer sun was already shining, though the settlement was still asleep, when the little caravan stopped to rest for a moment before continuing on its way.

Tamsen had something to say to Devon. Walking away from the others, she led him down toward the water's edge. A nervous hand pushing her long hair back, revealing her face in all its purity, she looked up at him.

"I believe I owe you the truth, Edwin," she said. "Ned McGowan was quite correct in everything he said. I—I am what he claimed me to be. I ran a—a brothel in San Francisco. Nell, Dusty, and the girls

205

worked for me. And we're going now to set up a—a place of entertainment, in the mining camps. You're free to leave us, you know. You can take ship from here—"

"I can't believe this," he said jerkily, his eyes dark with hurt. "You're not the kind—"

"Kind?" she asked, angrily, "*What* kind! If you mean do I engage in the business myself? Take money for sleeping with men? I do not! I own the business, sing and dance a little—and leave the other to those who see nothing wrong with giving a man something he doesn't get somewhere else! I'm the kind who had two sisters depending on her and had to find a way to support them! And now there's Dusty, Nell, the girls! They're broke, haven't got a dime between them! And I've tried the respectable life, and where did it get me?

"Go on, Edwin! Tell me! *What kind am I?* Because I don't know—I don't know!"

She was weeping now. He put his arms around her, holding her dark head against his chest, drowned in an infinite wave of pity.

"I can't judge you. And I won't. All I ask is to be allowed to come with you, to watch over you, for"—he swallowed hard—"the rest of my life."

She raised her wet eyes to his and blinked the tears away. They dissolved into a gamine-like grin. "Well, then, what are we waiting for? Let's go!"

Nell, watching, saw the embrace. "Well, I'll be damned," she said, pleased. "Looky there, wouldja!"

Everybody looked, and Nell smiled. Maybe things were going to turn out all right for her Tamsen-girl after all. She hoped so, because she sure as hell guessed wrong on Tallant, the sonofabitch! The Devon-feller was a puny sort, stacked up against Dan. But he was English, wasn't he? Like Dusty.

206

And that made him a real man in her books.

Maybe when they got their business paying off, Tamsen would let Devon take her away. She'd have the kind of life she belonged to, like her sisters, Em and Arab, did. A slight frown passed over Nell's features as she recalled the girls' last visit. But maybe things weren't as black as they had painted them. By now, everything ought to be roses back home.

No need in dwelling on what couldn't be helped. Tamsen needed looking after now, and maybe Devon was just the feller to do it. For a going-away present, hell, she just might give them her sammyvar.

BOOK II
BARANOV CASTLE
REVISITED

CHAPTER 1

Despite Nell's hopeful calculations, things had not improved for Emmeline Alden or Arabella Narváez. San Francisco was still in the grip of depression, its busy hubbub dwindling to a sullen mumble. Former millionaires hung about on street corners, looking seedy in run-over, worn boots from better days. Donald Alden's office building, now converted into living quarters for both families, had been for sale so long that it had begun to be a pathetic joke.

One day, it was a joke no longer, for someone had finally appeared with enough cash to purchase it. The buyer, oddly enough, was Alden's old manservant, Lin. He'd saved his salary for years and, supplemented with his winnings from a Chinese lottery, it was sufficient to meet Donald's last stated price.

The dignified office where respectable business had been transacted for many years was slated to become a Chinese laundry—as soon as the present occupants were packed and gone.

Time was running out, Em thought morosely. She stood in a patch of sunlight as Arab knelt to turn up the frayed hem on a gown that would be mended and packed away. The sunlight also pointed out the shabbiness of the place with a merciless finger. More

211

than a year of living here, all of them crowded like so many sardines, had taken its toll.

Yet even these small rooms had taken on an aspect of home. Em had walked by the old house today, the one she and Donald had occupied before the banks failed. She'd stood awhile, trying to recapture the feeling of belonging, but she couldn't. A child had come out of the house, a toddler, about the age Martha was when they lived in the house. But a shrewish voice shrilled after the little girl, mixed with profanity—

No, it was someone else's dwelling now. And this converted office was home. She wondered frantically if Lin would reconsider the deal and sell it back. For she had come to a decision.

"Ouch!" Arabella said. "For goodness sakes, Em, stand still! If we're going to be a credit to Tamsen at the Russian court, we've got to—"

"I'm not going," Em said.

Arabella sat back on her heels, looking up at her sister's determined face. "You don't mean that!"

"But I do. This is my home, Arab. I can't leave it, go off to a strange land—"

"You no longer have a home. It's sold! And Juan and I have no other choice. We can't have Donald saddled forever with all of us!"

"You go, but I'm staying."

"Em!"

Em burst into tears. "Arab, you can't imagine what it's like! I don't think Donald wants to go. *Everything* is wrong. We're like strangers, Arab! Polite strangers! I don't think he even loves me any more."

"Of course he does," Arab scoffed. Though, privately, she'd been wondering much the same thing. The magic she'd associated with Em and Donald

Alden was gone. He seemed more like a father to Em. Maybe, she thought wryly, even a grandfather, but there was none of the closeness of husband and wife.

"Staying here won't solve anything," she offered. "And there's Martha to consider. You know how it's been for her. No place to play but the streets. And the language she's picked up lately—"

"I know," Em said, subdued. "But I'm afraid, Arab! If only Donald would go at the same time we go! But this notion of his to wind up his affairs and follow us a month later—it scares me. I don't know why—"

"I have my problems, too. Juan isn't too happy about letting Donald pay our way to Tamsen—or being dependent on Dan and Tam when we get there. But Em, there's nothing else we can do!"

"You can go," Em said. "I will stay, and wait for Donald, if nothing else."

Her words broke off at the sound of a shot in the street outside. "My God! Martha!"

Running to the door, her unhemmed gown trailing, she screamed her daughter's name. Half a block away, a man lay in the street, with another bent over him holding a smoking pistol. Horses reared in their harness, panicked by the sound of shooting and the smell of blood.

"Martha!"

Martha came running, crossing directly before the hooves of a plunging horse; its hooves narrowly missed her small, pigtailed dark head. "Here I am, Mama."

Em knelt to embrace her. "Oh, Martha, thank God!"

Martha poured out her story. Old Whitfield, up the way, was drunk again. He'd approached a man on the street, claiming he owed him money. Martha acted the scene, graphically.

" 'Get away from me, you goddamn panhandler! I don't owe you nuthin'!' Then Mr. Whitfield grabbed the man's arm, and got shot, dead."

"Oh, honey! What an awful thing for you to see."

"It was 'citing. Lots of cussing, an' lots of blood. Mama, what's dead? Can we fix Mr. Whitfield again?" Her lip quivered and Em hugged her fiercely. "Don't you worry about Mr. Whitfield, honey. Think about where we're going! To see Aunt Tamsen, in a real castle!"

"And you'll marry the prince, an' we'll live happy ever after," Martha giggled, clapping her hands.

"But I'm married already, sweetheart. To Daddy."

"D'ruther you'd marry the prince," Martha said candidly. "Daddy's no fun any more."

She was right, Em thought drearily. For the past year, it had been like living with a dead man. Even the child had felt his deliberate attempt at estrangement. And Em knew, too, that she would take the steamer, even though Donald must remain behind. The shooting was just one more in a series of gruesome happenings. Only last week, a friend of Donald's, broken and destitute, had hanged himself from a lightpost in front of his business down the street. Neighbors found him there at dawn.

"Come help Aunt Arab hem my dress," she said. "We have to get things packed, so we can go—"

Leave-taking was not as difficult as Emmeline had feared it would be. When they left Donald's office, which had become home to both couples, she paused to look back. The place looked cold, empty, as though it had never been occupied. Donald had moved his own things to a rented room, to await the closing of the business transactions he'd stayed behind to handle. One would never know that people had lived here, had loved here, had wept here....

Donald accompanied them to the ship. For the first time in months, he seemed like his old self. He dressed in his best clothes for the occasion; his face below its crown of white hair was composed, serene. He's come to terms with what's happened, Em thought, smiling at him with affection. Now that his office space is sold, he's facing the fact that it's all over.

"There'll be a new beginning in a new country," she reminded him gently.

"I know," he said. "Castles and kings, the kind of life you deserve, Em."

"And we'll have it together."

But he had turned his attention to little Martha, admonishing her to be good and not give her mother any trouble. She promised, and he swung her giggling into the air with something of his old manner, then set her down with a small swat behind. "Go to your Aunt Arab," he said. "I want to say goodbye to your Mommy."

His goodbye was rather stiff and formal, but it was typical of Donald, who hated any public display of emotion. Em longed to throw herself into his arms, to beg him to forget his unfinished business and go with them now. But she held her feelings in check. After all, it wouldn't be long. And the short space would give Tamsen and Dan time to find something for him to do, something that would make him feel important once more.

The bell rang to announce it was time for guests to go ashore. A hasty kiss on the cheek, and Donald was gone. Em could see the sun glinting on his white hair as he made his way through the crowd on the dock; she bit her lip with exasperation. He was already in a hurry to get on about his business, whatever it was. One would think he would at least stand there, waving, as others did, straining for a last glimpse of his wife and child.

No point in her standing here, just to watch the city of San Francisco fade away, Em decided. She collected little Martha and made her way to their cabin. Arabella and Juan remained at the rail. Juan was silent as he looked at the skyline of the city they were leaving; his eyes were sad and remote.

"What is it?" Arabella asked, finally. "Do you hate leaving so?"

Juan shook his head. "It's not that. I was just thinking I've become something of a parasite. Living off Donald's bounty, and now—counting on your sister and brother-in-law for help—"

"Don't be silly," Arab said hotly. "You worked for Donald! And you did a good job! He said so! It isn't your fault his reputation suffered—and some of the stigma rubbed off on you! Dan will be glad to have someone like you to work with him!"

"Will he? Then why hasn't he written to that effect? Surely you told Tamsen we were coming. Long ago."

"I didn't mention it," she lied. "I wanted it to be a surprise." She hadn't heard from Tamsen for a long time. But after all, ship's mail was not all that dependable. And Russian Alaska was a foreign country. Tamsen would be overjoyed to see them. She knew she would.

"You told me you would write her," Juan said. "*Dios*, Arab! We cannot just appear and say, 'We're here, feed us, give me work to do for pay!'"

216

"She's my sister," Arab said sullenly. "Let me be the judge."

"Very well. Except that I cannot take charity."

"You and Donald," she huffed. "Two of a kind! Stop being so—so damned noble!"

Juan smiled at her small display of temper. His beautiful green-eyed princess, usually so loving and tractable. Sometimes he would swear that she, too, had Spanish blood. Then his mouth straightened.

"You speak of Donald. I think there is much of the source of my worry. I do not like leaving him alone. I feel something is wrong—"

Arab laughed. "Are you a *gitano*, then? A gypsy? Then tell my fortune, oh wise one!" She held out a small hand and he placed a kiss in its palm.

"Your fortune is not in your hands, but in mine," he teased. Then his eyes took on their dark moodiness again. "Arab, there is something I must tell you. A thing I do not understand. Donald gave me a letter, a message for Em. It is to be kept secret until we are in sight of foreign shores. The letter—it gives me a bad feeling—"

Arab exploded with merriment. "It's a love letter, my blessed idiot! Just the kind of thing poor old stiff-necked Donald would do! Didn't you see him say goodbye? Like an elderly uncle seeing his niece off on a cruise! He's written all the things he wanted to say and couldn't!"

"Then you don't think I should give it to her now!"

"And spoil all the romantic effect? When he probably sat up writing all night? For shame!" She danced away from him. "Have you forgotten, so soon, what it's like to be in love?"

He reached for her. "I have not forgotten, and I

217

shall never forget. And I do not have Donald's disinclination for making love to one's wife in public."

His brown hands held hers, the sun striking sparks of gold in his dark eyes, and she caught her breath as the old feeling of being two enchanted lovers, caught in a glass bubble, timeless, set apart from the world, returned.

"I think," she said in a small voice, "perhaps we should go to our cabin."

"Yes," he said. "I think we should."

Reaching their quarters, Juan carefully put Donald Alden's letter in a safe place before he turned to his love. The letter could wait.

It lay undelivered, even after the first sighting of alien shores. A place of land and sky and water, low, tree-clad islands, that gave way to snow-capped mountains which framed the inland waterways, their crowns stained rose and gold in the diffused light of the already shortening day.

The sounds of the small steam-powered ship seemed subdued in the vast grandeur through which it traveled; it lightly skimmed the slaty waters as if it were enchanted. Arabella and Juan stood close, lost in a romantic dream as they watched the shoreline. A white bird rose from the waters and seemed to hang suspended for a moment against a backdrop of towering trees.

A picture to remember, Emmeline thought, coming on deck with little Martha's hand held fast in her own. A moment to share. Trying to shut out Martha's prattle, she imagined herself and Donald in Arab and Juan's places, drinking in the beauty of this strange new world.

Probably, she thought crossly, he wouldn't like it

at all. Donald, admittedly, had little imagination, but it would be enough for him to be here. Whatever they faced, they should face together. It didn't seem fair that he'd made her come ahead without him. The ease with which he'd managed to send her away had aroused an anger in her. And gentle Em was uncomfortable with that sort of feeling.

"Aunt Arab," Martha called.

Arab turned from the rail and concealing her disappointment at the interruption of her thoughts called, "Martha! Em! Come join us."

But Em had caught the minute hesitation. "Not now," she said. "I just wanted to take another look before I return to my letter. I'm writing to Donald."

Donald's letter! Arab looked at Juan, whose face was suffused with guilt. How could they have forgotten! "Wait here for a moment," Arab laughed. "Juan has a surprise for you."

Em moved to her sister's side, gratefully relinquishing Martha's hand to Arabella. They talked, admiring the view, until Juan returned with the message he'd promised to deliver in his hand.

Tactfully, Arab drew Martha and Juan to one side when Em gasped with delight at the sight of Donald's tidy hand. Love letters should be read in private. . . .

Em's smile faded as she scanned the pages in the half-light. Then her face grew suddenly old. She read them once more. Finally she took a step toward the waiting trio, half-stumbling. "Here, Arab," she said thinly, "read it. Come, Martha."

She led the rebelling child back toward their cabin as Arab looked after them, blank with shock at the letter's reception. Bad news?

She began to read Donald Alden's words to his wife. "Oh, God," she whispered. "Oh, my God!"

219

The pages fell from her nerveless fingers, and she crumpled, sobbing, against the rail. "Arab," Juan pleaded, "Arab, what is it?"

When she couldn't answer, he sought the fluttering bits of paper. He would find out for himself.

My dearest wife, the letter began. *I have failed you once more, choosing a coward's way to deliver my last words to you. Before you read on, I must assure you this is not a whim. I am not an impulsive man. My plans have been made for a long time. I have merely awaited a moment that would be less painful and embarrassing for you and for Martha.*

I cannot live with failure, or with the knowledge that my honor has been weighed and found wanting. Pray forgive me for what I am about to do.

When you read this letter, you will be free, no longer tied to a dull, old, and broken man. Free to begin anew in a new country.

I have instructed Lin as to the disposition of my body. All expenses incurred by my death have been paid; all arrangements are made.

Bless you for those happiest of years.

Juan folded the letter slowly, carefully, and placed it in his pocket. Then he hurried to his wife, lifting her, holding her close.

"It's not true," she wept stormily against him. "Oh, Juan! He wouldn't! It isn't so!"

"I'm afraid it is," he told her, his own eyes wet. The letter befitted Donald Alden. Neat, methodical, unable to live in an untidy world, he had planned his demise in the most minute detail. Lin had been instructed. All expenses had been paid. Juan had felt the coming of tragedy—had felt it, and then forgotten, so soon.

But it could not have been forestalled, he knew

that with certainty. Donald Alden, dressed in his best, had told his wife goodbye, then gone straight to his dismal rented room. There he had died by his own hand.

"Em!" Arab wept. "Oh, God, poor Em!"

Holding her, soothing her, as they went to find Emmeline, Juan looked over her head at a misted flamingo sunset, at the new land, which was to have been a land of promise for them all.

CHAPTER 2

The first sight of Sitka with its little settlement of Novoarchangelsk was not an impressive one. Sheets of blinding rain hid the snow-crowned cone of Mt. Edgecumbe and the small outlying islands that lay like emeralds in the sea. Water and sky were much the same color. The small, sad group that disembarked from the ship's landing stage was soaked to the skin.

Passing through the long warehouse tunnel, they emerged into a landscape of unpainted, moisture-blackened structures rooted in a sea of mud. All about them were Russians who had gathered to greet the coming of a ship. Bows and compliments for the ladies were uttered in a strange tongue, while tremendous whacks on Juan's shoulders were joined with offers of drinks from bottles. Efforts at conversation only left their greeters with blank looks and shaking heads. Until the name *Baranov* worked its magic.

"Ahhh!" Bearded faces split in smiles. Fingers pointed toward a sprawling wooden structure on a high hill. "Baranov!" Then their attention turned to the seamen who were beginning to unload the cargo; they shouted welcoming, though incomprehensible, remarks with tremendous goodwill.

"At least the natives are friendly," Arab said, an amused smile on her rain-wet face.

"Donald will enjoy this when he comes," Em said. Arab sighed. After a terrible night in which the young woman would not speak or cry, Emmeline's mind had taken the least painful course. The letter had never existed. Donald was not dead. Nervous, brittle, she prefaced every sentence with "Donald thinks," or "Donald says." No one dared shatter the wall she'd built around her grief.

Poor little Martha was confused. Something had happened, but she wasn't certain what it was. There had been a night when Aunt Arab and Uncle Juan had stayed up all night with Mama. In the morning, Mama looked different. Black rings around her eyes, a fixed bright smile on her face. And now, she hugged too hard, hurting, sometimes—

"Is that the castle?" Martha asked now. "It doesn't look like one. Castles 'sposed to have shiny towers."

Arab answered. "There is a tower. See? On top?"

Martha's face was disappointed as they climbed the steps. Then she clapped her hands with glee at sight of the glitteringly uniformed sentry standing in the rain. "A prince," she shouted with excitement, "or a king! Oh, Mommy, it *is* a castle!"

Em's head thudded dully, a fragment of memory shredding at her mind. *Castles and kings,* Donald had said. *The kind of life you deserve, Em.* With a look of anguish, she put her hands to her ears as though to shut out his words. Then, seeing the concerned expressions around her, she painfully erected her protective wall.

"It will be so good to see Tamsen! Donald says—"

The sentry did not speak English. At the mention of the Tallant name, his eyes showed recognition, but he only made gestures of negation. A mention of the governor-general's name brought a pointing finger in the direction of the newly arrived ship. Juan's

223

heart sank. Evidently the ruler was one of the richly dressed group who had boarded the ship just before they had left.

Now what were they to do? Surely they couldn't remain standing here in the rain. He must find shelter for the girls somewhere, especially for Em. His anger rising, he turned to his earlier tack.

"Tallant," he said. "Daniel Tallant. *Tal—lant!* Tamsen. *Tam—sen!*"

He hadn't seen the richly caparisoned young nobleman who had emerged from the castle and stood just around the turn leading down to the parapet. The newcomer stepped toward him, his eyes bright with welcome and curiosity.

"You are having difficulty? And you are friends of Tamsen? May I offer my services?" His English was excellent, only a slight accent betraying his foreign origin.

"We're Tamsen's sisters," Arab interrupted. "This is Emmeline Alden, my husband Juan Narváez, and Martha, Tamsen's niece. We're trying to locate Tamsen. It—it's a surprise." She floundered. "If you could help us—"

The gentleman bowed. "Prince Igor Mischerski, at your service, ladies, sir. And a close friend and confidant of your sister, if I may be so bold as to say so. Her husband"—Igor pursed his lips, sourly—"I did not know so well. Any feelings I might harbor toward him are due to his actions toward the poor lady."

"What in heaven's name are you talking about?" As Arab's breast heaved with agitation, Igor studied her admiringly. Taller than he, her head a red-gold halo, this was a female to his liking.

"Daniel Tallant deserted Tamsen. Left her sick

224

and alone. He went off to Russia with a woman I am not proud to claim as my sister."

"Tamsen! Oh, God! Where is she?"

"Somewhere in New Caledonia, I believe. In the gold fields." He went on to explain that she'd left in the company of an Englishman and some rather odd people from the States. A woman named Nell—

"Up to her old tricks!" Arab looked at Juan, her eyes flashing with anger. "And we thought marriage would change her! I can't blame Dan—"

"Tamsen's morals or lack of them is her own affair," Juan said. "We came here in hope of finding work, through Dan's influence. And now we have no place to turn. With Donald gone—"

Em made a little whimpering sound and wilted. Juan caught her and stood helplessly, wondering what to do. Igor moved to the rescue.

"You cannot stand in the rain," he said practically. "I apologize for my dilatory hospitality. As a representative of the tsar's court, I have some influence here." He spoke to the sentry in a babble of Russian, and the castle door was thrown open. Martha gave a cry of delight as they entered the sumptuously furnished structure. Arab sighed, a ragged sigh of homesickness, recalling the palatial home in Spain that she had shared with Juan— before the political leanings of his uncle, General Narváez, had driven them away.

With authoritative commands to the servants, Prince Igor soon had them established in adjoining apartments. He had assigned them a servant, an Indian girl, who spoke English of a sort. She had worked for Tamsen, the girl, Helena, said shyly.

"At the moment," Arab said, close to tears, "that is hardly a recommendation."

Helena's eyes went hard, and, from that moment on, she spoke only when spoken to, and then in monosyllables.

A bit of brandy brought Em back from her faint, and she chose to ignore the cause of it, once again speaking of Donald in the present tense. As if he were still alive.

It was just as well, Juan told Arab after he returned from a consultation with the governor-general. His mention of their relationship to Tamsen hadn't seemed to elevate the group in Voedvodski's estimation. But he was delighted to have the wife of a well-known senator as guest. He hoped that, even though the person they came to visit had gone, they would remain as his honored guests for a time. And that Mrs. Alden would then convey his good wishes to her husband, who in turn might convey them to the ear of the new President.

"I did not have an opportunity to inquire about work here," Juan said ruefully. "Our conversation was purely social. I do not know what I might even do, with the language barrier."

"You will find something," Arab comforted him. "And in the meantime—look!" She and Em had both received hand-written invitations from Voedvodski himself to a fete to be held in their honor that night. "I'm wondering what to wear," she said, distractedly.

"Surely your sister does not plan to attend."

"Em? Of course."

"But propriety—"

"Propriety be damned," Arab said angrily. "Em doesn't choose to believe Donald's dead. And perhaps it's better that way! The truth will come home to her soon enough. Let her enjoy life while she can!"

"Perhaps you are right," Juan said wearily. He hadn't slept well since reading Donald Alden's letter.

In San Francisco, he had been responsible only for Arabella and himself. Now he had the added responsibility of the widowed Em and little Martha. And no way to make a living for them. Not that he'd done so well in the States. After Donald's business failure, he'd worked at anything he could find, unloading at the docks, clearing garbage from behind a casino, gutting and cleaning fish. Work not exactly suited to the talents of Juan Narváez, reared to head the *cortes* in Spain.

Here all menial labor was performed by Indians and Aleuts. And he didn't even have enough money to get them back to San Francisco. He would have to tell Arab of their financial situation, but not now. Not when her eyes were sparkling in anticipation of a festive evening. "I will wear this," she said finally. "Now I will go help Em decide."

He watched her go, smiling. Arab, his elusive nymph, a will-o'-the-wisp. She was made for love and delight, for dancing. It had been hard for her these last years. She'd been the darling of the Lola Montez troupe when he met her. They had fallen in love, and he had refused the marriage General Narváez had arranged for him. He followed Arab to San Francisco and married her. The marriage had brought her nothing but poverty and privation. Let her have one gala night.

He was proud of his women that night when he entered the banquet hall. Em and Arab, one on each arm. At Arab's insistence, he had worn his scarlet Spanish uniform. Arab was clad in his favorite green, echoing the color of her sparkling eyes. And Em, in blue, a faint touch of color in her cheeks, walked with a regal bearing.

"This is Donald's favorite gown," she'd said, smoothing the skirt.

A highly rebellious Martha had been left in

Helena's care. "One day it will be your turn to attend parties," Em comforted her.

Juan hoped so. *Dios*, how he hoped!

He soon lost his ladies. Governor-General Voedvodski was paying his respectful attentions to Em. And Igor followed Arab from group to group with worshipping eyes. Juan was amused. The dapper little prince was obviously smitten. Notions of jealousy never entered Juan's mind. He knew with all his heart that Arab was his own dear love.

Instead, he speculated on Igor's influence in the community. He might be able to aid him in finding work—a prospect that seemed nebulous in this place. In a more barbaric way, it reminded him of Isabella's court with its fun-loving, decadent noblemen and its richly uniformed officers who were sycophants engaged in a lifelong ball that never ended.

Tallant must have hated this place, with its social pretenses, its glitter. Tamsen, like Em and Arab, would have been in her element for a while. Then the glamor would have faded. Tamsen's basic honesty would have brought it into proper perspective.

Arab would not understand Juan's thoughts. In her disappointment at finding her sister and Dan gone, she was unable to think clearly. In Arab's mind, Tamsen had, by returning to her old profession, deserted Dan, rather than the other way around. Yet it did not make sense, either way. There was a mystery here.

Igor joined Juan after he was unable to get near Arab for the admiring throng about her. "I will escort your lady to table. You do not object?"

"She will be honored," Juan answered mechanically.

"She is a beautiful woman. Three such lovely

sisters, and all so different," Igor mused. "Your wife—she is like fire. The lady Tamsen, delicate, but with a touch of fine steel. And Mrs. Alden—"

He paused, and Juan prompted him, "Em? Yes?"

His face was a study in comical bewilderment. "I do not know. The lady puzzles me. An enchanting, gracious lady, yes. But one feels another person there, behind a mask."

And there was, Juan thought sadly. A woman desolate with grief which she would not admit. "You mentioned Tamsen. I would appreciate hearing her story again. I find it hard to believe Dan would leave her—or that she would leave him."

Igor gave him a few more details, but the story remained essentially unchanged. Tamsen had been injured. Tallant had left her and gone to Russia with Princess Anya. When Tamsen recovered, she journeyed to the gold fields with her friends.

Only one new facet appeared in the telling. Igor suspected the governor-general of having a hand in Tamsen's leaving. With Tallant gone, Tamsen had no official reason to remain, and Voedvodski was antagonistic toward the Americans and the English, seeing them as a potential danger to his rule. As guests, they were acceptable. But as permanent residents—Igor shrugged.

"I had been thinking of making our home here. Perhaps finding employment," Juan said steadily.

Igor looked at him in amazement. "Employment, here? Even if the governor-general should allow it, there is nothing. This is a dying colony, no longer a source of income to Russia. The fur trade is disappearing, the lumber filled with damp, not suitable, really, for building. Our industries, the building of ships, the casting of bells, have been allowed to deteriorate. We are trapped here between

229

the Hudson's Bay Company and the sea. We cover our failures with pomp and ceremony"—he gestured at the crowded hall—"pretending to be a power. When actually, we are deteriorating. Soon there will be only a colony of fishermen."

Juan looked about the room with its elegant furnishings. With liquor flowing freely, many of the noblemen had dropped their exquisite manners. Bearded men hung on each other's shoulders, roaring with laughter. There was something of desperation in their attitudes, as if they lived only for today and were determined to wrest all they could of enjoyment in their brief time.

"I suppose Tamsen saw this," Juan said slowly. "Perhaps that is why she went away."

Igor shrugged, "Perhaps. I have heard the area she went to is rich in gold. And where there is gold, there is new life. I should have accompanied her, but I am a coward. Ah! If you will excuse me, I will rejoin your wife."

As the diminutive prince scurried to enter an opening in the group around Arab, Juan considered their conversation. The governor-general did not like Americans; he would suffer them as guests, but not as permanent residents. There was no employment to be had in a dying settlement; therefore, he must find some solution to their problems. In the back of his mind, he filed another piece of information. In the gold fields to the east, where Tamsen had gone, he might find a chance to make his fortune.

Later, sitting between two Russian noblewomen, neither of whom spoke a language he could understand, Juan watched his wife and her sister. Clearly, they were both in their element. Arab was enthralled with the attentions of so many men. And Em, sitting with the governor-general, appeared as gracious as a hostess, the role she'd filled so well in the senator's home. If uncertainty flickered occasionally in her eyes, if her hands trembled on the heavy, ornate silver, it went unnoticed.

At the end of the feasting, Voedvodski rose to his feet and called the company to attention to formally introduce the wife of a famous senator from the United States, together with her companions. The city is yours, he assured her, offering his hospitality for as long as she might remain.

Em rose and gave a small speech in return, lauding the generosity and friendliness of the Russian people. In fact, she intended to write her husband to that effect this very night. For the senator himself would soon arrive in Novoarchangelsk. Perhaps her message would speed him on his way.

She turned pink at the applause her words evoked, then sat down, not meeting Juan's or Arab's eyes. Donald was coming soon. Of course he was.

Much later, they returned to their various apartments. Em looked in on the sleeping Martha, with a twist at her heart as she noted, again, how like Tamsen the child was. Bending over the little form, Em placed a kiss on her flushed cheek, soft as a butterfly's wing.

"Your father is so proud of you," she whispered. "So proud!" Then she wondered at the tears on her own cheeks. This was no time for crying. She was tired, that was all. It had been a wonderfully exciting evening, but so exhausting. It would be easier when Donald came.

In the Narváez apartment, Arabella was too excited to sleep. Tonight she had met barons, princes, and Russian generals. They would all help

231

Juan in finding gainful employment, she was certain. He would become a very important man in Novoarchangelsk. Despite the way Tamsen and Dan had let them down, coming here had been the right thing to do.

And had Juan noted the paintings on the walls? Priceless! The wonderful furnishings imported from across the seas. A far cry from their former quarters behind Donald's office, she said wryly. Then, soberly, "If only Donald could be here. Juan, do you think Em will be all right? I'm afraid for her."

"She will come to an understanding, sweetheart. We all do what we have to do. Maybe it's easier this way. She's gaining a little time, and time eases everything."

"I suppose so," Arab said sadly. Then, "I guess I feel ashamed of myself because I'm so happy here."

This was not the time, Juan decided, to discuss the idea that was beginning to form in his mind. That they should leave this place and go in search of Tamsen, and perhaps of gold.

CHAPTER 3

In the week that followed, feasts were held each night to toast and admire Arabella and Emmeline. Arabella and Juan had their first serious quarrel over the sisters' discovery of the company store.

"This velvet for me," Arab told Juan, holding the tawny material to her cheek, "and a blue taffeta with matching lace for Em. She's going to make them both up. I'm hopeless at sewing."

"How much did it cost?" Juan's voice was sharp. "And how did you pay for it?"

Arab looked at him, startled. "Why—I don't think I asked," she said, uncertainly. "The man said our credit was good. I told him you'd be in to take care of it."

"And what do I take care of it with?"

"Juan! We have some money! And we must keep up appearances. Everything we have has been seen!"

Juan's face was flushed with suppressed anger. "You're forgetting we're paupers," he threw at her. "We're living here as guests, off the governor-general's bounty. And what happens when he finds out Alden's dead? That the senator he's expecting to arrive will never come? What are we supposed to do then? *Dios*, Arab! We cannot even pay our passage home!"

"But you will find work. The bill will wait."

"Arab," he gritted, "there is no work! And you are letting the way we are living addle your mind! There will be no more bills! No more new gowns! I will pay this, but it will be the last. Do you understand?"

Arab stared at him, something in her thrilling to the steel in his voice, so masculine, so commanding. But the sensation only served to heighten the anger she felt at his words.

"Don't worry," she said, "I'll find a way to pay for it myself! My gown and Em's too!" She stamped her foot and ran from the room.

She was still angry when she met Igor in the tea gardens. Igor smiled, thinking how her temper became her, her eyes glinting, her untamed red hair catching the flame from her disposition.

"Something has upset you, my lady?"

Arab forced a smile. "Something trivial. Sometimes husbands are not . . . understanding."

"A pity. He suffers from jealousy, perhaps?"

"No," she answered honestly. "He knows I would never look at another man."

Prince Igor's face fell. For years, he'd cut a figure among the ladies of Alexander's court. Perhaps, he thought ruefully, it had spoiled him. For he'd never been able to feel a genuine interest in a woman until he met these three sisters. Toward Tamsen he'd developed a deep and profound feeling of friendship. Em intrigued him. But Arabella—Arabella was the only woman who had ever touched his heart.

"If I can be of aid," he said quietly.

For an instant, Arab thought of borrowing the money to pay her bill. But that would solve nothing. She would only be ridding herself of one debt and gaining another. But she'd told Juan she'd manage to pay what she owed, and she would do it. If she could only find a way...

"Igor," she said, leaning toward him, "there is something you can do. Did you know I once danced professionally—once I appeared before Queen Isabella of Spain? I miss it so!"

Before they parted, Igor, enchanted and bemused, had agreed to drop a hint to the governor-general himself. He was certain Voedvodski would be delighted to ask her to perform.

Arabella hurried home and carried her bolt of tawny velvet into Em's room. "I want it made like this," she said, her eyes shining as she made a small sketch. "See, like a gypsy gown." There were some beautiful gold hoop earrings in the company store, bought for the noblemen's wives. She'd buy them now—and pay later. Also, there was an enveloping Spanish shawl.

Several days passed in which both Em and Arab absented themselves from festivities. On a night when a new ship docked in the harbor, Arab's dress was done. Em's could wait, she said, smiling. She would not want to wear it until Donald came.

Arab dressed in Em's room, leaving her red-gold hair to hang down her back, the hoop earrings shimmering against it. And at last, she wrapped herself in the Spanish shawl.

Martha was delighted. "You look pretty, Aunt Arab! I wish Mommy had a dress like that."

Em blushed. "I don't think your father would like it," she said. "Not for me. But it seems to suit Aunt Arab very well."

Juan wouldn't like it, either. He would wonder at the earrings, and where the shawl came from, but he would say nothing until they were alone. She'd told

235

him to come for them here, counting on Em's presence to keep the peace.

His lips tightened as she had expected, and she saw the question in his eyes. Let him wonder. She would pay for her things as she'd promised, and she would be able to, after this night.

In the banquet hall, Juan, as usual, found himself an inconspicuous corner where he might keep an eye on Arab and Em. He had been immediately contrite over his blow-up at Arabella. She had made her purchases, charging them in good faith, believing there would be funds to pay for them. It had not been her fault, but his. He'd been too much of a coward to tell her they were nearing the end of their money, or that, though he'd been looking—*Dios*, how he had been looking—there was no employment in this small settlement to support a man, two women, and a child.

Arab had not known that. How could she? But after he had warned her of their plight, forbidding her to make more purchases, she had apparently gone against his will. His Arab, upon whom he could always depend for understanding! What was this place doing to her?

A Russian lady approached Juan, smiling. His blind, unseeing eyes seemed to rebuff her. She turned away. Igor, seeing Juan's bleak features, thought how odd it was that the sisters had chosen such grim, forbidding husbands. He wondered what Donald Alden would be like.

The evening dragged interminably. And finally, seated at the festive board, Juan found himself unable to swallow. He felt a sense of relief when the last course was removed. There would be speeches, entertainment, and dancing afterward. Then it would be over.

236

When the governor-general stood to announce the entertainers, Juan Narváez was startled to find his own wife would head the list. He folded his arms and knitted his brows as she moved into the center of the floor.

"Governor Voedvodski, will you interpret for me?" she asked prettily. At his bow, she continued. "I am going to sing and dance for you, as I did for Queen Isabella of Spain. In this dance, I will be a *gitana,* a gypsy girl of the streets. And at the end, to make it authentic"—her breath caught on a little laugh—"I will raise my skirts, so"—she gestured with her hands—"for the watchers who will shower me with coins."

With a swift motion to the musicians, a whirling step to twirl the cape from her shoulders and into the hands of an appreciative nobleman, Arab was transformed. A poor little street waif, forward, yet shy at the same time—but oh, so very much aware of her physical charms. The dance was suggestive, provocative, as she stamped and whirled, the full skirt revealing well-formed limbs, her clear voice chiming in a naughty little song.

With a crashing chord, the music ended, and Arab gathered up her skirts. The audience roared with delight as they showered her with rubles, with rings hastily pulled from noble fingers, glittering with gems.

Juan Narváez rose and left the room. It was almost an hour later when Arab burst into their apartment. Her face still wore a flush that might have been one of success, but instead was of fury.

"How could you!" she choked. "How could you embarrass my by leaving like that!"

"I embarrass *you?*"

The incredulity in his tone stopped her, then she

began again. "I was a dancer when you met me! You know that! You've never minded before."

"But now you're my wife, Arabella." His eyes were hard in the flicker of candlelight, his brown hands clenching and opening as if he would like to close them about her throat. "I do not care to have my wife begging, whether it be in the streets or in a castle hall. It is much the same—"

"Begging!" Arab's voice rose. "Begging! I earned what they gave me!"

"And at the expense of my pride."

"Someone must make money in this family." Arab heard her voice speaking. It seemed separate from her mind, for she was thinking, wildly, that this was Juan she faced. Her beloved Juan. And this nightmare must stop. They could not be talking to each other like this!

Juan's voice was quiet, deadly. "You are quite right. Perhaps I should thank you for coming to a decision for me. I spoke with some seamen off the ship this afternoon. There is truth to the rumors of gold in New Caledonia. I cannot find employment here. I have tried. Therefore I am taking ship in the morning."

He had said I, not we. Arab tried to keep the terror out of her voice. "In the morning? We—we can't be ready by then. And Em still believes that Donald . . . Oh, Juan, we can't go! I won't!"

"You will not be accompanying me," Juan said, sighing. "You need not have any fear. I am going alone."

Arab, weeping, let go of her skirts. Rings and rubles rolled to every corner of the room as she flung herself into Juan's arms.

"You can't leave me," she sobbed. "Juan, you can't!"

238

"Someone must have money in this family," he said. She recognized her own words.

"I didn't mean it," she moaned. "Oh, Juan, nothing's important enough to separate us again. I don't need new things. And I won't dance any more."

He looked down at her sadly. She still didn't understand a man's feelings. "Dance if you want to, little one. But not as a beggar." He smoothed the tangled copper curls away from her tear-wet cheeks. "I only want to be able to provide for you, little *gitana.*"

His face had been pale, stone-like. Now it was flushed with the beginnings of desire. A shred of hope entered Arab's mind. There was a way to keep him here....

Her hands went to his shirt front, unbuttoning it deftly. Her fingers traced the muscles of his hard brown chest until she felt them begin to quiver. Then she slid the ruffled gypsy gown from her shoulders, pressing her own whiteness against him.

Dios! No wonder she'd been such a voluptuous *gitana!* She'd worn nothing underneath! The thought surged through him like an electric shock as he crushed her to him, feeling the throbbing of her body like an echo of his own. He carried her to the big bed and she drew him down, her hands hot against his shoulders, her burning mouth seeking his. He was startled for a moment, with the confused feeling that Arab *was* a gypsy lass, that this might be taking place on a grassy slope beneath the stars. Then, as her nails clawed into his flesh, he met the fire that was in her with a violent passion such as he had never known.

Sated, exhausted, Arabella finally slept, secure in the knowledge that Juan would not leave her now. But Juan lay beside her, dark eyes fixed on the

239

ceiling. In the morning, he rose before daylight, taking a long look at his wife's sleeping face. How he loved this girl! He would not wake her. It would be easier this way. There would be no parting then, and there would be last night to remember—until he returned.

He dressed, stepping on spilled coins and jewels before he pulled on his boots. At least there would be this, he thought. Perhaps it was as well. He had little to leave. He took enough money for his passage, and enough for whatever supplies he might need. He must meet with success on this journey. He left the castle silently, passing by the sleeping sentry unchallenged, and made his way to the shoreline.

As he stood at the rail of his ship, watching the settlement of Novoarchangelsk fade into the distance, an odd thought struck him. In all the days he had been here, it had done nothing but rain. He wondered if the sun would ever shine on Sitka and his love again.

CHAPTER 4

Rain beat against Governor-General Voed-vodski's window as he studied the three letters on his desk. An unheard-of event had occurred at this late date in the year—not one ship was anchored in the harbor, but two. One was from Okhotsk; its captain insisted he would return across the icy seas no later than tomorrow. The other was from San Francisco.

With the ships had come a series of messages. The Russian vessel carried two. One was from Baron de Stoeckl and stated that he and Daniel Tallant had arrived safely in St. Petersburg after a long and eventful journey. It commended the Tallant man for his actions during the voyage. Then it went on to say that a tragedy had occurred, that the Princess Anya Mischerski had fallen to her death. Tallant's young aide had also lost his life in an attempt to rescue her.

"Please convey the news to Prince Igor Mischerski, along with my sympathies," it ended.

The governor-general had not liked the girl. She had been a source of trouble during her stay. And the scene she made in the banquet hall on that long-ago night had been an embarrassment to him, but still, the news was shocking.

Yet it was not as shocking as that contained in the other message from Russia. The letter from Daniel Tallant to his wife, sealed, with a notation on the

241

cover to send it on, should she have returned home.

Unsealed now, the paper crackled in Voedvodski's hand as he read it once more. Abducted? Placed in irons! God in heaven! What the American press would make of this! It could not happen under the auspices of Holy Mother Russia! The man was lying, to cover his defection. With Anya dead, he was once more seeking the good graces of his wife.

Tallant's protestations of love did sound sincere, but one who could invent a tale such as this would have great writing talent. The governor-general consigned Dan's letter to the fire.

The last message troubled him even more. When the Narváez fellow left several months before, without a word to anyone, Voedvodski had been disturbed. The proposed visit of Senator Alden had not come about. He began to wonder if the guests in his house were imposters. They could be spies, perhaps, on some nefarious mission, so he had sent a message to his contact in San Francisco, and now he had his answer.

Senator Alden died by his own hand. He had placed his family aboard a vessel bound for Russian Alaska, returned to his rented room, and taken his life. The governor-general studied the message somberly. It had been a long time, and Mrs. Alden had sent out letters with every ship, though she'd received no answer in return. Was it possible she did not know?

He called to his aide. "Please bring Mrs. Alden to me," he said. The man turned to go, and Voedvodski called to him to wait. He'd grown fond of the gracious Em and little Martha, and he was a sentimental man. The thought of tears filling the woman's lovely lupine-blue eyes was more than he could bear.

"Instead, bring Mrs. Narváez."

Arab's heart was pounding as she entered the governor-general's presence. It nearly stopped when she saw his lugubrious expression. "I have some sad news for you," he said.

She went white, her hand going to her breast. He leaped up and guided her to a chair. "Juan?" she asked, her lips white. "Something's happened to Juan?"

"No, madam. But I regret to inform you that Senator Alden—"

"I know."

"You—do?" His amazement was almost comical. "But—when did you learn this?"

"My brother-in-law saw us off, then left to take his own life. He had given my husband a letter for Em. Oh, Governor Voedvodski!" She was weeping now as she clutched at the startled gentleman's hands. "Em refuses to believe it! As long as she doesn't face it, she can pretend nothing's happened, that he will join us soon—"

Disengaging himself, Voedvodski produced a clean linen handkerchief. Arab wiped at her streaming eyes as he walked to the window, his back to her.

"What are your plans?" he finally asked. "What do you intend to do?"

"I haven't the slightest idea," she admitted forlornly. It was all out in the open now, and she might as well level with him. "We arrived here virtually penniless, hoping to find something to do— some way to make a living. My husband has gone to the gold fields in New Caledonia, since he found

243

nothing here. If—if we could be allowed to remain until his return—we will repay you."

Voedvodski blinked rapidly. He'd been spared the sight of tears in Em's blue eyes, but he'd suffered as they spilled from slanting, long-lashed green ones. They would not be the lady's last tears, he was certain. Slender, courtly Juan Narváez was not a miner, but an aristocrat. The wilderness had swallowed up far rougher men than he. It was not likely that he would find gold—nor that he would even return. And he, Voedvodski, would have two unattached women on his hands—and a child.

But he had grown fond of Mrs. Alden and her little girl. And Arabella was a welcome addition to his banquets. It flattered him to introduce an entertainer who had danced before the crowned heads of Europe.

"I beg you to remain as my guests," he said gallantly. "It will be my pleasure."

It was only after she had gone that he dared to admit to himself a third reason for his invitation. It would make up in some small measure for the disasters that had befallen Tamsen and Daniel Tallant at Russian hands. The story Tallant had written could not be true. But if it were, it was a tragic thing. And he still felt some guilt over blackmailing the woman into copying her husband's maps.

At least, he could afford to be generous now. The maps were in the hands of the tsar. They would have reached St. Petersburg long before Dan did. And he, Voedvodski, would surely be commended for his devotion to his country.

Emmeline, who had moved into the Narváez apartment when Juan left, sat sewing, but looked up anxiously as Arabella entered. "The governor-

244

general—what did he want? Is there news of Donald?"

"Only to make certain that we were at the banquet tonight," Arab lied. "There are two ships in the harbor. One from Russia, the other from San Francisco."

"Are there passengers?"

Arab tried to remember what Igor had told her. "Two miners, from San Francisco, I think, hoping to winter here."

Em put down her sewing and went to the window. "If Donald doesn't hurry," she said fretfully, "he will have to wait for spring."

Arabella ignored her sister's plaintive remark. "I'm meeting Igor at the tea gardens," she said hastily. "Will you be all right?"

Em looked at her in surprise. "Of course. Why wouldn't I be? I have Martha here, and Helena—"

Igor was late for their meeting. And when he entered the tea house, his face was pale. He had come from the governor-general's office, where he'd learned of Anya's death. As he relayed his grim news to Arab, sympathy touched her eyes. She had no pity for Anya, from what she'd heard of Dan's involvement with the girl. But she was Prince Igor's sister, and Arab was very sorry for him.

"I am sorry," she said.

"Sorry? You needn't be. I am not. There has never been any pretense of love between us. It is only a—a shock. People like Anya do not die. They live on forever, feeding on other people's hurts." His mouth twisted with a bitterness new to Igor. "Do I surprise you? Please, do not think less of me. You did not know her. I am only honest with you."

"Then I will be honest with you," Arabella said in

245

a low voice. "As I have not been since we arrived." She told him of the financial situation in San Francisco, their plans to join Tamsen in Novoarchangelsk, the way they'd learned of Donald's death aboard ship, and that Em refused to accept it. The governor-general had learned of Em's widowed state only this morning, but had graciously extended his hospitality—until Juan returned from the gold fields, with enough funds to buy their passage home.

"So you see"—Arab blinked rapidly—"we are nothing. Just a group of poverty-stricken people, depending on the governor-general's generosity. Beggars, if you like—"

"Ladies," Igor corrected her. "Very lovely ladies, who have fallen on unfortunate times. My sister was in control of our fortunes, but now that she is gone, I am a wealthy man. If I may offer—"

"You may not!" Arab said, softening her refusal with a smile. "But I will remember your kindness. Helena says Tamsen made some money by sewing gowns. Em is an excellent seamstress, though I am the world's worst, but I am quite good with design."

Igor struck his palm against his temple. "Your talents lie in quite another direction," he said eagerly. "In St. Petersburg, your art would be respected! Admired! You would become famous, wealthy! Perhaps appear before the tsar himself! Oh, Arabella—please allow me to call you by your name—let me take you there. I will return there now that my sister is gone. Let me take you with me and introduce you."

His excitement was contagious. For a moment, Arab almost believed the things he said were feasible, that they might come true. Then she drew back, laughing a little sadly.

"You forget, sir, that I am a married woman. That I have a husband to consider. And that I must be here waiting when he returns."

Igor's face fell. "You might leave word here for him to follow," he said hopefully.

"I do not think it would meet with his approval. And now, I think we should return to Em."

They walked along in companionable silence, Arab thinking how fond she'd grown of the mercurial little prince; Igor glum with the knowledge that he'd developed into such a serious fellow. The old Igor would have boarded that vessel returning to Russia, despite the wintry seas it must endure. He would have returned to St. Petersburg, to become once more the mischievous darling of the court.

Instead, he would remain in this dreary, rain-soaked place, seeing the same people, the same faces, attending those interminable dinners that were beginning to be a bore. And all because, for the first time in his life, he'd had the misfortune to fall in love.

Immersed in their separate thoughts, they didn't notice the crowd gathered before them until it halted them. From the thudding, grunting sounds, it appeared a fight was in progress in the midst of the cluster. Arab halted, and Igor put his hand on her arm, protectively, the other going to the short sword at his side.

"Hi—eee—yah!" a man's voice gleefully shouted, and Arab leaped backward as a bearded, shirtless *promishleniki* came flying over the heads of the watchers and landed at her feet. The crowd parted as a figure forced its way through. He was a blond giant, his massive naked shoulders gleaming with rain, his face alight with a savage joy. Reaching the fallen man, now trying to get to his knees, the giant picked him up and shook him like a wet puppy.

"Had enough?" he asked. "Ready to call it quits?"

The dazed Russian, almost as large as his attacker, but wilted in defeat, was quite ready to surrender. The blond man gave him a mighty shove. "Then get the hell out of here. And don't try startin' anything you can't finish after this!"

Catching sight of Arab, the conqueror's eyes widened. "I'm sorry, ma'am. But it was either him or me—"

She wasn't looking at him, but at his fist. It was bruised and battered, his knuckles bleeding. He followed her fixed gaze and half-lifted the offending hand, then held it toward her.

"Hell, lady," he said, "it ain't all that bad—"

His words stopped short. Arabella had fainted dead away.

She woke, dazed, in her own bed at the castle. It had been a dream, she thought, lifting a hand to her throbbing head. She sat up, despite the efforts of a solicitous Em. Helena stood by with an armful of towels. Against the far wall stood Igor, white and frightened-looking, in the company of a small, roughly dressed stranger, a man with a nut-brown face, as wrinkled as a walnut.

Arab stared at him. "It was the other man," she said, haltingly. "The man who was fighting. Where is he? Where did he go?"

"Carried you in, then lit a shuck outta here," the small stranger said. "Figgered if he was so ugly he skeert a purty gal like you—"

"Find him," Arab moaned. "My God, you've got to find him!" And to her sister's worried face, she whispered, "Em! Oh, Em! that man—he was wearing Juan's ring, the one like mine."

The strange man came closer to inspect Arab's hand. "Just like the one Duke's wearin', I'll be

248

daggoned! Close enuf t'be its twin sister. I'll tell him it must be wuth somethin'. He'll be right proud—"

"Where did he get it?" Arab shrilled. "Tell me! Where did he get it? Go find him! I've got to know!"

"Now, don't go gettin' all het up agin. You don't need Duke. I kin tell you that, 'cause I got the thing myself. Took it off a dead man, somewheres a-twixt Douglas an' Lillooet—"

He ceased with a look of consternation, for Arabella had fainted again.

CHAPTER 5

That evening, at precisely five o'clock, Duke Courtney presented himself at Baranov Castle. He was freshly shaven, and his blond hair was combed and fastened at the back of his neck with a leather thong. He wore his best set of clothes—the ones he wore for hellin' around in town: a blue wool shirt from the Hudson's Bay store and corduroys to match.

When the sentry challenged him, refusing him admittance in incomprehensible language, Duke didn't argue with him. The sentry didn't see what hit him. Duke looked at him for a moment, then dragged him over and propped him against a wall. Looks more fitting that way, Duke thought.

Then he marched into the castle and bullied a servant into directing him to the two American ladies. His partner, Mac McCandless, had returned with the details of a tragic story. And Duke Courtney had come to make things right. Because of the ring, a poor little girl had learned she was a "widder-woman" the hard way. He hadn't wanted to wear the damn thing, anyway. But old Mac had worked on it all one night, cutting it, piecing it out with a hammered silver dollar so that it would fit his massive hand. Couldn't turn it down after that.

Duke also had a small black book Mac had taken

off the dead man's body. It had his writing in it, something his woman would surely want. The third thing he carried was a nugget, the size of a turkey egg. It had not been in the dead man's possession, but Duke figured he'd lie a little. Hell, two American women in a furrin' land could probably use a little ready cash, and he could always get more where that came from.

He didn't look forward to facing the widow in her grief, but he hoped he'd get another look at the other one, the lady-one, with big blue eyes and silky brown-blond hair. The glimpse he'd had, when he had carried the girl who fainted to her bed and then skedaddled, had remained with him ever since—like a soft, sweet tune running through his head. Hell, I'm a damn poet, he thought, reddening. He rapped on the door.

Em answered his knock. Her eyes were enormous in a white, drawn face, but Duke thought she was the most beautiful thing he had ever seen in his life. Feeling outsized and bear-like in the presence of her fragile femininity, he tried to subdue his booming voice as he stated his errand. On the first try, his voice didn't come out at all.

Then he was following her into the room, feeling his boots scuff on the soft carpets, elbows held close in fear of sending some priceless object crashing to the floor. The red-haired girl, now clad in a flowing green robe, a fur thrown over her knees, sat before the fire. Her eyes were swollen, but her head was high. She reminded him of someone, he realized, some other girl he'd met who held her head like that.

"I'm glad you came, Mr.—?" The sentence ended on a question.

"Courtney, ma'am. Just call me Duke."

"And I am Arabella Narváez." The last name was

uttered with just a hint of a quiver in the soft voice. "I'm so glad you came. I've been wanting to ask you how—how—"

"Reckon he fell, ma'am. It was about the time of the first snow, start of September. Winter's rougher'n hell in there. Figured he slipped. Mac seen this shiny boot sticking out of the snow—"

Arabella shivered. "What type of boot? I have to be sure—"

"Some kind of furrin' lookin' boot, ma'am. Real tall, black an' shiny, like I said. Purty things, but they ain't worth a damn on the trail."

Arab leaned back in her chair, the green eyes closed. "And did you see his face? Can you describe him?"

"Dark," he said uneasily. "Slim type. Figured him fer Eye-talian, or Mex—An' ma'am, we buried him nice—"

"Thank you," Arab said faintly. "I'm sorry. I—I can't talk any more. Em?"

Em saw him to the door and he remembered, belatedly, the items he intended to deliver. "Here's the ring," he whispered hoarsely, "and a notebook the feller carried. An' this." He put the nugget in her hand, and she thanked him, laying the things he'd given her on a small table. When he still stood there, she looked at him, questioningly.

"I don't think I got your name, ma'am," he said awkwardly. "It—it would be nice to know."

"I am Mrs. Alden. Mrs. Narváez is my sister. And now, thank you again for coming."

He was in the hall, the door shut against him, before he knew what happened. And it was all done so lady-like and nice, slick as a whistle. It was easy to see, he thought morosely, what the lady thought of a man who went around robbing dead bodies. Mac took the ring, but he'd taken the book, with the idea of finding the owner's identity. Nothin' wrong in that. As for the nugget, the donor of that was very much alive, alive enough to burn a little at the brush-off at the door.

Mrs. Alden, she'd said. The lady was married. But hell, she wasn't for the likes of him, anyway. Maybe it had been worth the price of the nugget, though, just to get a look at a woman like that.

He was frowning as he turned to try to retrace his steps to the castle entrance, and he caught only a brief glimpse of the small figure that flashed by, eyes wide and dark above a laughing mouth, black hair flying as she entered the door of the apartment he'd just left, shouting, "Mommy!"

He stood for a moment in shock, because he suddenly recalled who the child resembled. Tamsen Tallant, the girl who ran the house over near Dangerous Rapid, a madam—and hell, he should know! She'd made him pay through the nose the night he started a fight and busted up the place!

It was Tamsen Tallant he'd been reminded of when he saw Arabella Narváez. Not in looks, but something in the way she held her head. And now the kid—He shook his head. That little blue-eyed Alden woman had him dizzy. He was imagining things. Two ladies like that being any relation to a girl who ran a whorehouse—hell, he was losing his goddamn mind!

He found the entrance and went down the steps. The sentry was still sitting where he'd propped him. Duke checked his pulse and lifted an eyelid, then smiled in satisfaction. He'd wake up in ten minutes or so. With a sense of the proprieties, he carefully straightened the fellow's headgear.

Back in the Narváez apartment, Em shushed little

Martha. "Aunt Arab has a headache," she said. "We mustn't disturb her." She didn't see Arabella stiffen in her chair at the words.

Martha had been for a walk with Helena, but she'd escaped, playing a mischievous game of hide and seek throughout the castle. When the servant arrived, finally tracking down her charge, the little girl was glad to leave the somber apartment for the rainy out-of-doors.

When she had gone, Em took the black notebook to Arab at her request. Arabella opened it and flinched at the sight of the familiar hand.

"I can't read it, Em—read it to me, please?"

"I don't think—"

"Please, Em."

Em smoothed the first page. It was water-stained, and almost illegible in spots, but she began.

"*Watched Novoarchangelsk fade into the rain this morning. A bad feeling, as if I would not see my little sweetheart again. Stood so long at the rail, I was chilled through. Thought of her sleeping, all snug and warm. I feel as if I shall never be warm again.*"

"*Ah, God!*" Arab choked.

Em snapped the book shut. "I can't go on, Arab! I can't do this to you!"

"Read it. I have to hear it."

Em read on, through the random thoughts Juan had on the trip, thoughts in which Arab figured largely. He had landed at Asquamalt and walked to Fort Victoria, where he camped for the night in a rock valley.

"*I am writing this by firelight. I purchased a canvas drop today, supposedly to make a shelter. Surprised to find myself most inept. It sags somewhat, but at least is effective against the rain.*

"*Advised at the fort to find a partner, since I am*

254

what they refer to as a cheechako, or greenhorn. A good idea, since I would not recognize gold if I found it. It is my intention to locate Tamsen, if I can."

"He didn't find her," Arabella wept. "If he had, she might have stopped him!"

"Juan was a man, Arab. He had a sense of pride. He would do what he thought he should, in spite of Tamsen or anyone else, you know that." Her lips whitened. Her voice had sounded like an echo of Donald's. Shaken, she returned to the book's pages.

"*Have found a partner,*" the next entry read. "*I am not at all certain he is trustworthy. He boasts of his career as a bandido in Mexico and of his prowess with the ladies. But, though he is unfamiliar with this area, he has had experience in the gold fields of California. So he will do to travel with.*

"*I am uncertain of where to search for Tamsen. The miners I have met are going upriver, not coming down. And I have learned there are several ways one might go. One route is via the Harrison to Douglas, making use of boats and portage. The other, by paddlewheeler to Yale at the end of navigable water, entails much foot-travel.*

"*My partner, José, favors the first route. Therefore it is the one we will take. I hope Tamsen will be found somewhere along the trail.*

"*We leave in the morning.*"

There followed a terse account of their journeying. "*Arrived Harrison River, 8 A.M. Left by another steamer, the Union. Got to Douglas, 7 P.M.*

"*Left Douglas, each carrying 70 lb. pack. Steep hills. Walked eight miles and stopped for dinner, beef tainted. On to camp at 14 mile stone. Bread, tea, Indian meal for supper.*

"*It is snowing, an eventuality California José did*

255

not anticipate. He says we must return. I refuse. Found the first colors of gold in the creek this morning, though the ice had to be broken. How long are winters here? How severe? Can we sit this out and wait for spring?...

"Snow to the knees and drifting. José and I quarreled today, about my rationing of supplies. Shot a rook today, made a stew. Told José he is free to leave if he wishes. Think he will go."

The last entry read:

"José is going. It is nearing the end of September, and I have never known such cold. The snow keeps putting out the fire. I warm myself by thinking of Spain, and Arabella in my arms. Those thoughts will see me to the end of my journey—"

Em turned the page and gasped. There was only one word. *"Today."* It was barely visible, since the double spread was encrusted with a great rusty stain.

Blood! Juan's blood.

She closed the book quickly. "That is all," she said. She carried the volume to a bookshelf behind Arab's chair, slipping it behind other books. Tomorrow, she would remove the offending pages. It was something Arabella should never have to see.

Then, moving like a sleepwalker, she returned to Arab, kneeling in front of her chair. "I know how you feel," she said, "because—you see, I know Donald's dead, too... I know it now." The tears began to fall, the tears she'd stored away for so many months. They cried together, two sisters, both newly bereaved.

When Helena returned with Martha, Arab and Em had both composed themselves. Em put her arms around her little daughter. "There's something we have to tell you, sweetheart." She told her the whole story of how her daddy had died a long time ago and now Uncle Juan had gone to join him. Martha listened gravely, then asked, "Are they in grave houses, like Helena's mommy?"

Grave houses? Em thought of Donald, seeking death by his own hand, lying somewhere in an unvisited grave; of Juan, lost in the New Caledonian wilderness where his burial spot might never be found.

"Something like that," she said shakily.

"Then God will have to fix them," Martha said. In her mind, the two men had been gone such a very long time. Grief didn't enter into it. To Martha, months were years. Em knelt before her and sat back on her heels in relief.

Then Martha began prattling away with the details of her walk. Helena told such wonderful stories. Today, she'd learned the story of Keet, the Killer Whale. And another story of Raven who made the world and who played such tricks! Was Raven like Prince Igor?

While Em was readying her for bed, Martha remembered something else. Today she and Helena had met a man. An American man—"This big"— she stretched her arms wide. "He was a nice man. And guess what, he knew *Aunt Tamsen*. He's been to her house."

Em's face paled. Today they had lost one loved one and found another. She would not mention this to Arab. But tomorrow, she would have to seek out this man and question him, despite her distaste for robbers of the dead.

CHAPTER 6

Em's interview with the rugged Duke Courtney did not produce the desired results. Through inquiries, she learned that he was staying at the soldiers' barracks. Obviously she could not go there, and she did not wish him to come to the apartment again. So she settled on a tea house as a meeting spot and sent a messenger to relay her invitation.

Courtney was waiting at a table in the corner when she entered. He rose clumsily to his feet, looking outsized and uncomfortable in the tea house atmosphere.

Em tightened her lips in a spinsterish manner as Courtney awkwardly conducted her to her chair. This man belonged to the out-of-doors, while Donald was an intensely civilized man. And Duke Courtney would not give way before public opinion as her husband had—no, he wouldn't take the quick way out at the approach of failure. He would fight back. A survivor—

Duke Courtney was both bemused and amused. Little bit of an act, he thought. No sister of Tamsen Tallant's would be so prissy-nice. Then, studying her face with keen blue eyes as they ordered their tea, he decided he was wrong. This was a woman who'd spent a lifetime setting rules for herself. He'd bet that on the inside, she had all the feelings a pretty girl should have. All she needed was a little loosening up. He wished to hell he was the man for the job. Probably, she was married to a poor excuse of a man.

Feeling his eyes on her, Em flushed. "I have no desire to prolong this meeting," she said. "So I'll get to the point. My daughter tells me you know the whereabouts of my sister, Mrs. Tallant—"

"Tamsen? Hell, yes. Been to her house plenty of times before I decided to try the Harrison."

"I am certain you have."

He grinned at her icy tone. "Not for the reasons you're thinkin', lady. Tamsen runs a clean house, but there's some of us goes just for social reasons. Good talk, a drink that ain't doctored. A little entertainment. Just to look at a pretty woman, an' know there's still some, somewhere. But I don't hold with payin' for something—"

"That you can get for free," Em finished for him, her color high. "I find this conversation offensive, sir. I did not come here to discuss my sister's business, but to learn her whereabouts."

"You thinking of joining her?" He had leaned back in his chair, his eyes speculative.

Em flushed again. "I might be," she admitted. "Just for a short visit," she added hastily.

He took a tobacco pouch from his pocket and rolling a cigarette, he called for the plump Russian waitress to bring a candle to light it with. The whole time his eyes were on Em; it made her feel most uncomfortable.

"It's a rough, rugged country in there where she is. And no place fitting for a lady when you get there. How does your husband feel about this?"

"That is none of your business," she said sharply. "But for your information, I am a widow."

"Sa-a-y!" His eyes brightened and his mouth

259

widened in a delighted grin. "That being the case, I'll take you there, myself. No way to get in until spring thaw, but—"

"We will not need your services."

"Who's we?"

"My sister, Arabella, my daughter, and I," Em said, flustered.

"Three women packin' into the wilderness? Hell, no! Look, lady, you bring me some man—a man who's been there and knows the ropes, and I'll direct you right to where your sister lives. Otherwise, forget the whole deal."

Em stood, her face taut with anger. "Then our conversation is at an end. Goodbye, sir."

She snatched up her cloak and walked out into the rain. Duke Courtney, his cigarette burning forgotten in his fingers, watched her go. "If you change your mind, you'll know where to find me," he called. She gave no indication of hearing him.

It was his fault, he thought morosely. His pleasure at learning she was a widow had been undisguised. Probably thought he was still after a dead man's leavin's.

And Tamsen had been wrong about this place. Listening to her tell about Novoarchangelsk one night, he'd got the notion of wintering here, and now here he was stuck until spring. Big Duke Courtney, with the only woman he'd looked at twice mad as hell at him, sitting in a tea house, looking out at the goddamn rain.

Em was furiously flustered as she hurried back toward the castle. That awful man! How dare he think he would take her to Tamsen! Ha! That would be the day! But she had to get the information, someway. Perhaps if Arab talked to him. No! She shook her head, decisively. Despite his obnoxious

260

qualities, he was a most attractive man. Attractive enough to set any young widow's heart beating faster. Except mine, she amended. True, her heart was pounding like fury, but that was from anger at his insolent inference that she, Arab, and Martha could not be trusted to take care of themselves. Well, she would show him! She and Arab would find Tamsen. They had to.

Her steps slowed as she considered alternatives. She could no longer pretend that Donald was alive, and Juan would not return. The ship from San Francisco had already left the harbor, and there would probably not be another till spring.

So where did that leave them? Two women and a child dependent upon the charity of the ruler of a foreign land. They could not live like this forever. They had two choices: to return to California, where nothing awaited them, or to find Tamsen and build some kind of life on the fringes of hers. Neither alternative was acceptable, but the latter made more sense. Tamsen always knew what to do.

In Em's absence, Arab had taken matters into her own hands. She dressed in her best gown and requested an audience with Voedvodski. Dry-eyed, elegantly poised, she told him Em had, at last, faced Donald's death as a reality, and that her own husband, Juan Narváez, had died in his search for gold.

"We must impose upon you until spring," she said firmly. "But we intend to pay our own way. I do have this"—she extended the nugget, clasped in her hand—"and I understand my sister, Mrs. Tallant, once lived in a small house in the settlement and that it is now unoccupied. Perhaps this might be used as a form of rental—"

"But my dear lady"—the governor-general was

261

disturbed—"please remain with us. The very pleasure of your company—"

"It would not be seemly to open a dressmaking establishment in the castle. And this is what we intend to do. Though I thank you."

Voedvodski finally accepted her terms. He would miss them in the castle. He would miss having Em at his side at his banquets, and Arabella to dance—but perhaps they were right. Two bereaved widows might need such a project as the sewing establishment to keep them happily occupied.

Together, Em and Arab went to see the house that would be their home for the winter. The roof had leaked and all the rooms smelled of mildew, but fine furniture stood against tapestries hung to hide unfinished walls. It was not the palatial atmosphere they'd been living in, but with a little work, it would serve them well.

When they had finished, the place had the cozy atmosphere of a real home. They moved in with Helena accompanying them. She would accept no salary. All she wished was to be near the child, whom she adored. Arab and Em were dubious about having an extra mouth to feed, but it soon became apparent that Helena more than paid her way. Their meager diet was supplemented by Indian foods, dried fish, and berries. As they got to know Helena, truly for the first time, they developed a deep fondness for her.

Rain turned to ice, and it was pleasant to stitch at winter gowns for noble wives before the light of their own fire. When Christmas arrived, Igor found a small Sitka spruce for them. He and Martha had great fun decorating it with scraps of silk, velvet, and ribbon left from the sewing. Like two children together, Arab thought, watching them fondly.

On Christmas Eve they had a small party. Em made a cake, and the table was set in festive fashion. Beneath the tree were gifts they'd all made for each other and for Igor and Helena. There was a new warm cloak of many colors for little Martha; it was pieced together from remnants. Em bit her lip, thinking of other Christmases. Even in hard times, they'd somehow managed toys for the child. But now—the cloak must be her one special gift.

They attached the candles to the tree. Igor would be coming soon. He'd said frankly that he was looking forward to the occasion, and Helena was like a child herself with excitement at the preparations. Em and Arab had an unspoken pact that there would be no talk of Donald or Juan tonight. Nothing of grief... it was Christmas Eve....

Igor arrived to find an atmosphere he had never known, a cozy home filled with the scent of spices and greenery, bursting with love and good cheer.

It was well worth missing the banquet at the castle, he thought. He wondered what his life would have been—his and Anya's—if they'd grown up in a home such as this, rather than as the two spoiled darlings of the tsar's glittering court.

He blinked back tears as he knelt to place his small gifts with the others. How he'd wanted to come laden with wealth, with gifts of emeralds and diamonds! But his intuitive good taste had prompted him to make minor purchases at the Tlingit market. Sewing baskets for the women, a pair of fur boots for Martha, food treats for all.

The candles were lighted and Martha rushed from her room to fling herself into Igor's arms. "Merry Christmas!" she shouted. Then there were kisses all round, and she stood back to survey the tree.

"It's the prettiest ever, and I helped. Oh, Mommy, can we open the presents now?"

Gifts were opened and exclaimed over. Later they sat quietly with their refreshments and listened to the sound of singing outside. The members of St. Michael's Church were walking the icy streets, carrying a star and caroling to the homes around the village.

A hush fell in the room as they listened to the miracle of Christmas. They were all startled by a loud knocking sound at the door. Em went to answer it and opened it to find a strange, enormous creature framed against the night.

"What in the world!"

White fur had been cut to form hair and beard, and a red stocking cap was pulled over the head. The beard spilled down over a red plaid shirt, obviously stuffed with something, while another strip of fur surrounded the artificially inflated middle. Blue corduroys were tucked into miner's boots, also decorated with fur. Behind the disguise, recognizable by his immensity and his wide grin, was Duke Courtney.

"You—," Em sputtered, "are you drunk? What do you think you're doing—"

His voice rose over hers. "Ho, ho, ho," he shouted gleefully. "I'm looking for my friend Martha! Does she live here?"

Martha catapulted across the room. "Santy Claus!" she screamed with delight. "You found me!"

"Couldn't come down the chimney," he told the excited little girl. "Too damn hot. Look here, you been a good girl?"

Martha nodded, clasping her hands in anticipation, and he thrust a clumsily wrapped package in her hands. Then, raising his eyes to Em's stunned ones, he gave a broad wink. "Reindeers a-waitin'," he said. "Gotta go. Lot more work to do tonight."

Then he was gone, the doorway frame empty. There was only the distant sound of singing. Em turned. Martha was busily tearing wrappings from her gift. It was an enormous Russian doll. Em had seen and coveted it at the company store. Hugging it to her, Martha repeated the words she'd been saying all evening. "The best Christmas ever!" But this time, they seemed to have a special meaning.

Em returned to her place, for some reason unable to swallow. "Perhaps the cake is a little dry," she said. She was shouted down. It was perfectly delicious! The best she'd made for a long time.

Em put her fork down, knowing what was ailing her. Somewhere outside, there was a very lonely man, and she hadn't even considered inviting him inside. A stranger at the door on Christmas Eve, and she hadn't let him in.

CHAPTER 7

Christmas brought about another change in the little family living in Tamsen's previous home. Helena, in silent Indian fashion, had been observing Arab and Em for a long time. The words uttered by Arab upon arrival, which blamed Tamsen for their plight, had put Helena off. She had been businesslike and remote with all but the child, who reminded her so of her adopted sister, Tamsen.

Now things had settled in her mind. On Christmas Eve, she was treated like one of the family. And so on Christmas morning, using an odd mixture of Tlingit, Russian, and English, she told them of her closeness to Tamsen. She related how, at the wedding ceremony of her relative, her own mother had accepted Tamsen as her child. They heard about how Tamsen had attended her adopted mother's funeral services, mourning with the rest, and distributed gifts according to custom.

Em's eyes blurred. For everything Helena said brought dear Tamsen clearly to mind. "Do you know where she is now?" she asked.

The girl shook her head. "I wished to go with her. She would not take me, saying she wished to spare me that kind of life. I would have gone. I have nothing here—"

"You do know what kind of business Tamsen

intended to begin," Em said carefully. "It is not exactly—"

"I knew. And I would have gone." The girl blushed. "And I would have done anything necessary to help her. Here, I am nothing. Not Russian, not Tlingit. If she could have placed a value on my services—"

Em opened her mouth to scold the girl, then thought better of it. The things Tamsen had done she'd done for the sake of others. Perhaps this Indian-Russian girl was more of a true sister than she. She had no right to judge her, as she had judged Tamsen so many times, without knowing her real motives.

"All I ask," the girl said unhappily, "is that if you go to her, you will take me. I will repay you."

Em found herself promising. She could not detect the expression on Arab's face, a kind of holding back. For Arabella had begun to consider other plans. Igor had been pushing the trip to Russia. She had enough confidence in her abilities to realize he was right when he said a fortune could be made there. There was nothing now to hold her, no beloved Juan to wait for. Only Em and Martha need follow, but Igor had solved that problem, too. He would pay for their passage. Arab could repay him later, when she was a rich and famous favorite at court.

Since they'd moved from the castle, invitations to the banquets had not been extended. Possibly the governor-general considered it poor taste in view of their bereavement. But Arab missed the glamor and glitter of those feasts—the dancing and the adulation of the noblemen—more than she would admit. Since Juan was gone, she must make a life for herself. And since fate had willed it this way, it might as well be a life of her choosing. She held back, though; something was telling her not to mention her new dreams to Em.

Emmeline, in the meantime, continued to take steps toward discovering Tamsen's whereabouts. She made an appointment in the tea house to meet Duke Courtney's partner, McCandless. He evaded her question neatly by saying he hadn't been up in them parts himself. Em knew he was lying. Duke Courtney had already warned him he would be questioned and had coached him on his answer. She couldn't make him give her information he had no intention of divulging, but his words fueled her anger toward his stubborn blond friend.

January passed, its ice-slick frozen ruts occasionally peppered with snow. February came, and toward the end of it, the rains ceased freezing. The warm current that protected Sitka from the rigors of the wintry north seemed to envelop the landscape in a haze of opalescent mist. There was a feeling that the world trembled at the edge of spring. Em and Arab both secretly nursed a sensation of emptiness. They would never see a Sitka late spring and summer such as Tamsen had described, with its brief burgeoning of bloom and berry. They would not be here when the Sitka roses bloomed around the tea houses on the hill.

The governor-general had weighed the nugget and scrupulously returned what he thought to be the difference in rubles to the young women. With that, and with the amount they'd realized in their dressmaking, there was enough money in the house to return to San Francisco, to seek out Tamsen if they knew where to look for her, or to go to Russia. Finally, at Igor's urging, Arab made up her mind.

She broached the subject to Em one pleasant

afternoon as they sat sewing companionably by the fire. Em dropped her needle, her mouth opening in shock. "Go to *Russia?* To St. Petersburg? Arab, you're out of your mind!"

"You don't understand," Arab said doggedly. She outlined Igor's plans in detail, the way he would present her at court and how the tsar would find her charming. Then the sky was the limit as far as their fortunes were concerned.

"I never heard anything so idiotic," Em gasped. "To want to be a common showgirl again! Juan would be furious!"

"Leave Juan out of it! The point is, we can't stay here forever. Somebody's got to earn a living, and that is the only thing I know that I do well." She looked disgustedly at the hem she was stitching and threw the material from her. "One thing for certain, I can't sew!"

"But Russia! How would we get there?"

"We've enough for one fare. Igor has offered to advance the rest."

"Arab, are you in love with Igor?"

"No."

"Then you cannot become indebted to him," Em said, decisively. "It's out of the question, If you go, you go alone."

"I suppose you have a better idea?"

"I suggest we go to Tamsen."

"And I suppose her money's better than Igor's," Arabella flung at her.

"She's our sister. And she would have no reason to expect something in return."

Arab rose to her feet. "Em," she stormed, "you're a prissy idiot! And you know good and well we can't go off hunting Tamsen! If Juan couldn't find her, how could we? If you want to go on thinking like a—a silly jackass—go ahead! But when spring comes, I'll bet you're ready to go along with me."

She left the house, and Em sat staring at the crumpled gown Arab had thrown to the floor. This was the first time they'd quarreled in years. Maybe this idea was just a whim of Arab's. Perhaps her anger was nothing more than one of her tantrums of old, but Em had a frightening feeling she meant what she said.

She was afraid that this would be the worst mistake of their lives. Igor might be correct as to the success Arabella would have in Russia, but a dancer's career was a brief and passing thing. What of the future? The best Arab could hope for would be to become the mistress of some member of a dissolute court. And what would life hold for little Martha?

Em set her lips and called for Helena. "Please send a messenger to tell Mr. Duke Courtney, at the soldiers' barracks, that Mrs. Alden would like to see him at once."

The messenger located him down on the docks where he'd been engaged in helping a fisherman unload his catch. His old clothes were faded and soiled, and his boots glittered with scales as Em led him into the house that appeared so elegant to him.

"Please sit down." She indicated a chair upholstered in a satin material. Duke eyed it dubiously. "If you don't mind, ma'am, I'd rather stand."

Em shrugged, "As you wish." She walked to the window and stood looking out, away from him. "Some time ago, I approached you to get some information about how to find my sister. You refused to answer me at that time unless I proved I

270

had a proper guide to the area where she lives."

"Yes, ma'am, and what I said still goes."

She held up a silencing hand. "At that time, you agreed to lead us in, yourself, in the spring."

His heart leaped at the tack she was taking. "That offer still stands, ma'am."

"Very well. I will accept your offer. But it must be understood that this is a business deal. I cannot afford to pay much, but you will be paid. If your partner wishes to accompany us, and you wish to divide your fee with him, that is your affair."

"It's a deal, ma'am." His quick grin flashed, and he reached out, capturing her small hand in his massive grip. "We'll shake on it."

Em pulled her hand away and placed it behind her back to hide its trembling. "That won't be necessary," she said loftily, "as long as we understand each other."

Duke had been quick to catch her reaction, the widening eyes, the softening of her mouth at his touch. Maybe the woman wouldn't be so hard to loosen up after all, he grinned to himself. Then he said jauntily, "And who's going? How many in the party, ma'am?"

"Myself, my daughter, and Helena." Another long pause. "Perhaps my sister, Mrs. Narváez."

So that's it, he thought. She wants to get little Sis out of here. Maybe she doesn't like the idea of her getting mixed up with that fancy-pants Russian prince. Or maybe they each got ideas of where they want to go, and for Sis, this ain't it. But as much as he looked forward to escorting the lady to the wilds, he had to be honest with himself and with her.

"You still got time to think this over," he cautioned. "If you back out on the deal, it's all right

271

with me. That place of Tamsen's, like I said, she keeps it clean, but it ain't the prime spot for a little girl—"

"And you can mind your own business," she snapped. His face hardened, and she looked at him helplessly, her anger fading. "No, you're quite right. And since you've shown concern for my child's well-being, I suppose I owe you an explanation. Tamsen has a—a knack for keeping her family and business life separate. And she loves Martha more than anything in the world. She won't let anything hurt her."

She dropped her eyes. "I suppose you wonder why I'm going there at all," she said dully. "I guess it's because Tamsen's always been the strong one. With Tamsen, I feel—safe. And the known isn't as frightening as the unknown, while Russia—"

Duke nodded. He'd got the picture now. Sis was pushing for Russia, but Emmeline lived in fear of the unfamiliar. She didn't have the slightest idea of the hellhole she was going to. The black canyon above Yale was enough to give the devil himself nightmares, though it wasn't only the country. The gold-seekers themselves were rougher than hell. It would take more than Tamsen to make a girl like Em feel safe. He groaned as he tried to think of a way to explain.

"Look, honey," he said, with the familiar endearment he'd murmured to a thousand girls in a thousand bars, "you don't understand—"

Em's head jerked up, the wide blue eyes frosty. "*You* don't understand! And the name is Mrs. Alden. Mrs. Donald Alden. Just as you are Mr. Courtney to me, an employee. I shall figure what I consider to be an appropriate salary. If it is satisfactory to you, then I suggest you begin to make

272

preparations for our journey. For now, this conversation is at an end."

"Yes, ma'am." Duke backed away before her furious gaze, reaching the door. Outside, he expelled a breath. "Whew!" For a lady who was weak and helpless, she sure was a hellcat when she was mad. Maybe, just maybe, she'd make it over in New Caledonia after all. And maybe he'd just stick around to watch the fireworks.

After he had gone, Em tried to compose herself. Why was it that that man always brought out the worst in her! Her hand still burned from his touch. For a moment, he'd looked like he might be going to put his arms around her. What would she have done? The very thought gave her a melting sensation. She would have—have *struck* him, of course! Fought herself free as any true lady would! However, for a moment, she had longed—oh, God, she was going to have to travel with him for a long distance. How would she keep him in his place?

Arabella, returning in contrition, noted the brightness of Em's eyes, the jerky, nervous way she spoke as she scolded Arab for going out without her cloak while she grabbed a towel to rub mist from her sister's long, luxuriant hair. Nothing was said of their earlier quarrel, but Arab was unable to contain herself.

"I'm sorry, Em," she wept. "You're right. We have no business going to Russia. It's so far, and the people aren't our kind. It's just that Igor made it seem so exciting, and Em, I'm so tired of being poor!"

"I know," Em said, stricken. Oh, God! Had she done the right thing? There was still time—

"And it's not only that," Arab said in a muffled voice. "I think I wanted to run away from myself, be

273

somebody else for a while. Oh, Em, I feel so guilty!"

"You, guilty? Why, Arab?"

"I feel guilty about Juan." Arabella's face was streaming with tears. "We had an awful fight the day before he left. He was mad because I—I took money for that gypsy dance. I screamed to him that somebody had to make some money—the same way I did to you. And I didn't mean it, Em, either time. I don't know what makes me say such things!"

Em rocked the girl in her arms. "It's all right," she soothed. "And that's not why Juan left, I'm sure of it!"

"But that's not all I feel guilty about," she confessed. "Sometimes I think I'll die without Juan! Oh, Em, I loved him! Loved him! And then sometimes I get angry because he went off like he did, leaving us behind—"

Em heard her out, dry-eyed. Then she said, "You're only human, Arab. Maybe guilt is a part of grief, I don't know. But I feel better, knowing I'm not the only one."

Arab lifted her head, startled, as Em went on. "I tried to keep Donald from doing what he thought was right—paying off his friends who had lost by taking his advice. Instead of telling him I was proud of him, that we'd manage some way, I—I immediately thought of Tamsen, telling him *she* could help us regain our fortunes.

"I didn't know what I was doing to him, Arab! I helped destroy him! And—worse, I feel the anger you mentioned, too. I feel sometimes that he deserted me, left me to face life alone . . . and the way he did it, with no warning—"

"Oh, Em!"

"And I have something worse on my conscience," Em went on doggedly. "I loved Donald like a—a

274

wife. A nice dutiful little wife. I loved cooking for him, keeping a tidy house, playing hostess to his dinners, making him proud of me. But—we didn't have what you had, Arab, you and Juan. Maybe it was his fault, maybe it was mine—maybe I'm not capable of loving a man—that way."

Arab put a small hand over Em's mouth to stop her flow of words. "We're not thinking, Em, not really thinking at all. If Donald and Juan could hear us now, wouldn't they forgive us? You know they would, so why do we torture ourselves?"

Em looked shocked, but her face finally brightened. "You're right, I never thought of it that way. We've both been such awful fools!"

"And we'll cease being fools at this moment," Arab said practically. "No more self-recrimination. No more running away. But what are we going to do?"

"I've already made arrangements to go to Tamsen. Duke—Mr. Courtney knows where she is, and I've made arrangements to employ him to guide us in."

"Duke Courtney? The big man with the ring? Well, I'll be switched!" Arabella was surprised to find that gentle Em had taken the reins in her hands to such an extent. And most surprising of all, that the name of Duke Courtney had brought a definite blush to her sister's fair cheeks.

CHAPTER 8

When, Helena was told of the impending journey, a few un-Indian-like tears rolled down her cheeks. "I am happy," she said. "I will pack."

The difficult task was to tell Igor. Arab delayed it for as long as she could, despite Em's constant prodding. "The man's in love with you, Arab. Don't keep him dangling. It isn't fair."

Finally she summoned up her courage. They met at a tea house, and he listened to her decision, the impish laughter fading from his eyes.

"How did he take it?" Em wanted to know when Arab reached home.

"I don't know," Arab worried. "I really don't know." She had grown quite fond of the handsome little prince and wouldn't want to hurt him for the world. For a time, his visits made life almost bearable; his harmless flirting, the way he entertained Martha, were special times in their life in Sitka.

They didn't see him for several days. Then one night during a banquet at the castle to celebrate the arrival of a Russian ship anchored in the harbor, he appeared at their door. Arab gave a sigh of relief as she took his cloak. "We've missed you," she said. She led him to his favorite chair before the fire, and Em excused herself to get refreshments, taking a reluctant Martha with her.

Prince Igor waited until the door closed behind them, then, with a comically desperate expression, dropped to his knees before Arabella.

"I assume this is the proper position," he said wryly. "For it is something I have never concerned myself with, nor ever thought I would." He took her hands in his own, and looked at her with a yearning sincerity. "Arabella—I love you. I want you to be my wife. I will be boarding the ship in the harbor when it returns to Russia. I want you to come with me, to come to Russia, not as an entertainer, but as my wife. I can offer you riches, a place at court—"

Arab's breath caught on a ragged sob. "Oh, Igor, I can't! Don't you see, I like you. I like you so much! But love—" Oh, God! He looked as if he might be going to cry!

The door opened and Martha bounced in, followed by Em with a tray. They both stopped, staring at the kneeling prince in astonishment. In a trice, he grinned his impish grin and threw his hands up in a dramatic gesture.

"Caught in the act," he groaned. "The first time I have made a marriage proposal, and I have an audience. Worse." He clapped a hand to his forehead. "I have been spurned!"

Rising, he went to Em, still standing in the doorway, unable to move. He knelt once more. "I don't suppose you would have me, dear lady? Out of pity?"

Em turned pink, then laughed. "Igor, I'm very fond of you. But I think—no, not at the moment."

"Spurned once more." He rolled his eyes in mock tragedy. "Strange that I only feel romantically toward the women of this family! Tamsen, Arab, and you, Em. Ah!" He moved toward Martha on his knees.

"Young lady, I know that I am older than you, but I can wait. Would you consent to become my princess?"

Martha giggled, her eyes shining. "Would you kill a mean old dragon for me?"

"Indeed, my lady! With my trusty sword. Where is he?" He made a show of looking about the room as if expecting to be attacked at any moment.

"And would we live happy ever after?"

"Most definitely."

Martha put a fist beneath her small chin and studied him carefully. "Thank you for asking me, Prince Igor, but I'm 'fraid I can't. I thought I wanted to marry a prince, but I've almost d'cided I'd rather marry a Duke."

Em, making the connection between Martha's statement and Duke Courtney, gasped. Igor carried on with his role of rejected suitor. "My heart is broken," he said. "Only a cup of tea and a cookie will mend it." He looked meaningfully at Martha. "And it can only be brought to me by the hand of the most beautiful girl in the world." Giggling, she ran to do his bidding.

Igor did not stay long. He had to prepare for his journey. He would not have time to call before leaving, since the ship sailed the day after tomorrow. But he would be pleased if they would come aboard to say farewell. Then he said, "And remember, my proposal still waits, should any of you fair ladies change your mind."

Arab stood at the door and watched him go, feeling a pang at seeing the fair head bent, the strutting walk missing. It would hurt to say that last goodbye.

The Russian ship sailed, with full ceremony. The governor-general himself came aboard to hear the speeches. Generous dispensations of rum brought tears to the eyes of the many sentimental bearded men. Prince Igor and his staff were surrounded by well-wishers.

Arab, Em, and Martha stood quietly to the rear, wondering whether they'd be able to say goodbye after all. Then the crowd parted and Igor saw them. He made his way to them. Behind his mask of merriment, his eyes were dark and haunted.

"My favorite ladies!" he sang out. "Is it too much to expect a kiss to speed me on my way, young Martha?"

The little girl complied, and he turned to Em. With a small embarrassed laugh, she touched her lips to his cheek.

He looked uncertainly at Arab. She threw her arms around him in an agony of loss. Lifting her mouth to his, she said, "Oh, Igor! I'll miss you so!"

He kissed her, holding her tightly for a long time, groaning, "My dear one! Oh, my dear one!" Then he stepped away. "It was very kind of you to see me off," he said almost formally. "It is a memory I will treasure." Looking at Martha, his impishness returned. "I shall tell all the ladies who pursue me at Alexander's court of the young woman who broke my heart!"

Once again, he was swept off into a group of departing noblemen. Em, Arab, and Martha returned to shore. They stood watching as the vessel began to move, waving at the prince who remained at the rail, his small figure diminished by distance, and finally fading away.

The women returned home in silence; except for Helena, Igor had been their only true friend. They would miss him more than he would ever know, though they, too, would soon go off to an unknown

279

country, under the guidance of a man they did not know.

Without Igor's lively presence, the days passed dully. Em tried, where possible, to conduct her business with Duke Courtney by messenger rather than in person. She sent a list of belongings she planned to take for his approval. It was returned to her with nearly everything crossed out. *"Take only necessaries"* was written at the bottom. *"Two outfits. Best get men's clothes. Flannel underwear. Heavy boots. 1 frypan, tin plates and cups for along trail. What you take, you carry."*

"Of all the nerve," Em raged. She shot back a note. *"What you ask is impossible. Many items I mentioned are mementos of our late husbands, possessions we treasure. They cannot be left behind. And dressing as men is out of the question! You forget yourself, sir!"*

The return message was terse and laconic. *"Remember your late husbands ain't carrying the load. You are. From Westminster on, is deck passage. Couple of women, lots of men. Dressed fancy, you ask for what you get. Men's clothes best for trail, unless you want your drawers to show when you fall down."*

Em was speechless with anger. Arab took the wadded note from her hand and read it. "It makes sense, Em. I think we should do what he says. We could get the clothes a little large; put our hair up, no one would ever know we weren't—"

"I would know," Em seethed. "It isn't decent! And that man knows it! He's sitting over there in the barracks laughing at us right now!"

"Well, I'm going to go along with his orders."

"And I'm not!"

Emmeline almost succumbed when Arabella

280

returned from the company store and emerged from the bedroom in her newly purchased clothing. In a heavy wool shirt of gray and green plaid over gray corduroy trousers, her hair up, with a wide-brimmed man's hat covering it, she looked like a slender, very handsome boy. But to Em's consternation, she walked like one, her clean limbs swinging freely without hampering petticoats as she strode back and forth on parade.

Em would wear her blue wool, with matching bonnet. At least it was serviceable and covered her decently. She did accede in lightening her load. The items on her original list would, according to Arab, require a dozen mules. And Em, realizing that Courtney meant what he said, that she would have to carry what she brought, reluctantly weeded them out. Donald's stepmother's tea service was eliminated; the bulky manuscript of a book he'd begun on the new state of California went; his old smoking jacket to which she had clung, things she'd brought with her in anticipation of his following— once again she had to accept merely the memory of her life with Donald.

Oddly enough, Courtney had left one unserviceable item on the list he'd marked over, which was little Martha's doll. Only because he gave it to her, Em thought bitterly. Yet in her heart, she knew it wasn't so, because the child and the doll were inseparable. It would add to the child's feeling of security in a strange new place. Damn the man! So—so obnoxious in some areas and so sensitive in others. The first attribute overshadowed the second, and she must never forget it.

As winter advanced toward spring, there was nothing to do but wait for a ship to touch these shores and head for the coast of another country, where their real journey would begin. The waiting wore on Em's nerves. For one thing, she had taken for granted that Tamsen would still be in the gold mining area. What if she'd gone? Returned to San Francisco, with Nell, Dusty, and the girls? Or she might even come back here, hoping against hope that her husband had returned from Russia to start over with her.

To cover the situation, she insisted that Courtney draw a map for her, pinpointing the area where they were going. She made copies, sending one with a message to Madam Franklin's parlor in San Francisco in case Tamsen was back there. Another she took to the governor-general himself.

"In case anyone needs to find us," she told him. He looked at her, pityingly, and she knew that he was thinking she still hadn't come to terms with Donald's death. But it wasn't that, not at all. They were going into a wilderness with a man she didn't quite trust. And it suddenly seemed important to let someone—anyone—know where they were going.

The maps had been a stupid idea. Tamsen would know where she had lived and how to find it. The message would have sufficed—a full description of their guide, so that if they were murdered, his name and appearance would be on record. But it had seemed the thing to do. Surely someone, somewhere, would care enough to seek them out if they disappeared forever on this journey....

Arabella tried to quell Em's fears. The man was honest, or else he would have pocketed the gold nugget he found on Juan's body. And Martha liked him, didn't she? Children had an innate sense about people. If the man was less than polite, it might be possible Em's own attitude had put him off. Had she thought of that? Duke Courtney didn't seem the type who enjoyed being bossed by a woman.

Maybe Arab was right, Em thought. She considered sending a messenger, asking him to call for a discussion of their journey, then changed her mind. She would only be doing what Arab said, ordering him to come at her beck and call. She would take a walk with Martha. If they happened to meet the man, she would be friendly—not familiar—just friendly. After all, they would be forced to endure each other's company for some time.

She heard him before she saw him. "Hi—eee—yah!" No mistaking that immense, booming, gleeful voice. She turned a corner just in time to see a huge Russian crash into the side of a building. He gained his feet, shook himself, and bored back toward his opponent, who shook his blond hair back with a laugh and struck him again.

"It's Duke!" Martha shouted. "Look, Mommy, he's winning!"

Em turned her daughter about with a firm hand. "Don't look at those—those ill-bred ruffians," she choked. "We're going home!"

She got even angrier later that night when she heard his "Hi—eee—yah!" sound in the room she shared with Martha. She found the child in her nightdress, fists doubled, in a pugnacious stance as she threatened her shadow on the wall.

Settling her with a spank followed by a hug, Em returned to an amused Arab. "I swear, I don't know what I'm going to do with that girl. Or about that man! If I can't stand him for five minutes, this is going to be a miserable trip!"

They didn't see or hear from Courtney again until a peremptory message came. *"Ship in harbor. Be ready to leave Wednesday morning."* The sisters looked at each other in consternation. Waiting for a date of departure had seemed interminable, but now it seemed all too soon.

They boarded the ship as directed. Arab and Helena were trim and boyish-looking in their male clothing. Em had made a special point of her and Martha's appearance. The child wore her Christmas cloak and boots, with a warm alpaca gown beneath. Em had donned her serviceable blue wool. Courtney's eyes flicked over them all, and Em set her jaw defiantly. Let him say something about the way she was dressed! Let him just dare.

He did not. He looked instead at the size of the burden she carried; she staggered a little under its weight. "Packed wrong," he said. "Have to show you how."

"I am the one who will carry it," she reminded him. "And I prefer it this way."

He only shrugged. "Suit yourself," he said.

As the ship lifted anchor, there was a minor miracle, of sorts. This morning the small island chose to give them, in parting, what it had not offered them in welcome, or during their stay. The sun beamed through the mist in pale lemony rays; Mount Edgecumbe stood sharply defined, its snow-crowned cone clear against the sky; the mountains to the southeast wreathed in soft haze were a study in cool pastels. The settlement they were leaving looked like a watercolor painting, the weathered wood of its buildings picking up tints of rose, of pink and blue. Light struck the windowed belfry of Baranov Castle, reflecting in cool flames. And for some reason, the bell of St. Michael's was chiming.

"It's strange, isn't it," Em said softly. "Everything

284

seems so much more beautiful when one looks back."

Arab agreed. But Duke Courtney did not. He had hefted the pack an exhausted Em had set down on the deck. "Mrs. Alden," he yelled, "what in the hell have you *got* in this thing!"

CHAPTER 9

Duke Courtney's attitude persisted throughout the steamship journey. Em, sensing that Arab and McCandless were perhaps laughing at her, remained in her stateroom until she heard Duke believed her to be seasick. That brought her on deck in a hurry. Em was discovering hidden parts of her nature. She was short with Arab and unusually cross with Martha. That fact did not go unremarked by Courtney.

"Leave the kid alone," he would growl. "You're only young once. She's goin' to have a tough enough time on the trail."

"I will not have her talking to every sailor and—and low-life on the boat," Em flared. "It is—unseemly."

"So you want to turn her into a damn little prissypants, too good to associate with the people she's going to be around? She's gonna be goddamn lonesome, you can count on that! Lonesome as hell."

"Your language is offensive! And I'll thank you to remember she's my daughter, and her upbringing is my responsibility."

He looked at her oddly, hurt. "Suit yourself," he said, but in the end, he had his own way. Martha was as easy to restrain as the wind, and finally, Em gave up. Thank God, the voyage would not be much longer.

Another side to her character that she discovered was an avid, burning curiosity. Whenever she found Mac McCandless alone, she somehow managed to turn the subject to Duke Courtney. Only because she wanted to know what made a man like that tick, she told herself. He was so unlike Donald.

McCandless was only too happy to oblige. Duke's ma and pa were real class, his pa sent out from England to a position in the Hudson's Bay Company. His ma was a teacher, taught the few children in the little settlement. That's why Duke had so much education. Mac had been a fur-trapper then, coming often to the fort, so he'd known them all. Knowed Duke since he was a leetle shaver.

There was a raid on the fort. Indians. And Duke's ma and pa were killed. "I was there at the time," the older man said. "And that young devil didn't cry er nuthin'. Jes' took his pa's gun and lined hisself up alongside me." Mac went through a pantomime of shooting and reloading. "Bang! Bang! Musta got twenty, thirty of them heathens his own self.

"Then him not having nobody, me not having nobody, we teamed up. Best thing I ever done. He musta saved my old hide a dozen times er more. He's hell on wheels, Duke is."

His talk went into a meandering version of Courtney's supposed heroic actions. The time he'd taken on a gunfighter in a St. Louis bar, and the bear he killed with nothing but his knife and his bare hands, yesiree! How he'd gone into a blizzard after two men who were lost and appeared out of the snow, carrying one under each arm. "An' I sez, 'Duke, boy, is that you?' an' he sez, 'Well, it sure ez hell ain't Santy Claus,'"

The tales were all highly embroidered, Em was certain of that. For a time, though, she felt a deep pity for the child who had lost his parents in such a terrible way. She caught herself up short. It was impossible to think Duke Courtney had *ever* been a child. He was born rude, crude and overbearing.

When Courtney appeared on one side of the deck, Em went to the other. Arab finally began to tease her about her game of hide and seek. Yet when Em saw the man in conversation with Arab, she felt compelled to join them. It was an older sister's duty to protect a defenseless young widow—

It was a relief when they landed at Asquamalt. From there, they had to walk to Fort Victoria. They set out, Martha running far ahead, circling back to announce new discoveries. Courtney, Arab, Helena, and McCandless walked with easy strides, carrying their packs with ease. Em, red-faced, her blond-brown hair escaping its moorings to curl in tendrils about her perspiring brow, stumbled after them. Her skirts were heavy and hampering; the pack was far too heavy. She would have to lighten the load somehow. And that—that ill-mannered boor might have offered to lend a hand. Mac hadn't offered, either, probably on Courtney's orders. Only Arab had dropped back, asking, "Em, can I help you? Switch packs for a while?"

"I'm doing fine," she'd said shortly. And Arab took her at her word.

When they reached the rocky valley where they would camp, it was filled with white men and a multitude of Indians. Courtney, Helena, and McCandless, Martha in tow, went in search of firewood. Em and Arab tried, futilely, to erect some sort of shelter for privacy. A group of rough, jeering men gathered around. They ignored Arab, dressed as a boy, but leered at Em; they ridiculed her as the shelter collapsed.

"Go to it, Sis," one cried. And they began to make bets between them on how long the shelter would stand. "Put it up for you, sweetheart, if I kin share it" and "How about rentin' me a room fer the night?"

Duke Courtney returned, set his firewood down, and walked toward the knot of onlookers. The ringleader backed away before his bulk. "No harm intended, mister," he said. "Didn't know the lady was yer wife."

The watchers melted away. Courtney built up the fire in silence. Then, his anger barely restrained, he said, "I will fix your shelter, if you will cook. You *can* cook?"

Em didn't deign to answer. She would show him! Within minutes, she had a fire going, bacon sizzling, and was making biscuits as she'd learned to do on the trail. Duke soon appeared and she was conscious that he was watching her with her sleeves rolled, flour to the elbows; she had a feeling of pleasure at the sense he approved.

He only said, "Use a lighter hand on the cooking from now on. Supplies gotta last us a long time."

She was slightly mollified when, after a meal that they all attacked voraciously, he said, "Best grub I've had in years." Mac echoed his words.

It was nice sitting in the firelight. Only a faint mist was falling, a relief after the heavy rains they'd become accustomed to. Courtney's features, across the fire, seemed blurred and softened. Again Em was struck by the thought that he was a very handsome man in repose, and her pulse began to beat a little faster. Then he rose and with Mac went to their own shelter, leaving Em and Arab with the mess to clean up. Em was tired, almost too stiff to move, and Martha must be put to bed. By the time she returned from kissing Martha good night, Arab had things well cleared and cleaned. Finishing the last details, banking the fire for the morning, they went to their tent, where Arab fell into bed, fully dressed.

After a few minutes, hearing Em rummage around, Arab asked, irritably, "Em, what *are* you doing?"

"Trying to find a nightdress in this mess," Em snapped.

Arab groaned. "You'll have to sleep in your clothes on the trail, you idiot!"

Em intended to observe the proprieties. And besides that, her stays hurt, and her petticoats were bedraggled with mud. She kept on searching. Finally, lighting a lantern, she located her long, high-necked flannel gown and donned it, not realizing her figure was cast against the canvas in silhouette and that a watching ruffian was enjoying the view. He had seen the men go to one tent and the women to another. And he was not one to let a poor lady spend the night in loneliness—

The watcher waited an hour, two, as he fortified himself with the bottle of whiskey he'd brought along. In darkness, he stumbled across the way to the small shelter, dropping to his hands and knees to crawl through the opening. Then something caught him by the ankles and he was pulled out backwards, scrabbling for a handhold as he went.

"Musta made a mistake," he said, grinning foolishly up into Duke Courtney's irate face.

"You sure as hell did!" Picking the man up by the seat of his pants and his shirt collar, Courtney pitched him into the darkness. And Em emerged from the shelter, a ghostly figure in her white flannel nightdress, a stick of stovewood in her hand. Duke stared at her, at her apparel, his gaze moving from her head to her feet.

He shook his head a little as if he couldn't believe his eyes. "Well, goddamn," he said slowly. "Goddamn!" He turned on his heels and went back to his own bed.

The next morning, Em felt stiff and ached all over. Just getting to her feet was an effort. She bent over the cookfire while Arab and the men dismantled their shelters; Martha raced around with delight at a new morning. At last, breakfast was over and the plates were wiped clean; she went to put hers and Martha's in her pack.

It had been reduced from a burdensome bundle to a small neat package. Two of her four gowns, the velvet and the taffeta, had been wadded up and thrust in the mud beneath a bush. Along with them, her two nightdresses. The flannel, and the muslin with lace insertion. Petticoats, corsellette, chemise, all her lovely handmade underthings, ruined! And she knew who had done it. The thought of those big hands rummaging through her intimate clothing made her blood boil. And where was her Bible?

She marched to where Duke Courtney stood waiting and placed her hands on her hips, demanding to know the Bible's whereabouts. Or did he sully the Good Book, too, as he did everything else he touched?

"Mrs. Alden," he sighed with exaggerated patience. "I hefted that thing. Weighed five pounds or more. God will have to step in to get you where you're going, but that much dead weight sure as hell won't help." He jerked a thumb toward the drunk across the way, snoring in his blankets beside a dead fire. Her Bible lay atop his recumbent form. "Figured there might be somebody that needs it more'n you. Found one right off."

Em froze him with a look, then took a step toward

the sleeping man. He yawned and stirred, and she retreated nervously. Let it go, she thought, her eyes burning with tears of loss and humiliation. Let everything go! What does it matter, anyway?

The pack was much lighter, and after a while she was grateful for it. In Fort Victoria, while Duke Courtney made arrangements for a steamer to Westminster, she made a few more purchases that added to its weight. A man's shirt, trousers, a soft felt hat that she could fold away and conceal. For she wasn't certain she would be able to bring herself to wear such clothing, after all. She would wait until they were farther from crowded places, if she decided to don them.

She had bought boy's clothing for Martha, too, but her daughter's transformation would also be delayed. Her pack was larger and heavier, with the addition of her purchases, and she waited for Courtney's disapproval. He just looked at it and at her and said nothing.

The journey to Westminster was uneventful. There they boarded a sternwheeler that would take them to the end of navigable waters—to a small town called Yale. The vessel was overloaded, packed with rough and rowdy men who had come from all parts of the world to seek their fortunes. At the sight of a woman, their jaws dropped, and more than one lewd comment reached Em's ears.

Finally, she turned on Courtney. "Did you hear what that man said to me? Are you going to let him—?"

Duke Courtney wore an expression of unconcern. "None of my affair. I'm paid to guide—an' advise. You didn't take my advice, so you're payin' for it now. Hell, it's not my problem."

She whirled away from him and forced her way

through grinning men toward the rail. At the sight of the tumbling yellow water, carrying broken chunks of ice downriver, she choked back a cry. A slab struck the side of the ship with a resounding thump, and Em shuddered at the sound. Mac had pushed his way to stand beside her. "Don't let it skeer you missus," he said, amused. "You think this is sump'n, wait'll you git a squint at Hell's Gate."

He gestured toward the canyon walls, growing steeper, more terrifying as they proceeded. "Black Canyon makes this here look like a durn hole pissed in th' sand." Catching her look of outrage, he lowered his eyes and mumbled, "S'cuse me. I keep fergittin' yer a woman."

I wish everyone else would, Em thought forlornly, as she fought her way back to where Martha waited with Arab and Helena. She would change to men's dress the minute she reached Yale.

They were not destined to reach the town at the end of their journey by water. It was raining, and the majority of the passengers had huddled away from the wet, seeking every shelter and overhang to catch a few winks before beginning the long trek by foot. The small party seeking Tamsen had the railing to themselves. Duke Courtney was giving a running commentary regarding their surroundings. "Hill's Bar." He pointed to a group of buildings. "Wickedest place in the world right now."

Martha, standing on the lower railing, bending over to view the floating ice, looked up with interest. "Mr. Whitfield, back home, used to go to a bar. He got drunk." She gave a parody of a drunken man, and Em snapped at her.

"Be careful! You'll fall. And it's not that kind of bar!"

Courtney laughed. "This is a gold bar we're talkin'

about, missy. Sometimes sand or gravel builds up in a river and catches the gold when it washes down. Makes it easier to find. Then people come to look for gold, and build a little town. That's what Hill's Bar is."

"Could I find some?"

Duke grinned at the excitement in the little girl's voice. "You betcher boots you can. I'll help you look for it myself." Em had turned deaf ears. Her whole being concentrated on those swirling chunks of ice on the tawny river as they moved away from the ship and back again—A heavy thump jarred the vessel and it suddenly yawed, swung sideways, and struck a rocky projection. With a thud Em got knocked off her feet. She screamed and snatched for Martha's skirts, but it was too late—

The child went over, head first into the ice-studded Fraser beneath them. There was a glimpse of her small upturned face, mouth open in a cry of fear, and then she went under, dragged down by the weight of her skirts.

Em regained her feet and climbed the railing, and was about to follow her daughter into the water when she found herself pulled back, gripped tightly in Mac's lean old arms. She fought and kicked, screaming at him to let her go.

"It's all right, ma'am," he kept saying. "Duke'll git her. Now, you jes' gentle down—"

Now she saw two heads in the water, Martha's—and Duke Courtney's. He'd reached her. Her black hair streamed out across his shoulder as he battled against the current that was sweeping them downstream. The stern wheel had stopped and the vessel drifted with them, still out of control. A chunk of ice bore down upon the pair in the river, and Em closed her eyes.

"Oh, my God!"

But when she opened them, she saw a rope had been thrown from the ship's stern. Martha was slung over his shoulder like a sack of meal and Duke was climbing the rope, hand over hand.

Em's knees went slack for a moment, but she was at Martha's side when the little girl was laid upon the deck. Courtney barked at her to stand away as he worked over the small limp form. Martha returned to life with a strangled scream.

Em dropped to the deck beside her, holding her shivering body close. Blood was bright on the forehead below the tangled hair, and Em wiped it away with the hem of her skirt—dear God, she'd been hurt. But it was not Martha's blood; there were no cuts or abrasions. Looking up at Courtney towering above her, she saw a deep gash at the side of his head where floating ice had struck him. "You're hurt," she said, half-rising—but he was gone to lend a hand to the seamen who were fighting to keep the crippled ship in midstream.

A large piece of ice had swung in toward the stern wheel that powered the boat, striking a blow that put it out of commission. The vessel wallowed and floundered like a beached fish and moved steadily backward downstream. They had reached Hill's Bar once more.

A coil of rope was thrown to watchers on shore. A man leaped to catch it to secure it to a mooring post. When the stern was secured, the nose of the vessel started to swing out and away, so another rope had to be tied for the ship to stay lengthwise against the bar.

Em, Arab, and Helena were oblivious to the dangers they'd passed through. They were busy chafing the child's hands, trying to warm her. Martha's lips were blue, and she shook with a chill. "We've got to get her someplace where there's a fire," Em said distractedly. "Get something hot inside her."

Courtney and McCandless appeared. Duke Courtney picked Martha up as though she were weightless. "I've found a place," he growled. "And we've got to get off. This boat isn't going anywhere for a long time. Get your packs."

He strode away and the girls obeyed, then went hurrying after. When they reached the two-story house, Duke entered before them; he disappeared up the stairs with the little girl still in his arms. They all followed, taking no notice of their surroundings or the men who watched them ascend.

"I'll be damned," one man said to the other. "Did you recognize that girl? That's Mrs. Alden—the senator's wife."

John Bagley's jaw dropped. "No," he said. "It can't be! Mrs. Alden, here? Aw-w, Ned! Hell no, can't be!"

Upstairs, the men waited outside while the women stripped wet clothing from the shivering little girl and wrapped her in warm blankets. When they entered, Courtney built up a roaring fire in the stone fireplace; Mac produced a bottle from his pocket. "Give 'er a swig," he said. "Help ward off pneumony."

Em looked at it doubtfully, but Arab put the bottle to Martha's lips. The child strangled and sputtered at the first swallow, but she soon stopped shaking.

After her daughter was no longer an immediate concern, Em assessed Courtney's condition. He was still in his wet clothes, his head wound bleeding.

"Let me fix that," she murmured, reaching out a

296

hand to touch his face. He flinched as though she'd struck him, his eyes going dark.

"It'll be all right, ma'am. Mac here'll take care of it. He's done for me before." He started to back through the open door.

"Wait—do you have a room?"

"We'll bed down in the stables, ma'am."

"Mr. Courtney, Duke!" He turned at the sound of the urgency in her voice. "I want to thank you! To tell you how everlastingly grateful I am to you for my—my baby would have drowned. I wish there was some way I could express—"

"But there is, ma'am," he interrupted.

She looked at him in surprise. "Anything," she whispered.

"Get rid of that damn-fool get-up that almost sunk us both today! My God! Ten yards of clothes on a kid that size? Get her some decent stuff—pants, shirt, something she can move around in. Might save her life. Hell, she ain't gonna shock nobody's modesty!"

"Mr. Courtney—"

"I know. My language offends you," he said. "So if you'll excuse me, I'll take my offensive self down to the stables, get out of these wet duds, and have myself a good stiff drink!"

"He's right, you know," Arab said seriously. Helena nodded her head in agreement.

"Yes, I do know. I was going to tell him so. But it is very difficult to tell Mr. Courtney anything!" Em's color was high. "Right now, I'm going downstairs to see if I can find someone to fix Martha a nice hot cup of tea."

She descended the steps, stepping out into the enormous common room. There were tables and chairs and a bar along one end of the room with a pimple-faced boy behind it. Besides the stairs was a rolltop desk, a man with gartered sleeves working behind it. Another gentleman sat watching him, astride a chair. They both leaped to their feet at her entry; Ned McGowan's face split into a grin as he bowed mockingly.

"You see, Judge, I was right. Hill's Bar is being treated to some mighty fine company these days. First a whorehouse madam—and now, her sister, the senator's wife. Wouldn't surprise me a bit if that redhead didn't show up."

Em had been struck dumb at the sight of the two familiar faces. Frantically, she searched for their names. Donald had despised them both. McGowan, that was one of them. And Judge? Judge Bagley. Both of them had been run out of California for their nefarious activities."

Em had regained her poise. "It's always nice to see old friends," she said, "but as you know, there was an accident. My daughter nearly drowned. I wonder—I wonder if you could tell me where I might find a cup of tea. She's thoroughly chilled—"

"Shanks'll bring it up." McGowan's evil mouth twisted in a grin. "Then later, maybe, we can have a little get-together. Talk about old times."

"I'm afraid that will have to wait for another visit. I must return to my daughter. If she recovers sufficiently, we will leave in the morning."

McGowan's smile turned nasty. "Sure," he sneered. "Well, Shanks will bring your tea."

Em returned to their room, trying to swallow back terror. She felt as if she'd landed in a den of thieves. But why fear thieves if one had nothing worth stealing? Nothing at all.

Perhaps she should tell Duke Courtney that their hosts were of dubious character. Still smarting at his last remarks, she decided against it. But she wished there was a lock on the door.

CHAPTER 10

Duke stopped in the stables just long enough to change his clothes and have his head attended to. Then he went down to the diggings where the miners worked like ants, to look for somebody his size. Since the killing of his parents, compulsive fighting had become a way of life with him, a way to let off steam.

The Alden woman had no idea what a close call that had been today. It hadn't just been a question of rescuing the little girl, but of sorting her out from her tangled skirts that had wrapped around them both and hampered his movements. A narrow squeak. For a while, he'd thought they'd both go under.

Right now, he felt like hitting somebody, and he couldn't hit a lady. He found his match down on the docks, a giant black-bearded man named Pierre. First a shove, then, "What the hell are you doing?"

"Minding my own t'am business, fren'. W'at you t'ink you're doing?"

Words led to words, a blow to blows, and soon they were engaged in a joyous rough-and-tumble that drew a crowd. Above the sounds of fists smacking against flesh rose Duke's gleeful shout. The onlookers cheered stranger and friend alike, until at last the two men came together in a grip neither could break. As if by mutual consent they

300

released their holds at the same time, stepping backward, eyeing each other in admiration.

"One t'am good fighter, you," Pierre grinned, despite a bloodied lip.

"Purty damn good yourself," Duke said ruefully, rubbing a blackened eye.

"Come, I buy you dreenk, eh?"

The two walked away, arms draped over each other's shoulders in comradely fashion.

"Nevair have I had fight so good," Pierre told Courtney as they entered his shack. He took a bottle from a chest and opened it, handing it to his guest, who choked on the first swallow.

"Nor whiskey so bad," Duke said wryly.

Pierre had an explanation for that. In his broken English, he explained that everything in Hill's Bar was controlled by two men, McGowan and Bagley, two cheating cutthroats who had been chased out of California. They had a monopoly on everything. Land, whiskey. Even the Hill's one woman, who had men lined up for her favors, had to pay them a share of her income.

Old Indian Annie was dead now. McGowan and Bagley had sent outside for replacements. Time had passed and they hadn't arrived, but Pierre knew the way the two brigands operated. One day, a man would come through with his wife and take a room at their place. Then, "Ze husban', poof!" Pierre snapped his fingers. "Ze woman, she stay."

"Their place, these men you mentioned; it's the big house?"

"*Oui.*"

Duke was on his feet. "Goddamn! Out of th' fryin' pan into the fire! You're sure of this, my friend? That these men commit murder and then—"

"Zere is no law 'ere, my frien'."

301

Duke Courtney made his way back to the stables, head lowered, thinking hard. They would try to make it on foot to Yale, but from what he remembered, things weren't much better there. And it wasn't a good idea to move Martha until they knew she'd recovered from her shock. It was possible that the talkative Frenchman was a bigmouth like Mac, he thought, grinning, but it wouldn't hurt to keep an eye on things.

He walked about the house in the fading light. It was built with its back against a solid wall of rock, sheltered by a natural projection at one side. Duke looked at that wall, musing. It was steep, but it could be climbed. There was a narrow ledge two feet from the window of the room where the women would sleep. A man could spend the night there, if he had to, and be at hand if an emergency arose.

He went back to the stables to discuss the situation with McCandless. Maybe he'd got some kind of slant on the situation.

McCandless had. That pimple-faced boy who worked behind the bar had come to him with a message and a sizable sum of money. The ladies had decided the journey ahead was too rough for them and hoped he and Duke would consider this sum sufficient recompense for their trouble in guiding them this far. They were now to consider their obligation fulfilled and to go on about their business.

"What do you think, Mac?"

He grinned. "Bullshit."

"My thoughts exactly. Now, look, here's what we're gonna do."

They repacked their gear and went down to the waterfront where Pierre was already back at work. As they went, Mac was arguing loudly all the way.

302

When they found Pierre, Duke told him they were leaving and that he just wanted to shake his hand once more.

"Damn-fool idea," Mac growled. "Had me a notion to get in a good night's drinkin' before we hit th' trail."

Duke looked at him belligerently. "I said we're headin' out. You travelin' with me, or not?"

"I'll go along," Mac said. "But hell, Duke—"

"Then it's settled." With a punch to the shoulder and a crunching handshake, Duke Courtney said goodbye to his new friend and they headed away from Hill's Bar.

Reaching a spot about a mile away, they found a small rift in the canyon wall. There they stowed their gear, sat down, and waited until after nightfall. McCandless took a slug of whiskey and poured the remainder down his front; they retraced their steps. At the outskirts of Hill's Bar, they separated, and Duke drifted from shadow to shadow until he reached the house backed against the rocky cliff. Mac didn't attempt to hide his entry.

A small shambling figure, who appeared to be very drunk, Mac wove his way to the front door and entered the common room. McGowan looked at Bagley in consternation and signaled Shanks to the table where Mac sat, after negotiating his way there with difficulty.

Shanks got a rambling, incoherent account of how Mac and his partner had fought about staying in Hill's Bar for the night, seeing a little action. Finally, Duke had said to hell with it. He'd made camp up the canyon quite a ways and told Mac to go ahead, do as he wanted. But if he didn't have his scrawny ass back by daylight, he was going on without him.

303

"He'll do 'er, too," Mac slurred. "But I'll ketch up t' him. He's my frien'. My bes' frien'. Bes' frien' I got in this world." His eyes blurred with sentimental, alcoholic tears.

Shanks made his way back to Ned McGowan. "Harmless old coot. Drunk as a skunk. Big one's gone fer good."

"Tell the old drunk I like his spirit. Drinks on the house. See that he has enough."

An hour later, McCandless was face down on the table, his last drink spilled where he lay. McGowan looked at him and laughed. "Pitch him out," he ordered.

Two men obliged. Mac struck the ground like a sack of laundry, limp and relaxed. Then raising his head feebly, with an expression of infinite hurt, he said, "Why'd you fellers do that?" His eyes were unfocused, his tone maudlin. Then he sank back and began snoring where he had fallen. The men who had ejected him laughed, reentered McGowan's place, and closed the door.

McCandless lay quiet for a while, then drunkenly got to his hands and knees. He would crawl for a while, then his hands would give way, letting him down. His performance continued until he reached a patch of black shadow, then he was instantly on his feet.

"Duke?"

"Here."

Mac told him what he'd learned. There was a kind of auction going on. The three highest bidders had the three girls for tonight. Afterward, it would be on a wait-your-turn basis. Duke cursed, fluently. "The child—Martha—what are they going to do with her?"

"They said she had a habit of fallin' in th' river,

anyways," McCandless said in a tight voice.

Courtney looked at the projection from which he could reach the second-floor window. "I'd better get on up there," he said grimly. He adjusted a coil of rope around his shoulders and began to climb the slippery rocks.

In the second-floor rooms of the McGowan-Bagley house, only Arab, Helena, and Martha were sleeping. Em had relayed her concerns about the honesty of their hosts and had insisted on preparations for a hasty departure should one be indicated. They had all dressed for the trail, including Martha. Their packs were ready, placed by the door. And Em had assigned the girls to watch, in shifts.

"I don't know why," Arab said. "Good heavens, we have nothing to steal!"

"It's just a feeling I have. Indulge me."

And they had. It was not in Em's nature to be forceful like this. Em sat now, watching the door. She had pushed an old chest in front of it, but it wouldn't keep anyone out for long. For extra protection, she had a club, a leg she'd laboriously wiggled loose from a rickety chair. She was torn between nerves and a desire to laugh at the picture she must present. For she had donned the clothing she'd purchased in Fort Victoria, men's dress. And she supposed it made some difference. Because if someone came through that door, she'd be able to swing with that club!

She looked fondly at Martha, sleeping like an angel. A boy-angel, for she, too, had been transformed by means of clothing. A resilient child, she'd made a rapid recovery after her frightening experience. Perhaps Duke Courtney would now realize the extent of her gratitude.

She was grateful, she told herself, but that did not

305

mean she was deliberately currying favor with the man! She gazed toward the door, alert at a sound.

But the sound had come from another direction. She whirled at a thudding noise. An enormous, black figure leaped through the bedroom window! With a shrill gasp, she rushed toward him, the chair leg raised to strike him.

It didn't happen. A hand gripped her wrist, twisting it, and her weapon fell clattering to the floor. She felt herself pulled close against a massive chest, heard her name. "Em! Oh, Em!"

Duke Courtney! She leaned against him in a wave of relief, feeling the very bones of her body melt at his touch. Then sanity returned. What was he doing *here?* To climb through a window into a room where women were sleeping—he could have come for no good purpose! She fought herself away, opening her mouth to scream. He put his great hand over her mouth until she quieted, then gave her a little shake.

"We've got to get you out of here!" In a few terse words, he told of McGowan's plans for her and the other women—and for Martha. He did not have time to deal with hysterical females. He had to get them out of here, and he told her how he intended to do it.

One by one, the girls were lowered to the ground by means of the rope he carried. Then the packs. And finally, only he and Em were left. "Your turn," he told her.

"Mr. Courtney," Em said, "Duke—we may not get out of this. I know the records of these men. In—in case anything happens, I want you to know—"

"Shh. Listen!" The big man's head was cocked to one side. "They're coming up now. Out of the window with you! Go with McCandless. Hurry!"

Em clung to the rope as he paid it out, her heart beating like a triphammer. Hurry, she thought. Oh, God, let me reach the ground so he can defend himself!

The chest barring the doorway bought a little time. Duke was in mid-room when the door crashed open, three would-be lovers, blinded with lust, crashing into the dark room at the same instant. Duke caught the first with a mighty blow, knocking him backward into the others. Taking advantage of the element of surprise, he quickly disposed of another. The third managed to get off a quick shot, and a bullet sang past Courtney's ear as he swung once more.

The winners in the contest for the girls' favors were finally disposed of. Duke waited. Surely the shot had alerted someone below. It had. Ned McGowan mounted the stairs, swearing. "No gunfighting, lads," he sang out. "There's enough to go 'round—"

His voice broke off as he poked his head in the door, seeing a sprawl of bodies. Duke Courtney, standing to one side, brought the chair leg down. Two more to go before they would be assured of a head start on their journey. The big man went downstairs. Bagley and Shanks stood talking at the bottom of the stairs. Duke caught Bagley's collar and pulled it up tight. Shanks turned to make a frantic sprint for the gun he kept behind the bar, but Courtney reached for him and held him by his shirt at the back of the neck. He disposed of them neatly by knocking their heads together. Now he was ready to go; nobody would be in shape to follow them for some time.

He caught up with the others a short distance up the trail, catching the stumbling Martha into his arms. "You're gonna have to ride for a while till you wake up, missy," he said.

"McGowan and Bagley—do you think they'll follow us?" Em asked fearfully.

"Nope."

"What—what happened?"

"Took care of things." His voice was vague with disinterest. Then to Martha, "Put your arm around my neck. That's right, honey, and lean your head on my shoulder so you can get a little shuteye."

When they reached the spot where the packs were cached, Courtney shouldered his own in addition to the burden of the sleeping child. With an admonition to make haste, he strode on. Em was hard put to keep up with his long strides. She looked at him admiringly and wondered that she'd ever questioned his character or bothered to compare him with Donald.

Donald would have tried to deal with those men back there on a reasonable basis, perhaps threatening them with the due process of law. And Donald would have gotten himself killed. She and the girls would have been at McGowan's and Bagley's mercy. And little Martha—she shuddered.

Duke Courtney hadn't waited or reasoned. He had taken the law into his own hands. She missed Donald, and would always miss him, but right now she was glad it was this man at her side.

"Mrs. Alden—"

"I think, after what we've been through, you can call me Em."

"Well, Mrs.—Em, ma'am," he said awkwardly, "I wanted to tell you you look mighty good in them clothes. Real nice."

"But you haven't seen me in the daylight," she laughed.

"Don't need to. Reckon you'd look good in anything." He stopped in an agony of shyness and paid careful attention to the trail. Em walked along beside him with a feeling of wings on her feet, of a new strength that surged through her and gave her a sense of power to overcome all things.

They had gone several miles before she remembered the others and looked back to see how they were managing on the tortuous trail. They were still following, but they were far behind.

CHAPTER 11

Farther up the Fraser River, much farther, Tamsen surveyed her small domain. She had carefully chosen this site between two of the gold-bearing bars of the river. To the north was Fargo Bar, beyond that, Mariner. To the south, Yankee Bar, Boston Bar, and a number of others clustered close together.

Nell had wanted to set up in the middle of a miner-populated area, but Tamsen had chosen this spot. "Better to have them come to us," she said. "Anything worthwhile has to be worth a little effort." She was right; they had come.

The men were delighted to have women and a place of entertainment in their midst; they even donated their labor to build a small log structure. Then, one crowded night, someone had come up with an idea. "Hell, let's build a bigger one!"

So the small shelf in the gigantic ditch the Fraser ran through now held a small structure in which Nell and Tamsen lived and a large two-story edifice with rooms upstairs for the girls and downstairs entertainment. A new small building that housed the two new girls had been set cornerwise. Just before winter, Tamsen had made a trip to Yale for supplies. She found two women there, just off a sternwheeler in the harbor, who were asking for Ned McGowan's place. By their appearance, Tamsen could recognize them for what they were, so with a brief description of the life they'd have at McGowan's, she persuaded Pinkie and Dollie to join her troupe.

From the main shelf where the major buildings stood, a rather chancy footpath rounded a rock wall to a smaller shelf. There, a long, low building housed Dusty and Edwin Devon.

Tamsen ran this establishment differently. She would not take money the girls had earned. Her income was derived from a charge to her patrons for sitting in on the gambling games; it was a fee for entertainment. She also received a small remuneration for writing letters for lonely illiterate men, far from home. A few even paid for evenings of being allowed to sit and talk in her parlor, sipping tea from Nell's samovar. It had been a long winter; her funds were almost depleted, and she felt torn, uncertain as to what steps she should take after what she'd learned recently.

Nell appeared beside her and Tamsen turned, smiling. "Take a deep breath, Nell. You can almost smell spring!"

"Good thing," Nell grumped. "I was beginnin' t'feel like a goddamn mole!"

"Well, the snow's almost gone. The customers are starting to come in at night. We'll soon be having all we can do to cope with it."

"D'ruther work my butt off than freeze it off," Nell said. "Wasn't fer gittin' a fresh load of splinters, I'd head back to someplace where th' sun shines."

Tamsen suppressed her mirth. In all her life, she would never forget that incident on the trail. They'd come to a spot where the mules had to be left behind, where a small roaring stream poured down through a cleft in the cliffs to join the tumbling Fraser. The only crossing was a foot log.

The others had safely negotiated it, carrying their packs. But Nell sat down and refused to go another step. Finally, threatening to leave her, they'd evolved a plan. With Dusty and the girls on one side and Tamsen and Devon on the other, they held the end of a rope tied snugly about the woman's ample waist. Even then, she refused to walk, but sat flat, inching herself along, her chubby knees bobbing up and down. She clutched the samovar in her arms, since, she said, it brought her luck. She'd complained of splinters ever since.

Tamsen kicked at a patch of dirty snow. "It's almost gone. And Edwin says, above us, there are flowers at the foot of the trees."

"He ain't doin' so good, is he?" Nell asked bluntly. "He shouldn't oughta waste his strength foolin' around up there."

"He says it makes him feel better, seeing something God made—"

Nell snorted. "Do better restin' hissef, er takin a good physick, if you ask me. What th' hell's wrong with him, anyways?"

"I don't know," Tamsen said gloomily. "I don't know!"

Edwin Devon had been growing thinner and paler since they arrived. This winter had taken its toll. He'd developed a persistent cough, and his eyes were darkly circled. Tamsen worried, believing him to be conscience-stricken at his involvement in what he considered an immoral business. But now she was beginning to think there was something more. She'd heard there was a doctor among the gold-seekers at Lytton, which was far above them. She'd suggested

312

that Edwin go to him when the snows thawed, but he refused.

He had been a great help in the building. He brought many loads of moss from the forested areas to chink the buildings against the cold. He kept books, and she'd taught him to run the gambling games, but she was beginning to wish he'd remained in Novoarchangelsk and made life easier for himself—and for her. His constant protestations of love were disturbing and hurting. Tamsen had but one love in the world. He had deserted her and destroyed her desire for any other. She liked Edwin Devon far too much to love him out of pity.

"Still think he oughta see a doc," Nell grumbled. Then, in a different tone she pointed away from herself and exclaimed, "Who th' hell's that?"

Tamsen, startled, followed her gaze. A massive figure, blond hair shining in the spring sun, rounded a huge stone that bulged across the southward trail. There was no mistaking the outsized man who raised a ham-like fist in greeting, his teeth flashing in a wide smile.

"Duke! Duke Courtney," Tamsen said. "He's back again. Hide anything that'll break," she laughed as she ran to meet him. He stopped as those who followed him caught up: three young men, and a small boy.

Tamsen reached him, not giving the others a glance. "Hey," she said, smiling, "welcome home!"

"Thank you, Tamsen," The voice came from behind him. Tamsen stared at a young man with long curling blond lashes framing eyes misted with tears, a mouth that trembled with emotion. One hand went up to remove a wide, soft-brimmed hat, and gold-brown hair tumbled forth.

313

"Em! It's you! Oh, Em!" Her arms went around her sister, pulling the travel-stained cheek against her own. Then her eyes widened as she looked at the others. "Arab!"

The scene was reenacted, amid laughter and tears. Then there was little Martha to hug. How she had grown! And Helena—!

"I swear, I haven't been so happy in a long time," Tamsen said, wiping her eyes.

"We know about Dan," Em told her "And, Tamsen—Donald's dead. And so is Juan. We're all in the same boat."

"Juan?" Tamsen's voice was shrill with incredulity. *"Juan* dead? What do you mean! He—"

"He died along the trail," Arab said in a hopeless voice. "We'll give you the details later. But right now, Tamsen—we're very tired."

Tamsen's expression of shock gave way before a rather odd, contrite smile. "Of course! Let's go on to the house. Nell's back there bursting with curiosity—and if we don't hurry, she'll split a seam! Arab—" She paused, looking at her younger sister. "Dusty will be almost as excited as I am to see you. Why don't you go around and surprise him?" She pointed toward the footpath that led around the rocky extrusion. "I'll take the others on."

Arabella's joy at seeing her sister was touched by exasperation as she followed her direction. The last five miles had been accomplished only through stubborn endurance, one step at a time. She'd been looking forward to a bath, a bed, more than anything in the world. But she'd humor Tamsen, who was just as bossy as ever.

The path was narrow, tilting down toward the river at its outward edge. Arab couldn't help smiling

314

at the thought of Dusty trying to negotiate it. It would be hard for him, she thought wryly, only if he were sober. And that was an unlikely eventuality. The footpath turned sharply inward. And there, nestled in the curve of a cliff, was a long, low log structure. Arab stopped to rest her weary legs. Ten or fifteen more steps. One at a time. Perhaps if she called—

Then she saw the figure of a man at the brink of the ledge. He stood quietly, hands in his pockets, watching the great chunks of ice in the swirling river. Something in the shape of his shoulders, the poignant grace of his slim body, touched her heart with a searing pain.

She would have to get over seeing something of Juan in other men. Stiffening her resolve, she called out to him. "Is Dusty here?"

The man jerked erect, then turned slowly with widening eyes. "Arab!"

Arabella made a small moaning sound, closing her eyes and reaching out to brace herself against the rock behind her. It could not be! It could not be!

"Arab! Oh, my darling!"

She opened her eyes once more. He was coming toward her. She reached out a hand to touch him. This was not a hallucination, not a dream. He was real!

Then she was in his arms, his dear familiar arms, struggling to get closer to him, to feel every plane of his body pressed to hers. Her hands went up to cup his face, feeling the fine bones beneath the flesh as she began to cry, harsh racking sobs that shook her from head to toe.

"You were dead," she said wildly. "You were dead!"

315

At last, he picked her up and carried her into the house, placing her on his rumpled bachelor's bed. Dressed in men's clothing, trail-worn, tear-stained, her glorious hair spreading around her, he thought she was more beautiful than she'd ever been.

He sat beside her, stroking her hair, and soothing her until the shuddering hysteria faded. For a long time, she lay quietly, her green eyes dazed. Then she said, "I still can't believe you're here, alive. I don't understand—"

"I was hurt. Robbed. Shall I tell you what happened?"

She shivered again. "No, just hold me. Love me. Oh, Juan!"

He raised her to a sitting position, her cheek against his. "I've dreamed about that night in Novoarchangelsk for a long time," he said in a low voice. "I've gone half-crazy missing you. And I thought it was something like that I was wanting. Now that you are here, I know it wasn't. All I want to do is hold you—like this, to thank God we are together again, to get used to my own good luck."

He held her for a long time and wiped her tears away. When her trembling ceased, he put his mouth against her cold cheek until it warmed beneath his lips. Then he laid her gently back against the pillow and lay down beside her, moving his hands over her familiar body until he heard her catch her breath.

"Now?" he asked softly.

"Now."

It was not the earthshaking tumult of that night in Novoarchangelsk, but a coming together with tenderness, with love.

Later, Dusty and Edwin Devon approached the house they shared with Juan. They'd made a trip

316

upriver to Fargo Bar to check out travel conditions. For days, a short stretch of the journey had been blocked by snow. Now it was clear, and Tamsen's place was assured of a good clientele tonight. She would be pleased to hear their report, but first they'd stop off to change their trail clothes. Their boots were soaked through.

The sound of a woman's low laugh did not trouble them. Evidently Tamsen was here, in anticipation of their arrival. They entered and came to an immediate halt. From beyond the partition that surrounded Juan Narváez's bed came the unmistakable sounds of lovemaking. Juan's voice, a feminine answer—

Devon backed outside, his face red with embarrassment. Dusty followed, his face also flushed, but with anger. The man was Arab's husband! How dared he! And the woman, who was it? Carmen, Maggie? Pinkie or Dollie? Strumpets! Whichever it was, Nell would have a thing or two to say to her. And as for Narváez, he needed a good horsewhipping!

They rounded the footpath in silence, Devon with his head down and Dusty strutting like an irate bantam rooster. When they reached Tamsen's door, Dusty bypassed his friend and burst inside, his white hair standing on end. "Our house!" he shouted. "That blighter, Narváez, has got a woman in there. He's being false to his vows, and with one of your girls, Nell! I tell you, I don't intend to stand for it!"

He stopped short, hurt at the laughter his pronouncement had induced. And his eyes widened as a tall boy came toward him, blond hair falling to a slender waist. "My word," he stammered. Then, at a loss for words, he borrowed one of Nell's. "I'll be a sonofabitch," he said fervently. "It's Em!"

317

"Don't cuss," Nell said virtuously. "It sounds like hell on you."

Around some light refreshments, Tamsen told the newcomers what had happened to Juan. He had been suspicious of the partner he'd taken up with from the beginning, and when the going got rough, José took more than his share of supplies and left. One night soon after, as Juan was seated beside a fire, preparing to make an entry in his notebook, he was struck from behind. He remembered nothing more until he awoke; his boots, ring, and notebook had been stolen along with his remaining supplies. While a great gash on his head had bled copiously into the snow, his fire had gone out. Eventually he found José's discarded boots and staggered along the trail, retracing his steps.

Luckily, he had joined up with a party of miners who were promised "free grub and free tripping" by Governor Douglas in return for cutting a trail from Port Douglas at the head of Harrison Lake to Lilooet. Each miner had given Douglas's clerk twenty-five dollars as proof they wouldn't quit on the job. Douglas had also promised them mules, which never arrived; it was a sour, grumbling crew of men, who depended on the wildlife of the area to supplement their diets.

"I'm gonna take the man back," one growled, "Hell, if someone don't, he'll die."

"You'll lose your deposit," another warned.

"Douglas can keep my deposit," Juan's new friend said. "An' I've got a few ideas as to what he can do with it! I'm takin' him back."

He took Juan along as far as Yale, where a returning miner told him of Tamsen's whereabouts. Juan had just gotten his strength back and had

318

planned to go upriver in a day or two.

The irrepressible Martha, still fresh after a grueling journey that had worn her elders down, now came running inside, her eyes as big as dollars. "Aunt Arab's coming!" she panted. "And she's got Uncle Juan with her!" She paused and said, judiciously, "He isn't dead. I guess God fixed him."

Em put her arm around her small daughter. She and Tamsen went to the front porch to watch the two approach. They walked hand in hand, caught up in a kind of rapture. There was an invisible wall around them which separated them from the world. The watching sisters each felt a pang of envy: Tamsen thought of Dan; Em thought, strangely enough, not of Donald, but of Duke Courtney who, now that his mission had ended, would soon go on his way.

CHAPTER 12

Duke Courtney had no immediate intention of leaving. That girl, Em, had shaped up pretty good on the trail, but a high-toned lady like her wasn't for the likes of him. The more he hung around like a moony sick calf, the more miseries he'd pile up on himself, but it didn't seem like a good idea to move on just now. He had an idea Ned McGowan wouldn't be standing still after the way they'd outfoxed him. Tamsen, he figured, could probably hold her own, but the men around here weren't up to snuff in his books. Dusty was a nice old guy, but always half-seas-over. Devon was a gentleman, and a sick man if Duke had eyes in his head. Juan Narváez—good stuff there, but unused to the ways of men and mining camps. Look at the way he got himself knocked in the head—

After a talk with Tamsen in which he learned how she and the others had escaped McGowan's clutches, and how she'd snatched McGowan's imported girls right out from under his nose, Courtney was certain sure there was bound to be trouble. So he guessed he'd stick around, if they'd let him. He'd give old Mac his d'ruthers, but he figured Mac'd stick around, too.

Housing arrangements had to be worked out. There was room for Em, Martha, and Helena in the house Tamsen shared with Nell. Pinkie and Dollie were in their separate structure, and Carmen and Maggie remained in the big house on the second floor. Arab and Juan were given privacy in the full occupancy of the long, low house on the second ledge. Dusty and Devon chose to move into an empty storage shed. It was nearly a mile upriver to another ledge where a house might be built. Duke and Mac built a small structure there. Too far for Duke's peace of mind as to the girls' safety, but at least it was near a sand bar where they could prospect a little.

Scouting around at Fargo Bar, Duke began to worry a little. Out of ten men, six were returning home, broke. It made no difference how they worked, panning the flume or tunneling into the cliff; there was color, but that was all. Two of the ten men were staying right here, and two were moving on upriver, still following the scent of gold.

Word filtered down that the big bonanza lay ahead. A pack of lies, perhaps, but if it were true, Tamsen's little settlement would be left high and dry, a lonesome, unproductive spot in a wilderness.

Duke tried to talk to Tamsen, and she laughed. "Twenty thousand men in this area. Do you think they'll all go? And this place is just beginning to cash in. I've got my own gold mine!"

He had to admit she had a point. The big house was jammed every night. Lots of dirty, sweating miners who would take out twenty dollars during the day—and come to Tamsen's place to spend it. He didn't blame them, he thought nightly, as he watched the entertainment. That Tamsen had a real knack for holding a feller's attention, and also for holding a pack of wolves at bay, he thought admiringly. He often watched her fend off would-be suitors. They said nobody had been able so far to unlatch the lady's bedroom door, and he believed them.

Her sister, Arab, was pretty good, too, but he guessed having a Spanish husband glowering in the back of the room did put a damper on her act.

He wondered about Em, who was conspicuous by her absence at the doings in the big house. She had never approved of Tamsen's business, and she stayed far from it now. Every single night she watched Duke Courtney enter the front door, and he knew she watched. He also guessed at the disdain in her mind. What was wrong with a man having a drink, sitting in on a hand or two, watching the byplay between women-hungry men and a few pretty girls. If some of those girls traded their favors for money, that was their affair. Not his. Nor Em's.

He had to admit that the woman's holier-than-thou attitude took a hell of a lot of enjoyment out of his evenings. And it could be that that attitude was the reason he showed up every night. For some reason he felt driven to do things that would arouse Em's disapproval. Maybe some night he just might go into Pinkie and Dollie's—and let Em stew! He was telling himself that the night he was dressed in his best walking past the house Em shared with Tamsen. He turned on impulse and knocked at the door, for he thought he had seen Em's face at the window.

She answered, and he bowed awkwardly. "It come to me you might want to go on over an' join in th' fun. If you had you a man to go with, that is."

"I'm afraid not," Em said, coloring. The memory of the day she and Arab went to Nell to ask for a loan was still fresh in her mind. But she'd been desperate then, needing the money to help Donald. Here, she was earning her keep, cooking, cleaning, freeing

Tamsen from the household chores. She'd keep away from the dirty fringes of Tamsen's business.

"Figured you'd say that," Duke said. "Well, to each his own." Em felt she'd been measured and found wanting. As he turned away, she reached a hand to touch his sleeve.

"I would like a walk," she heard herself saying, "if you could spare the time. Martha's asleep, and it gets rather monotonous being cooped up here all day."

To his astonishment, he found himself walking along the trail and down a narrow defile that led to the river, a woman's soft hand on his arm. The late summer light enabled him to see the parting in her hair, now demurely braided and coiled over her ears. The nape of her neck seemed so tender, so vulnerable, as she gazed at the turbulent waters at their feet.

"I—I'm a little frightened of this country," she confessed. "It's all so big, so violent. The river, the rugged cliffs and canyons—the people—"

"Folks are the same all over," he reminded her. "A lot of us good with some bad, another bunch bad with some good. All of us got our likes an' dislikes, our happy times and our troubles."

"But why did the worst have to gather in one spot?" Em cried. She looked back toward the direction of the big house and shivered. "Such a group of low-lifes, of scum!"

He stiffened. "I'm one of 'em, Mrs. Alden." He addressed her formally, deliberately. "Hope you ain't forgot that. An' here you are, out with a low-life scum in the dark. Ain't you scared?"

She laughed, suddenly self-conscious. "You know I didn't mean you! You're a very fine man. I think my whole family agrees to that."

"An' how do you know them others ain't the same?"

323

She looked up into his earnest face, seeing the sincerity in his blue eyes, wanting to touch the curve of his mouth with her fingers. How was it he always made her feel so guilty, as if she were in the wrong?

"I don't know," she said slowly. "I—I suppose you're right." She searched for a way to change the subject. "What do you think of Edwin Devon?" she asked.

"Like him," was the prompt answer. "Good man. Though I don't figure he'd be worth a damn in a fight."

Em stifled a giggle of amusement. Trust Duke Courtney to reduce everything to the simplest elements.

"I've noticed something," she told him. "Helena is in love with Edwin. I wondered why she insisted on coming with us, and now I know. I don't think he even guesses, though."

"Maybe she ought to tell him."

Em gave a shocked little gasp. "But that would be wrong! A woman couldn't do a thing like that! He wouldn't respect her! Why, what would you say"— her face felt hot and flushed but she continued—"if I stood here, right in front of you, and told you a thing like that!"

His big arms went around her, lifting her. She struggled a little, pressed against his massive chest. Then his mouth fastened on hers, and she felt a throbbing sensation, a roaring filled her ears, and she clung to him. When he put her down, she backed from him, her eyes dazed, her hand on her burning lips. "How—how dare you!" she said weakly.

"You asked me what I'd say, and that was my answer," he said. "I'm a man of action, not words."

With a strangled sound of fury, Em ran from him. He followed behind her until she reached her door, then made his way grimly to the big house. But it was not his night. He sat in on a game and lost heavily. When Tamsen sang a plaintive tune that had men sniffling all around him, he sat dry-eyed. He wondered if it was true what he'd heard about those rooms upstairs—that the girls had their beds made up like little nests all lined with fur. Well, sometime, he just might see for himself!

For now, he was haunted by a pair of long-lashed blue eyes and the feel of a small-boned fragile body in his arms. He heard her voice saying, "Such a group of low-lifes, of scum." There was no place for a lady in his life. He shouldn't have done what he did tonight, scaring the life out of Em that way.

Somehow, though, he was glad he had. It would be something to think on, during the long winter nights after he left this place. He would leave soon, he decided then and there. He sat nursing a drink and glowering until the place closed down in the wee small hours. Devon joined him, and they talked for a while; Duke studied the Englishman, envying him his polish if not his physique. If he were more like Edwin Devon, he might stand a chance with Em.

The room had emptied. It was time to go. Duke looked forward to his long walk home. It might cool him some. He and Devon left together, and found Arab and Juan bending over something on the ground.

"Drunk?" he asked. "Passed out?"

"I don't think so," Arab frowned. "He had been drinking. But his forehead's burning. I noticed him earlier. Someone said he's a new man, just in today."

Duke knelt beside the man, putting a huge hand on his brow. "Man's sick," he said. "Maybe I'd better try to get him up to my place."

"Take him to ours," Arab said. "I don't think you

should try to take him that far. And we have a spare bed."

Courtney and Devon got the man to his feet and half-walked, half-dragged him to the house on the smaller ledge above the Fraser. He roused long enough to mumble his thanks and his name, then lapsed into delirium.

"It's something like I had once," Duke said. "Only time I ever been sick in my life. Kind of a grippe. I was sicker'n hell. It could be catching."

Arab looked a little worried; then her face cleared. "After all, we couldn't let him just lie there!"

Three days later the sick man had recovered and gone on upriver to seek his fortune. His coming had made little impact on the residents of Tamsen's place. His going left less, until Devon fell ill. Then Juan.

It was decided to move Devon into the Narváez household, so that Arab, already exposed, could care for the two of them. But one day when Tamsen left a basket of invalid foods at the door, no one answered her knock, so she entered. Arab, too, was flushed and muttering, out of her head with fever.

Tamsen went to the turn in the path and, seeing Dusty, called out to him. She would be caring for the sick, and Nell must handle things the best she could. Each day, she would appear at this spot at about the same time, and, unless she failed to come, no one was to come near. Whatever they had was highly contagious.

That night, all hell broke loose at Tamsen's place. At Fargo Bar, one man had found a nugget of unbelievable size. Word had gone downriver to Mariner Bar—and even as far as Boston Bar. The downriver miners had stampeded toward the discovery site; the Fargo men came to Tamsen's to

326

celebrate, and they all converged at the same time.

Duke Courtney and McCandless, entering the big house, found a distraught Nell and a state of chaos. The mirror behind the jerry-built bar, packed upriver at great expense, had been shot full of holes. Chairs were overturned, and the crowd was in an ugly humor.

"They spected some singin' an' dancin'," Nell said, wringing her pudgy hands. "Arab's down sick, Tamsen's over t'take care of 'em all, an' the girls here can't sing worth a damn. I got a voice like a turkey buzzard in matin' season, an' as fer dancin'"—she looked ruefully down at her bulk—"if I ever got all this started movin' I'd never git it stopped. In th' meantime, they're bustin' hell outta th' place!"

Duke looked at the crowd, dangerously on the verge of becoming a mob. "Got an idea," he said. "Gimme a minute."

He ran to Tamsen's house, banging on the door until Em appeared. Her eyes went big, her mouth tight at the sight of him. "Dammit, don't go all prune-faced on me," he thundered. "All I want to do is ask you a question. You sing?"

"A—a little," she said doubtfully.

"Figured you could. Figured it run in th' family. Get some fancy duds on an' come with me. Nell needs you."

"Duke Courtney, if you think I'm going in there— put on a show in front of those ruffians—you're out of your mind. I'll have no part of Tamsen's business!"

"There won't be no business left if you don't hurry," he interrupted. "The crowd up there's tearing the place all to hell. I can't make you go"—he looked at her with dislike—"I just had you figured for somebody that might come through when the chips were down. Tamsen would, if it was the other way round. Forget I asked."

"Wait a minute. Do you—do you think I could stop them?"

"That's what they're yellin' for. They come here expectin' to be entertained, an' that's all they'll settle for."

"Give me a moment."

Em went into Tamsen's room and stood for a moment, leaning her head against the door. Then she went to the curtained alcove where Tamsen's wardrobe hung. That dress—the one she'd chided Tamsen for wearing. An apricot velvet, cut too low, slit to the knee. She donned it hastily and went to join Duke, acutely self-conscious.

She needn't have been. He didn't look at her. She ran to keep up with him as he strode toward the big house. Inside, she was lost in the swirling maelstrom until he put both hands at her waist and lifted her to the bar.

"Gentlemen." She lifted her hands. "Gentlemen!"

The surly mood quieted. Someone gave a soft, low whistle and the tension lifted. Em's face glowed above the apricot gown, the creamy shoulders above the low-cut bodice tinted a shell pink. She couldn't know what she looked like—a lovely frail innocent with a touch of wantonness in the dress she wore that made her seem enchanting and deliberately artful.

"I'm sorry, gentlemen, that I was late. Perhaps a song—?"

Her words were drowned in thunderous applause. She began a tune she'd learned in her childhood; Carmen in the background listened, then joined in with soft strumming chords.

Em's voice was not the low, husky, breaking voice of Tamsen or the pure soaring one of Arab. It was

328

softer, weaker, lacking in volume, sometimes almost becoming a whisper, but it was highly effective. The room was absolutely silent except for her singing, and the small voice, with its whispering interludes, gave even the simple old song a hint of suggestiveness.

Nell, watching, had her mouth open. "Be gawdamned," she muttered. "Didden know the girl had it in her. Hell, she could give Tamsen a run fer her money! Mebbe even keep th' change!"

The song ended with the watchers exploding in hearty appreciation. Em felt an odd surge of pleasure, and for a brief space, she loved them all, these rough brawling people with whom Duke Courtney identified.

Some more songs brought similar reactions from the crowd. They were calling for more when her mind suddenly went blank. For the life of her, she couldn't think of another refrain! She, whose singing had been restricted to hymns—or lullabies—but they were waiting, clamoring—

"Perhaps something different," she said hesitantly. Then in a soft voice she began an old, old hymn, one they had sung in church back home in Pennsylvania.

"Migod," Nell groaned. "She's blown it now, sure as hell."

Em sang on to the end and finished to dead silence. Then a choked voice said, "My mother used to sing that." Another man sniffed and wiped his face with the back of his sleeve. "Say, do you know—"

As she finished the hymn he mentioned, she noted a humming accompaniment. Several of them were singing along with her under their breath. She began another, pausing at the refrain to ask, "Won't you sing with me, please?" Her small hands beckoned to draw them in. They sang uncertainly at first, then from their throats the words issued with a will that shook the rafters.

Nell rolled her eyes toward the heavens. "May God fergive us," she said piously.

Pinkie and Dollie had waited at their place in vain. They'd watched the crowd entering the big house with gleeful anticipation. Normally, by this time, the customers would be filtering toward their small domicile. When they didn't show, the girls decided to join them—advertise their charms a little. Dressed in their finest—tight pink satin gowns with plumed hats to match—they headed toward the big house where games and entertainment predominated.

Entering, they might as well have been invisible for all the attention they received. Tamsen's prissy-prude of a sister, too good to associate with the likes of *them*, had the crowd in the palm of her hand. They listened a while, unable to believe their ears, then began to cast a few practiced glances among the crowd. Their usual brushings of bosom and thigh against a lonely miner did not work tonight.

Finally they left; the night aided them in coming to a decision. They'd halted the idea of being stuck here through the long winter with so few men and no place to shop. They'd catch the first sucker going downriver and sweet-talk him into taking them along. They should have gone to McGowan in the first place.

Duke Courtney walked Em home in the gray light of dawn. "I was right proud of you tonight," he said soberly.

"Th—thank you. Would you care to come in?"

330

"Better be getting on home." He touched his forehead in a kind of salute and strode away. Em watched him go, trembling with fatigue—and something else. She would never understand that man. Juan didn't like for Arab to dance and make a display of herself, Em knew that. As for her own performance this evening, Donald would have been scandalized! Yet Duke had said he was proud—and meant it!

Duke Courtney rounded the curve in the path that led toward the shack he shared with Mac, whistling tunelessly. The lady was loosening up, all right. She had the makings of quite a woman!

CHAPTER 13

In the long, low house on the smaller ledge, Tamsen looked out at the morning with distaste. The sun had risen in a rosy glow, touching the rock and clay walls of the big ditch with tints of pink, amber, and blue. Even the yellow rushing waters looked inviting. A rare day, and she must miss it with her sickroom chores. She put a hand to the small of her aching back and sighed. It had been a long night. Juan was recovering well, though he was awfully weak. Arab felt miserable, temperish and fretful, asking for small attentions and then deciding she didn't want them. She would be all right in a few more days.

It was Edwin Devon she worried about. He alternately chilled and burned, and his face had a gray look to it that frightened her. Again it was time to look in on him. She entered his small partitioned-off room and spoke to him softly. He answered. His eyes were clear this morning, though enormous in his wasted face. A scarlet splash on either cheek showed that the fever was still with him.

"I was out of my head last night, wasn't I?" His voice was soft, questioning.

Tamsen reddened. "Yes, you were."

"I remember." He had a confused dream of gripping Tamsen's hands and babbling out his need

332

for her. And she had held him to her, soothing him like a child.

"You're very kind," he said unexpectedly.

Tamsen put her hands on her hips, assuming a mock frown. "Only because I'm very fond of you, sir! And you can repay me by getting well as soon as possible, so I'll know I'm a good nurse."

Devon sighed. Fondness . . . it was not enough. If he were only well, he would make the lady love him. But he knew inside himself that there was little possibility of his recovery. He'd been steadily going downhill during these last months, roaming the cliffs above in order to fix the beauty of things in his mind for his dark journey. This illness would put an end to it all. He only hoped he'd manage it without making a fool of himself—as he had last night.

"Could you manage some broth?"

He didn't want any. It wasn't worth the effort. But for Tamsen, he would try. She left the room, and he lay thinking of the girl he'd seen across the room at Baranov Castle, outshining the ladies of the court, of the laughing lady he'd walked with along the Indian trail in the summer sun, of this woman who had saved his life by facing down his would-be murderers with a gun.

Tamsen ladled a cup of broth from the pot boiling over the open fire and carried it to him. He willed himself to manage a few sips. Then she performed a similar duty for Juan, going at last to Arab.

"It tastes awful," Arabella complained. "If we only had a decent cup! Those things make everything taste like tin. And, Tamsen, my feet are cold."

"Arab, for heaven's sake!"

Weak tears filled the younger girl's eyes. "Oh,

333

Tam, I'm sorry! I have no right to fuss when you're working so hard. It's just—I'm so miserable."

"I know," Tamsen soothed. "But you're getting better. Now, drink this."

A teaspoon of broth down Devon, a cup for Juan, a half-cup for Arab was a pretty good record this morning. Tamsen went about her duties, bathing feverish faces, performing the functions of a nurse despite the embarrassment of the men. Somebody had to do these things.

It was late morning when she stepped out into the sun. The ache in her back had intensified, and her eyes felt hot and dry, the landscape seeming to blur around her. Probably from lack of sleep, she thought. She went back into the house and sat down for a moment, only to find she couldn't get up again. In a moment, she began to shiver, and then she knew.

She must contact someone while she was still in control of her senses. Someone who could help the others, especially help Devon. She forced her way to her feet and leaned against the chair for a moment, then staggered toward the door.

Later that afternoon, Dusty waited in his accustomed place for Tamsen to appear. She was late, but then maybe she'd got tied up with one of the invalids. He waited as long as he dared, then, squinting at the sky, estimated that she would have come by now if she was coming at all. He went to Em; something was wrong at the house on the smaller ledge.

Em was all for going herself, but Helena reminded her that her first duty was to Martha. She would go in her stead. Perhaps Tamsen was only asleep, worn out from serving as nurse both day and night, and had missed appearing at the appointed hour. If this were the case, Helena would remain to help her, but

Martha must be spared any contact with the infection.

Em reluctantly agreed, and Helena set out with a basket of medicines, barks and herbs to be boiled into bitter healing brews. Rounding the stone obstruction jutting into the narrow path, Helena stopped short, then ran forward.

Tamsen had collapsed near the edge of the precipice. She lay face down on the ledge. Helena helped her adopted sister into the house and to the pallet where Tamsen had rested so little before illness caught up with her. Making the sick woman comfortable, Helena went her rounds. Arab was in one partitioned alcove sleeping fretfully. Juan managed to raise himself on one elbow when Helena looked in on him.

"Tamsen?" His voice was weak.

"Tamsen rests. I will help her." Helena's voice was calm and reassuring.

"Arab?"

"Your wife is well. She recovers. Now, sleep."

The last alcove sheltered Edwin Devon. Helena gazed at him for a long time, her lustrous dark eyes filled with love and pain. Soon they would sound the drum for this one. She prayed that her mother might take him by the hand.

He turned blank eyes toward her. "Tamsen?"

"Sleep," she said, touching his hot cheek with cool fingers. *"Ach-tu wassigu."* My heart cares.

Helena built a bed of decayed cedar wood in the center of the stone-floored structure. On this, she laid hot stones, to prepare a specific Tlingit remedy for rheumatic fevers. For their coughs, she prepared a warm effusion of sweet cicely, and one of wormwood to ease pleurisy. In addition, she used the medications Em had sent: camphor wood,

335

eucalyptus, and camomile. Either due to Tlingit methods, Em's methods, or to the fact that the grippe had run its course, the patients began to improve. . . .

All except Edwin Devon.

Helena, now that the others rested well, sat with him nightly, listening to his ravings. And finally, one night, he clutched her wrists. "Love me, Tamsen," he pleaded. "Then I will die happily. Just love me."

A spasm of agony passed over Helena's stoic features. He does not know who I am, she thought. Then lying down beside him, she took his wasted body in her arms. "I am here," she comforted him. "I am here."

She was not aware that she'd slept at all. But when she opened her eyes, it was day, and Edwin Devon was looking at her, his eyes clear, with an almost transparent look. She extricated herself with embarrassment and arranged her rumpled clothing. "You wanted Tamsen," she said in a low voice. "I—I took her place. I am sorry."

"But I am not," Devon said, his voice holding a new husky note. "Please—don't be sorry, Helena."

At the look in his eyes, her own blazed with a sudden happiness. "Then I will not be. I must hurry now. There is much to do."

Helena went about her work on light feet this day. She allowed Juan a few minutes out in the sun. Arabella could sit up for a while. And Tamsen had a few lucid moments. All was well.

Arab insisted upon returning to her husband's bed that night. Helena helped her, tucking the blanket around their shoulders as they lay sleeping, clinging to each other like children. And then Helena went to Devon.

Tamsen woke in the night with a burning thirst. It

336

took a moment to become oriented to her surroundings, to remember Helena was here, caring for her. She called faintly, surprised that she had no more voice, and then she called again.

There was no answer. Then Tamsen remembered how sick Edwin Devon had looked. Perhaps he was worse; she must see to him. There was a faint candleglow from Edwin's partitioned cubicle. Rising, Tamsen held to the wall, almost too sick and dizzy to stand. She made her way to Edwin's room.

For a long moment, she stood staring at Helena's golden arm flung across the pale chest of the Englishmen. The significance of it did not penetrate her fever-dulled mind. But suddenly she was no longer thirsty, just terribly, terribly alone and forlorn. With weak tears coursing down her cheeks, she found her way back to the haven of her bed.

The keening began three nights later. The ailing ones were recovered enough now to navigate under their own power. Helena sat cross-legged before the opening of Devon's room; her face was blackened with ash from her medicine fire. She was mourning her dead, for the spirit of life had passed from the pale body on Devon's bed.

It was her wish to cremate him, according to Tlingit law. But Tamsen convinced her he should be buried according to his own customs, in the softer lands above the valley cliffs where he had so often wandered. It took half a day, and the combined efforts of all of them to carry him there, but he was laid to rest in a small glade beneath tall trees. Here the vines and flowers grew in profusion. The snows would come and another summer, with its green blanket, and the grave would be lost forever, assimilated into the wilderness—as Devon would have had it.

Tamsen whispered what she could remember of her father's burial service. Juan muttered a Latin prayer and crossed himself. Arab wept, while Helena stood by stoically. But when the others had walked away, she remained behind. She had carried a little basket containing a book in which Devon had been writing, some small sticks of firewood, and a tin cup with live coals from the fire. She knelt and arranged a miniature pyre, placing the book in the center. After the small blaze was going, she threw her dark hair back and began to sing.

Tamsen, at a distance, recognized the thin column of smoke for what it was and listened to the dirge sung to speed Edwin's spirit on its journey. Helena, half-Tlingit, half-Russian, was taking no chances with the soul of the man she loved.

When the girl joined them for their journey home, her face was as impassive as always. For a few brief days, she had known the love of a man. Now he was gone, and she had done what had to be done. She was at peace.

The burial had taken its toll on the small, weakened troupe. It was nearly a week before they felt free of the illness that had plagued them. Then they took turns carrying water from the river, washing themselves, sunning blankets and clothing, and scrubbing the house until they felt it was free of infection. Only then did they feel safe to return to the other ledge with its cluster of dwellings.

Nell took the news of Devon's death hardest of all. She had grown quite fond of the quiet Englishman. Migawd, she thought, thunderstruck. It coulda been Dusty! "That feller," she sputtered, "that damn walkin' case of plague! Shoulda left him lay where he was! Shoulda kicked his butt in the river!"

"Nell, you don't mean that," Em said. "He couldn't help being sick."

"Guess I don't," Nell said disconsolately. Then her face brightened. "But if he ever shows his goddamn face around here agin', when he ain't sick, *then* I'll kick his butt in the river."

Em groaned. "Nell, you're hopeless!"

The reunion of the group, so long separated, was a joyous one despite the subduing news of Devon's death. Nell's report on how Em had taken over the entertainment left Tamsen speechless. For a long time, she'd sensed a gradual change in Em, and now the mousey, straightlaced girl was gone. In her place was a vibrant, vital woman, who waved aside Tamsen's thanks. "I've enjoyed it," she laughed.

"I'm still a little weak," Tamsen confessed, "and so is Arab. Could you manage to carry along for a while?"

Em could, and would. There was other news not so welcome. For one thing, Dollie and Pinkie were gone. They'd just picked up one day and joined a group of miners heading downriver, without a word or a by-your-leave. On top of that, things weren't so good for business. The nugget found at Fargo Bar proved to be a fake. Oh, it was real enough, but it was put there—salted—by a man who wanted to sell out and go home. He'd cleared a pretty penny on his claim.

Now there were more miners going downriver than there were coming up; word was out that the big strike would be farther along. "Purty soon, we'll be sittin' here, high an' dry, all by our goddamn lonesome," Nell said sadly.

"Duke Courtney is still in the neighborhood," Em said, her color high, "and his friend McCandless."

339

"Well, Duke ain't stayin' fer gold," Nell said meaningfully. "He says there ain't much here, an' he's got a nose fer it. He thinks it's gonna be a damn sight farther upriver. Tamsen, I think we oughta hightail it outta here, one way er another."

Tamsen considered the big woman's advice. "There's nothing at home to go back to," she sighed. "And as for moving on, it's September now. The trails to the north won't be fully developed yet. Juan, Arab, and I are still not quite strong. And there's Martha to think about. . . . We can't do it, Nell. Not now. Maybe if we just holed up until spring, then after the snows—"

Nell's face fell. "Figgered you'd say that. Well, we better get us some firewood in. Gonna be colder than a welldigger's ass if this winter's anything like th' last one."

Nell's dire predictions regarding their clientele proved true in the next few weeks. Their nightly visitors dwindled to ten, to five, and then one night there were none. In the meantime, they prepared for the winter ahead. Helena had dried berries and fruits garnered from the lands above, earlier, when it was still spring. Now they all worked with her as she taught them to preserve the meat from wild game brought down by Duke, Mac, and Juan. The meat was cut into thin strips and hung on drying poles above a small smoking fire. Helena especially prized their acquisition of a fat black bear. Its fat was rendered down and made valuable for both cooking and medicinal purposes. The remaining meat was dried, and the fur tanned carefully, Indian-fashion.

Their larder was full and running over, and still the good weather held. "We've lost a hell of a lotta time," Nell said reproachfully. "Coulda awready been moved an' set up somewheres else."

340

"But we wouldn't have had time to put up our buildings—or preserve food," Tamsen reminded her.

"Food, hell," Nell snorted. "If you think I'm goin' t'eat that gawdam bear!"

Tamsen herself had had some misgivings. It would have been sheer folly to move upriver at this time of year, but they might have wintered in some more populated spot, like Yale. She had an idea, though, that Ned McGowan's memory was long and that he hadn't forgotten his humiliation at her hands, the stealing away of his imported girls, or the beating he'd received at Duke Courtney's hands.

No, they would be safer here, isolated though it might be. They had plenty of supplies. They could sit the winter out snug and warm.

CHAPTER 14

Tamsen had been right in judging Ned McGowan's temper. Pinkie and Dollie had found their way to his place at last. Not plush, they admitted to themselves, but after being stuck out in the howling wilderness, it looked pretty good. As they paraded through Hill's Bar, they picked up an admiring, catcalling group of men. The pickings looked rich.

They simperingly told their newly concocted story to McGowan and Bagley, two gentlemen if they ever saw one. They'd been lost and scared when they got off the boat, not knowing where to find their new benefactor, and they'd asked this woman, who introduced herself as Mrs. Tallant, for directions. She'd led them on a wild-goose chase, far upriver, where they'd been virtual prisoners, forced to work for her at her place. They'd only just now escaped from her vile clutches.

Ned McGowan didn't believe a word of it, but his spirits soared in sudden elation. The miners who came downriver from deserted claims usually didn't make it as far as Hill's Bar. They shipped out on the first available vessel from Yale, above. He'd known Tamsen Tallant was in business up there somewhere, but he wasn't quite certain of her location, or the

342

extent of her entourage. Here was his opportunity to get some real information.

Pinkie and Dollie responded to his smiling flattery. When he had finished with them, he had a complete map in his head. He also had a pretty good idea of Tamsen's holdings: one big house, one medium-sized house, and a house that Tamsen herself occupied—all snug as a bug on a ledge above the Fraser.

"Thank you, ladies," he said gallantly. Then, "Shanks! Shanks, show these ladies where they go. And then get the word out that they're here."

Shanks hastened to obey his command. Pinkie and Dollie walked willingly into a trap that meant a life of penury and servitude. McGowan settled back in satisfaction. The men who won at auction the previous spring hadn't trusted him since. He'd returned their money, but they still held the beating they took in his upstairs room against him. Not that he blamed them; he still had headaches himself. He was pretty sure they wouldn't mind going along with his plan. It meant revenge—and more. They'd be bringing back a lot of pretty girls in one bunch. He wouldn't mind taming that wildcat, Tamsen, himself. Em he'd gladly throw to the wolves to even the score with her husband, Senator Alden. He frowned a little, wondering what kind of crusade the old boy was waging now. And why he had let his wife and child come to this wilderness alone.

Ah, well, that was none of his affair. There was enough to do, scaring up some help and plotting a course of attack. He reached for a piece of paper and began sketching the layout of Tamsen's place as it had been described to him.

As he worked, some changes were being made upriver. With Dollie and Pinkie gone, their small shack stood empty. It was Em's suggestion that Duke Courtney and Mac be invited to move down and make their winter quarters at Tamsen's place. It would be safer to have two extra men in the area, with Devon gone and only Juan and Dusty remaining. Supposing there was a recurrence of the summer's illness, or an Indian attack? Wandering renegade miners, who saw a settlement composed mostly of women might think them easy prey.

The idea did not set well with Courtney. It was better to stay far from Em, if possible. Close enough to keep an eye on her, and far enough that he didn't succumb to temptation. He dreamed of her almost nightly as it was, and would rise early in the morning to climb upward into the trees and chop wood until he was too tired to think.

But the housing arrangement made sense. Especially since the women cooking was included in the bargain. Next spring, he'd see them settled away up the Fraser, then he'd get the hell out as fast as he could.

There wasn't much to move down. Courtney stood, his pack on his shoulder, taking one last look at the cabin that had been built around a tree stump which, surrounded by a couple of flat rocks for chairs, served as a table. Like the Tlingit houses, it had a smoke hole in the roof. He was going to miss this place. His thoughts didn't keep him from hurrying down the trail to the settlement of which Em was a part.

The girls had cleaned the small shack and fixed it up as well as they could. A mouth-watering pie was waiting on a cloth-spread table. Duke glowered at the sight of feminine fripperies. Then Dusty appeared with a bottle, and the women left. Maybe it wasn't going to be so bad after all....

Toasting their moving in, they talked man-talk, mostly about the weather. Odd, the way it kept holding off. "But, when it goes," Dusty said, blearily, "it will go, don't you know! Lucky you made the move now, in time."

Taking another drink, Duke Courtney agreed. His surroundings were beginning to appeal to him. He settled back, growing mellow. Em was standing at her window, wishing she were not a lady and therefore excluded from the gathering down there. She could visualize the scene. Dusty, red-faced and talkative, McCandless, telling tall tales, and Duke—he would be lounging back, smoking in silence, with that terrible aura of leashed power he had—the thought set her tingling.

"Em," Tamsen called, "aren't you ever going to go to bed?"

Em turned reluctantly from the window. At least, the light burning down there gave her a feeling of safety, of security. Duke Courtney might be a rough, very willful man, but she had a feeling there was no situation he couldn't handle ... nothing he couldn't do.

Time passed. Em and Courtney met and spoke in passing, but that was all. The two miners, Duke and Mac, fiercely guarded their privacy in the little shack. When they came to meals, Courtney spent his time chatting with Martha, while McCandless told tales of other mining areas to Dusty and Juan.

The women remained unnoticed. They were left out of the stream of masculine conversation so often that sometimes Em thought she would scream. She took to remaining in the house, indulging in a flurry of housekeeping. Tamsen was glad to escape her activities on these late, unbelievably warm mornings. Helena, too, seemed moody and at loose ends.

They awoke one morning to a sea of mist. A warm mist, to be sure. But Tamsen knew it presaged a change. Thoughts of last winter, imprisoned in a small space with drifts higher than the windows, were still with her. All of a sudden she could not get enough of the out-of-doors.

It was her suggestion that she and Helena climb to the top of the canyon, to the forest line where Devon lay. She had such an odd feeling—that either they would not be here, or that his body would be gone by spring. She felt an urgent need to say goodbye. Helena was happy to accompany her. Though she had not mourned aloud, her loss showed in her face. She had lost weight. Her fine bones were prominent in her cheeks, but she made no mention of her grief. If only she, Tamsen, hadn't been standing in the way, Devon and Helena might have had a brief life together. If only the man's infatuation with her hadn't persisted almost to the end. Tamsen tried to be honest with herself, wondering if she'd encouraged that infatuation. Or if it was only the fantasy of a man who knew he was dying.

For she had read the little book Helena burned the day of his burial. It described days of agony, alone with his pain; it illustrated ecstatically the emotions he felt in her presence. And in words that sang like poetry. Devon had, indeed, the magic of words.

Those final days when he turned to Helena were unrecorded. A pity. Tamsen had a feeling those pages would read like a psalm of peace and contentment. She hoped so.

They climbed through the narrow defile that lay

just beyond the house Arab and Juan now shared, and finally reached the top of the canyon wall where a grassy meadow lay like a narrow ribbon between the big ditch and tall spruce and hemlock, dark with shadow. Helena stood silent at Devon's grave, but Tamsen was nervous. She had an eerie feeling that someone was watching. Perhaps Devon's spirit, with his shining, translucent eyes? A ridiculous thought, she told herself. But still, there was something. The back of her neck prickled, and she shivered. Then a small squirrel moved in a tree above, chattering at their human intrusion, and she relaxed, laughing at herself.

They stood for only a short time at Edwin's grave, then Helena, dry-eyed, straightbacked, said, "It is enough. We will go."

Tamsen reached a sympathetic hand to her adopted sister, and together they made their way toward the opening to the glade, which was criss-crossed with shadows. Tamsen heard Helena's cry of warning, but she didn't see the blow that struck her down, turning the day into darkness.

McGowan, Shanks, and Judge Bagley had developed their strategy well. Six men from Hill's Bar followed the canyon trail below. They would enter Tamsen's settlement in the guise of miners seeking a place to stay for the night, thus having the element of surprise on their side. However, McGowan knew the three of them would be recognized and the game would be up. Therefore, the party had split and his own group climbed to the canyon's rim. A ravine led downward to the house where Arab lived with the Spaniard. They would kill him, take the girl, then converge on the settlement from another direction.

Time was an important factor. It had taken them longer to climb to the brink than McGowan had anticipated. He was cursing a little as he tried to hurry the portly Judge Bagley, who was having difficulty keeping up. Then his sharp eyes caught sight of something ahead. Women's skirts, disappearing into the trees. Weighing one factor against another, he immediately changed his plans. The fellows below could take care of that chore themselves. This was too good an opportunity to miss.

He stationed himself at one side of the trail, sheltered by a gigantic tree. Shanks and Bagley were to wait at the other, and they were not to shoot. This prey must be taken alive. He grinned as he listened to the sounds of the girls' approach; he judged from the voices that Tamsen would emerge on his side. His face hardened as he reversed his gun, holding it by the barrel, ready to swing with the butt. He would take no chances with the little hellcat—

There, it was done! Tamsen lay unconscious on the ground. Helena struggled in Shanks' and Bagley's grip. McGowan tied her wrists, slipping a noose around her that held her arms to her sides. The other end of the rope he gave to Shanks to keep. Then he bound Tamsen's wrists and ankles. Helena would walk, but this one would have to be carried.

A rattle of gunfire sounded from the settlement below, and McGowan jerked to attention. Too many guns for the number of men who'd attacked the place. He heard the sharp crack-crack-crack of a Henry repeater, the dull, cannon-like boom of a Sharps fifty-caliber. Good God, *his* men had gone in with handguns. All hell was breaking loose down there. A column of smoke rose in black puffs above the rim. The damn fools had fired a house, probably with the women still in it.

348

Well, he had two of them in hand. And he would get the hell out of here with them, while the getting was good. He picked up Tamsen's recumbent body and placed it over his shoulder. Didn't weigh much, but the others would have to take their turn later. "Come on," he said shortly. "Let's go."

They moved out, Helena walking like an animal on a leash. But a wild thing, with hating eyes. Tamsen's dark hair hung down McGowan's back, lolling with each stride he took, all streaked with blood. Moving downriver, they headed away from the settlement where the spatter of weapons had died away, leaving only the crackling of flames as log structures burned.

The settlement had been taken by surprise. The men were all gone, working to build a storehouse behind the house Arab and Juan occupied, on the smaller shelf. The other storeroom was bulging with foods prepared for winter, and they required more room.

Carmen, Maggie, and Nell were lazing before the big house, taking the sun now that the mists had faded, making plans for the move in the spring. And little Martha, running to join them, fell, skinning a knee. Maggie scooped up the crying child and hurried to take her to Em. Carmen and Nell followed, with Nell clucking like an old hen. To their mutual relief, the cleaned and bandaged wound seemed slight. The house was warm and clean with the smell of baking and, reluctant to leave, they remained to visit.

"Where the hell's Tamsen?" Nell wanted to know.

Em told her that Tamsen and Helena had gone to visit Edwin Devon's grave.

Nell looked sad at the memory of the Englishman.

349

"Goddamn good thing they went today," she finally said. "Figger it's gonna snow us in, purty soon. Hell, you can smell it a-comin'."

"I hadn't noticed." Em laughed, pretending to inhale. "But then I'm in the house so much." She paused, an odd expression on her face. "Does anybody else smell *smoke?*"

She hurried to the window. "My God, the big house! It's on fire! Look!" Then she saw the capering figures of men around the flames.

Ned McGowan's followers had entered the settlement without being seen. They had gone first to the two-story building. There were two girls there, Ned had told them. But now the structure was unoccupied. A fire burned in the big front room, near the bar. They had a few drinks on the house as they pondered their next move. And then one of them came up with the idea of burning the place down.

The deed done, they boiled out onto the ledge. Duke Courtney spotted the pillar of smoke and left his work at a dead run. Followed by the other workers, he was the first one to round the narrow footpath. One of the intruders, seeing his gigantic figure, took dead aim.

Em, in the house, had taken charge, alerting the terrified women. Two guns leaned against the fireplace, and she grabbed them, giving one to Nell. "Maggie," she commanded, "get Martha to the floor, under the table. Carmen, go to Tamsen's room. See if she left her little gun behind."

Then she turned to the window, in time to see Duke's arrival, the other man's pistol aimed, in a deadly tableau. She fired without thinking. Duke's would-be killer spun and fell—but not before he

350

squeezed off a shot that sent Duke Courtney staggering as it struck.

Em's fright was replaced by a cold, deadly fury. She snapped off another shot as Duke headed for his house in a low crouching run. Another man down. Beside her, the gun Nell held boomed like a cannon, hitting a target, but knocking Nell to the floor.

"Hell," the big woman groaned. "Thing's gotta kick like a gawdamn mule. Now, how th' hell do you reload th' sonofabitch?"

Maggie left Martha and wriggled to her side, reloading for her. It was ready as Em, having fired off shots in rapid succession, was ready to reload her own. Their shooting had drawn the attention of the attackers from the footpath. As their fire was returned, Juan, Dusty, and Mac scurried to join Courtney. Bullets began to penetrate the room, striking the walls behind Em and the girls, all of them strangling on the smell of black powder. The invaders then turned to face a new threat—a barrage of gunfire from the shack that had been Pinkie and Dollie's, but where Duke and Mac now lived.

Caught between two fronts, the remaining men attempted to flee; one went down, followed by another. The last intruder raced for the narrow footpath leading to the smaller ledge. Once around the bulge of rock, he would be free—

Em drew a bead on him. Her rifle clicked. Empty. And Nell's was in the process of being reloaded. He was going to get away.

The fugitive met his nemesis in the form of an angry, red-haired girl. Ordered to remain behind, Arab had obeyed—but not for very long. Fearful for her husband's safety, she'd snatched up an old musket Dusty had won at cards and given to Juan. She'd

351

watched the men load and fire it, but she was uncertain as to the amount of powder they used. Too much was better than too little, she thought, pouring it in with a lavish hand. Then she shoved the wad and lead ball home. The sounds of shooting on the other ledge had intensified. She must hurry. She ran out the door and rounded the path. She met the fleeing gunman midway.

He stopped, gaping, the smoking gun in his hand hanging at his side. Arabella froze, too, but only for a moment. She raised the musket and fired point-blank. There was a terrific explosion. Arab found herself sitting on the path, the man nowhere to be seen. He'd been blasted over the edge of the cliff, cartwheeling until his body reached the river. And the waters carried him away.

Dazed, smoke-blackened, Arab trudged on, still carrying her empty gun. Juan was running to meet her. He caught her and held her close, one hand smoothing her tangled, singed, once-glorious hair; he murmured little broken words of love.

The others emerged, and they took stock of their casualties. Duke Courtney's arm was injured; the bullet went through cleanly, though, not touching a bone. Dusty and Maggie had been struck by flying wood splinters, which inflicted superficial wounds. Arab had powder burns, to which Em applied bear grease and a badly bruised shoulder that was turning purple. Nell made light of Arab's injury. "Hell," she said cheerfully, "you oughta see me. Black 'n' blue all th' way t' my butt. But I got me one of them bastards."

The most critical wound was the damage done to the samovar. It had gotten a sizable dent from a ricocheting bullet. Nell had to be restrained from going out and shooting the dead men all over again.

Mostly the small group felt pretty lucky. The big house was gone, true. The thing to think about was the way they'd escaped with their lives. "It was lucky," Em said, "that Tamsen and Helena had gone—"

Duke Courtney frowned. "Where did they go?"

Em explained, and he felt his blood run cold. From up there on the rim, they couldn't have missed the smoke. And the firing from below would have sounded loud and clear, now that miners were no longer working the valley. Knowing Tamsen, he knew she would have come running at the first alarm; they would have been here by now.

"Think I'll mosey on up an' walk 'em home," he said quietly, reaching for his gun. McCandless jerked his head up at his friend's tone. "I'll go with you," he said.

Courtney shook his head. "Them sonsofbitches might not have come by themselves. Could be more waitin' to move in." He settled Mac and Juan to guard the lower trail, Dusty the upper; he cautioned the girls to get their guns reloaded. Then he went along the trail and climbed to the rim.

Nobody in sight. He crossed the strip of meadow toward Devon's grave, walking slowly, on tenterhooks, ready to take a dive if someone fired at him. His eyes missed nothing, the movement of a branch, a blade of grass, the scurrying of an animal. The skies to the north were heavy and bulging now, a dirty white—

At the entry to the little glade, he found what he sought. Two men had been here. There had been a scuffle to his right, where they were, and here was a button from Helena's gown. To his left, where one man had waited, the grass was singularly undisturbed. Except here. Courtney knelt to identify

353

what he'd found: a pool of blood with a long, black, lustrous hair that coiled around his finger like a living thing. Tamsen's.

He scouted the area. Here a bloodied stem, there another. They pointed off downriver like an arrow. He began to run. And like an explosion, the skies broke loose with the belated storm.

It was twenty-four hours before he made it back to the settlement; stumbling through waist-high drifts, the snow still falling. He had failed in his search, stopped by stretches of snow and ice that couldn't be negotiated. He'd fought his way onward, finally stopping to curse and shake his fist at the sky before he was forced to return.

The news he brought back was devastating. Tamsen was not to be found. The women wept. The men paced with frustration. Em had directed that the dead men's pockets be searched. In one, they'd found a paper signed by Ned McGowan.

Tamsen was dead now, Em said in a tight voice. Or both girls were in Ned McGowan's hands. She didn't see small Dusty turn paper-white at her words, or Nell move to his side sensing the depth of his emotions. Em's eyes were on Duke Courtney, praying he would refute her statements.

Dead? It was likely, Duke thought, evading Em's pleading gaze. With all that blood—he walked to the window. "At least, we won't have to bury those men out there until spring. The snow will keep them."

"They're not there," Em said dejectedly. "They came from Hill's Bar, and we sent them back where they came from."

Far below, hidden by a curtain of driven snow, the yellow Fraser carried its gruesome cargo downriver.

CHAPTER 15

Ned McGowan was an astute man who believed in covering all eventualities. His keenness was, he believed, the only reason he'd survived so long. On the way upriver, his eyes worked with his brain to catalogue every slight deviation that might be taken along the trail, should their mission fail and they be followed.

Now, assuming that his men might have lost the battle, it would not be long until someone came in search of the girls. He drove the others unmercifully, taking evasive action whenever possible. When the snow began to fall, he went forward more confidently. Blowing as it was, it shielded his tracks and made the small group invisible from a distance.

He had a destination. On the way up, he'd noted several abandoned mine shafts that appeared tenable. He'd left a cache of supplies in each. It was late night when they stumbled into the first of these shelters, half-frozen and blinded with snow. But it was already occupied. The place was rank with smoke and the smells of wet furs and of cooking. Behind a small blaze where a hare was roasting on a stick sat an Indian.

Ned McGowan's hand went to his gun as the Indian rose, then hesitated. The man was making a gesture of welcome, pointing to the food, indicating his willingness to share. His dark eyes touched the bound girls and moved away with disinterest as if there was nothing unusual in the sight.

Ned relaxed, grinned, and dumped his burden in a corner. "Come in, Judge," he said jovially. "You too, Shanks. Think we've been invited to make ourselves to home. Take the noose off that one." He pointed to Helena. "She ain't going no place. But leave her hands tied. Maybe she can still give her friend there a hand."

Helena, released, dropped to her knees at Tamsen's side, catching her breath at sight of the terrible wound. She was so cold—but she still breathed. The Indian, good-naturedly, brought a thin cup of melted snow water and Helena tore a bit from her skirt to wash the blood from Tamsen's face. The Indian's features looked Tlingit, but he could be Kenai, Haidi, anything—many of them drifted into the mining camps, forgetting their proud heritage, to pick up the gold-miners' leavings . . . .

"*Haiti-deschi*," she whispered. "Help us."

Ned McGowan's gun had leaped into his hand. "What did you say?" he grated.

"I only thanked him. But he is not of my people. He did not understand."

McGowan studied the Indian's expressionless face. At last, satisfied with what he saw, he put his gun away. He didn't relish the thought of spending a night in the shaft with a dead Indian. The morning would be soon enough. They would leave him here where nobody would find him. Besides, he was fashioning snowshoes; finished with one pair, he began another.

Ned McGowan appropriated Bagley's gold watch and held it to the Indian's ear, watching his expression of amazement at the ticking sound. Then, with gestures, he pointed at the snowshoes, holding up four fingers. He managed to convey that the watch would be a reward for four pairs of snowshoes—if they were done by morning.

"You damn fool," Bagley exploded. "Not my watch! You could trade him something else."

Ned grinned slyly. "You'll keep your watch. In the morning, he won't need it."

The Indian worked at his craft until the hare was done to a turn. Then he tore it apart with his fingers, passing the choicer bits to his guests. Helena refused her portion, and he thrust it at her, grunting incomprehensibly, until she accepted it. In the days ahead, she thought forlornly, she would need all her strength if she were to find some means to escape.

After they had eaten, McGowan went farther back into the shaft, finding the cache he'd left on his earlier journey. He removed a bottle from it, then, after deliberation, took two more. One each for the night, to ward off the chill they'd suffered in the snow; there would be a long trek tomorrow.

He offered the Indian a drink. Surprisingly, it was refused. The man pointed to his work, to his head, and then pointed to the bottle, pantomiming that he would wait until the morning.

"Intelligent fellow," Ned told Bagley as he put the bottle to his lips. "Makes me wish I didn't have to shoot him." The Indian worked at his snowshoes. The other men drank and discussed their foray on Tamsen's settlement, wondering what had gone wrong. The others had run into trouble, or they would have shown up by now. But for sure, they'd burned the place down, and with all that shooting, they'd accounted well for themselves.

Helena, listening, was sick at heart as she wondered who was listed among the dead. From

357

time to time, the Indian replenished the fire. Its warmth spread through the small shaft; it was sleep-inducing after the cold they'd endured. Helena found herself nodding. With a generous gesture, their host had spread his furs for the renegades. The men took off their wet boots and set them near the fire to dry, then proceeded to drink themselves into a stupor.

Their snoring filled the shaft as the Indian finished the second pair of snowshoes. Then he rose, stretched, and came toward her, cat-footed as he stepped over the recumbent forms, with a knife in his hands. She felt immobile with fear, but he took her wrists and slit the ropes that bound them. She was free.

Her first thought was of Ned McGowan's gun. She would kill them all! But seeing her glance toward it, the Indian shook his head and beckoned to her. Picking up Tamsen in one arm, his snowshoes in the other, he led her out into the blowing snow. Then he left them and went back inside. He came out with three pairs of boots, and as Helena looked at him questioningly, he tossed them into the turbulent Fraser below.

Helena followed him numbly as he led the way south, to a place where the trail was blocked by drifting snow. Then they turned west, away from the Fraser valley, and kept close to the sheltered flanks of the high mountains; they followed ravines and creeks that curved and twisted like endless mazes. He knew where he was going. For on the first night, he brought them to a small, deserted shack that was shelter of a sort. Here, snow water was boiled and broth made from an an owl he brought in; he had found it by the simple expedient of seeking out the bones of small animals the bird regurgitated near its nesting place.

Tamsen was made as comfortable as possible and broth forced between her pale lips; the Indian told Helena who he was, and where they were going. His name was Dan-e-wak, or Silver Eyes. His kwan were a lost people. Long years before, in his grandfather's time, they had lived on the island of the Kiksadi. Driven from their homes by the Russians, they had moved to Shisk-kee-noo, the fort at Indian River. There was a battle there, and the Indians had dispersed. He had heard many had gone back, but his family, along with others, desired to be free. They had sought another home, and it was there he would take them now.

That was the gist of it. His story was difficult to follow. There were other accents mingled with his own, those of Haida, Tsimshian, and Kenai. Apparently the customs of the Tlingit had merged with other customs. Helena felt a chill. Among one of these types, the medicine men were rumored to be dog-eaters and flesh-eaters. It was a part of their religious ceremony. What would they find when they reached the haven toward which this man was taking them?

She was even more concerned when he looked at the sleeping Tamsen. "They will rejoice that I have aided you," he said soberly. "But our homes are well hidden away. They will not like my bringing a *Koltschanen,* a stranger."

Helena opened Tamsen's dress at the throat, withdrawing the raven amulet. "She is of the Raven kwan, my sister, the adopted daughter of my mother whose spirit watches over her. She mourned our mother's death and brought gifts to the funeral feast. She is one of us."

She had convinced their guide, but how would she fare when they reached the village?

Tamsen woke for a short time that night. Though

she did not recognize Helena, or seem to know who or where she was, they got her to take more broth. It was a good sign.

In the morning, the snow had stopped. It was bitterly cold; the landscape was a dazzling white expanse. Even the trees bent beneath a concealing mantle of white. Taking soot from the dead fire, Dan-e-wak painted his face and Helena's to protect them from snow blindness. Leaving Tamsen's wet cloak behind, he wrapped her in furs from the shelter and lifted her to his shoulder; they set off again with Helena following.

The next night on the trail was a repetition of the one before. And finally, the next afternoon, they reached a summit. Here, Dan-e-wak turned to enter a tunnel-like defile, almost hidden from view. Shoulder-width at first, it went down and down. They finally came out on a small plateau. Dan-e-wak gestured at the scene below.

"My home. My people."

Helena gasped, first at the terrain, then at the houses and the people. They were located near a hot spring. A haze of steam lay over the valley floor; here and there were patches of green. An overhang of the mountain shielded the valley from snow. Helena's eyes, half-blinded by the glittering expanses they had traversed, had difficulty in focusing. But through the mist, she saw houses, constructed and painted in the old way, painted with the kwan signs. The people who moved among those houses dressed as they did in her childhood, before she had been taken away to Veniaminov's orphanage. The men with their mantles of tanned skin wore fur caps with the hair on the outside. The women in their top-to-toe under-garments of skins wore apron pieces that reached to the waist, their over-cloaks.

She had not realized how many of the Russian ways her people had adopted. Her eyes blurred. It was like going back in time—to a happier day. Then a new thought struck her. The scene was so hazy and unreal that she thought perhaps she had died, and landed in this spirit world. Maybe her mother would be there to greet her; maybe she was truly going home.

Dan-e-wak removed his snowshoes, and Helena followed suit. Then, picking up his slight burden once more, he led the way down a winding path. The warmth of the valley came up to meet them.

At the base of their descent, Dan-e-wak placed Tamsen at his feet and stood with folded arms as two regal-appearing men approached them. "My grandfather, my father," he said with dignity, "these are women of the Raven clan. I will take them as my wives. The one," he pointed at Helena, "because I wish it. The other because of my responsibility. I will be her brother-in-law."

Tamsen stirred and opened her eyes. Her head hurt, and for a moment, she thought she was back in the hospital at Novoarchangelsk. But these were alien faces bending above her, frightening figures dressed in peculiar clothing. They did not like her, she could tell. They wanted her to go away.

A woman's arms went around her shoulders as she struggled to sit up. Helena. Where were they, and what were they doing here? Tamsen made a small sobbing sound. "Where's Dan?" she moaned. "Helena—please find Dan."

BOOK III

PALACE OF
THE TSAR

CHAPTER 1

Dan Tallant stood on the floating bridge that spanned the Neva River and looked down into its shadowed waters. The climate of St. Petersburg was deemed temperate compared with most of Russia. But he was cold; it could not be less than twenty-five degrees at the moment, but the damp seeped through the padded jacket he wore, chilling his very bones.

He felt very much alone. The Baron de Stoeckl had been sent to Washington immediately after their arrival in Russia. Dan himself was instructed to wait for an audience with the tsar—an audience that never occurred. Tsar Alexander II was at present deeply involved in drawing up articles of emancipation for Russian serfs. His drafting committee had been in session for months. All else had to wait.

Not that the emancipation wasn't a good idea, Tallant thought. He'd grown to despise the arrogant Russian aristocracy and its treatment of downtrodden peasants. He longed for his own country, where he wouldn't be kept cooling his heels while a ruler tried to set up something that wouldn't work. How the hell could it? A little bit of freedom was worse than none at all. And even that would probably be withheld. The tsar couldn't seem to make up his mind about anything.

At least Tallant had accomplished one objective. He'd given the maps he'd carried so long to de Stoeckl, to deliver to a senator in Washington. He believed in the baron's sense of honor. The sealed packet would be delivered safely, and his friend, the senator, would know what to do with them. De Stoeckl would never know he carried the key to the treasures of Russian Alaska, or that the maps might be the deciding factor in the purchase of the country. Though the baron was in favor of selling, he might change his mind if he knew the true richness of the Alaskan territories.

The maps turned his thoughts to Tamsen and her betrayal of him. He had forgiven her long ago for making copies for Voedvodski. There was much to forgive on both sides. Looking into the dark waters, he was able to resurrect a memory of her small face. It shimmered there until a passing boat shivered it to fragments.

How he longed for his Tamsen... imagining her beside him, though he still didn't even know whether she was dead or alive. A communiqué from Voedvodski had only stated that Mrs. Tallant was no longer with them in Novoarchangelsk, and he hoped Mr. Tallant did not feel the need to excuse his actions with such imaginative tales as his abduction story. It did not make for good relations between countries.

So, Tamsen was no longer with them. Had she actually gone away? Or had something happened to her? Tallant didn't know, and it was driving him out of his mind. He'd requested permission to return to the Russian-American colony and permission had been denied. He must wait upon the indulgence of the tsar.

Dan Tallant was as much in prison as when he had

been in irons. His keeper was Alexander Nikolaevich, emperor of Russia, who walked the tightrope of public opinion, which changed with the wind. He might not get around to the discussion of Alaskan territory for weeks, months, years.

Tallant left the bridge and walked through the streets of one of the most beautiful cities in the world. It was famous for its severe and stately architecture, its straight streets, its wide avenues and lush gardens. The banks of the Neva were framed in pink and gray granite, and the surface of the river was smooth as glass. But Dan walked with blind eyes; too many times he'd traversed the three wide avenues radiating from the Admiralty Building to the Neva.

All his life Dan had been something of a loner. It was a necessary trait in his profession, but he'd never felt so alone as now, in a strange city among alien people. At the moment he had two choices: to return to his high-ceilinged, marble-floored room, which was always cold despite the charcoal burning on its hearth—or to walk some more. Tonight, though, he felt badly in need of companionship. He considered a third alternative that he'd often rejected before—an invitation to attend a secret meeting....

Before he departed for Washington, Baron de Stoeckl had introduced him to several writers and intellectuals; among them a man called Turgenev and another called Tolstoi. The gentlemen had fired question after question at him about the way of life in the United States. Bitter at the exile of their friend and comrade, Fedor Dostoevski, for his "reactionary views," they spoke out angrily against their government, pointing out the corruption that lay beneath its surface.

Dan had been invited to a secret meeting by

Turgenev, who told him their usual time and location. Dan hadn't gone before because he did not wish to align himself with a radical element in the eyes of the tsar. Well, to hell with the tsar! He would go tonight!

He left the broad thoroughfare and moved into a narrower street. He walked until he came to a shabby area, but even here attempts had been made at beautification. The scenic canals, however, were still filled with refuse, the gardens trampled, the fountains dry. Around him wandered men from the shipyards, the mills, kerchiefed women bent from scrubbing floors, their skirts still wet from kneeling. There was a smell of poverty here, of sweat and of lack of proper sanitation. One of the poorest lanes was the one he'd been directed to. It was a certain number of houses down, in a basement room at the rear of a tall house. He began to count.

He whirled at a sound behind him, the sound of galloping hooves striking stone intermingled with a scream. "The Guard!" It took a minute for the Russian word to translate itself in his mind. In the same moment, he saw the lane crowded with mounted men; they were Cossacks and they rode over fleeing people, striking out with the flat of their sabers. The lead horse brushed Dan's chest, knocking him backward into a doorway. Then more galloped by. The white night was filled with them, and with the moans of the citizens they'd ridden down.

A flurry of soldiers on horses thundered past. Then something happened. A big Russian caught the bridle of one horse, and turned to block the lane. Its rider cursed him, and struck out, swinging blows that the man ducked nimbly. Politic or not, Tallant stepped out to help him.

368

But the courageous Russian worker was felled. Horrified, Dan watched the Cossacks ride over his prostrate body. Dan turned to go back to his own sanctuary, then stopped. A small woman had tried to cross the lane during the brief pause—or was it a child? Now, she stood still, frozen at the sight of death thundering down on her—a baby in her arms. He leaped forward, grabbed her, and pulled her toward the doorway, absorbing another stunning blow from a horse's front quarters as he covered her with his body.

Then the Cossacks were gone, the lane swept clean before them; all the other residents had scuttled for shelter.

Dan looked at the remains of what had been a brave man. "Good God," he said, swallowing. "Good God!" Then, in Russian, "Where do you live? I will take you home." The girl only looked up at him, still paralyzed with fear. He tried to take the baby from her and she clung to it fiercely. In the process, the ragged cloth around it fell away, and he saw it for what it was—a loaf of black bread.

Suddenly, she began to speak. "I am sorry. It was my fault. I knew it was not wise to venture out at this hour. But I—I had hunger."

All Tallant could see were two great eyes in a small pointed face. As he tried to follow her Russian, he realized she was still frightened—and of him. It was the way he was dressed, he decided—in the expensive clothing of the aristocrats; but he wanted to get her to a safe place before those monsters returned. At his insistence, she pointed out a house, two doors away from where they stood. Its door opened on a steep stair, and he followed her as she climbed, casting wary glances over her shoulder.

"Does this happen often?" he asked.

"The Guard? Those who would make revolution gather here to better our lot," she said a little bitterly. "So the Cossacks come many times. In this place, hope and death are old friends."

She pushed open a warped door that scraped against bare boards. He entered behind her, watching as she placed the bread on a table and lighted the stub of a smoking candle. Then she turned to face him, dragging the scarf from her hair.

The candle revealed a small figure in a large, ragged gown. The girl's hair was like Tamsen's, long and dark. He knew it would be silken to the touch. The eyes that met his were an odd shade of turquoise, and they were filled with a hopeless fear.

"Do as you will and be done with it," she said listlessly. "You saved my life, and I am tired of fighting—"

As he stared at her, the meaning of her words finally dawned on him. She thought he had followed her here, hoping for a night of dalliance as a reward. His first impulse was to explode, to tell her he had no intention of raping a pitiful little waif of a girl, but she was frightened enough.

He bowed, as he would to a great lady. "I'm afraid I have some business to attend to, so now that I've seen you safely home, will you excuse me?"

Her eyes grew even bigger. "You do not like me?"

He reddened. "I find you quite charming. But I have a pressing errand."

He backed through the door. Reaching the street, he decided to return to his room. The basement meeting had broken up, no doubt. He hoped they had all escaped. He walked past the place where the courageous Russian had fallen. A little knot of people were gathered around his body. An elderly

370

woman, a black shawl thrown over her face, was weeping over the dead man.

His had been a futile gallant gesture. Tallant despised this country. He had no respect for its court, with its petty intrigues and posturing; he had little patience with the revolutionaries who played their games for which innocent people suffered; he feared the Cossack guards who ruled the streets through terror.

As he came out into view of the magnificent structures along the Neva, he shook his head in confusion. St. Petersburg consisted of many worlds, each almost ignorant of the others. One day they would all come together. The Neva would run red with blood. And what would come from the bloodletting? Something better—or far worse.

His head ached as he tried to dismiss the events of the night from his mind. But when he reached his room and readied himself for bed, sleep would not come. He kept thinking of a small ragged girl, bread clutched in her arms as though it were her most precious thing. He had felt her bones sticking out in the brief time she had pressed against him in the doorway, for protection. And his trained eye had retained a picture of her room: dark, squalid, an empty hearth, and a few moldy cheese rinds on the table where she placed the bread.

There was no sign of another occupant; she was alone. A child like that! No, not a child, but a woman. She must be Tamsen's age. And there was something about her that reminded him of Tamsen. The way she had faced him, looking him straight in the eye, despite her fears—

He sighed. Tamsen was separated from him, perhaps lost forever. He was trapped here and couldn't

371

search for her or help her. But he might be able to do something to aid this girl. He would go there in the morning, take some food and a few rubles, see if there were any way he could get her moved into a less dangerous area.

He fell asleep, dreaming of Tamsen bending over a campfire, her dark hair down her back. At his approach, she raised her head and smiled. He reached a hand out to trace her lips, her tawny cheeks. "Getting to know you," he said.

Then he noticed that her eyes were an odd turquoise blue, that the gown she wore, a ragged, rusty black, covered an emaciated little body. She stared at him in a hopeless resigned fear.

"Do what you will and be done with it. You saved my life, and I am tired of fighting."

Dan Tallant woke up swearing and threw his pillow at the far wall. He slept no more that night.

In the morning, a long-awaited summons came. Daniel Tallant, representative of the government of the United States, was requested to present himself before the tsar.

CHAPTER 2

Tallant approached the Winter Palace with a good-sized chip on his shoulder. In this job, which required diplomacy, he'd schooled himself to think as a gentleman would; the new language in which he was now so adept added a formality to his thoughts and actions.

Now the facade had slipped. The long months he'd been kept waiting were vivid in his mind, as was the incident of the previous night. Right now, Tsar Alexander Nikolaevich would catch the brunt of his anger. Dan forgot the elegant Russian garb he was wearing, the exalted person he was going to meet; he reverted to the kind of anger he would have expressed in his role as a footloose ruffian in the cantinas on the Rio.

He had come to the conclusion that the tsar was a sonofabitch. A little tin god sitting up there on his throne throwing his power around, doing whatever amused him. *Kill a few helpless people. Deign to talk to that fellow from the States.* Emancipation of the serfs? Hell! The bastard probably had never seen one!

Pausing at the entrance of the palace, Dan presented his credentials to a guard. The Russian inspected them while Tallant scowled fixedly out at the Neva. The city of St. Petersburg was situated in a

373

low swampy area, and he'd heard they had some pretty catastrophic floods. He wished the waters would rise and wash the whole goddamn place away.

The guard gestured curtly, and Dan followed him. Another guard swung in at his other side. Was he a guest or a prisoner? Tallant wondered as he marched along between them. He had a sudden impulse to grab both by the collars and crack their heads together!

He just might do it, after this interview. How would it be conducted? He could see himself being forced to walk across miles of floor toward a man on a jewel-studded throne, being pushed to his knees by the guards, forced to make obeisance to a sonofabitch with a crown. He'd be damned if he would. He would kneel to no man!

The corridor turned and turned again, and at last they stood before a door. It opened; the guards stepped in with him, saluted, and then retreated. He was left to face the tsar alone

But the man who sat behind the desk was dressed in the uniform of an officer of the guards. Dan feared he was getting the brush-off again. Either that, or he was to be placed under arrest. He glowered as the officer rose and came forward with his hand outstretched.

"You are Mr. Daniel Tallant," the man beamed, giving him a hearty handshake. "I am Alexander. And this"—he introduced an aging gentleman standing behind him—"is my old tutor, poet, friend, Zhukovski, in whose opinions I have great confidence. Please, sit down."

Dan sat, his knees suddenly undependable. The anger he'd built up had no target. It felt like swinging at someone, he thought ruefully, missing, and finding one's self hurtling into space.

374

The tsar returned to his seat behind the desk, and Zhukovski provided tea from a steaming samovar. "Now," Alexander said, "tell me about your country."

Dan found himself talking as he would to any ordinary man. The tsar asked questions as fast as he could answer them.

"Are your people satisfied with their rulers?"

"We elect our government. But I suppose all people are never satisfied."

"What do you do if you are not."

Dan grinned. "Then we just stand up on our hind legs and say so."

"I do not believe that would be an effective system here."

"No," Dan said, recalling the events of the previous night, "I don't think so."

After a while, he began to wonder if Alexander would ever get to the point. When the change came, it was so sudden it caught him by surprise. The tsar slapped a stack of papers on his desk and said sternly, "Mr. Tallant, would you like to explain *these?*"

The maps of Russian Alaska, Tamsen's copies, with the locations of minerals and precious metals designated on them, had reached the tsar, and for the moment, he was speechless. Alexander fanned them before him. "These have been in our hands for months, but they only came to my attention yesterday. I am a very busy man and have tried to deal only with the emancipation situation for some time, giving orders that all else be laid aside. But *these!* If I had known of their existence, of the riches to be found in Russian Alaska, I would not have allowed de Stoeckl to treat with your president."

Tallant stalled for time, shuffling through the

papers. Then he frowned, puzzled. He did not recall marking this location. As he remembered, the whole area was nothing but muskeg. And this! Purportedly a rich gold find, the designated site lay in a country of great glaciers, rivers of frozen ice that shifted, producing thunder as it shaled into the waters. Immense, dangerous, impenetrable. Good God!

Turning the paper over, he studied the other side. Had he not known what to look for, he might never have found it. There were definite signs that the map had been traced. And he understood what Tamsen had done. Brave, loyal, foolish woman. She had copied the charts, but the locations of value were not marked for distinction.

"These are your maps?" Alexander looked at him, keenly. "Of your making?"

"Yes," Tallant said. "And no. I made a large set for Governor-General Voedvodski, and a smaller for myself. But if you will please look at the legend at the bottom of each, designating the general area—that is in my hand. While this," he pointed to a tiny, neat printing at the site locations, "was most definitely done by someone else." He turned the paper over, showing the marks of tracing. "And, as you can see, this is a copy, perhaps from my original. Except for these. There are no telltale signs beneath these." He tapped the X-marked areas.

Zhukovski moved forward, studying the charts. "He is quite correct, Alexander."

Dan concealed his elation beneath a disturbed expression. "I do not understand it. Perhaps it was done as a jest. Or someone may have had something to gain by such a forgery."

The tsar and his old tutor exchanged glances, and Alexander stood. Extending his hand once more, he told Tallant he had enjoyed their interview and only regretted that pressing business forced him to cut it short. He extended an invitation to dinner that night, with his family, and once more, Dan found himself escorted down the corridors.

Behind him, Alexander looked at Zhukovski. "What do you think, old friend?"

"Our man there, Voedvodski, isn't it? He has opposed the sale of the Russian Americas, has he not? Yet, would he dare...?"

"I do not know." The tsar sighed, looking suddenly tired and old. "But send a message. Furuhelm is to replace him, since he is at hand. When Captain Lieutenant Golowin is free from his present duties, I will send him out to look at the situation." He closed his eyes, pinching the flesh between them with his fingers, then, with his customary self-doubt, asked, "Do you think that would be wise?"

Zhukovski gently reassured him. Replacing the charts in a drawer, the emperor of the Russias returned to his other duties.

Dan Tallant didn't go immediately to his lonely room. Instead, he went to the Neva bridge and stood looking at the water with blind eyes. He thought of the accusations he'd thrown at Tamsen. "You'd sell anything, wouldn't you?" And then, "You can set up all the paying customers you want from now on, because, my dear, I'm through!"

Good God, even if he managed to convince her that he'd been abducted, that he'd had no intention of leaving with the despicable Anya, how could Tamsen ever forgive him?

Somehow he must obtain permission to leave Russia, to seek her out if she still lived. To go down on his knees to her. The tsar had seemed a reasonable man. Perhaps he would have an opportunity during dinner to talk to him, to ask for release.

The opportunity did not arrive. For the tsar had been quite literal in stating his invitation to dine with the family. It was not the sumptuous banquet Tallant envisioned, but a simple meal in a small but beautifully appointed room. The party consisted of the tsar, his wife, Maria Alexandrovna, their six sons and two daughters; in addition, there was the old tutor, Zhukovski, and the children's governess, a robust Swedish girl with a fine command of English, who was seated at Tallant's right.

Looking at him from beneath blond lashes that curled over pink cheeks, the girl, Ingrid Larsen, liked what she saw. There was nothing effete about this man with his bleak, scarred face; a look of pain was in his dark eyes and about his mouth. Alexander had teased her about her disinterest in the gentlemen of the court. Here at last was a man she found exciting. All laughter and blushes, she set herself to capture his attention.

Ingrid could not know she reminded him of an errand he'd failed to perform. That her well-nourished body contrasted sharply with that of a ragged little waif, or that Dan Tallant was unable to swallow the food before him as he thought of a girl in a room with an empty hearth—and a loaf of bread.

The evening ended with Maria Alexandrovna and the governess shooing laughing children toward their beds. A pretty sight, and especially welcome. Now Dan had a chance to speak with Alexander, but apparently their going was an announcement of the end to the evening. The tsar stood and extended his hand.

"So kind of you to come. We must do this quite often."

"Your Highness," Dan blurted, "may I request

permission to return to Novoarchangelsk, now that we have spoken? I have urgent business there—"

The ruler looked perplexed. "Are you not happy here? The Baron de Stoeckl wished you to remain until his return—"

"Your Highness, I am a married man. My wife—"

Alexander's brow cleared. "Ah, that is it! You are lonely! We have been remiss in our hospitality, and that we shall remedy. You will be our guest tomorrow night—a ballet, featuring the Frenchman, Marius Petipa! A master at the art. And you will escort our little Ingrid. Yes?" He beamed at his solution to Dan's problem and Dan forced an answering smile.

"Thank you, sir. I appreciate the invitation."

A handshake, and Dan Tallant found himself in the corridor.

That night he dreamed he was in the Winter Palace. A woman stood in the shadows, calling him, her voice echoing through the palace halls. First she was Tamsen, in her gown of satin and tulle. Then it was the waif he'd rescued, clad in ragged, rusty black. He must go to her. But he couldn't move. His wrists and ankles were manacled—bound tightly in Ingrid Larsen's flaxen braids. He woke, half-smothered, ill with frustration.

CHAPTER 3

The dawn was gray and cold. Fedor, Dan's manservant, had already started a fire on the hearth, but the marble floor was chilly beneath Dan's bare feet. How much colder it would be in a dreary room in a shabby lane—no heat, no tea brewing in a samovar, no warm winter clothing.

"Fedor," he said crisply, "I want you to do some shopping for me." He made a quick list and handed it to the man who studied it with astonished eyes: a large basket, tea, charcoal, beets, turnips, a cabbage, smoked fish, cheese, and some small Russian cakes—and a woman's cloak?

Fedor had been a nobleman's valet before he'd been assigned to the mad American. He'd felt a great deal of his dignity had been lost in the assignment. But to be sent to shop! And for such items! It was the ultimate in humiliation.

"Sir," he said, elevating his nose.

Dan looked at him steadily. "I will expect those purchases within the hour."

Fedor's hauteur crumbled. "The cloak," he asked meekly, "what size or color?"

"Small, I suppose, and the color doesn't matter. But it must be warm."

Curiosity consuming him, the supercilious Fedor tried again. "For an aristocratic lady, sir? Or for—"

Dan cut him off, his voice harsh with anger. "For a lady. There's only one kind! Now go!"

Fedor went to do his bidding, his pride destroyed. Only the large number of rubles the mad American gave him drove him to do his duty. If he shopped most carefully, there would be lots left over. The American was crazy, he would confide to the shopkeepers, given to charitable impulses. He himself had deigned to offer his services since it was in a good cause, thus keeping the American from being cheated. "I want the best," he would say. "And at the least price!"

Perhaps his employer would reward him further, and his gains would be doubled. He returned to Dan Tallant, carrying a basket filled with the best of produce. The cloak he had purchased was of crimson wool, with gold braid for trim and warmly lined with fur. It was a cloak suited for a princess.

Apparently, Dan Tallant thought so, too, for Fedor did receive an additional reward. He could almost forgive his new master for being less than a gentleman.

Tallant left the house, carrying the cloak and basket and made his way to the back street of St. Petersburg. Today it did not seem as menacing as it had the night before. Only sad. Ragged children played in the street still stained with hero's blood. At Dan's approach, they froze like frightened mice, their faces blank and expressionless.

The memory of last night's dinner, with the tsar's exuberant children, haunted Dan. How could such disparate ways of life coexist? He was tempted to pass out the contents of his basket. But there were so many! Spread so thin, it would help no one. So, he continued on his way and found the house with no difficulty.

The stairs were as he remembered, steep, scuffed, and warped with dampness. The smell of cooking clung to the walls; years of cooking tainted by time. Cabbage, onions, meals long vanished, haunted the halls like tantalizing ghosts to the starving.

He tapped at the door to the girl's room, and there was no answer. Finally, feeling a bit foolish and apprehensive at what he might find, he pushed the creaking door inward. It went its limit, hanging up on the warped floor. But it was sufficient to see that there was no one there.

Dan entered the room, stricken at its poverty, and placed the basket on the table. He would wait, and while he waited, he would set a fire on the hearth. He was kneeling, fanning the crude charcoal into a blaze, when he heard a gasp behind him. He rose to see the girl he had rescued standing in the door, her eyes wide with fear. And like the children of the street, her face was expressionless. It was clear she was terrified out of her wits.

"I—I beg your pardon," he said huskily. "I thought perhaps a fire—"

She entered warily at his words, her eyes going hungrily to the basket he'd put down. "It is nice," she said in a hopeless voice.

He knew what was in her mind. He'd left before without claiming a reward, and now he had returned. He cursed himself for his clumsiness.

"I have been longing for a home-cooked meal," he said stiffly. "I thought perhaps you might not mind...so I brought some things." His words trailed off at her expression. She went to the basket.

"Cabbage, beets, fish, cheese...!" Her tone grew fainter, and she reeled, her face white.

Leaping up, he took her arm and led her to the one broken chair. She hunched forward, her arms crossed, tightly pressed to her middle. "Are you all right?"

"Yes," she whispered. "Yes."

"Then stay where you are," he said harshly. He set to work, brewing tea, lacing it lavishly from a bottle in his pocket. She drank it thirstily, her color returning.

"I will cook," she said.

"No," Tallant answered. "I will."

His days on the trail enabled him to produce an adequate meal on the Russian hearth. The girl ate daintily, trying to control her hunger as he watched. It was just as well, he thought, or she would be ill. There was something about her that didn't fit with her surroundings. Her body was slender and aristocratic, unlike the lumpy limbs of the peasantry. She might have been masquerading in her rags, from the appearance.

She stopped eating and wrapped a remaining morsel in a bit of cloth. "I thank you," she said, still with an odd fear in her huge eyes. "Why are you so kind to a stranger?"

Why? A good question. But maybe he could answer it and set her mind at rest at the same time. "You are very much like my wife," he told her. "Except that her eyes are dark. Her name is Tamsen. By the way, I am Daniel Tallant, a representative of the United States."

"And I am Olga, wife to Pavel Stepanov—if he still lives."

Little by little, he got her story. Her husband was a seaman. He had sailed away and not returned. Though she was certain he was dead, she waited. His pay had stopped, but there had been no official notification. It had been difficult living here in this rough street, alone, yet she had managed.

"Your husband—I'm sorry. You loved him very much?"

She had an expression of bewilderment. "I do not know. We had been married only a week when he sailed. My parents had died, and he was kind, though he was not of our class—"

Our class. It was a clue to her appearance. But he must not ask too many questions, not this time. She was a bundle of nerves, close to tears. Probably because she was still afraid of him. He could ease those fears by taking his leave.

"I must go. I have many things to do. And an appointment this evening. The ballet—"

"Ballet," she said dreamily. "I have never seen it, but my mother told me of its beauty. How wonderful for you."

"Perhaps I might take you one day," he blurted.

She began to laugh, a harsh bitter laugh. "I shall never see it. Thank you. You have done quite a lot already. And do not think I am more than what you see. It is true my parents were of the court, in the time of Nicholas, but my father's sympathies were with the Decembrists. He was banished to Siberia, then returned here where I was born. So I am nothing, but I am grateful, all the same."

Embarrassed, he took his leave as soon as possible, his anger directed at all tsars, past and present—and at himself. He should not have brought the glitter of the tsar's circle into that small dark room, pointing up all the shabbiness the girl had to live with. Parents exiled and now dead; widowed after a week; cold, hungry, good God!

He wondered gloomily what his own wife was enduring. Then, returning to his room, he tried to shut it all from his mind as he dressed for the evening of ballet.

He did not enjoy it. The women on stage were graceful, blossoming, then wilting like flowers. It was a hell of an occupation for a man. He made the mistake of voicing his views to the astounded Alexander.

He was wrong, he was told. Ballet was directly descended from the court festivals of the Italian Renaissance. Perhaps as long ago as 1749. And as for Petipa! His brother, Lucien, was *premier danseur* of the Paris Opera, his father, Jean Petipa, ballet master in Brussels before coming to Russia to teach in the Imperial Academy of Dancing.

Sensing his remarks had been sacrilegious, Tallant folded his arms and watched in silence. There was grace there, he thought grudgingly, and even beauty, but all too precious for his taste.

He was aware of Ingrid's amused eyes on his face. She leaned toward him. "I understand your thinking," she whispered. "But you must also understand ours. See only the loveliness of it all!"

He smiled at her, enjoying her understanding and the touch of her warm fingers on his arm.

Despite his feelings toward the gentlemen of the ballet, Tallant found his interest drawn to the stage as the dance wove its way to a romantic ending. The soft lights and music got through to him, making him let his guard down. He was surprised to find himself misty-eyed.

Ingrid leaned toward him, tapping him with her fan. "You see, you did enjoy it! How I would love to see it again! But then, I cannot attend without an escort."

Neatly trapped, Dan volunteered his services for the following night, and Ingrid's cheeks were pink with triumph. Alexander sent him a fatherly look of understanding that made his blood boil. He swallowed his anger, knowing that part of it was directed at himself. He had been pleased at the thought of an evening spent in female company, after all those nights alone.

They left the theater with guards on either side of them to protect the tsar and his guests. The street was filled with ragged, solemn-faced people, gathered to view the pomp and ceremony. Those who crowded too closely were beaten back. Dan's fists clenched at the sight. Then he saw, huddled in the shadow of a building, a white face lifted above a red cloak . . . Olga!

Dan had made an involuntary sound. Ingrid put her gloved hand on his arm, following his gaze. "Someone you know? A friend, perhaps?"

"A chance acquaintance," he growled, his mind seething with anger and concern. Had she followed him here? To wait outside in the street like that? And now Olga would be going back to her room, through those dark and dangerous alleyways at the mercy of the roving Cossacks—and unscrupulous men who lay in wait for young women alone. It was a damnfool thing to do!

Tallant handed Ingrid into the tsar's coach, mumbling something about an errand he'd forgotten. Would she forgive him if he asked to be excused? Tea tomorrow? Of course, he'd be delighted. Then he shoved his way through the crowds, which was easy for a tall bronzed man in an opera cape with an important air like his to do.

Another woman, Ingrid thought. She'd known Dan Tallant had a wife, but that had not troubled her. The wife was not here, therefore, no one to be reckoned with. She, herself, had left a husband and a small neat house in Sweden, preferring life in a palace. If there had been love, she would not have considered such a choice. She'd thought herself incapable of love. Until now.

This woman, whoever she was, could be found and sent away. A word to Maria Alexandrovna would suffice. Ingrid knew she was loved by the royal family and that her happiness was important to them all.

But she discarded the notion. A man was worth having only if he came of his own desire. And tomorrow, there would be tea— She rode in silence, her fine blue eyes misted with tears, her fan, a gift from Alexander's children, a ruin in her lap, shredded by her nervous fingers.

Dan Tallant hurried through the darkness, seeking a small girl in a red cloak. Damn her, he thought glumly. When he caught her, he'd shake her until her teeth rattled. A freezing rain had begun to fall. How long had she stood out there in this? What a goddamn stupid thing to do!

Was that a flicker of color? He hastened his steps, slamming into a stone projection. The blow only increased his anger. He ought to let her go on alone. Serve her right! Ought to grab her and dunk her in the icy waters of the Neva! Maybe that would shock some sense into her head. Goddamn little idiot! Hell, why did he even bother to follow? She was no concern of his.

He followed doggedly, through a maze of canals, gardens, cracked fountains, and broken statuary, and at last she turned into the narrow, sinister lane that led to her home. Dan breathed a sigh of relief. She'd made it. Now he would retrace his steps. She'd successfully ruined his evening. Dumping Ingrid like that was inexcusable, hardly the act of a gentleman.

How the hell was he going to explain? Say he'd gone off chasing a green-eyed little chit of a woman who somehow reminded him of his wife?

A small scream brought him to his senses.

Whirling, he saw two struggling shadows, one large and bulky, the other very small. There had only been the one sound. Olga fought, silently, as the man who stepped from a dark doorway, smelling of alcohol, attempted to drag her inside. Kicking, clawing, she knew she was losing the battle. Then someone else entered into the fray. She was thrown aside as her attacker turned to meet the newcomer.

Daniel Tallant, her rescuer and friend!

Now the street was filled with the sound, of the two men swearing, one in Russian and one in English; their blows were loud thuds. The lights of flickering candles appeared in the windows above. And a woman's voice screeched. "The guard! Call the guard!"

Finally Olga's attacker lay sprawled out on the ground. Dan Tallant swooped her up and hurried her to her own door as the streets filled with people.

Inside her room, he lashed out at her in his own language. His words were incomprehensible to her, but the emotion behind them was clear. He was furious at her for having ventured out to see his exit from the ballet. She apologized in her own language. Had she been an embarrassment to him? She had not intended to be seen.

Dan groaned. "Good God, no!" Then he managed to compose himself and speak to Olga's bent head so that she could understand. The streets were dangerous at night. She had no business being out there in the cold. He had followed to ensure her safety. Why had she done such a stupid thing?

388

"I often go to watch the people come from the theater. My mother took me when I was very small. It is a glimpse of another world. And—I went tonight because I had a warm cloak."

He shut his eyes, seeing a haggard woman holding a little girl high above the crowd to show her what life had once been for her family.

"I'm sorry," he said. "I should not have shouted at you. Forgive me. But please, do not go out unattended again."

"If you wish it." She bowed her head, obediently, and he saw the pale parting of her hair. She had managed to subdue it, braiding it into neat coils over her ears. She, too, had dressed for the ballet.

"I must go," he said. "Try to get some sleep."

She raised her eyes to his. "You cannot go now. Not until the commotion dies away. Stefan, the man who caught me, has friends. They will be watching. The Guard will come to disperse the crowd with force. You must stay."

Tallant went to the single window and looked down. He had to admit she spoke the truth. A dozen or so ruffians milled in the streets below. He stepped back as a stone crashed through the already shattered window. In his stained opera garb, he would be a prime target out there in the streets. He could probably fight his way out of it, but it might bring danger to Olga. He would wait.

He went to the hearth and built up the fire, then motioned the girl to the pallet of rags that served as her bed. He moved the single straight chair to the door and sat down in it. From time to time, he cast a furtive glance toward the girl. Olga's blue-green eyes were closed, and her face was a pale oval against the midnight of her hair; she brought back hurting

389

memories. A wave of longing surged through him, but he fought it back; it was not this girl he desired, but Tamsen.

After a while, his longing was replaced by pity. He'd been a fool, lashing out at her like that. She was probably as starved for beauty as she'd been for food. There was no law against standing outside a theater. No law against a girl like this attending the ballet, if she were properly dressed. He wondered if she might have just one night of magic. Perhaps Ingrid Larsen might help him—

The hoarse sounds from the street grew louder. Hopeless, poverty-stricken people fighting for the sheer need of something to do. Then he heard hoofbeats, a terrible moaning as the street people realized the guards were upon them. Screaming was followed by hooves retreating. Then silence.

He went to the window. The lane below was empty in the gray light, an icy mist still falling. It was safe to go.

Tallant turned to look at the girl, sleeping peacefully in the unaccustomed warmth of her dreary room. His heart gave a little bump as he thought of her smallness, her vulnerability. If it had been any other man here this night—

He found himself wishing he could kneel beside her and at least touch his lips to her cheek in farewell. He shook his head resolutely, and put the thought from him. The best thing to do was just to get the hell out of here.

It had been a close call, he told himself as he finally reached the wide avenues that were St. Petersburg's pride. He would have to stay away from the girl.

CHAPTER 4

Next morning, Dan arranged for the delivery of a supply of charcoal to Olga's address, enough to last out the winter. It was over and done with now, he told himself; the girl was not his responsibility. If only she didn't remind him so much of Tamsen, for whom he *was* responsible.

Yet he found himself wavering in his resolve not to see Olga again; he fought his desire to return. This afternoon he joined Ingrid Larsen at tea in the Winter Palace. Her small sitting room adjoined the children's suite and was warm, beautifully appointed. The lady herself was lovely; her voluptuous body was gowned in soft blue matching her eyes.

Though Ingrid's mind was full of questions regarding Dan's defection the previous night, she kept the conversation light; they discussed books, plays and the bailet that they would attend again tonight. Her face glowed as she talked of the music, the costumes, and the dancing.

"Women like that sort of thing, don't they?" Dan asked, unexpectedly. "All women—"

Ingrid smiled. "I suppose we do," she admitted. "I suppose it is because we can put ourselves into another world where everything is beautiful and romantic for a time, with no ugliness to mar it. And then we feel beautiful."

Dan gallantly assured her that, in her case, he didn't think such substitution was necessary; he was rewarded by her warm smile. But in the back of his mind was the thought of a ragged girl who had said much the same thing. She had come to stand in a freezing mist to catch a glimpse of that other world, one she could never enter. It did not seem fair.

That night, attending the ballet with a radiant Ingrid on his arm, he found himself studying the women in the audience; their rapt faces, the gowns they wore. Leaving the theater later, he searched the crowded street for a glimpse of a small figure in a red cloak, an action that did not escape the notice of his astute Swedish companion. It was clear he was looking for someone, and that the someone had not materialized.

Tallant returned Ingrid to the palace, unable to ignore the fact that her every action spelled invitation. A strapping girl, glowing with health, she was both warm and willing; she reminded him of a girl in his past, Katie Ryan. He almost wished he didn't have two other women on his mind. Olga—and Tamsen.

Ingrid wilted in disappointment as Tallant took his leave. Again she thought of seeking the aid of the tsarina. The girl who'd drawn his attention the first night at the ballet could be found—and sent away. The problem was that Ingrid was in love. And she was not a girl to be content with half a loaf. Love on his side could not be forced. She was certain of that. She must attract him on her own merits—or not at all. She went to bed, but not to sleep.

Dan Tallant, too, had trouble sleeping. He kept seeing a white face above a red cloak in the shadow of a building, watching as the elite poured from the theater. When morning came, he knew what he was going to do.

A scandalized Fedor was sent to locate a dressmaker, a fastidious lady who drew her skirts aside as she accompanied Dan through the miserable lane that led to the place where Olga lived. Accustomed to sewing for noblewomen, she was aghast at the sight of Olga's ragged gown, her shabby room. Only the rubles that had been promised in return for her services persuaded her to enter the door.

Olga, herself, was both surprised and humiliated. She'd sensed, when the charcoal was delivered the day before, that it was a farewell gesture. She did not expect to see Dan Tallant again. Listless, uncaring about anything now that he had gone from her life, she'd neglected to comb out her hair. It hung in gypsy tangles, and her fingers were black with charcoal.

Yet here he was, and in the company of a grand lady who turned up her nose at the scent of cabbage cooking on the hearth. When she learned the lady was there to measure her for a gown, she could not believe her ears.

She looked at Dan. "I do not understand. Why?"

He grinned. "When it is finished, will you do me the honor of accompanying me to the ballet?"

Numb with shock, she stood still for the dressmaker's ministrations. This was all a dream—it could not be real.

The gown was ready within the week. There were no fittings. The seamstress refused to return to such a shoddy, sinister neighborhood. Whatever she produced from this first visit would have to suffice. She did unbend enough to select slippers and underthings to go with the dress. And because the red cloak would not go with aquamarine ... perhaps another one to match?

The things were delivered. And on a designated evening, Tallant hired a small enclosed carriage, shabby enough to be inconspicuous in Olga's neighborhood, yet adequate for their arrival at the ballet. Leaving a driver, nervous at the surroundings, to wait, Dan climbed the creaking stairs.

The girl who answered his knock glowed against the background of her barren room. Her form had filled out a bit with these last days of adequate food and warmth. The gown, of soft velvet, echoed the color of her eyes and bared her gently rounded shoulders. Her hair was washed and shone with blue lights. It had taken Olga the whole day to prepare for the evening. She had traded some of her precious hoard of provisions to a small boy in return for buckets of water to be hauled up the steps, and she had heated it laboriously, with a reckless use of charcoal.

She clasped her hands together in panic as Dan looked at her, first in admiration, then distractedly, as if something was wrong.

"I didn't think. You should have jewels."

"I could not have accepted them. I have taken too much from you. And here, I would fear for my life with such things in my possession." She lifted her head proudly. "Perhaps we should not attend the ballet, then?"

Despite her apparent calm, Tallant saw that she was afraid. A pulse beat hard in her throat, and her eyes were big and dark ... afraid she wasn't good enough to associate with the nobles and the wealthy. It made him angry. He wanted to put his arms around her and assure her she would outshine them all. Dammit, she deserved a better life!

The coach, too, was a new and frightening experience. She had not ridden in one before. He wished it were less shabby, and that he hadn't deliberately purchased inexpensive tickets for the ballet, in order to be in the least conspicuous spot. She belonged in the tsar's gilded box.

Olga's fears had abated by the time they reached the theater and were seated. She was very quiet as she tried to take it all in: the luxurious surroundings, the ladies with their beautiful gowns and glittering escorts. And when the curtains opened and a dancer drifted across the stage like a leaf on the wind, her lips parted. She leaned forward, eyes wide with wonder, lost in the magic of the dance.

Tallant, eyeing her, thought she looked as Tamsen had the day they entered Baranov Castle for the first time—young, and in love. He made a small groaning sound, and Olga turned to him, perplexed. He forced a smile, and she turned once more to the stage, her features gilded with enchantment.

On the way home, she leaned back against the cushions of the coach, exhausted. It had been the most wonderful moment of her life. But Tallant was oddly silent.

"I did not embarrass you tonight?" she asked. "I was a credit to you?"

She sure as hell had been. He'd drawn more than one envious glance. He told her so. There was no dissembling, no coy denial calculated to draw more compliments. "I am glad," she said.

Tallant was troubled. He'd like to give the girl a further taste of the glamorous world she craved, but perhaps he was meddling in something he shouldn't.

He would leave St. Petersburg at the first opportunity, and then what would happen to Olga? Perhaps he was making a mistake.

Sensing that something was wrong, Olga reached out to him and placed her small hand in his. That, too, he thought glumly. He'd seen a deep affection in her eyes several times this evening. He must make it plain that there could be nothing between them. Yet he dared not destroy the pride she now felt in herself.

At her door, he said, "Olga, I want to come in. But only for a short time. I want to tell you a story."

Seating her on the one chair, he sat on the floor by the hearth; he lit his pipe with a coal from the fire. And he told her about Tamsen, beautiful, wrongheaded Tamsen who had first stolen his horses, then his heart.

He told her of their marriage and how they'd gone to Novoarchangelsk, of the Princess Anya's pursuit of him, and of the misunderstanding that led to his estrangement from his wife. That Tamsen had been injured, was perhaps dead. He left nothing out, showing her the scars on his wrists, caused by the irons when he was chained in the hold of the ship that had brought him from Russian America.

"I love my wife very much," he said simply. "And I want to thank you. In allowing me to do things for you, you've helped me. It is as if I were able to do things for Tamsen. Do you understand?"

She did...enough to shed tears after he had gone...tears of relief, not unmingled with grief. Her pride had hurt at accepting things from him, yet her need had been great. He had not been like other men, asking for something in return. She had no idea what he expected, yet she had taken.

Now she understood what was behind his dark, haunted features, and she was grateful that he had confided in her. Now she could allow herself to feel toward him a deep and growing friendship.

Tallant didn't return to his room immediately, but walked up and down the Neva, his face lifted to the chill air. It was dawn before he made his way to his lonely bed.

CHAPTER 5

In the weeks that followed, Tallant was a busy man. He approached the radical element, hoping to persuade them to help him find a way to leave Russia. They sympathized with his plight, trapped as he was at the tsar's whim, but could offer no solution. If he were smuggled aboard a ship, he would most certainly be discovered on a long journey around the world from St. Petersburg. It was dangerous, crossing Siberia at this time of year. And even then, reaching Okhotsk, he would have to find a way to board a ship without the tsar's permission. If he weren't so unmistakably American! There was no question of disguise.

It wasn't possible to treat with Alexander. Any mention of Tallant's leaving was answered with a vague, "When de Stoeckl returns." Then the subject was changed. Alexander Nikolaevich was adept at keeping the peace. Although he liked the man, Tallant often longed to take him by his officer's uniform collar and try to shake some cooperation into him.

At last, Dan turned to Ingrid, hoping that she would have some influence with the Russian ruler. He had been too long away from home, he told her, and he wished to return. Perhaps she might intercede on his behalf. Ingrid, sitting before an embroidery frame, stitching with bright colors, smiled. She knew of Tallant's involvement with an unknown girl; she had watched them through her glasses at the theater, and she also knew she had time on her side.

"There is no hurry," she said tranquilly, "since there will be no ships leaving the harbor until spring. You may as well enjoy what St. Petersburg has to offer."

It was a blatant invitation, and he hastened to leave her presence. She had been right, he thought dismally. There was no way open for escape. Now all he had to do for the next few months was to try to stay far away from women.

Dan found he was unable to maintain such a resolve. Olga's enjoyment of the arts was contagious. He found himself escorting her to museums, to plays, just to watch her bemused small face. And again they attended the ballet.

One night, leaving the theater, he spotted a familiar face. It could not be! He asked Olga to wait and pushed his way through the crowd.

"Igor!" he shouted. "Good God, Igor! It is you?"

The small prince turned, his eyes widening in shock as Dan went on, "Tamsen! Can you tell me anything about my wife? My God, man, it's good to see somebody from—"

Tallant! Igor stared at him. The man had run off to Russia with Anya, his sister, leaving his wife poverty-stricken and at death's door. Now he had the effrontery to show up here, calling him by his first name like an old friend, pretending concern for the woman he had deserted.

Igor's glance turned to Olga, who had moved to stand at Dan's side. Obviously Tallant had already found himself another woman! Well-fed, well-dressed, attending a ballet while Tamsen was trying to keep herself alive. Holy Mother of God! Igor's small frame trembled with anger as he deliberately ignored Tallant's outstretched hand.

Dan paused at the prince's expression. Igor's eyes had narrowed while his mouth twisted into a snarl. "In your own language," he spat, "you, Mr. Tallant, are a son of a bitch!"

Dan flinched, his hand dropping to his side. "I don't know what your problem is," he said baldly, "but I want to hear about my wife! Is she—"

Igor's hand flashed up. He tapped Dan's cheek smartly with the gloves he carried. "We'll meet tomorrow morning at the bridge over the Neva," he said crisply. He glanced down at Dan's doubled fists. "With a *gentleman's* weapons. Your choice, naturally. If you will name your second, mine will call upon him."

Dan was still stupefied. The prince's reception had been unexpected. And a duel? Good God! "My valet, Fedor," he finally choked, anger before his eyes in a red mist. "But first, you're going to tell me—"

"I will tell you nothing. You do not deserve to know!"

Tallant stood choked with fury as Prince Igor Mischerski walked away. The little sonofabitch! He should have tried to knock it out of him! They had never been friends, but there was no reason for his animosity—unless... unless he'd learned the circumstances of Anya's death and considered Dan at fault. After all, the girl was his sister. Tallant suddenly felt ill. But he didn't want Igor's death on his conscience.

To hell with a country where something couldn't be settled with your fist! He slowly came back to an awareness of his surroundings. He and Olga were the center of attention, and her face was white and strained. He had to get her out of there.

In the carriage, he explained the situation. Olga was terrified, but she forced her voice to remain calm. "What are you going to do?"

"Meet him. What else can I do? I cannot run and hide."

"The weapons? You have your choice—"

"With pistols, he'd be a dead man. He's got to have a chance. Swords, I suppose."

"You know nothing of fencing. You have told me—"

"Don't worry." His voice was grim. "I can take care of myself."

He left her at the door with only a brief farewell. His dark face was closed, as his mind raced ahead to what he had to face on the morrow. He'd fought an Indian once with knives, and had bested him. This shouldn't be much different. If he could draw the first blood . . .

He didn't sense that Olga, too, was making plans. She stood at her window after he had gone, pondering the thing she was going to do.

Prince Igor woke swiftly at his attendant's call the next morning. Normally, he was a late sleeper, but the anger that had seethed in his small frame all night brought him instantly awake. Fueled by his fury, he pulled on the dark, inconspicuous clothing dictated by the occasion and hurried from his rooms at the Winter Palace. It was still gloomy in the long Russian night. He didn't see the girl until a hand touched his arm.

"Please," she said. "I must talk to you!"

Tallant's mistress! Perhaps the man was a coward

as well as a wife deserter and woman chaser! Had he sent the girl to plead his case? Igor looked at her with loathing. "Well?"

"Mr. Tallant did not kill your sister. It was the other man." She babbled out Dan's tale of his kidnapping, his whipping, and his being chained in irons. "Please do not do this terrible thing," she finally moaned, twisting her fingers. "Give him the opportunity to explain."

Igor heard her out, intrigued by the way her eyes seemed to glow in the dimness, like a cat's. Her story, of course, was too wild to be true, but she seemed sincere. Perhaps it was something Tallant had invented to impress her. Maybe that was the man's secret with women, setting himself up as a heroic figure.

"I believe you have been reading cheap novels, my dear," he said rather spitefully. "And I'm afraid you have not found a sympathetic ear. This affair has nothing to do with my sister, but with another lady the man has wronged. In fact, if all goes well, I may be doing you a service."

He bowed and walked on, summoning up a picture of Tamsen's face when he told her Tallant had gone off with Anya while she lay in a critical condition. He'd seen the light die in her eyes. They'd been like smudges of charcoal in a death-white face. He thought of the way she'd struggled to survive, hurt, alone in a country that was not her own. Tallant would not live to hurt her again. Igor was an expert swordsman. This was not his first duel, nor would it be his last.

His second caught up with him. "The girl is following us," he said nervously. "Should I speak to her? Try to send her away?"

402

"I do not think she would listen. Let it be." Mother of God, that devil Tallant had a way with women.

They met in mid-bridge, over the Neva; the tall American and the little prince greeted each other with cold formality. Fedor presented Dan with his sword. Tallant faced Igor, who had assumed a professional stance, his own weapon at the ready.

Suddenly, Dan couldn't go through with it. He hadn't known Igor well, but he had been Tamsen's friend. He threw his own sword clattering to the bridge floor. "Dammit, I've never fought anybody without a reason." Walking straight toward the prince, he took the weapon from his startled hand and tossed it to lie beside his own.

"I'll fight you if I have to. Hell, I'd probably enjoy it. But we're going to talk this out before we act like a couple of damn fools! Now, if this has anything to do with Anya—"

"My sister's honor does not concern me. Your wife's honor does."

"Tamsen?" Dan's face was perplexed. "I don't understand—"

"Mother of God!" Igor began to hurl accusations at him; the way he'd gone off with Anya, leaving his wife in sickness and poverty; she'd been exiled from Novoarchangelsk and gone with a party into New Caledonia, a wild and dangerous country. Then her sisters had come, in need. Em a widow, Arab's husband killed in his search for gold—and Tamsen.

Tallant heard him out, only a tremor in one cheek betraying his emotion. Tamsen did, then, think he had deserted her. And Donald was dead. And Juan. Good God!

"And I find you here," Igor hissed, "attending the

403

ballet, living off the fat of the land. Already you have found yourself another woman—" He gestured, and Dan followed his pointing finger.

"Olga!"

"You are surprised? You did not know she would accost me with a pack of lies? I think," Igor's eyes glinted with malice, "that you invented them between you, in an attempt to hide behind a woman's petticoats."

Tallant's fist doubled, but he forced his voice to remain calm. "Lies? What did she tell you?"

"That my sister kidnapped you and put you in irons. That you did not leave Novoarchangelsk of your own accord, when it was rumored everywhere that you planned to do so."

"Then the rumors were planted," Dan said soberly. He peeled back his sleeves and extended his wrists. Even in the darkness, Igor could see the scars that encircled them like bracelets.

"Holy Mother of God," he said, this time in a whisper. "I think I have made a mistake. We must talk, but first"—he turned gallantly toward the small figure that had followed him onto the bridge— "first, you must introduce me to the lady who saved us from our hasty tempers."

After Olga was introduced, the prince went on to tell of Arab and Em's arrival, that Donald had committed suicide and Juan died in the gold fields, that Tamsen, Arabella, and Em were all alone.

"I proposed to all of them," Igor admitted candidly. "But none of them would have me, not even little Martha."

Dan sat with head bowed. Em and Arab, husbands dead. Igor said they planned to join Tamsen. The burden would be on her shoulders once more. He had an idea why she'd headed for the gold

404

fields when Nell and Dusty arrived. She was back in business, most probably. It was the only thing she knew.

His thoughts jolted to a halt. "That Britisher, Devon. Where is he?"

Igor had changed, but not that much. He looked at Tallant with guileless eyes. "Devon? He went along with Tamsen. Didn't I mention it?"

He missed seeing Dan's reaction because Olga began to shiver. "You are cold," he said. "I will see you home."

"Oh, no," she said. "I cannot—I cannot!" She looked to Dan for help.

"Let him," Dan said. "I think it would be good for him."

Doubtful, a little frightened, she took the arm the young prince extended to her. They left Tallant sitting alone and hurried off to the Winter Palace, where Igor ordered a guard to provide a coach. They set off in one of the tsar's glittering vehicles.

Left alone in the garden, Dan buried his face in his hands. He'd thought he'd lose his mind if he didn't hear news from home. Now, he had, and it was worse than before. It was all his fault; he couldn't think of a thing he hadn't done wrong.

First, he should have taken that week in bed he'd promised himself upon his return from the wilderness. He'd vowed to put his arms around his wife and never let go. Instead, he'd tried to act like a goddamn diplomat. Something he wasn't. Instead of wooing the Princess Anya to gain her good will, he should have said, "Here's what we'll pay for your cooperation." And if she balked, then to hell with it!

Above all, that night when he found Tamsen with the charts, he should have picked her up, carried her back to bed, and held her, listening to her

405

explanation. Five minutes of closeness might have made the difference.

He groaned, imagining her close, her tears on his cheek. He mopped his face, realizing the tears were his own.

"Dan!"

He jerked, thinking it was Tamsen's voice. Ingrid Larsen bent over him, her face bright with cold, a Nordic princess in her scarves and furs. "I did not mean to startle you."

Dan smiled painfully. "I'm just surprised to see anyone out at this hour."

"I often walk in the mornings." It was true. Ingrid did love the cold freshness of the dawn. But today, she was out early for another reason. Gossip had reached her ears; word of Igor's challange to Tallant at the theater had reached her. Seeing him leave with the girl who had been Dan's companion, she hurried here, fearing for Dan.

From his expression, she could see some type of encounter had taken place. Apparently, he had no desire to mention it. "Will you walk with me?" She smiled.

He extended his arm, grateful for human company, his mind torn with worries. Tamsen. Arab and Em. Donald committing suicide? Good God! And Juan Narváez dead. And he was also concerned that he had let Olga go off with Prince Igor, uncertain about the attentions the prince would pay a young defenseless girl. He should have seen her home himself.

In the tsar's golden coach with guards riding ahead and behind, Olga felt extremely shy. She'd been driven to speak with this royal personage in order to stop the duel, but now she wondered at her temerity. She was embarrassed at the thought of his seeing how and where she lived.

Igor was not one to allow a woman to put up a barrier of silence. He chattered away, nonsensically, drawing out with a few adroit questions the story of how she and Tallant met. He learned that she had been married to a man who disappeared at sea and might—or might not—be dead. He filed that away for future reference, for suddenly it seemed most important to him.

The basic statistics taken care of, he set himself to making her laugh, delighted by the merest sign of a dimple when he succeeded. It was some time before he took note of his surroundings; the coach turned into a narrow lane.

"Mother of God!" he whispered at the signs of poverty around him, seeing the closed faces of people, already risen to go and labor. He watched them with unfathomable eyes. "You cannot live here! I did not know a place like this existed in the city!"

Few noblemen did, Olga thought bitterly. But she said, "There is my house. The gray one with the broken window. It is my window."

The prince escorted her to her room, aghast at the barrenness of it. Yet the girl was gracious as she thanked him for accompanying her home. He found himself outside her door without having made an opportunity to see her again. She was obviously a lady. Her eyes, though a different shade, reminded him of Arabella's. He made up his mind to find out more about her.

His first act was to contact the commander of the Imperial Navy. By giving him the name of Olga's husband, and his ship, Igor learned that the vessel had been lost at sea with all hands.

Igor thanked his informant, but lectured him about informing the widows of such men. He was guiltily elated that the lady was free. His next step was to speak with Alexander himself. Amnesty was assured, and Ingrid could use help with the children. She was delighted to cooperate, having learned Olga was her competition for Dan Tallant's attention. If Olga were at the palace, she would be under Ingrid's watchful eye.

When she met the girl and sensed her shyness and awe of the Winter Palace, Ingrid Larsen's cold heart melted. Especially when she saw the way Olga and the young prince looked at each other. In fact, she guessed Igor's feeling toward her young protégée long before he did.

Walking into the nursery one day, Igor found Olga, her smooth head bent over the tsar's youngest, another small one at her shoulder. There was an aura of warmth about her, something that made him think of that Christmas night with Emmeline and Arabella, when he'd wondered what it would have been like to have had a family. Holy Mother of God! He was in love again!

In the meantime, Tallant simmered with frustration over his detention in St. Petersburg. He was also concerned about Igor's attentions to Olga. Though he and the prince had reached a basis for a rather uneasy friendship, he was still not assured of the man's moral character. Prince Igor appeared to be a creature of whims. If it had suited Igor to play Lord Bountiful for a while, he would, Dan thought grimly, but as soon as he lost interest, he might dump Olga on the street again.

Dan demanded to know Igor's intentions and received an infuriating grin for answer. "Damn it to hell," he exploded, "I know I'm making a fool of myself. But I introduced you to the girl! I'm responsible for her!"

"Ah! And I was wondering how I should observe the proprieties! It is you I should ask, since you feel for her in such a fatherly way!" Igor's face beamed with mischief. "Sir, may I have permission to request Olga's hand—"

"Olga's hand?" Dan looked at him in confusion.

"I plan to marry the girl."

His sincerity stopped Dan dead.

"Do you have Alexander's blessing?" Dan asked.

"Indeed. Through the intercession of the divine Ingrid—along with my own persuasive charm."

"And Olga is willing?"

"There she is now. Ask her yourself."

There was no need to ask. Olga's face glowed with the enchantment it had worn the night Dan took her first to the ballet. And in the green eyes she turned on Igor, there was something more. Tallant took his leave as quickly as possible, leaving them alone. The Olga he had known was gone: the small ragged girl who clung to a loaf of coarse bread as though it were a child was destined for the life of a princess.

Ingrid found Dan in the garden and seated herself beside him without a word. Finally, she said, "Do you approve?"

"I certainly do," he said soberly. Then he grinned at her. "Do you know something, Ingrid? I like you. I like you more than anyone I know."

Those were the closest words to love that she would ever get from him. She forced a smile. "I like you, too. More than anyone." She blinked back tears.

Igor and Olga were married at Easter time, a period of joyous celebration after the fasting of Lent.

409

The holidays caused a run on the gantlet of kisses from family and friends. Alcoholic beverages were partaken of freely, and one person meeting another said, "Christ is risen." The answer would follow, "He has risen, indeed." All carried eggs boiled into stones and painted, gilded, or dyed, to present to their friends. Through it all sounded the continuous ringing of bells.

The bells were pealing in accompaniment to the wedding ceremony. Igor was unnaturally pale in his ornate uniform; his radiant bride wore blue. Watching them, Dan felt a lump in his throat. Ingrid's hand slipped into his, and he held it tightly, listening to the responses, the bells . . . .

Afterward, there was a bridal cake bedecked with mystic signs, and tea, coffee, chocolate, and champagne were served. The tsar himself, as highest officer present, led the little bride into the dance. Igor was trapped by a buxom Russian dowager. Dan caught the look Olga shot her new husband, an expression of mischievous glee. They were well suited, he thought. Their happiness was suddenly more than he could bear, and Dan made his apologies to a disappointed Ingrid and returned to his lonely room.

Slowly, time passed. The ice broke up on the Neva. Spring came, and with it a ship, ice-sheeted from its wintry voyage. It landed its cargo and passengers, and Dan Tallant was summoned before the tsar. Baron de Stoeckl had returned. Tallant faced them with his heart thundering in hope of immediate dismissal, for some word regarding the success of the baron's mission. De Stoeckl looked old and tired. There were new lines about his mouth. Dan suffered through Alexander's ponderous social comments impatiently.

"The sale of Alaska to the United States," he finally said. "It has been considered?"

"Unfortunately not," the tsar said. "It has been set aside, to be studied at a later date."

Dan's temper flared. He forgot he was talking to a ruler. For an instant, Alexander Nikolaevich was only another man in uniform, a military man who persisted in entangling a situation in red tape. "Good God!" he exploded. "Can't you ever make up your mind? No wonder—"

He stopped, appalled at himself. De Stoeckl's face was white, the tsar's stiff with anger. "I will try to overlook your outburst," Alexander finally said slowly, "in consideration of your disappointment at the moment. I will even venture a further explanation of the situation. De Stoeckl has appeared before your senate in an effort to sell the Russian Alaska territory, at my express orders. But the United States has asked for the delay in its time of trouble."

"Trouble? I don't understand—"

"Your country," the tsar said, "in which—and I quote—'one stands up on his hind legs and says so, if he is not satisfied,' is on the brink of war."

"My God," Dan whispered. "My God!"

Somehow, he managed to make a stumbling apology for his harsh words to the tsar. It was accepted with good grace. Alexander had never been one to hold a grudge, but the horror of what he'd learned stayed with Tallant until he returned to his room. Then, like seeing a light in a dark tunnel, he realized he was free, at last, to go. He summoned Fedor with a whoop that brought the dignified gentleman on a dead run. "Pack my gear," he said exuberantly. "I'm leaving."

Two days later, Dan Tallant said goodbye to St. Petersburg. The tsar had provided a troika and guards. There would be changes of horses across the Siberian steppes, and Tallant would carry some messages to Okhotsk and some others to Novoarchangelsk, all with the tsar's own seal. Tallant was to be treated with honor and consideration.

Tsar Alexander Nikolaevich, Maria Alexandrovna, and their children saw him off on his journey. Olga and Igor were there. Olga's eyes were red from crying. And Ingrid Larsen stood solemnly quiet. Her face was serene and tranquil as she kissed Dan goodbye. After all, she'd known for a long time that this moment would come. Now she had one other obstacle to overcome: to tell the tsar she'd decided to return to Sweden. Maybe there she would find what she was looking for. She prayed Dan would be successful in his search for his wife and that there would be happiness for him forever.

Tallant had begun his journey to St. Petersburg in irons and chains. Now he was returning with honor. Without incident his entourage made its way to Perm, at the Russian border. In Siberia, they traversed the rutted *tracht* that led through the *taiga,* a gigantic wilderness of trees and swamp, where they came to an area of vast nothingness. It was to stay with them until they reached the grubby little port of Okhotsk.

. Even here, at what seemed the end of the world, the carriage marked with the tsar's seal and the papers Dan carried paved the way for royal treatment. He was put up at the best Siberian inn, and there he waited for a vessel to carry him to Novoarchangelsk.

He took the first that came to port, a rusty little tub that wallowed its way to the island of Sitka and arrived during the fall rains. After he disembarked,

Dan stood for a long time looking at the home he'd shared with Tamsen before his enforced trip to Russia. The place had deteriorated badly in the few months it stood empty. Some kind of animal had been at the roof, and the windows were blank holes that caught the drizzling rain. Dan supposed he'd been expecting some miracle. He knew Tamsen was gone from the settlement, but somehow he'd felt that he would come here and the house would be shining with warmth—and Tamsen would be at home.

Wearily he made his way to the castle thinking this was not the end of his journey, but the beginning of his search for the woman he loved more than anything in the world.

Ivan Furuhelm, the new governor-general of Novoarchangelsk, welcomed him warmly. After all, the man carried papers from the tsar that clearly stated he was to be treated with all honors and that his every request should be met. All Dan wanted was a ship, a request that was easily met.

Armed with the map Em had left behind, he boarded a small vessel for Asquamalt, from where he walked to Fort Victoria and took ship to Westminster; then he traveled by sternwheeler to Yale. There he paused only to fill his pack with food before he set out once more. Tamsen had been here before him; she had brushed against the same rocky projections on this narrow trail.

The skies began to spit with the winter's first fall of snow, but he forged onward, his wife's name thundering in his mind. At last he rounded the bend in the Fraser that led to Tamsen's place. He found a burned-out shell of a house, with several other structures that had been pillaged nearby. Nothing but ruins where he'd expected to find his love.

He was exhausted from his journey. Anticipation

had lent strength to his feet during these last long miles, but now it drained out of him. On a rock he sat and studied the map drawn in Em's hand; he tried to shelter the paper from the snow that settled on it and made the ink run in a wash of purple tears. This had to be the place, he admitted to himself, but its occupants were gone. And must have been, for a long time.

CHAPTER 6

Upriver, at a spot near the head of Anderson Lake, not far from Lilooet, two people wrestled at setting up a flume for mining gold. It consisted of a long narrow trough, head-high at one end where it caught a small ribbon of a waterfall. It sloped down to the sluicebox, a larger trough, its bottom stripped with lath-like pieces of wood.

Juan Narvaéz had constructed it. Never having done such work, he was justifiably proud. He had explained its principle to the women over and over again. Sand and gravel was dumped into the sluicebox, then the flume was allowed to flow into and over it. The debris washed away while the gold remained.

It was good that he had shown them, Em thought a little crossly. If any gold was found, it would be up to the women of the family to find it. Two supports had cracked at óne side the previous day, toppling the flume, which broke Juan's arm in several places and injured his head and shoulder. Arab was with him now, and Em would be damned if she'd go to Duke Courtney for help.

With a system of slender wood poles, the bark tearing into her hands, Em managed to lever the flume into position. It teetered and swayed as she

415

called, "Quick, Martha! Do what I told you! The post under it now! And now the other—"

The child moved obediently, unaware that her mother was at the end of her strength. And the flume stood upright, solid once more.

"Now," Em said, "let's see if it works." She heaved a shovelful of sand and gravel into the sluicebox and opened the flow of water to it as she'd seen Juan do.

"We can do it, honey! We can do it!" she sang out, her face flushed with triumph beneath the battered man's hat she wore.

"Are we gold-miners, Mommy?"

"You can bet we are!"

"Better than Uncle Juan—and Duke?"

Em thrust her thumbs in the suspenders that held up a pair of baggy men's trousers, strutting a little. "Better than anybody," she laughed.

"If you're all that good," an amused voice sounded behind them, "I'd suggest a few cross-braces, here—and here."

Em turned to face Duke Courtney, her face flaming. "I didn't know you were there!"

"So I figured," he grinned. "I was just up to Arab's. She told me what happened, an' that you could use a hand. So I moseyed on down."

He moved toward the flume and pushed against it with his enormous strength; he shoved the wedges in a little tighter. Then he began to hammer cross-braces home, humming under his breath. Em, feeling the chill of the day now that she was no longer exerting herself, sent Martha toward the shelter of the small shack they shared with Arab and Juan. At least, she thought, she could feel as though she was earning her keep, for she intended to take over here until Juan was well.

Her hand went to the small of her back. Dear

God, how it ached, but sore muscles would go away. It would take a few days for her to break in.

"There you are." Courtney had finished the job, and Emmeline had to admit it looked more secure. "Thank you," she said formally, "I'm sure Juan will appreciate it."

"Will he appreciate what you're doing?" Duke came closer to her, and she felt her usual flush at his nearness. "He doesn't strike me as a man who would like having a woman do his work for him."

"I'm working for myself," she spat. "I'm earning my keep. And you know there's nothing I can do up there." She pointed toward Nell's place, which was a tiny two-room shanty, the back room partitioned off for Carmen and Maggie, the front room only big enough for a couple of gaming tables. But it was the best Nell could manage at the time they'd come.

"Tamsen had a way a-doin' things," Nell had said gloomily. "But hell, we're bound t'expand!" But Nell had picked the wrong spot to set up business. It had sounded good when she put forth her arguments: here at the joining of two trails, the Harrison and the Douglas. "Catch 'em comin' an' goin'," she boomed.

She hadn't counted on the fact that most of them had passed them by and were headed upcountry—just as Duke Courtney was planning to do. He was leaving them. He had no right to tell Em what kind of work she could or couldn't do! He didn't pursue the subject, but drew her to a tree stump where he sat her down, looking at her bleeding hands as he did so.

"Look, Em, I'm gonna bring up the subject once more. Can't hold Mac back any longer. He's fit t'be tied, wantin' t'get on up to Quesnel, maybe further. There's gold up there, a-plenty. I can smell it. I can't leave you here—"

"You were paid to take us to Tamsen's place." Her

voice was a little shrill, and she tried to tone it down. "You did. And you came this far with us. You have your own life. You don't owe us anything."

"Then do what I asked. I've got some money, not much, but enough to get you all to San Francisco. You can't winter here with a hurt man, just a couple-a women and a little kid—dammit, Em! If I can't go with a clear conscience—"

"Get away before I tell you where you *can* go with your conscience," Em exploded.

His blue eyes hardened. He bowed his head and walked away. Em sat still, her shoulders slumped, examining the torn, grimy hands in her lap, but not really seeing them. Why did Courtney always make her feel like a silly, incapable female? Like something dragging on him, holding him back. He couldn't leave with a clear conscience! Had he ever thought that she might go with him?

Her mouth began to tremble and she leaped to her feet, shoveling material into the sluicebox until blisters formed on her hands. The wind had risen cold off the mountain snow, but it felt good on her hot face. Em, the lady! In love with a great brute of a mining man! He was going to leave her, and she didn't know how to hold him. Tamsen would have known....

She stopped and leaned on the shovel, a dull, empty feeling coming over her at the thought of her younger sister. What had happened to Tamsen and Helena, they would never know. Courtney had headed south at the first opportunity, and he had met up with a Frenchman from Hill's Bar. Tamsen and Helena were not there, not in the hands of McGowan and Bagley as they had thought. People assumed that the two died somewhere in the snow.

Grimly, Em returned to her shoveling. Her hands

hurt, but not as much as her heart. The move, the labor entailed to set up here, had been the only thing that had saved them all. Even Nell had aged some, her heavy features fining down, to Dusty's consternation.

Closing the sluice-gate, Em studied the profit of her day. Between ten and twenty dollars' worth of gold. Nell would know the exact amount. But with supplies coming up the trail at more than a dollar a pound for transport, it wouldn't go far. They needed blankets, flour—

"I beg your pardon," a voice said behind her. "I am looking for—"

Em whirled at the sound, her mouth agape as she looked at the man who spoke. "Dan!" she said in a strangled voice. "You!" When her surprise faded, she took the shovel she had leaned against the sluice-box and brought it down on top of Tallant's head with a resounding whang.

Then, bursting into tears, she ran toward the house she shared with Arab. Tallant, staggered for a moment, rubbed his head. What the hell was the matter with that damnfool kid! Then he saw the hat fly away, caught on the wintry wind, the mass of blond-brown hair that tumbled to the flying figure's waist. Not a boy, but a girl!

His eyes widened. It could not be *Em!* He took off in determined pursuit, only to meet a giant figure of a man who charged from the cabin door roaring like a bull. Perhaps he had been wrong. Panting, Tallant raised a placating hand. "I am looking for—," he began again.

He never ended his sentence. A hamlike fist swung toward him, and he failed to duck. When he woke, he found himself lying flat on his back, surrounded by a group of ragged men and boys. No, that *was* Em, still with her shovel. He flinched. And the one with the frying pan—Arab? The little boy! It was Martha. And beside the big man who'd flattened him—Juan, his arm splinted. Juan—who was supposed to be dead, according to Igor!

He started to struggle up, his mouth forming words that went unheard as Nell arrived like a runaway stagecoach. She looked him over, panting, recognition reaching her eyes.

"It's him," she said scornfully. "Didden figger he had th' guts. Kill th' sonofabitch."

Tallant lay back and closed his eyes, folding his hands on his chest. "Before you finish me off," he said conversationally, "would you mind telling me where I can find my wife?"

There was a long low moan, and Emmeline began to cry.

CHAPTER 7

The big man finally provided the solution to the impasse. He stood over Dan, studying him carefully. Apparently, he was satisfied with what he saw. He extended a hand to help the fallen man to his feet. "I'm Duke Courtney," he said brusquely.

"Glad to meet you." Dan's voice was dry. "Now—and some other time when I'm not outnumbered."

There was a flash of appreciation in the man's blue eyes. "I believe in giving the devil his due," he said. "Folks, I think we oughta hear the man out. Could be he had his reasons for runnin' off an' leavin' the little lady. S'pose we take a listen—an then I'll beat the hell outa him if you want."

Dan entered the shack, moving warily. Good God, he should have expected this. They all thought he'd walked out on Tamsen, just as Igor did. He was guilty until proven innocent. But, damn it, he admired their loyalty to his wife, even this Duke what's-his-name, with the lethal punch—whoever the hell he was. Dan rubbed his jaw ruefully as he sat down on a proffered bench. Arab flounced to the fire and returned with a steaming cup of tea, slamming it down before him. He took a grateful sip of it, surprised to find he was shivering. The months of worry, cold, and fatigue had caught up with him, but he had reached his goal. He would see his wife after he disposed of the reception committee.

He began to talk to the hostile group ringed around him. He told it all. Anya's arrival, his stupidity in trying to cope with the girl, the estrangement between himself and Tamsen because of her. He told how he'd caught Tamsen copying his maps for the governor-general's use—

"I don't believe that," Arab said flatly. There was an ominous murmur from the others, and Dan said, "Wait!"

He spared himself nothing in the telling, repeating the things he'd said to her. They were engraved on his mind, and he went over their quarrel word for word.

He described the night Tamsen was injured, and at last the way he was taken from her, holding out his hands to show his scarred wrists. He told of the whipping, of Ivan's and Anya's deaths, how he'd thought he would have to stand trial for murder when he reached Russian shores. His discovery that Tamsen had rigged the charts she'd been blackmailed into copying brought murmurs of approval from his listeners.

"And it was all for nothing," he finished grimly. "Fell through. The States are at war."

He stopped on a weary smile. "That's it. That's the story. Now what? Still going to beat me to death with a skillet and a shovel? Or are you going to tell me where—"

Em threw herself to her knees, clasping her arms around him. "Oh, Dan! I'm sorry! I'm so sorry!" Arab, too, moved forward, putting her cheek against his. It was wet with tears.

"Hell," Nell grumped, her eyes screwed up, "we

422

shoulda knowed better. We're a buncha gawdam fools! Ain't got th' sense God give a duck!"

Dan's voice cut through their apologies. "It's all right. It's worth it—anything's worth it. But now—when can I see Tamsen? She's got to hear this from me—if I can keep her from braining me first." He grinned. If her sisters were this riled up, facing Tamsen would be something! He stood. "Where is she?"

His smile faded as he looked at the faces surrounding him. "What is it?" His voice shook a little. "Something's wrong—that Devon fellow? She hasn't—"

"Devon's dead," Em whispered. "And Tamsen... Tamsen..."

"Em, shut up!" Duke Courtney's voice thundered in the small room. He turned to Tallant. "Ain't room here. You can put up at our place up the river. Can you walk another couple miles?"

"*Tamsen?*"

"I'll fill you in as we go." Duke scowled around the room. If he'd figured Tallant right, this was something he oughta hear from a man with a right straightforward approach.

Taking the dazed man by the arm, Courtney led him outside and away from the house. There, mist freezing on their faces, he told him the flat truth. McGowan's men raided and burned their settlement; Tamsen and Helena were captured and presumed dead.

Dan's face fined down to the bone as he talked, his eyes blank, lifeless shadows. It was like watching a man die. Duke felt the reflection of his agony.

"Hell, man," he blurted, "nobody knows for sure. I heard a wild story about a white woman livin' with the Injuns, just the other day—"

423

"You think—there might be something to it?" Dan spoke for the first time.

"Buncha bullshit," Duke said succinctly, the hope in Tallant's eyes making him feel guilty for even bringing it up. "Forget it. Now, let's get on down the trail and see if Mac's got the coffeepot on—"

In the morning, Dan barely remembered his introduction to Mac. He had rolled into the blankets before the fire and slept a sleep of exhaustion. Toward dawn, he dreamed. Tamsen was running just ahead of him, flitting from tree to tree, laughing over her shoulder as he tried to catch her. The dream was so vivid that he woke, Courtney shaking his shoulder, with Tamsen's name on his lips. And he knew what he had to do.

He remained quiet as he took the cup of strong black coffee Courtney offered him, warming his hands around it as he considered his decision. The coffee was followed by a tin pan of fat meat and beans, topped with an enormous sourdough biscuit. Then Courtney hunkered down beside him, his rugged features sober. "Got me some talkin' to do," he said.

He described the sufferings the girls had endured. They'd borne them well. Like real troupers. But they didn't belong to this kind of life. Hell, only one man in the bunch, unless you dealt Dusty in. Juan Narváez was a fine gentleman, but like Em and Arab, he was out of his element. He wasn't faultin' the Spaniard. He was as gutsy as they come, but every new problem that come up, he had to learn—

"I had heard he was dead," Tallant interrupted. "And Em's husband, Donald—"

"You only heard right about the Alden feller." Courtney squinted through the steam from his cup. "But the story on Narváez—well, it goes to prove what I've been sayin'. He took up with a damn low-life turkey buzzard an' got himself knocked in the head." He went on, telling the rest of the story, how they'd found the outlaw's body, and how he'd met Arab and Em.

"Been stuck with 'em ever since," he said dryly. "There's gold upcountry, sure as God made little green apples. Mac's on edge to get going, and I been holding back. Feel responsible for th' whole damn bunch. Hopin' you'll take 'em off my neck, get 'em back to the kind of life they're s'posed to be livin'."

"I can't go back now. I intend to look for my wife. I'm going to find her—dead or alive."

Courtney's face reddened with anger. "Good God, man! You've got to do some thinkin'. Them folks won't last longer'n a snowball in hell without somebody to look after 'em."

"I have to stay."

Courtney set his cup down with a sigh. "Come on. Let's get back down there. Maybe you'll take a good look an' get some sense in your fool head."

He strode out, and Tallant followed. They didn't speak until the small shack the women occupied was in sight.

"Look down there." Courtney gestured. On the gravel bar below, Em was shoveling sand into the sluicebox. She had a blanket draped around her shoulders against the cold. As they watched, she put her hand to the small of her back, relinquishing the shovel to little Martha, but only for a moment.

"The whole works is gonna be froze up pretty soon," Duke said brutally "Harder'n the hubs of hell. What's she gonna do then? They all been workin' like goddamn beavers. Narváez built him a haywire flume. Told him it needed bracing, but he put it off, too busy tryin' to make some money before the cold set in. Busted his arm on account of it. Know who put it up? Em an' th' kid—before I knew it happened—that's who.

"Arab an' her husband!" He jabbed a finger toward the shack. "Somethin' else Narváez put off. The wind blows through that buildin' like hell. Needs boardin' an' caulkin'. How's a one-armed feller gonna handle that? An' them—" He jerked a finger at Nell's place. "Nell's the only man in the bunch, an' she's a woman. Dusty won't freeze out or starve out as long as the likker lasts. But hell, man, we've already had our first snow—"

"I have money. I'm sending them all home."

"Home? Where's home? Em won't go back to Frisco, that's damn sure."

"I'll send them to Novoarchangelsk."

"Nell and the girls got run out of there once."

"They won't now. Furuhelm wouldn't dare go against the instructions of the tsar."

It sounded good, the big man told Dan, but it wouldn't work. The injured Juan and the little Englishman wouldn't be able to get the girls out by themselves. They'd never make it without some help. "I'm headin' upcountry," Duke added gruffly.

Tallant studied his face. He's seen a reluctant look on it when he spoke of heading out on the gold trail. And he'd detected the same expression when Em was mentioned.

"You're going to take them back for me. I'll pay you well for your trouble."

Courtney's jaw dropped. "Hell, no! Me? You're loony, Tallant! A goddamn loony! Mac's headin' off, with or without me. And there's gold up there, Tallant! Gold! You think I'd give up a chance at it to ride herd on a bunch of petticoats?"

"Yes," Dan said, "I do."

Mumbling a swear word under his breath, Duke stalked away. He walked down to the sluicebox and snatched the shovel from Em's frozen hands. "Git the hell in the house," he snarled. "An' git the kid inside, too. You want her down sick?"

Em's first impulse was to tell him to mind his own business, but something in his eyes stopped her. Calling for Martha, she headed toward the house and its welcome warmth.

Duke Courtney didn't feel the cold. He wielded the shovel expertly, trying to work out his dilemma at the same time. Dammit, he loved Em, but he had sense enough to know she wasn't for the likes of him. He had to get away from her! He tossed a shovelful of gravel into the box... but he couldn't let her go downtrail without some protection! Another shovel...

With a sad half-smile, Tallant turned toward the shack where his wife's sisters lived. He understood Duke Courtney all too well. There was something in the man that had been in himself long ago. He would work out his frustrations in physical activity, and in the end, he would do what Dan asked him to do.

Two days later, Dan shook hands with Duke Courtney and said goodbye to the small group ready to set out for Yale. He'd given Courtney a sum of money to see them through the winter and a letter to Furuhelm that was not a request but a command. They would be all right now.

In the end, it was Tallant who had difficulty concealing his emotions. Once more he was cutting himself off from all close ties. When they had gone, he would be alone. He looked around at the loved faces. How Em had changed! No longer prim and flowerlike, her face darkened by wind and weather, there was a new look of purpose about her—a kind of rawhide toughness. And Arab was no longer the wild, impulsive child he remembered. Adversity had softened her, revealing a core that was unexpectedly tender. And Martha—Martha was a delightful tomboy! He swung her high and kissed the tip of her freckled nose, then turned to the others. The girls, Dusty, Nell...

Nell had prepared for this journey by making herself an enormous pair of trousers out of canvas. She looked like a ship under sail. Seeing Dan's grin, she defended herself. "No gawdam splinters *this* time," she said, enigmatically. In her arms, she clasped a bullet-dented samovar, which she refused to leave behind.

"Take care of them, Duke."

The big man met Dan's eyes with a level gaze. "Like I told you," he said meaningfully, "until spring."

Dan watched the party depart, his mind on the things he had to do. He had six months to search for Tamsen, before Duke would leave the others. He would begin working his way south. When he reached the burned-out shell of Tamsen's place, he would fan out from there, crossing and recrossing his own path.

Returning to the shack, now emptied of all life, Dan Tallant took a charred twig from the dead fire and methodically began to mark out a chart on the dirt floor. So much territory to cover, and so little time. He'd give himself these six months to find Tamsen, dead or alive... Then he would have to face the truth... he also had a duty to the living.

CHAPTER 8

Tamsen was very much alive, and for the first time in a long time, she was suffering from heartache. The snow clouds hung heavy above the protected Indian village, which was swathed in steam from hot springs.

Climbing a narrow trail that led upward at the far end of the hidden valley, Tamsen looked back at the village and recalled the first time she had seen it. But she dared not go beyond that day. She must think of it as a beginning, a kind of birth. She wished to remember nothing of her former life. It hurt too much.

Tamsen sighed and went on about her business. She was awkward at so many tasks the Tlingit women performed, but she had finally found her niche. Her clever fingers made her adept at weaving the Chilkat blanket, so prized by the people. And her art had given her a status, even in the eyes of her father-in-law, which made her husband, Dan-e-wak, proud.

Dressed in a cedar bark apron over a full-length body-garment, a fur cloak over all, she toiled up the slope toward the treeline. Her feet felt strange in leggings and moccasins. In the Wolf House, she went barefoot, but to reach the hemlocks, she must walk through snow. It was necessary that she procure the bark at this time, for only from the bark of the hemlock could the black dye be produced.

The other colors she had in plenty: blue-green, produced by soaking and boiling copper in urine, yellow from a tree lichen, and white, the natural color of the wool. But there must be more black to complete her pattern.

She would be glad to return to the loom. It had sat idle through the summer while she worked with the others at gathering berries and preserving meats. But winter had come, and now she would kneel before her work, fingers busy-and mind blank, without having to think. Thinking was bad for her, she told herself as she cut the bark squares expertly, peeling them away. She'd managed to achieve a plateau of tranquillity that showed in her large dark eyes. She had become all Tlingit, she thought, fingering her amulet. Perhaps even more than Helena.

She was not surprised at the sound of a footstep beside her. Rarely did she leave the house of Dan-e-wak's father without being followed, lest she attempt to escape. The valley must be kept a carefully guarded secret. Only a chosen few were allowed outside. Though last week, Kita, a young boy angered at a punishment meted out to him, had run away. If they found him, they would kill him.

Tamsen had no intention of leaving. Here she was safe. She did not have to remember. She turned to see Dan-e-wak at her side.

"My husband," she said formally.

"My wife."

She finished her work, placing the bark in a basket, and he turned. She followed him down past the snowline and into the valley which still showed patches of green. Reaching the valley floor, the brave turned to her once more.

430

"You are content here?"

"I am content."

For an instant, her eyes swam with tears. And Dan-e-wak did an unheard-of thing for him. He touched her, laying his hand on her arm in a gesture of compassion. But it was enough to break down her barriers for a time. As she watched him go, memories of the outside world flooded in, beating against her ears with black wings. The older hurt of Dan's leaving, which she thought was scarred over and hidden, came gushing back. Donald, Devon— and the rest! The others she must not think of if she were to keep her senses. Em, Arab, Juan, Nell, Dusty—oh, dear God!

They were gone! All gone! And she didn't know where. Dan-e-wak had returned to her old home at the first thaw following that last long winter. The big house was burned, and there were shell casings everywhere. He'd brought them back and the women used them for ornaments. And he reported that there was no one there. He'd talked with a man who told him of bodies floating down the Fraser. . . .

She must not think! She must not think! With a little whimpering sound she put her hand over her mouth and stood there for a long time. Then she hurried to the house of the Wolf kwan. Like the house of her adoption, it was made of wood, with earthen banks thrown up to make a kind of hall along which were curtained partitions for various sections of the family. At the end of it was an enormous space where a fire burned beneath the smoke-hole. Like all Indian houses, it was hot and smelled of grease and cooking. But it differed from the Indian houses in Novoarchangelsk in its quality of decoration. Dan-e-wak's people had lived in this valley for a long time and were artisans in wood. The

431

impressively carved house poles were bright with color, echoed in gaily painted chests and basketry.

Tamsen entered her own cubicle, separated from the space Helena shared with Dan-e-wak by a cedar bark curtain. She looked at her loom, two beautifully carved posts with a crossbar to which the warp was tied, then at the pattern drawn, according to Tlingit law, by her husband. Her weaving was coming along well.

She must prepare the black dye. Soon she could return to this work: the weft would cross the warp, one strand in front, one in back, and would twist before it crossed another warp. Hands moving... hypnotizing the eyes, the mind, erasing all thought—

Lovingly she arranged her materials, seeing the design forming in her mind's eye. Then the bark curtain rustled behind her and she turned. "Helena—"

Her eyes rounded at the sight of her friend. "Helena! My God, what have you done!"

Helena's lower lip had been pierced, according to Tlingit fashion, and a small wooden plate inserted. It changed the expression of her once lovely features. "I believe we have a pact to speak only in our own language," she said, her dark eyes sullen.

"Language be damned," Tamsen cried. "Helena, take that—that thing out of there! Perhaps it will heal!"

Helena stiffened. "I do not wish it to heal. It should have been done when I was a child. I have done it to please our husband. I thought perhaps you would wish to please him, too."

"I?" Tamsen had a horrified impulse to giggle. For she had a vision of herself at her old establishment, making an entrance in a velvet gown—appearing before a group of admiring men, a labret in her lower lip.

"Before I'd do a thing like that to please any man, I'd see him in hell," she said. Then, "Helena, what would Devon have thought!"

Helena went pale. "We do not speak of the dead," she said finally. "That life is over. I am happy here. I owe our husband much—as you do. At least I am a wife to him."

Helena slid back through the curtain, leaving Tamsen to stare gloomily at her loom. Why couldn't she have complimented her friend and let it go at that? Why must she balk at so many of the Indian ways? Tamsen had not lied to Dan-e-wak; she was content here. And there was nothing left to look forward to. She should let herself be assimilated completely into her new life. But the labret—no.

She smiled crookedly. Perhaps a bit of vanity remained. Or it could be because of the meaning of the lip-piercing operation itself. Some said it was to keep down gossiping among the women, making speech more difficult. Others thought that it was meant to keep other men from looking at one's woman with desire.

She fitted neither category. She moved silently about the encampment most of the time, tending to her work. Adultery was punished cruelly here, so her marriage to Dan-e-wak gave her a mantle of protection—even though she was not his true wife. Helena was that; Tamsen was only a kind of honored guest in his household. But Helena had come with a purpose. The labret was Dan-e-wak's wish.

She could not do it! Anything but that.

In the big room outside the curtains a storyteller was chanting. He was telling the story of Raven; his listeners were roaring with laughter at one of

433

Raven's mischievous exploits. She shook her head in bewilderment. Even their notion of humor was beyond her.

Tamsen thought of Nell, hitching her way grimly across a log over a turbulent stream, the samovar in her arms, her complaints of splinters—now that had been funny! She looked wildly around the room that had become a prison. Dear God, what was she doing here! Would she have to live out her life like this? The noise from the outer room, the stifling smell of smoke and grease—

She ran from the room and out into the daylight, where she walked from one end of the village to the other. The stoic greetings of the women had become something else. In their dark faces she read dislike, suspicion. Among them, she had no friends except Helena.

And only last week, Helena dared ask Tamsen if she had incited the young Kita to run away. She hadn't even spoken to him! It was he who was unable to fit into the life here, not Tamsen. A born renegade, he'd been in trouble all his life. But she'd probably been talked about, the blame placed on her shoulders. Helena should have known! It was another wedge between them. Tears glistened on her cheeks as she leaned against a log wall, moist and clammy with the valley steam. Out of the swirling mist, Dan-e-wak appeared.

"My wife?" he said formally.

"My husband." Tamsen's voice was listless.

She followed him back to the house where the storyteller still held forth, where the smoke rose in choking clouds and where everything smelled of grease...to where the richer men had more than one wife, and they were expected to wear labrets.

CHAPTER 9

No more mention was made of the labret. The weeks passed, and the blanket grew beneath Tamsen's fingers, glowing with color. Dan-e-wak's father came to see it, giving a grunt of pleasure. It was to be a gift for him.

"A woman of value," he told his son. "You have done well."

Tamsen caught a glint of jealousy in Helena's eyes at his words, and her heart sank. The girl tried so hard to be a perfect Indian wife, even submitting to disfigurement, and yet she was unable to master the art of weaving.

"It is the result of my years at sewing," Tamsen told Helena after the others had gone. "And it is all I can do." But Helena's eyes were hard as she left the room. They had not been close since the incident of the labret. Tamsen wished she hadn't been so shocked at Helena's action in having her lip pierced. If she'd only held her tongue. After all, it was Helena's affair.

Helena remained cold and distant for a few days while Tamsen worked doggedly, trying to blank out her mind against this new concern. So she was surprised when Helena slipped into her room, her face shining above fresh garments of finest doeskin, her hair braided and fastened with an ornament. She looked almost beautiful despite the disfiguring labret. She knelt beside Tamsen, exclaiming over the beauty of her work. "One would be certain you were true Tlingit," she said, admiringly.

"I try to be." Tamsen smiled.

"And you are!" Helena hugged her with the affection of the old days. "Tamsen, I have something to tell you! Something wonderful! I am going to bear Dan-e-wak's child!"

"Helena! I'm so happy for you!" Tamsen's eyes grew bright and she began to laugh with delight. There would never be friction between them again. For what was a Chilkat blanket compared to bearing the first grandson of a tribal leader? "It will be a boy, I'm sure," she said. "And I will have a nephew!"

Helena's eyes were misted. "I am so happy that you are my sister. I would not want another woman to share our husband's bed—"

Tamsen rocked back on her heels, staring at her friend in amazement. "What do you mean?"

"You know our customs here. As second wife, you will take my place when my time draws near. Perhaps you, too, will bear a child. They will play together, yours and mine—"

"Like hell I will!" The inelegant phrase might have come from Nell's lips, but it conveyed Tamsen's feelings.

Helena's face tightened. "It is your duty. If you do not fulfill it, you are not a true Tlingit." Her composure shattered. "Don't you understand? He can put you from him. You will become a *kŭchu,* a slave! Or worse! Old Sach-a-hãn has approached him, asking permission to become your second husband! I cannot protect you! Or Dan-e-wak may take a third wife. I can share him with you, my

436

beloved sister, but not with some strange Indian woman—"

"Then you are not a true Tlingit," Tamsen said angrily. "If you cannot accept their ways, why should you expect me to?" With a choked cry, Helena turned and fled the cubicle that was Tamsen's room.

That night, Tamsen could not sleep. Always the house was filled with the sounds of movement. She lay crouched in her blankets, watching the bark curtain that seemed to sway at times. The gentle motion reminded her of waiting for another man, not with fear, but with longing and desire. What would she do if Dan-e-wak came to her? Could she pretend he was someone else? Might she perhaps even learn to enjoy his attentions? Wasn't anything better than a lifetime of being alone?

Or would she struggle, rail out at him, damage his tremendous Indian pride? To do so might mean death. He was a fine man. She had developed a deep affection for him. But not this! Dear God, not this!

He did not come to her. And in the morning, Helena entered, her face a mask. "You need not worry. I have convinced our husband that you are a madwoman, fit only for weaving blankets. That if you should bear a child, it would have evidence of its mother's injury, mindless, as you were when he brought you here. He will not touch you, nor will any other Tlingit man!"

"Helena—"

"Within the week," Helena continued stonily, "our husband will take Kaskoé, daughter of Chlūnat of the Raven kwan to wife."

Then she was gone, and a door had closed between them forever. For with acceptance of a third woman in the household, Helena had become all Tlingit.

Helena wondered if she should have told Tamsen the true reason Dan-e-wak had decided against consummating his marriage with her. He had listened with interest to what Helena had to say, and then he had told her of something new he had learned.

A man he trusted outside had gone to dispose of the unfortunate Kita. As he returned to the village he had paused to rest near the burned-out house where she and Tamsen had lived. And there the Indian had seen a *Kushtaka,* a captive of the land otter people—a man who moved with the wind. Bearded, ragged, the *Kushtaka* moved through the snow calling out Tamsen's name.

The *Kushtaka* had caught him and breathed upon him. Somehow the Indian had gotten away, but now he was ill, and talking nonsense. The *Kushtaka* had stolen his mind.

"It is a bad omen," Dan-e-wak said. "By bringing the girl here, I may have gone against the will of the spirits. I seek your wisdom."

Helena twisted her hands in her lap. "We must watch and wait," she whispered. "It is all we can do, my husband."

During the ceremony that attended Dan-e-wak's marriage to Kaskoé, the keening sounds of the death dirge arose. The Indian who had gone to punish Kita had died. The babblings of his delirium before his death had reached many ears, however.

"It is a bad thing," the old ones said. "And to happen at such a time. The marriage is ill-fated. This is not the end of the trouble."

Only Kaskoé was unconcerned. A round-faced,

lively girl of fourteen years, she'd married better than her family thought she would. And they'd honored her by presenting to her husband many more gifts than even a first wife usually brought. Secure in her new authority—the first wife set aside for childbearing, the second unnoticed—Kaskoé set herself to charming Dan-e-wak and to making life miserable for both Helena and Tamsen.

With reckless abandon, she appropriated Helena's possessions. Helena bore her invasions grimly. Dan-e-wak's attentions to the girl were a passing thing, she was sure. Helena knew she would rule once more when her son was born. She bore the third wife's malice in stoic silence, rather than carry tales. A man took pride in the peace that reigned in his house—

It was the Chilkat blanket that brought about the trouble. The blanket was completed in all its perfection and Tamsen sat tying more yarn in to lengthen the fringes, when Kaskoé entered her cubicle. Nodding to the girl, Tamsen turned to warm her fingers over a basket holding stones and a few hot coals.

"A beautiful blanket," Kaskoé said. "It will be mine."

"It is a present for our father-in-law," Tamsen said in a voice that was deceptively calm.

"I will have it. Our husband would wish it for me." Kaskoé smiled sweetly as she said it. "I think I will take it now." She jerked at it, pulling at the thong laced to the cross bar. Her hands were sooty, and they dirtied the virgin wool.

"Leave that alone!" Tam cried. She flung herself forward and the girl wrestled with her, trying to reach the blanket once more. Finally, Tamsen struck her with a resounding slap. The girl stood, glaring at her with hatred, and Tamsen backed away.

"I'll find Dan-e-wak," Tamsen said, her voice shaking. "Keep your hands off that blanket! We'll settle this!"

She returned with Dan-e-wak and Helena, to find the room filled with evil-smelling smoke. The scent of burning wool. The Chilkat blanket was burned, charred beyond redemption. And Kaskoé cowered in a corner.

"She did it." Kaskoé pointed an accusing finger at Tamsen. "I touched it, and she said, 'It was for the *Kushtaka,* and now it has been defiled.' She struck me. Then she looked at the blanket with eyes of fire, and it began to burn. Then she said, 'Your spirit will rise with the smoke.' And she left me—!"

Dan-e-wak was extremely uncomfortable. A man had no place in a quarrel between women, but the blanket that would have been his father's pride was spoiled. And the mention of the *Kushtaka* was too close to his fears. He turned to Helena, who saw the horror in his eyes. She smiled placidly.

"You have married a child, my husband. A child with great imagination. It is clear what has happened. An ember popped from the basket." She pointed at the container of stones and coals at which Tamsen warmed her hands as she worked. "It caught the fringe."

Turning to the girl, she said in a tone of affectionate chiding, "You need not invent a story, Kaskoé. Our father-in-law will be saddened by the loss of the blanket that was to be a gift for him, but you will not be blamed."

The interlude was ended, but Kaskoé was a talkative girl. By the end of the day, the story had spread throughout the village. And Tamsen found herself ostracized, eyed with fear and left alone. Doggedly, she set to work at a new loom. The new blanket grew slowly beneath her fingers, but it was a creation Tamsen would never finish.

In all of the houses of the village, keening began. Here a child had died; there, a young mother. In one house, a little boy coughed loudly during the night and a baby cried. In the house of Dan-e-wak of the Wolf clan, people began to fall ill. First the children and then a few young adults got sick. The house reeked with the smell of sickness, and Tamsen moved from bed to bed, doing what little she could.

She recognized the sickness for what it was. Measles. But the disease that produced red splotches and stole away mind and sometimes breath was new to these people. The *Kushtaka,* they whispered among themselves. Had he not breathed upon a man of their race—and sent him home to spread the poison and die?

A shaman was called. An old man with thick graying hair, the shaman wore a crown of wooden sticks, bent to resemble the horns of the mountain goat. They rattled as he moved his head. Around his neck was a garland of decorations that covered his naked chest; around his waist he wore a bright dancing blanket.

He squatted on his haunches, and the sick ones sat beside him. They looked on with uncomprehending, fever-glazed eyes as he moved the upper part of his body convulsively, breaking out in a heavy sweat. He sang a song, interrupted with periods of wild groaning, as he shook a wooden rattle in the figure of a crane.

With a pair of tongs, he moved to each sick one, gripping their head, their feet. Then he went to them, one by one, placing their hands on his hips, his abdomen. Calling out the names of various animals, he led them about the fire while other men, seated in a circle, beat time on a board and gave answers to the sporadic questions he asked.

Tamsen was frantic at her helplessness to interfere. The sick ones should be abed, their fever brought down with applications of cool cloths to their burning bodies. The man was killing them! It was the same as murder! The poor little ones, their faces splotched and crimson! Was this what Helena wanted for her baby?

She cast a sidelong glance at Helena. Her adopted sister's eyes were on the shaman, glowing with faith. And Tamsen remembered the girl who had blackened her face and cut off her hair at her mother's death—who had performed a token cremation rite at Devon's grave. There was nothing Russian about her now. Helena had come home.

Tamsen didn't feel Dan-e-wak's eyes on her as she watched Helena. Kaskoé was among the ailing. And he could not help remembering her story of the *Kushtaka* and Tamsen's threat that the girl's spirit would rise with the smoke. Perhaps there had been truth in his third wife's tale after all.

Tamsen, suffocated by the smoke from the fire, feeling the smell of sickness wrap itself around her, escaped to the outside. The green had gone, except for a few lush blades of grass about the spring. The valley was enveloped in a harsh, crackling cold. The vapors from the spring had settled on the walls of the valley, freezing into a sparkling mantle of ice. High above, on the far wall, trees stood weighted down with snow. Here and there, a dirty patch of it had fallen to the valley floor.

How could she have thought of this as a haven,

she wondered, the harsh chill biting into her arms. It was as if she had been asleep and was suddenly awake. Helena was content here, but Tamsen belonged to the world outside. Someway, she must manage to escape, to go back and face it.

That night, the keening began in the home of the Wolf clan. Dan-e-wak's uncle was the first to die. Then the daughter of his sister. The last to pass into the spirit world was Kaskoé, his young third wife, doomed from her wedding night when the deaths began. At the time of her passing, some freak current of air lay above the smoke-hole, and the room was filled with smothering fumes. Some said it was the scent of burning wool. . . .

CHAPTER 10

For a time, the valley of the spring was dark with the smoke of funeral pyres. The projecting cliff above lent the place an atmosphere of its own; air currents circulated and renewed their swirls night and morning. Now, the atmosphere was heavy with floating ash; the grave houses were filled, but there had been an end to the dying.

Tamsen was working on her weaving when a small boy summoned her to the fire. Puzzled, she entered the large room, to find herself the center of attention. At one side of the flames sat her father-in-law, Dan-e-wak, and other dignitaries. Others were grouped in less advantageous positions, and the women stood along the walls, except for Helena, who stood behind her husband.

As Tamsen approached, wondering at their solemn expressions, two men caught her, one at each side. She was forced to her knees, her head yanked backward and her arms tied with her long dark braids. She managed only one frantic, horrified word, "Helena!" And then a hand was clapped over her mouth. A shaman came toward her, shaking his rattles and muttering some kind of invocation as she stared in terror at him.

What was this? Dear God, what were they doing to her? Why? She tried to cry out against the restraining hand that was cutting off her breathing. Dan-e-wak stood, his face tired and old-looking. The hand was removed, and Tamsen gasped for breath as her husband spoke.

"I am embarrassed in front of my friends and family," he said soberly. "My second wife has been accused of witchcraft. Let her speak."

Her eyes rolled wildly toward the shaman who apparently stood as her accuser as he asked, "Are you guilty in the death of Jĕlch-tĕlch?"

"No," she whispered.

"Ratschenitla?"

"No, oh no!"

The list went on, interminably, ending in Kaskoé's name. Her accuser recited the story of the day the blanket was burned, telling it in the words of the dead girl. Tamsen closed her eyes and tried to swallow. It was almost impossible in her position, with her head bent backward as it was. "No," she said with dry lips. "I am innocent, I swear it." Her eyes sought Helena's. There was no pity there. Surely, in memory of their past friendship, she would come to her defense. She couldn't possibly believe Kaskoé's wild, trumped-up tale! Had she been the one who brought it forward?

"No," Tamsen said, with a small moaning sound. "No."

The shaman picked up an object and came toward her, lifting it high. She recognized it. It was a branch from the Devil's Club, a thorny shrub used to castigate those sentenced to punishment—or to make them confess their own guilt. She would be beaten until she confessed to something she had not done. Better that they kill her outright!

With a swift movement that felt as though her braids had torn away, she threw herself forward, straight at the shaman's knees, bowling him over into the hot ashes scattered from the fire. He leaped up, beating at the sparks on the fringes of his costume, his face livid with humiliation, then raised the club he carried high. Tamsen, lying on her side, waited for it to descend.

"Wait!" It was Helena's voice, proud and arrogant. "My husband, have I permission to speak?" Permission granted, she pointed a finger at Tamsen.

"We do not need an admission of guilt. She is a witch. I say it."

"Helena!" Tamsen's words came in a small, heart-rending sob. "Helena!"

"She is a witch. And her magic is stronger than all of us—even your own, Auktelchnĩk, whom she pushed into the fire. We should not have kept her captive here. That is why the *Kushtaka* who wanders, calling for her, sent death to us. He wishes us to return her to him."

"And how do you, a woman, know this?" The shaman's voice was sour, because Helena's remarks had elicited a titter that was directed toward his charred cloth.

"We have all heard of the *Kushtaka* who calls her name," Helena said with asperity. "And last night, I dreamed. The *Kushtaka* came to me in my dream. And I was afraid. 'Do not fear,' he said. 'There will be no more dying if you return the girl to the house that burned. And I will give your people much prosperity in return.'"

Her listeners stirred and muttered, but the shaman stood fast. "And if we do not?"

"Our tribe is lost, and we will join our loved ones in the spirit world."

Dan-e-wak moved forward, released the braids

446

that bound Tamsen's arms, and lifted her to her feet. "My wife is a wise woman," he said. "I have brought this woman to us. I shall return her to her proper place."

He led Tamsen to her cubicle. Once inside, she fell to her knees, sobbing her gratitude, but he returned to the fire, where the discussion went on all night.

She could not hear the words, only voices rising and falling in dissent. But she knew her fate would be decided by the morning. Helena, blessed Helena, had come to her aid, after all. But the one bit of her defense had been confusing. "We all know of the *Kushtaka,* who calls her name..." What did that mean?

Kaskoé, too, had mentioned the *Kushtaka,* spirit of a man held by the land otter people, a mad captive.

Was it possible someone had been wandering the countryside in search of her? Duke Courtney? Juan? Perhaps they had survived the attack of the year before. Dear God! Her heart leaped in hope, but she quelled it; after all, she might not be allowed to go free.

Finally Helena came to her with the news that she would be released. Her face was rigid and unwelcoming as Tamsen rose to go to her. Tamsen stopped, uncertain, as she spoke. "Prepare for a journey. Dan-e-wak will take you. I told them of a further portion of my dream. When you leave this place, your memory of it will be erased. You will tell no one of it, or where it lies. You will no longer be a member of our people."

She held out her hand, and Tamsen looked at her, perplexed, until understanding came to her. She lifted the Raven amulet from between her breasts and gave it to Helena. "I'm sorry I couldn't change."

447

Helena was already on the point of departure when Tamsen caught at her arm. "I know how honest you are," Tamsen whispered, "how it must have hurt to have to lie to your husband. I—I thank you."

"Lie?" Helena's eyes were unfathomable. "Lie? No, Tamsen, I didn't lie." The corner of her mouth quirked a little in the old way as she said, "I said I had a dream—"

A ray of sunlight had thrust into the little hidden valley as Tamsen turned for a last glimpse from the plateau. The warmth of it, with the heat from the springs below, had begun an early melting of the ice that glittered on its walls. It ran in small singing rivulets, like tears.

Tamsen felt a faint wave of trembling as she looked back. She had been safe here for a little while. When the shock of hearing her family and friends were gone, perhaps dead, had worn off, it had become a place to hide from her hurts. A shell.

Now she would have to discard that protective shell and return to the real world, naked and vulnerable, to face up to the sorrows she'd kept carefully shrouded in her mind. Dan-e-wak moved on ahead of her, and she hastened her footsteps to catch up with him.

CHAPTER 11

Dan-e-wak did not speak on the journey, nor did Tamsen. She had learned the art of silence in the House of the Wolf. They walked, pausing only to chew a bit of dried food and to scoop up a handful of snow to ease their thirst. At small shacks that served as rest stops along the way, the Indian slept soundly. Tamsen, rolled in her blanket, was unable to rest; her mind kept working at trying to create a miracle: there had been a mistake; they would all be there to greet her, to welcome her with love. She was going home.

As they left the line of trees and approached the canyon rim, she watched eagerly for chimney smoke. There was none. She stumbled a little, going down the defile leading to the shelf below, and for the first time on the journey, Dan-e-wak reached a hand to help her. She saw pity in his eyes.

When she reached the ledge, she began to run. Juan and Arab's house was first. Tamsen stopped and put her hand to her lips at the sight of it. The shutters that covered the windows had been blown down by the winter storms. The blank openings gaped like blind eyes, and the door hung crookedly on one hinge. She could not bring herself to look inside—not yet.

For the first time, she went ahead of Dan-e-wak

and rounded the projection that hid the buildings of Nell's old place from view. She could not suppress a cry of both anger and pain, for the big house was a rubble of charred logs. The other structures looked smaller than she remembered. Forlorn. Part of the roof of the house that had been built for Dollie and Pinkie had fallen in. Only her own house stood intact—and empty. A place of ghosts...

She entered her house to look about. The big main room was empty, except for a table—a table Devon had made—and a bench. The hearth was filled with cold ashes. An open tin stood on the table, its contents dried beyond recognition. Evidently the place had served as a kind of way station. She touched the tin—a link with civilization.

Flinching at a sound behind her, she turned to see Dan-e-wak. He moved past her and placed the bundle he carried on the table. After a moment's thought he placed the ornate hunting knife that was his pride beside it.

"I must go," he said.

Pain surged through her. This man had saved her life, and he had never been less than kind. He was a link with a past that had held some peaceful memories.

"I thank you," she said.

He inclined his head with dignity. "My wife."

"My husband." She complied with the old formality, and he reached a finger to touch a tear that glistened on her cheek.

"You are content?"

"I am content."

Then he was gone, disappearing into the shadows of approaching evening. Tamsen watched him until she could see him no longer. Then she turned to build a fire on the hearth. Tomorrow she would search the ruins of the other buildings and look for clues that her family still lived. But tonight she'd had all she could bear. She felt helpless, impaled on the sharp edges of returning grief.

Filling the empty tin with snow, she boiled it out and set it to boil again. Then she turned to the bundle Dan-e-wak had left for her. Someone had prepared the contents with thoughtfulness. There were blocks of dried meats and berries, compressed and preserved with bear grease, woven pouches of roots pounded finely into flour, and packets of herbs and bark for teas. In the bottom of the bundle was a skein of white woolen twine of her own making.

She looked at it, puzzled, wondering why it had been added to the supplies to be left for her. What use could she put it to? She lifted it; it was oddly heavy as if something were inside. And this protruding loop was not wool, but leather—a leather thong!

She wept as she used Dan-e-wak's knife to cut the cord that held the skein, spreading it carefully. She knew what she would find . . . the raven amulet. They had parted forever, but she and Helena were sisters, still.

That night, she slept in the echoing, creaking house, the amulet between her breasts, the knife of Dan-e-wak in her hand, its hilt pressed against her cheek.

In the morning, she prepared a cup of herb tea, then set out to inspect the premises. If she could only find one thing she recognized as belonging to a loved one! If she could only reconstruct the scene as it had happened . . . but there was nothing. The fire-gutted walls of the big house were packed with snow. She gazed at it for a long time, wondering where the fire

451

had started. Were the girls in those upper rooms? And where was Nell? Dusty? Did their ashes still lie there beneath the snow?

She forced herself to turn away. No clues yielded themselves during the rest of her search. The two structures still standing on the larger ledge were riddled with bullet holes. The low building that had been Arab and Juan's home had escaped somehow. They might have been spared.

By evening Tamsen had scouted all the dwellings, and unless something lay beneath the snow, there was no sign of the former occupants. Too much time had passed while she stayed, numb and unthinking, in the House of the Wolf, trying to ease her hurt by adopting another way of life.

Returning to her lonely hearth, she absently chewed a bit of the dried meat and berry mixture and washed it down with herb tea. There was only the haunted past here. She must begin to think of the future. She would go downriver in the spring. But to what?

What welcome would there be for a lone, bereaved woman dressed in Indian garb, without a penny to her name? Perhaps she should not think of the future, either. Now, it would be a struggle to survive.

As the days passed, she began talking to herself, to hear the sound of a human voice. From there, it was easy to progress to talking to others as her food supplies dwindled; she cut down until she was weak with hunger.

"Em," she heard herself say, "I would love one of your delicious apple pies." Then she would put her hand to her mouth. Dear God, was she losing her mind? There was no one here. No one!

But there was! One morning, when the snow had

452

reduced itself to a series of dirty patches, when the Fraser roared high above its normal level with the melting from lower ridges, when the ice was carried moaning and grinding on its way to the sea, she looked at the cliff above. It would soon be spring and there would soon be flowers up there, appearing as white patches melted away. The grass would soon be greening over Devon's resting place.

Devon!

Three days later, her hair carefully brushed with a twig and rebraided, face washed as well as could be with melted snow water, she climbed the small canyon that led to the ridge. It was awash with the run-off water from higher ground, and her leggings and moccasins were soon sodden. She seemed to hear Em's voice, chiding her for her appearance. "You are not dressed properly for a visit, Tamsen."

Tamsen shook her head to clear her thoughts. She must keep things straight. It had not been Em speaking, but her own mind. Things seemed so confusing lately. Yesterday she could have sworn she saw a body in the Fraser, but it turned out to be a fallen tree. But she'd even thought it wore a familiar face ... perhaps she should increase her rations. Spring appeared to be early this year. . . .

When she reached Devon's grave, she brushed the remaining snow away, delighted to see that she had guessed correctly. Small blades of grass were green beneath the white blanket, each blade separate, naked, shivering in the wind. Newborn—

As carefully as if she were covering a child, she replaced the covering. Leaning against a tree trunk, she thought how nice it was to be here. There was a companionable feeling about the spot as if Devon were actually there, looking at her with his clear, grave eyes, listening. She imagined that they were

453

not on a windswept ridge above the Fraser River, but sitting on the stone in Novoarchangelsk, along the Indian trail. . . .

"You must meet my husband, Dan," she told him. "He will be coming soon."

Her words chopped off with a little cry as she realized her mind had wandered again. Devon was not present. He was dead, and in his grave. Dan would not be coming soon—or ever.

She found herself running back toward the house on the ledge, splashing her way down the defile recklessly. When she reached the house, she saw the other grave for the first time.

She stood for a moment staring dully at the snow banked at one side of the building. There had been a few inches of branch sticking from it yesterday. Of that she was certain. But with the melting, more of it appeared. It was a cross. Two pieces of wood tied with thong, to form a cross! Unless she was hallucinating again.

She rubbed her eyes. The vision didn't go away. It was a grave! And just outside the wall where she'd been sleeping all this time. But who was buried there?

She hurried to the snowbank and dropped to her knees, trying to tear the icy covering away. But it was an impossible task. This ground was not the soft, feathery drift of the ridges above; melting, freezing, melting, then freezing again had created a barrier of ice.

Finally, Tamsen sat back on her heels with her fingers bleeding, and she sobbed with frustration. Then she remembered Dan-e-wak's knife. She hacked and chopped until she reached the frozen soil. Then she stopped, terrified. What lay beneath? And how far down? This could only be a shallow

454

pocket of earth on this ledge of rock. She must take care—

She forced herself to pause, to go inside, to chew a few bites from her stores that she was barely able to swallow. She drank a cup of hot herb tea and returned to her work, holding the knife horizontally, while removing one scant layer of earth at a time for fear of mutilating what slept below.

At last, she turned up an edge of cloth. A bit more. A thing of multicolored patches. She recognized it as Martha's. But she had to go on. She must be sure.

Face white, eyes like a madwoman's, Tamsen continued her work. Lifting the material she'd freed, she thrust her knife into a small pocket formed beneath, touching the hardness of bone, feeling the softness of hair. She jerked her hand back, hastily, and looked in horror at a black, silken hair twined around her finger. Only Martha had hair like this! Dear God, Martha! Poor baby!

She pulled frantically at the cloak; it was rotted by weather and damp and gave way in her hands. She seized another hold on it, her teeth clenched, and yanked once more. The cloak and its covering layer of earth came away, spilling her backward. When she regained her balance, she stared incredulously at what she'd unearthed. A small, obscenely smiling face, its forehead splintered by a bullet wound, arms gone and body trampled as if by heavy boots.

A doll. Martha's Russian doll!

Somehow, it intensified her horror—this *thing* from a nightmare world. She began to cry, hysterically, as she scrabbled earth back over the small battered object. Finding it had made her nightmare a real and living thing. They were dead, all dead....

Later, when she woke in the middle of the night from a fretful, disturbing dream, she suddenly realized the significance of the little grave. Someone had to have buried the doll. Who? It was the kind of thing a woman would do. For a moment, hope blossomed. Then she frowned, dismally. The house had been used as a way station. It could also have been the kind of rotten stunt a couple of drunken miners would indulge in. Time on their hands, at loose ends, it would be humorous to "give the little lady a decent funeral." She'd seen enough of their high jinks to know how their minds worked.

Her head ached. She must try not to think of it until the morning. Finally, she fell asleep again—to dream of the *Kushtaka,* bearded, ragged, faceless, running before the wind and calling her name.

The next morning, fearing that her mind was deluded, that she'd been mistaken in identifying the doll, she dug it up again, holding her breath as she laid the cloak aside. She had been right. It was only a doll. But supposing she began to doubt once more? She could not endure this macabre act again.

She brushed the soil from the wounded, smiling features and carried it into the house to wrap the cloak about it and prop it against the wall. It sat there stolidly, reminding her of the Tlingit dead.

A cold snap halted the early spring, and Tamsen's supplies were gone. She made her way down to the swollen river with the idea of weaving a net from her skein of wool. Watching the jagged pieces of ice swirl past, piling up on each other, she knew it would not succeed. A seine would be torn to shreds within minutes. Standing there made her sick and dizzy, so there was the danger that she would topple in herself.

Discarding that idea, she made her way to the ridge above and managed to dig up a few frozen roots and bulbs with the tip of Dan-e-wak's knife.

Boiled with bits cut from her leggings, they produced an evil-tasting, unsatisfying brew.

The doll began to take on human qualities as Tamsen grew light-headed with hunger. Some of the time, it became Martha herself, as a baby. Sitting on the bench, Tamsen would cuddle the creature, rocking her body back and forth, singing.

Finally, on a morning warm with sun, she came up with the idea of taking the child to visit Devon. Again, she washed her hair in snow water, sponging the thin body beneath the greasy Indian dress she'd worn so long. She scrubbed the doll's face and braided the ragged hair in a semblance of her own.

"There, you look beautiful," she said at last. "No, I won't tell you where we're going. It's a surprise, but you must be good."

In a few minutes, she was stumbling up the incline with the doll, in Martha's old tattered cloak, clutched tightly in her arms. Reaching the entrance to the glade where Devon lay, she ran forward, excitedly. "Devon," she called, "Devon—"

And from far away came an answering cry. "Tamsen!"

The sound shocked her to her senses. The dead did not speak! She had lost her mind! What in the name of God was she doing here like this? And this—this *thing* in her arms. She threw the doll from her and turned, sobbing, to run.

At the entrance to the glade, someone stepped from behind a tree and caught her in a rough grip. With a wild scream, she drew Dan-e-wak's knife and jabbed forward, feeling it grate into flesh and bone. Then she saw the astonished face of the man who held her and fainted dead away.

CHAPTER 12

For days, Dan Tallant had been doubtful of his own sanity. He had searched up and down the Fraser River, as far as fifty miles inland, covering the territory with a mapmaker's precision. He'd checked out every deserted cabin, every mineshaft, talked to everyone he met, and he'd come up with exactly nothing.

Finally, he'd gone downriver in an attempt to find the Indian who'd talked drunkenly of a white woman in a hidden Indian encampment. But the Indian was dead, killed by one of his own people. His listeners were unable to add any more to what Dan already knew.

At Hill's Bar Dan had learned that McGowan and Bagley had gone to Victoria; something to do with their illegal schemes, he was sure. But his interrogation of those he met proved unproductive. If he wanted a girl, there was Pinkie or Dollie, but he'd have to wait in line....

It was late February. If he was smart, he told himself, he'd hole up in Yale and take the first boat out to join the others. But hell, he hadn't proved himself too bright thus far. He'd head back upriver...take one more look around.

He'd set up camp at Yankee Bar, a few miles below Tamsen's place, and worked out from there, feeling like an idiot as he followed the same procedure he'd used before, dividing the terrain in sectors, making a sweep of each—and, from time to time, calling Tamsen's name.

He grinned a little, thinking of the time he'd scared hell out of an Indian who took off like a shot when he walked up to talk to him ... must have thought Dan was half-crazy.

Now, having exhausted the area below Tamsen's place, he'd about given up. He would make one more trip to the forlorn, deserted settlement, by way of saying goodbye. Then he would keep his promise to Courtney and free him to go back to his gold-hunting. Maybe when he got the others settled back in the U.S. he would come back. Somehow he could not get the idea that Tamsen still lived out of his mind. Each night, he had that same dream—of her running before him, just out of reach. It was driving him loony. There were times during his search when she seemed to appear out of nowhere, like a mirage.

Morosely, hands in his pockets, he skirted the canyon rim, his eyes on the ground, nudging every dirty patch of snow with the toe of his boot, fearing he would find bones. Once he had found some, and his heart had pumped wildly before he realized they were not human. And then one day he heard the cry.

"Devon!"

His head jerked up. A small, very dirty Indian girl was disappearing into the forest beyond. And again, the cry sounded. "Devon!"

Edwin Devon was dead! What the hell!

Tallant started to run. There was something familiar about the way the girl walked. And the name! He skidded to a stop at the entrance to the glade. He'd misheard, he told himself, disgustedly. But there had been a girl here, he was sure of that. The

459

new grass was still springing up from where she walked. But she was an Indian... what he'd heard was probably an Indian word. Perhaps she was meeting some young buck in a romantic tryst.

Dan started to leave, then thought better of it. He would not walk in on the occupants of the glade, but would wait here. Hopeless as it was, he would question whoever came out. Soon there came the sound of running feet, of sobbing. And when a small figure burst through the trees, he grabbed for her, automatically, turning her to face him.

The face that looked back at him was Tamsen's, eyes wild with fear. The lips that drew back in a grimace of terror were Tamsen's. The hand that sent a knife slamming home—Tamsen's.

"Goddamn," he said stupidly, looking at the girl who had just fainted at his feet. "Goddamn!"

Tearing off a piece of his shirt, he wadded it against his wound, then picked his wife up. She felt so little, so light! But that was all beside the point. He had found her! He had found her!

Holding her close in an agony of love, he managed to make his way down the defile and to the house where she had lived. He placed her gently on a bed she'd made of boughs and blankets and built up the fire. Then he stripped off her wet clothing, his hands moving gently over the familiar golden body of the girl he worshipped, need surging through him at the feel of her beneath his hands.

So thin! So pitifully thin. She appeared to be starving. Forcing himself away from her, he searched for some type of provender. There was nothing in the house. Good God, how long had she been here?

He took a bottle from his pocket and placed it to her lips. She came alive like a spitting cat, her eyes

460

insane as she clawed at him; her fingers dug deep gouges along his cheek. He held her until she quieted, then realized she'd lapsed into unconsciousness once more.

Watching her, seeing the lovely pointed breasts stir with her breathing, he gasped at her prominent ribs, each one showing beneath the smooth coppery skin. The words she had screamed at him were Indian. He was certain of that. But they had been unintelligible. One thing he did know was that she needed nourishment, and quickly. He had food and medical supplies to dress his own wound at his camp downriver, but he couldn't leave her. She wasn't in her right mind; that was clear. She might come to and run away, or do herself some injury. He did not intend to lose her, now that he had found her again.

Grimly, he sacrificed more of his shirt, tearing it into strips, and tied her wrists and ankles. Then he wrapped her blankets around her and knelt to lay his cheek against hers for a moment before he opened the door and began to run.

Tamsen woke to find herself naked and bound. She'd had a strange dream. McGowan had been waiting at the opening in the clearing once more. She had stabbed him, and his face had turned to Dan's. Now she was here, like this, or perhaps this was the dream. . . . She slept again.

Dan Tallant returned in darkness, laden with supplies. He was light-headed from his wound, worried that something else had happened to her. To think that Tamsen would still be there, waiting for him, seemed too good to be true.

Bending over Tamsen, he sighed with relief. He wanted to hold her close, to tell her his love for her had never failed, to apologize for everything that had happened.

That would have to wait. First he had to tend to her needs, then to his own wound which was bleeding again.

He pulled a kettle from his pack and set water to boil with bits of meat from a rabbit he'd roasted earlier. The can Tamsen had used for cooking still sat on the hearth. He sniffed it. For a long time, it had heated nothing more than water.

"Goddamn," he said. "Goddamn!" Poor little sweetheart . . .

The broth ready, he cooled it slightly and forced it between her clenched lips. She gagged a little and opened her eyes in protest for an instant, but he persisted. Some of it down, her eyes closed once more, and she appeared to be resting peacefully. He stood over her, thinking how exhausted he was from the long run and his bleeding wound, but he was afraid to rest.

She'd been like a wild thing. If he untied the bonds that held her, she might not be here in the morning. He couldn't trust himself in his weariness. Regretfully, he checked the strips that bound her, leaving them.

"I'm sorry, sweetheart. So sorry—"

Once Tamsen was comfortable, he put a new pad of cloth against the knife slash in his shoulder. He would bandage it more permanently in the morning. Wrapping himself in his blankets, he leaned against the stones of the fireplace, his shoulder and his heart aching, his eyes on Tamsen's face. It was a long time before he slept.

Tamsen woke in the night, her mind clear and lucid, to find herself a prisoner in her own bed. Then it had not been a dream. The fire had been built up, throwing grotesque shadows in the room. And above the crackling of its burning, she could hear the sound of a man's harsh breathing.

Turning her head, fearfully, she located the source. A bearded man wrapped in a blanket. He leaned against the fireplace in an uncomfortable position. Shifting a little, he groaned, and she recognized his voice.

Dan!

A wave of gladness rose in her, and she tried to sit up, but her bonds held her back. Tied! Tied to her bed like an animal. And he had done this! Why?

Lying back with her eyes closed, the joy she felt at seeing her husband dissipated into irrational anger. Step by step, she reviewed the things he had been responsible for. He had left her for another woman, when she lay at death's door. He had taken all the money they had with him. There had been no one to stand by her in her illness, no one to help when Nell and Dusty arrived, to help Juan, Arab, Em....

Tears streamed down her cheeks. Unable to wipe them away, she tasted salt on her lips. Tallant woke to find Tamsen's eyes on him. Her gaze held a sensible awareness. He stumbled to his feet.

"Sweetheart!"

Her steady look assessed his appearance. The beard. The padded jacket he'd donned over his torn shirt. He looked foreign. Russian. She turned her face away.

Dan crossed the room and fell to his knees beside her, burying his face against her breast. "Oh, God! Oh, Tamsen! I've got to explain—"

"Is that why I'm tied here?" Her voice was indifferent. "So that I'll be forced to listen to what you have to say?"

"I'm sorry," he whispered. "Oh, God, I'm sorry." He began to fumble at her bonds. At his touch, the old waves of warmth and yearning surged through her body. She came awake all over, like the hurt from a thawing frostbite. Clenching her teeth, she fought against the reaction to his familiar hands. Hands that had touched Anya like this—

Her hands free, she drew the blanket around herself and pulled away from him.

"I'm taking this too fast," Dan said. "I know what you think, and I've got some explaining to do. All I ask is that you hear me out, sweetheart."

"The way you heard me out?"

"Dammit, Tamsen!" He looked at her helplessly. "It can wait. The important thing is to get some more food inside you." He went to the fire and ladled up a cup of broth; gingerly he carried it to her.

At first, she turned her face from the cup; then she changed her mind and drank it slowly. She felt her strength returning. She needed that strength because she was going to tell him she wanted no part of him. That he was to go and leave her alone. Somehow, she'd manage. She'd managed this far alone.

The separation must be quick and clean. There was no need for discussion. The last time she saw him, Princess Anya was in his arms and they were planning to go away together. He had gone. That was clear enough.

The cup was empty. Again she turned her face from him, and he set the cup on the floor. "Now, sweetheart," he said gently, "are you ready to listen?"

"We have nothing to talk about, Dan. It's all over. Please go—"

He reached for her hand, and she pulled it away. "Dammit," he said in a fury of frustration, "I'll get down on my knees if that's what it takes. I didn't leave you the way you think. Hell, Tamsen, I've been going crazy, wandering around looking for you for months, praying we'd get a second chance! Your sisters believed me—"

Her thin body jerked. "My sisters?"

"Yes, Em, Arab—the others too, Nell and Dusty."

She lay still for a long moment, not daring to hope. These last days, she'd lived in a hazy dream world in which nothing was real. She shut her eyes against the tears that ran down her cheeks, slowly, effortlessly. How could they have survived in these bullet-riddled buildings? And there were the tales of bodies floating down the Fraser—

"I . . . I thought they were dead," she whispered.

Tallant saw the confusion in her eyes. She was still far from well enough to take it all in. He smoothed tendrils of dark hair back from her damp face. "They're alive and well, all of them. I sent them to Novoarchangelsk, with a fellow named Courtney."

Duke! Dan hadn't known Duke Courtney. It was true, then. Oh, thank God! Thank God! Her hand went to her lips to stifle a whimper. It was too much to learn all at once. Too much.

Dan stepped back, sighing a little. It was clear she'd had all she could absorb for the moment. Poor little kid, she'd been through one helluva time. And as usual, he'd gone at things like a goddamn bullmoose in season.

He wasn't going to push any excuses or explanations on her until she was well enough to listen. Then maybe she'd believe him, and maybe she wouldn't. It didn't seem all that important to justify himself now. All he wanted to do was love her and get her well.

"Try to rest a little," he whispered. "I—I have a few things to do."

He waited until he saw that she slept, a deep dreamless sleep. Then, taking a small hatchet from his pack, he went outside. There would be wood in plenty on the cliffs above, but he was afraid to go too far from the house. The structure that had been the

465

home of Pinkie and Dollie was falling down. He pulled a few logs from it and cut firewood for an hour.

She was still asleep when he returned. He built up the fire, then carried water from the Fraser below. When it was hot, he cleaned and dressed his wound thoroughly. He didn't know that she was awake and watching him, watching the hard-muscled body that gleamed copper in the firelight. It's Dan, she thought. It's Dan, come home! She wouldn't think of the man who held Anya in his arms and left her for another woman. That was someone else, a stranger—

"Dan," she whispered.

He turned to face her, the bandage incredibly white against his brown flesh, his eyes dark with mingled hope and fear.

"Dan, come here."

He walked to her and stood just a little out of reach, as if he were afraid to touch her.

"Dan, do you remember something you told me once, when we were in Novoarchangelsk? Something about how when we tried to talk, we struck sparks, but when you held me, all our misunderstandings flew out the window?"

"Yes," he said.

"Then hold me! Oh Dan! Dan, hold me!"

He sat down beside her and took her into his arms. When he tried to speak, she put her hand over his lips. "No sparks," she said. "Just—touch me."

He held her for a long time, the wan face against his shoulder, his rough hand running over the slender, fragile body he'd longed for all these long days and nights. When she finally slept, he put her down, gently, and lay beside her. She curled against him in the old familiar way, and his blood began to

466

heat. Intuitively, he knew this was not the time to give in to his male urges. This was a new beginning. Their relationship was as delicate as glass. When they came together, her nerves must be healed, and there must be nothing standing between them. He wouldn't volunteer any information until she asked, and in the meantime, he would hold her....

It was two days before she reached the question-time. There had been a warm wind that stirred the forests above, bringing down the scent of green growth to blend with the smell of the river. For a time, Dan and Tamsen walked outside, hand in hand. When they returned, Dan brought in a load of firewood for the night and looked up to find Tamsen's eyes fixed on him. She sat on the edge of the bed, her shoulders stiff, her hands clasped tightly in her lap.

"If you want to talk, I'm ready to listen."

He knelt before her with his face buried against her as he recounted his adventures. He could feel the tension leaving her body as he talked. And finally, when he was finished, she picked up his scarred wrists and put each of them to her lips.

"I love you," he said, choked with emotion.

"And I love you. I...I want you. Please, Dan!"

He reached for her with a strangled cry, his mouth bruising hers, pressing her to him until she cried out for breath. He dropped his arms and stepped back, fighting for control. "I'm sorry, sweetheart. I tried to be gentle. I guess I don't know how."

Her eyes sparkled as she laughed up at him. "Don't you understand? I don't want you to be!"

"Ah, Tamsen! Tamsen!"

Teasing, seductive, passionate, as fragile as silk and as strong as steel, she was his love. He tossed their clothing to the corners of the room and carried

467

her to bed. There, stirred by her touch, was a brief moment when he flew back in time to a hilltop high above San Francisco, to a high hill with a soft wind and a sky full of stars watching over them. A night like this, when all their differences had dissolved in love.

Then, as she did that night, Tamsen whispered, "Dan, please—," and he forgot everything; everything except that she was his again. They loved, then talked of the wonder of it, and then they loved again.

When morning approached, they were both still wakeful. Tamsen curled against her husband and felt him tense a little. Sensed a question in him. "This Dan-e-wak you mentioned," he asked gruffly. "Who the hell is he?"

She hid a small smile against his smooth chest. Womanlike, she reasoned that she'd suffered for a long time, imagining him with Anya. Let *him* have something to think about!

"Dan-e-wak?" she said in a sweet voice of drowsiness. "A Tlingit. My *husband*, of course. I'm sleepy now, sweetheart. Good night..."

BOOK IV

NOVOARCHANGELSK

CHAPTER 1

The party that contained Em, Arab, and little Martha, as well as Nell, Dusty, the girls, and Duke Courtney, had started out rather cheerfully for Novoarchangelsk. But their hopeful spirits did not sustain them for long, with the brusque Courtney in the lead. Courtney set up a pace none of them except little Martha could match. She ran along beside him, chattering and ignoring his surly mood.

He'd had to leave his partner to head on upcountry alone. And damned if he wasn't stuck with heading up a petticoat train again. Though the roughly garbed women behind him weren't wearing petticoats, hell, they were still female! He'd trapped himself neatly by agreeing to see this bunch home. Emmeline had got under his skin as no woman ever had before. Every time she got close, he wanted to pick her up and squeeze her until she couldn't breathe—and carry her off to the bushes! He guessed it was love. But love was something he didn't have any time for, especially with a woman like Em. Oh, sure, she'd loosened up a lot. There was good stuff in her, a lot of spunk he'd never expected. But she belonged in a parlor, all dressed up like a lady, serving tea . . . she wasn't for the likes of him.

He yanked savagely at a bush that had overgrown the trail, pulling it from its moorings and tossing it into the Fraser below. "Dammit," he groaned. "Oh, dammit!"

"Mommy doesn't like for me to say that," Martha observed candidly. "She says it's a naughty word."

He glared at her. That was another thing. He'd grown too goddamn fond of Em's kid. The little scamp was tougher than a boot, but she was still a girl. And girls had no business growing up in the wilderness.

He bowed low. "S'cuse me, ma'am." She followed him, still giggling, right on his heels, imitating his walk. He found himself suppressing a grin.

Em, some distance behind them, turned to look at the group that followed, straggling out along the trail. Juan's face was white above the injured arm he wore in a sling; Arab clung to his other arm, her face pale with concern. The girls stumbled behind them while a panting, crimson-faced Nell brought up the rear, urged along by Dusty.

He's trying to kill us all, Em thought angrily. Just because he's in a fit of sulks! Shifting her pack to a more comfortable position, she hastened to catch up to him.

"What do you think you're doing?" she asked fiercely. "The others can't keep up this pace! Juan's about to faint! Nell looks like she's going to have a stroke—"

"Then they better hold off a bit till I can get them under cover. I know what I'm doin'! Hell, look at that sky."

Em looked. The patch above them was clear, but over the mountains, the clouds were piling up like dirty gray wool. And anything could happen at this time of year.

He didn't wait for a reply, but went striding on, Martha dancing beside him, taking two strides to each one of his. Em tightened her lips and followed, hoping he was wrong about the coming weather—or if he was right, that they would reach shelter before it struck.

They did not. A wind sprang up and roared through the canyon with an icy breath. Rain interspersed with sleet came down and scoured their faces, soaking their clothes. It was a miserable group of people that stumbled into a deserted miner's shack long after dark.

Courtney built up a great fire, and they hunched gratefully before it, their clothes steaming. After they'd had hot coffee and recovered from the numbing cold, Courtney stood before them, with his hands on his hips.

"Ain't going to get no better," he growled. "An' there's one helluva long ways to go. Think you can make it?"

"Hell, yes," Nell said. Then, coyly, "Speakin' fer myself, a-course. I ain't like them." She jabbed a finger in the direction of the other women. "I got meat on my bones," she said with smugness. "Figger it keeps me warm."

A shout of laughter followed her statement. Courtney retired to squat against the far wall and roll a cigarette for himself. Em, watching, saw the worry in his eyes and felt pity for the big man. He was scared, she thought. Not for himself—he had the assurance of a man who was able to cope—but the responsibility of dragging a long train of inexperienced people along a dangerous trail in chancy weather had gotten to him.

The firelight glistened on his blond hair; his blue eyes darkened in the shadows. In repose, his mouth curved with a natural sweetness. Such a handsome man, with his massive shoulders, his lean waist. Em wanted to go to him, to kneel beside him, smooth that tawny mane—dear God, what was she thinking! She hurried to refill her cup, her hands trembling.

At first light the next morning, they moved out. Despite the lashing rain and sleet, the small train went doggedly on. Before them stretched one deserted bar after another, all with abandoned shacks or mining shafts that would provide shelter.

Below Siwash Bar the catastrophe occurred, where the trail narrowed at one point into a footpath that rounded a curve high above the Fraser's boiling waters. Duke Courtney, leading the way, his head bent against a winding sleet, stepped out confidently.

The wear and erosion of the path concealed the rock that was wedged closely though rooted separately from the cluster of rocks. Once it had been a part of the towering stone cliff behind it, but a bit of dynamiting below had started a rift, the vibrations of which had created a fault. For perhaps a year, the rock stood in place while thousands of feet passed over it. But ice had formed in the crack from time to time, and its pressure deepened the rift. And now, under Duke Courtney's great weight, it gave way.

Martha stood numbly at the edge of the chasm where the big man she followed so loyally had been a short time before. She screamed for her mother, whose scream in return electrified the others. She rushed forward to grab Martha and push her back. Then she knelt to look down.

There were no banks to the river here. Only a few stones, with yellow waters swirling around them. Duke lay, his face turned upward to the sleet, his eyes closed. The river tugged at his body in an effort to carry him away. It was Em who thought of the rope Dusty always carried, should Nell need its aid.

Commandeering it, she tied it to a projection, and, gritting her teeth, slid down it, feeling it sear her hands and her knees through the tattered trousers she wore.

Feeling the pull of water at her ankles, she swung forward, landing on a stone, slippery with a thin coat of ice. For a moment she swayed, dizzy with the thunder of the tumultuous river. She looked upward, seeing Arab's white face looking down, open-mouthed in terror.

Duke! Em pulled herself together and looked down. He lay just out of reach—and, oh, God, he was moving! Being carried with the water—

She slid waist-deep into the dubious shelter the rocks provided and found her footing, though the waters tore at her, pummeling her in an attempt to wash her off her feet. Was Duke dead? There was no time to find out. With numb fingers, she fumbled at the rope, knotting it around the big man's chest, beneath his arms.

"Pull him up," she screamed above the river roar.

"But Em—" Arab's plaintive wail reached her ears, "how will you—?"

"Dammit," Em shouted, *I said pull him up!"*

Her legs spread, she managed to hold his head out of the water until she felt the tug from above. He rose slowly, his toes pointed downward, his head hanging limply, the moisture from his sodden clothing covering Em's upturned face.

As if cheated of its prey, the current tugged at Em violently. She was terrified, her strength used up. She fell face forward across the stone, clasping it with her arms. Even when the returning rope fell across her, she had great difficulty in tightening it about her own body.

At the top, the whole group collapsed, winded

with their efforts. Duke Courtney was alive, but dazed, and he and Em were half-frozen in their soaked state. The trail was impossible. There was no way to cross the chasm, and nothing for them to do but return to their last campsite. There they would decide the best course of action.

It was a short distance, little more than an hour's walk. But by the time they reached it—Carmen and Maggie supporting Courtney, Em stumbling along with Arab's help—the spirits of the group had reached a low ebb. Once in the shack, Juan worked one-handed, with Dusty's help, to build a roaring fire. Arab held a blanket while Em stripped off her wet things and changed. Carmen and Maggie set to work undressing the semiconscious Courtney, much to Em's disapproval.

"It isn't decent," she hissed from behind her blanket.

"Hell, honey," Nell boomed cheerfully, "he ain't got a gawdamn thing they ain't seen a-fore."

All Duke's things had to be spread and dried. His pack had gone down with him. Em, emerging from her makeshift dressing room, was acutely conscious of the fact that the man was naked beneath the blanket he was rolled in. It bothered her. He did, however, seem to be coming to his senses, and the mood of the company had changed. After their narrow brush with disaster, they were almost in a state of euphoria, not thinking of the problems yet to come. For the moment, it was enough to be warm and alive. They laughed and talked—all except Dusty.

Em studied him. The little man looked terrible. He had aged since Tamsen disappeared, and lost all his jaunty self-assurance. His blue eyes looked old, dim. He had taken himself to a far corner of the room, where he sat in a heap of misery, silent in the midst of the merriment. She was worried about him.

Then Juan brought her attention back to the subject at hand. They were trapped here. The trail ahead of them had fallen away. They must begin to consider their alternatives. Em was for waiting until Courtney revived. She was certain he'd know what to do. Nell thought they should return to the place near Anderson Lake. Hell, they'd wintered here before. They could do it again. Juan thought they should backtrack along the way they'd come and find a spot where they could climb to the canyon's rim. It might be possible to follow along it, bypassing the chasm, then descend to the trail again.

While they were discussing the problem, Dusty Wotherspoon rose and left the house. His thin frame shuddered with the cold as he gazed at the lowering skies with blind eyes.

He had lost his Tamsen. And because he'd let himself deteriorate into a weak, bleary-eyed old man, he'd almost lost another of his girls. Tamsen had been the daughter of his heart, but he loved Em and Arab, too. It should have been he who went down to rescue Courtney. Juan, with his broken arm, could hardly be counted. He, Dusty, had been the only other man—

He'd stood there, his knees trembling, while a young girl did the thing he should have done. A bloody coward! He could not go back in there and face them—

He looked toward the shack. A lean-to had been built against it. It was of logs, the ends V-shaped, so that each fitted into another. The roof was gone and the shed half-tumbled down. Dusty stared at it for a moment, his eyes widening. Jove!

He hurried back inside and babbled out his plan.

Nell gazed at him in admiration. "Well, I'll be damned," she said.

By common consent, Em was left with the injured Juan and the semiconscious Courtney. The others, at Dusty's direction, managed to dislodge half a dozen logs from the dilapidated lean-to. They half-carried, half-dragged them to the gap in the trail. At the end of the day, a bridge of sorts had been thrown up across the chasm by the simple process of standing a log on end near the edge, then dropping it so that it fell to the other side.

Dusty was in his element. He had proven his manhood, and for a time he managed to overcome his fear. Lying flat on his stomach, he maneuvered the logs into position. Then he stepped out on the makeshift bridge to test it. The logs rolled beneath his feet; one crashed into the river below, sending Dusty scurrying for safety. Only Nell guessed that his heart was thudding madly. Well, hell, hers was, too!

Dusty solved the problem by lacing one end with rope, then crossing cautiously to the other side and repeating the act. With small stones wedged at either end, it proved to be satisfactory.

"Do you think it will hold us?" Arab asked.

Nell was proof of that on the next day, when the party set forth once more. Dusty crossed gingerly, and the others stood shifting their packs, looking at the frail bridge so high over the rushing water. "Lissen," she said, "I'll go first. Effen it holds me up, it'll handle anything!"

She crossed it, small feet close together, gigantic trousers billowing in the wind. She turned to smile back. "That's the kinda bridge I like," she said. "No gawdam splinters!"

478

Dusty took the lead, seeming a foot taller in his new pride, his white hair standing on end. Courtney, pale and bruised, deferred to the little Englishman. He had earned the right to lead. And Nell, proud enough to bust a gut, for once kept up with the group.

Their luck had changed. As if the territory and the weather realized they'd been bested, all began to go smoothly. The rain ceased in favor of a clear, crackling cold. Without further incident, they reached Dutchman's Bar, Spuzzum, Washington Bar—and finally, Yale.

There, a sternwheeler waited, ready to leave on its trip downriver within a few hours. Courtney watched as the women of the group reacted in typical female fashion. They headed straight for the general store and emerged, arms filled with materials for sewing. A pity, he thought, looking at Em, her straight, boyish figure in masculine clothes. But this change was to be expected. They couldn't go back to civilization as they were. And maybe a good thing. Em, dressed like a lady, would seem like a stranger, unapproachable once more. Then maybe he could sleep again. He'd had a helluva time on the trail!

The ship's route took them to Westminster, then to Fort Victoria, and ended at Asquamalt. The group that boarded a small steamer for Novo-archangelsk showed no sign of the privations they'd endured. Em and Arab were elegant in the simple dresses they had made while on board the first steamship. Nell had donned her own gown over her tremendous canvas pantaloons. She'd grown fond of them—like her sammy-var. Martha did not take to the change with good grace. Her freedom lost, she denounced the situation, fiercely stating that she was going to run away with Duke and be a boy. They landed at their final destination as a steady rain began to fall.

CHAPTER 2

The rain turned to snow, and back to rain again. Spring came quietly and allowed an occasional glimpse of sun. The group had been met, upon arrival, by an expansive welcoming party on behalf of Governor-General Furuhelm. They were his guests, he had insisted, and therefore, the guests of the tsar. Did they wish to stay at the castle?

They did not. They chose, instead, to return to the little house they had inhabited before. Nell, especially, beamed as she returned the samovar to its accustomed place. Scratched and dented though it was, she took a personal pride in it, feeling she was responsible for its survival.

Though the place seemed like home to Em and Arab after their adventures, it was not a happy time. They learned that a war was raging in their own country, the North against the South. It gave them a frightening, rootless feeling. For they had to acknowledge that the States would always be home. The idea of the serene beauty of Pennsylvania, their place of birth, ravaged by war, was unthinkable. And what of the boys they'd grown up with?

Juan was miserable for a different reason. He felt he'd failed them on the trail, with his arm crippled through his own negligence. It had healed slowly, but it was well now. And here he was, he and Arab

481

still subsisting on someone else's charity! If he could return to his adopted country, he might prove himself worthy in some manner....He waited impatiently for Tallant's return.

Duke Courtney was also impatient. When they finally reached Novoarchangelsk, he had deliberately cut himself off from the group. He sought out the rough company of the Russians who worked at the sawmill and the fish-preserving plant. He picked up enough of the lingo to enter some of their gambling games and took care that Em saw him, occasionally, in the company of his crude companions.

Whenever the thought of her got too much for him, he turned his mind to McCandless. Old Mac had probably struck it rich by now and was sitting on it, waiting for Duke's return. If that goddamn Tallant would just show up!

Em was irritable, and nobody knew why, Em, herself, least of all. She wished it could remain winter forever. With spring Dan Tallant would come, perhaps bringing proof that Tamsen was truly dead. Lost to them forever. Emmeline could not admit the rest of that thought to herself—that when Dan came, Duke Courtney would go, or that Duke's going had anything to do with her feelings.

As Em sat before a window in the house at Novoarchangelsk, the sun shining across her sewing, her mood suddenly caught up with her. Why was she doing this? It was Arabella's gown, after all! She stood up, tossing the material into her sister's lap.

"Do it yourself! I'm tired!"

Arab looked at her open-mouthed, and Em left the room, slamming the door behind her. Later Nell entered the room and found Arab weeping over her galloping stitches. "Em knows I can't do this," she cried out in vexation. "And I was going to wear it to the castle tonight! Nell, what's wrong with her? She's changed so much!"

Nell grinned. "You ast me, I'd say it was a man."

Arab looked at her, round-eyed. "A—a Russian?"

"More like a gawdam bullheaded big bastard of a miner, I'd figger."

Arabella stared at her uncomprehending; then her face was a mirror of astonishment. "Nell! You can't mean that! Not—not Duke Courtney!" At Nell's nod, her lips tightened. "You're wrong, Nell. He's nice enough, but he—he's a roughneck! And Em's a lady. He—he's nothing like Donald!"

"All the more reason," Nell chortled. "An' who th' hell says Em's a lady?"

Arab's face went pink with anger, and Nell waved a deprecating hand. "Aw, hell, keep yer shirt on. I ain't sayin' anything against yer sis. I've knowed the lot of you a long time, remember? 'Tamsen, the *responsible* one,'" she said, "'Arab, the *wild* one.' An' 'Em, the *sweet* one, the lady.' Hell, Arab, you've changed, ain'tcha? An' Tamsen—did." Her face contorted with grief for a moment and then she continued, "So why can't Em git a chance to be herself? The real Em's been corked up in a bottle so damn long she's a-startin' t'fizz!"

"You're wrong! Em's always been—"

"Been what? Tamsen told me that story about how a feller was after you when you was a kid, an' Em knocked him on the noggin with a rock. It wuz Em's idee to berry him an' hide th' evvydence. That sound like a lady? An' lately—who skun down a rope to save Courtney's bacon when th' trail fell in?"

Arab began to realize what Nell was saying and her voice filled with wonder. "Dear God—"

Nell nodded until her jowls jiggled. "You betcher

483

damn boots," she boomed. "Think on it, an' you'll see what I mean."

"Oh, Nell—"

Her words were interrupted. The door flew open to reveal Em, her face a study in joy and amazement. "Arab," she said in an emotion-choked voice, "Arab, Nell—Dan Tallant's back, and—and—" she burst into tears of happiness. "Tamsen is with him!"

This reunion was probably the happiest moment in all of their lives. Everybody was laughing, crying, and talking at once. Martha flung herself at Tamsen, almost bowling her over in her exuberance. "We're all here!" she shouted. "Aunt Tamsen, we're all here!"

"Indeed we are," Tamsen said. "Aunt Arab and Uncle Juan. Your Uncle Dan. Me. Your mother—" Her mouth whitened as she said, "Oh, Em, I'm sorry."

"Donald's been gone for a long time," Em said. "Martha, give Tamsen room to breathe! Now, sit down, all of you. We've got to hear what happened, how Dan found you. Duke Courtney looked—"

"Speaking of Courtney," Dan interrupted, "I imagine he's one happy man. Saw him the minute we docked. Guess he'll be heading out with the ship in the morning."

No one noticed Em's strange quietness. Finally, she said, "Go ahead and talk. I'll fix some refreshments. I can hear you from the kitchen."

In the kitchen, she stood for a long time, staring at the pies she'd made that morning without seeing them. Then, as they gradually came into focus, she thought, I made those pies.

And I hated every minute of it! Something any fool could do. And it's all I've got ahead of me! I'm just the Widow Alden, who can make a pie! And

484

Duke Courtney would be leaving in the morning.

With Martha's help, Em served the others, listening to their compliments as they devoured the results of her labor. Then they settled back to exchange stories of their experiences as she carried the empty plates back to the kitchen. There was nothing left to show for the work she'd put in . . . not like the bottom of a sluicebox, where there would be gold. . . .

Later, much later, someone asked, "Where's Em?"

Em had gone to her and Martha's small room and made up two packs, which contained only the barest essentials. She had pulled off her flour-dusted apron and thrown it in a corner, with an expression of distaste. Her gown and petticoats followed. Donning the male clothes she'd worn on the trail, she pinned her hair up and covered it with a soft-brimmed hat. The mirror reflected the image of a slim, long-lashed boy, with an expression of determination on his face.

She left by a rear entrance, but returned to shove the packs for her and Martha under the bed. If she failed in her mission, there was no point in advertising the fact, but she did not intend to fail. How good the sun felt on her shoulders! With a sense of euphoria at her new freedom, she made her way to the barracks where Duke Courtney stayed, and she climbed the stairs to his room on the second floor.

Courtney was not as elated at leaving as Tallant had assumed he was, though he tried to convince himself otherwise as he assembled his pack. Hell, he thought morosely, he'd ought to be kicking up his heels since everything had turned out all right. He'd bet the girls were out of their minds with joy, now that Tamsen had been found. Dan had invited him to come along to the house, to celebrate their homecoming—

But, hell, he had better things to do than watch a bunch of females hugging and crying. He inspected a worn-out shirt, and shoved it into his pack. Those boots, though, were sprung at the seams. Maybe he'd better lay over till the next ship went out. Give him time to get new supplies.

Dammit, he was stalling! He could make his purchases at Yale.

Someone knocked at his door and, irritated, he yelled, "Dammit, come in!" He heard it open, but no one spoke. He turned from his packing with a scowl. "What do you want?" The question trailed off as he looked at the figure in the doorway.

"Em! What the hell are you doin' here? And dressed—like that?" He finished lamely.

"Duke, I've got to talk to you," she said, stepping into the room.

"Not here, for God's sake! Em, are you out of your mind? This is a *men's* barracks." Taking her arm, he forced her from the room and closed the door behind them. As they hurried down the steps, he wiped the perspiration from his brow with a rumpled bandanna. It gave him a funny feeling, being alone with Em in a room. His heart was still thumping. It was not the kind of thing she would do, coming here.

"What the hell's got into you?" he demanded to know.

"I wanted to talk to you," she said in a low, mutinous voice.

"Then shoot."

"Not here—out in the street like this."

"Well, then, want to go over to your house? I don't have much time. Helluva lot to do." He sounded uncomfortable.

"Could we—take a walk?"

"I suppose so." As he fell in beside her, he wondered what the devil she was up to.

"Dan says you're leaving. What are your plans?"

He stepped aside to avoid a plump Aleut woman with a shopping basket on her arm. "Back to the Fraser," he said, "then on upcountry to join Mac. Up into Cariboo, like I been talkin' about. Why?"

"I just wondered. Oh, Duke, isn't it wonderful about Tamsen?"

"Sure as hell is," he said with feeling. Then, "Now that you're all back together, guess you'll be making some plans of your own."

"Yes, I suppose we will."

They were beyond the settlement now, keeping up a desultory conversation as they walked, until they reached the old Indian trail. Courtney could smell the blossoming vines, the green of vegetation borne on a soft wind. And it was something he knew he would always associate with the island of Sitka. That, and the woman beside him, beautiful in spite of the men's clothing she wore. She had taken off her hat, letting her hair fall about her shoulders. In the warm sun, it had the look and scent of ripe wheat.

A pulse in his throat throbbed at the nearness of her, at the magnificence of their surroundings; blue waters in the distance, snow-capped mountains above them, swimming in a mist of golden sunshine—dammit, he had to get back to the barracks before he made a fool of himself!

"You said you wanted to talk," he said. "So talk! Whatever it is, get it off your chest."

"Duke, I'm going with you."

He jumped at her flat statement, his mouth opening in surprise. "What the hell!"

"I mean it, Duke." Em's eyes met his squarely.

487

"My things—and Martha's—are all packed. Lightly, so we won't slow you down. We're both quite strong. You know that I can handle a sluicebox—"

Courtney shook his head as though trying to clear the cobwebs of confusion. He didn't know what was going on here, but the answer wasn't just no—but *hell,* no.

"Then Martha and I will follow you," Em said soberly.

"You can't do that!" Dammit, what was in her mind? What was she trying to do to him?

"And why can't I? Wait!" She caught at his arm. "You're going to hear me out, Duke Courtney! All right, so I'm not a man! But I'm an adult human being, maybe coming to my senses for the first time in my life! I've decided what I want out of life, and I'm going to do my damnedest to get it! Duke—" her voice faltered a little.

"Duke, do you remember a conversation we had once—when I told you that Helena was in love with Edwin Devon? You said she ought to tell him?"

Courtney suddenly found himself unable to swallow. "Yes," he said, his mouth dry.

"I said a woman couldn't do a thing like that." Her voice was low, but her eyes were on his, steadfast and shining. "But I was wrong. And I'm doing it now."

Only one time in his life had Duke Courtney taken a punch that almost knocked him out. For a while, his legs had felt rubbery, and he had been unable to comprehend what had happened. Emmeline's statement had much the same affect now.

With a low groan, Duke reached for Emmeline and held her tightly, his lips pressed against her wheat-scented hair, his big work-calloused hands stroking her slender shoulders. After a while, he carried her to a sun-warmed stone beside the trail, a stone for sitting on, for holding and loving on while birds sang above and butterflies swayed over blossoms, opening and closing their wings.

The long day of the northland had begun to melt into misty blue, and Em did not reappear. Her sisters were frantic. Juan went searching in one direction, Dan in another. They both returned without her. Their earlier notion that she might have gone out for some air was absurd. After all, she'd thought Tamsen was dead. Why would she disappear so shortly after learning she still lived? To be gone so long—it didn't make sense.

They were considering going to the governor-general and asking that he send a search party throughout Novoarchangelsk and the neighboring Indian village, when the couple arrived. Arab exploded as Em and Duke Courtney appeared in the doorway.

"Em! Where have you been? You might have had some consideration for—"

She stopped at the expressions on their faces. Em was radiant, her blue eyes filled with a kind of wonder. Courtney's smile was a mixture of pleasure and embarrassment.

"We've been looking everywhere," Arab said accusingly. "We thought something had happened to you."

Em didn't answer her. She was blind and deaf to all the occupants of the room, except one. Little Martha. She ran toward her daughter, and gathered her in her arms, crying softly. "Martha," she said finally, managing to quell her muffled sobs, "oh, Martha, guess what! I have a surprise for you!

"We're going to marry a Duke!"

The wedding was held in Baranov Castle, at Ivan Furuhelm's insistence. Terrified at the thought of a big affair, Duke Courtney fought it until Nell took him in hand.

"Weddings is important to a girl like Em," she told him bluntly, "So stop actin' like a gawdam mule!" And to the equally uncooperative Em, she said, "Hell, honey, when th' knot's tied, it oughta be tied good!"

They had submitted to the delay; two Russian tailors worked day and night on a suit to fit Courtney's big frame while the women stitched a gown for Em, of palest blue. It must be simple, Em had directed, and of course it could not be white. So Tamsen had chosen the color of the Russian wedding gown.

The night of the ceremony, the guests assembled in the great hall. The dining tables had been removed from the cedar-paneled room, and it glowed. Mirrors reflected the glittering assemblage of Russian officers, their ladies, and the friends of the bride and groom.

In one corner of the room, where swinging lamps of incense burned before ikons and holy images, an altar had been set up. And ministers of two faiths waited; the minister from the Lutheran Church, built in Etolin's time, and the Good Father from St. Michael's. Following the wedding, the bells of St. Michael's would ring.

He had covered every eventuality, Furuhelm thought, a trifle smugly. It should look good in Golowin's report to Tsar Alexander Nikolaevich. Now he had everything to gain and nothing to lose, with the sale of Russian Alaska tabled indefinitely and Tallant going home. Watching Tallant hurry across the room to join his wife, he smiled genially. He wasn't such a bad fellow after all.

The bridal music began, and Duke Courtney slowly walked up to stand beside the altar. He had pulled himself together and stood erect, towering above the others in the room. The fine suit sat well on him and, oddly enough, he looked like a handsome, prosperous gentleman.

Tamsen drew a ragged breath. For a space, it was as if she could see into the future. She need not worry about Em. Courtney would find his fortune, and Em would live like a queen....

Her odd moment of prescience was interrupted by a sigh as the crowd turned to see the bride. Em glowed as she walked to meet Courtney, her small hand on Dusty's arm. Furuhelm had offered to escort her to the altar, but instead she'd chosen the little man who had been her father's friend. Dusty's carriage was erect, his arm supportive, and he looked every bit the English gentleman.

"Look at 'im," Nell whispered with pride, "The l'il sonofabitch! Ain't he sump'n?"

No one heard her. They were all looking at the bride. Em no longer had the frailty of a fragile, drooping flower. The events of the trail had given her a look of strength, of shining radiance. She went to meet her husband-to-be with confidence, eyes raised to his, her mouth curved sweetly.

Tamsen, watching, felt a desolate sense of loss. For her gentle, loving sister, always so dependent, was gone. This was a stranger, with an inner core of steel, who wouldn't lean upon Duke Courtney as she had upon Donald, but would walk beside him as an equal, able to face whatever came. She just wasn't . . . Emmeline!

Dan, as if sensing his wife's bewilderment, slipped his arm around her.

The celebration lasted until dawn when Courtney, Em, and Martha boarded the ship that was to take them to Asquamalt. The guests gathered on the shore to strain for a last glimpse of the two sun-gilded heads and the small dark figure of the little girl between them. For a moment, the ship was framed, like a painting, against the snowy cone of Mt. Edgecumbe; then it was gone.

CHAPTER 3

Tamsen still felt disconsolate when they boarded their own ship a few days later. Mingled with her sense of loss was a feeling of envy—at least Em was going somewhere and knew that her husband would be with her.

Tamsen, Arab, and their husbands, and Nell and her entourage, were headed for San Francisco. After they reached the city, there were no further definite plans. Tamsen had questioned Dan, but he was evasive. He had a few ideas regarding their future, he admitted, but he wanted to think on them for a while. Arab told her Juan had been equally mysterious. Arab and Tamsen thought they knew why.

The war! The Southern states had seceded from the Union. The country was in process of destroying itself from within. And Dan, being the kind of man he was, would enlist immediately. Juan evidently planned to go along with him. It was the only obvious conclusion.

Arab came to stand beside her sister. "Juan hasn't been near me since we boarded the ship. He and Dan have talked to every crewman on this ship, trying to find out about the fighting. And now, they're talking to each other. War! Oh, Tamsen, I can't stand it! I know what they're planning." There was a note of hysteria in her voice. Tamsen looked toward Juan and Dan, standing together.

Juan was more erect than he'd been for a long time, a new pride in his dark face. Dan wore the old look of eagerness at a new mission. It was clear they were in agreement.

"Arab, maybe we're wrong, selfish. Do we have the right to ask them to give up something they believe in?"

Arab looked at Tamsen. For a space, Donald Alden's poor ghost hovered between them. Arab walked away to stand at the rail a little farther forward.

Tamsen looked back at Novoarchangelsk without seeing it. In a little while the engines would start and she would leave a place where she'd known the greatest happinesses and the greatest sorrows of her life. She thought of the memories she would carry with her, of Devon, Helena, Igor. The brightly painted bidarkas along the shore, the Indian village that housed a noble people—

Her hand went to the amulet at her throat as she remembered. And suddenly, Dan was beside her. The engines shuddered into life as he put his arm around her.

"We've reached a decision, sweetheart, Juan and I. But only on the condition that you and Arab agree with what we want to do. You know the kind of work I've always done for our government. They need those skills now—"

She braced herself for what was to come. But as he continued, she looked at him blankly, unable to believe her ears.

Even more they would need other things . . . beef, horses. He was thinking of establishing a ranch, a hacienda . . . somewhere in the green rolling country near the City of the Angels. Juan would be of great value, dealing with the Spanish-speaking vaqueros, providing them with an entrée into the society of the great Spanish landholders in the area. There would be a place for all of them, even Nell and Dusty, should they care to join them. And then, soon . . . children.

A small cry of happiness sounded above them, as Arab also approved of their plans. Tamsen hid her damp eyes against Dan's shirt. "Yes," she said. "Oh, yes!"

They stood like that for a long moment; then the ship began to move. Placing his hands on her shoulders, Dan gently turned her to face the shore. "Look, sweetheart."

The sun's rays had broken through the mist, bathing the small settlement in light. The windows of Baranov Castle refracted the sun in a glitter of gems, and the mountains holding the Russian-American colony like a cup were haloed in glory. Waves rippling below them were edged in gold.

For a space, the beauty of the scene remained static. Then the ship moved out, gently breaking the spell. Tamsen looked toward Juan and Arab. They, too, had felt the magic of it and stood rapt at the rail, holding hands.

"My God," Dan said huskily, "did you ever see anything like that?"

She never had. It was as if the island had reached out to her, saying, "You will always be a part of this place, and it will always be a part of you." It had left her with a moment to remember. She ached with nostalgia as Dan led her toward their cabin. Ahead of her was a country of summer, green rolling hills

495

that turned golden and hay-sweet in fall. Dan would be with her, and there would be children . . . one must not look back.

Still, she couldn't resist one last glance at the radiance of Novoarchangelsk, at the sunlight that turned the cupola of Baranov Castle into a beacon.

Dan, sensing her feelings, said, "Someday we'll come back. When it's part of the United States, we'll bring the children for a visit." He shut the cabin door against the scene that held her in its web of enchantment.

It was a moment to be strung along with others on the necklace of memories. There would be many more moments to come. She and Dan were together now. Their love had been tempered by the fires of doubt. But there would be no more misunderstandings. For if there were, she would know what to do.

She smiled up at her husband and returned the adoration in his eyes. "Hold me," she said, as the ship floated away smoothly on the quiet waters.